Also by Benjamin Alire Sáenz

Aristotle and Dante Discover the Secrets of the Universe

The Inexplicable Logic of My Life

BENJAMIN ALIRE SÁENZ

SIMON & SCHUSTER

First published in Great Britain in 2021 by Simon & Schuster UK Ltd

First published in the USA in 2021 by Simon & Schuster BFYR,
an imprint of Simon & Schuster Children's Publishing Division,
1230 Avenue of the Americas, New York, New York, 10020

5 7 9 10 8 6 4

Simon & Schuster UK Ltd
1st Floor, 222 Gray's Inn Road
London
WC1X 8HB

www.simonandschuster.co.uk
www.simonandschuster.com.au
www.simonandschuster.co.in

Simon & Schuster Australia, Sydney
Simon & Schuster India, New Delhi

A CIP catalogue record for this book is available from the British Library.

PB ISBN 978-1-3985-0527-8
eBook ISBN 978-1-3985-0528-5
eAudio ISBN 978-1-3985-0544-5

Printed and bound by CPI Group (UK) Ltd, Croydon, CR0 4YY

MIX
Paper from
responsible sources
FSC® C020471

Amanda, I See the rising of the sun and think of you. Sometimes I hear your laughter in the room and hear you say: "You're crazy, Uncle Ben."

This book is for you. I adore you—and always will.

EVERYWHERE I TURNED, EVERYWHERE I went, everybody had something to say about love. Mothers, fathers, teachers, singers, musicians, poets, writers, friends. It was like the air. It was like the ocean. It was like the sun. It was like the leaves on a tree in summer. It was like the rain that broke the drought. It was the soft sound of the water flowing through a stream. And it was the sound of the crashing waves against the shore in a storm. Love was why we fought all our battles. Love was what we lived and died for. Love was what we dreamed of as we slept. Love was the air we wanted to breathe in when we woke to greet the day. Love was a torch you carried to lead you out of darkness. Love took you out of exile and carried you to a country called Belonging.

Discovering the Art of Cartography

I wondered if Dante and I would ever be allowed to write our names on the map of the world. Other people are given writing instruments—and when they go to school, they are taught to use them. But they don't give boys like me and Dante pencils or pens or spray paint. They want us to read, but they do not want us to write. What will we write our names with? And where on the map would we write them?

One

AND HERE HE WAS, DANTE, WITH HIS HEAD RESTING ON my chest. In the stillness of the dawn, there was only the sound of Dante's breathing. It was as though the universe had stopped whatever it was doing just to look down on two boys who had discovered its secrets.

As I felt the beating of Dante's heart against the palm of my hand, I wished I could somehow reach into my chest and rip out my own heart and show Dante everything that it held.

And then there was this: Love didn't just have something to do with my heart—it had something to do with my body. And my body had never felt so alive. And then I *knew*, I finally knew about this thing called desire.

Two

I HATED TO WAKE HIM. BUT THIS MOMENT HAD TO END.
We couldn't live in the back of my pickup forever. It was late, and
already it was another day, and we had to get home, and our parents would be worried. I kissed the top of his head. "Dante? Dante?
Wake up."

"I don't ever want to wake up," he whispered.

"We have to go home."

"I'm already home. I'm with you."

That made me smile. Such a Dante thing to say.

"C'mon, let's get going. It looks like rain. And your mother's
going to kill us."

Dante laughed. "She won't kill us. We'll just get one of her looks."

I pulled him up and we both stood there, looking up at the sky.

He took my hand. "Will you always love me?"

"Yes."

"And did you love me from the very beginning, the way that I
loved you?"

"Yes, I think so. I think I did. It's harder for me, Dante. You have
to understand that. It will always be harder for me."

"Not everything is that complicated, Ari."

"Not everything is as simple as you think it is."

He was about to say something, so I just kissed him. To shut him up, I think. But also because I liked kissing him.

He smiled. "You finally figured out a way to win an argument with me."

"Yup," I said.

"It'll work for a while," he said.

"We don't always have to agree," I said.

"That's true."

"I'm glad you're not like me, Dante. If you were like me, I wouldn't love you."

"Did you say you love me?" He was laughing.

"Cut it out."

"Cut what out?" he said. And then he kissed me. "You taste like the rain," he said.

"I love the rain more than anything."

"I know. I want to be the rain."

"You *are* the rain, Dante." And I wanted to say *You're the rain and you're the desert and you're the eraser that's making the word "loneliness" disappear*. But it was too much to say and I would always be the guy that would say too little and Dante was the kind of guy who would always say too much.

Three

WE DIDN'T SAY ANYTHING ON THE DRIVE BACK HOME.

Dante was quiet. Maybe too quiet. He, who was always so full of words, who knew what to say and how to say it without being afraid. And then the thought came to me that maybe Dante had always been afraid—just like me. It was as if we had both walked into a room together and we didn't know what to do in that room. Or maybe, or maybe, or maybe. I just couldn't stop thinking about things. I wondered if there would ever come a time when I would stop thinking about things.

And then I heard Dante's voice: "I wish I were a girl."

I just looked at Dante. "What? Wanting to be a girl is serious business. You really wish you were a girl?"

"No. I mean, I like being a guy. I mean, I like having a penis."

"I like having one too."

And then he said, "But, at least, if I were a girl, then we could get married and, you know—"

"That's not ever gonna happen."

"I know, Ari."

"Don't be sad."

"I won't be."

But I knew he would be.

And then I put on the radio and Dante started singing with Eric Clapton and he whispered that "My Father's Eyes" was maybe his new favorite song. "Waiting for my prince to come," he whispered. And he smiled.

And he asked me, "Why don't you ever sing?"

"Singing means that you're happy."

"You're not happy?"

"Maybe only when I'm with you."

I loved when I said something that made Dante smile.

When we pulled up in front of his house, the sun was on the verge of showing its face to the new day. And that's just how it felt—like a new day. But I was thinking that maybe I would never again know—or be sure of—what the new day would bring. And I didn't want Dante to know that there was any fear living inside me at all because he might think that I didn't love him.

I would never show him that I was afraid. That's what I told myself. But I knew I couldn't keep that promise.

"I want to kiss you," he said.

"I know."

He closed his eyes. "Let's pretend we're kissing."

I smiled—then laughed as he closed his eyes.

"You're laughing at me."

"No, I'm not. I'm kissing you."

He smiled and looked at me. His eyes were filled with such

hope. He jumped out of the truck and shut the door. He stuck his head through the open window. "I see a longing in you, Aristotle Mendoza."

"A longing?"

"Yes. A yearning."

"A yearning?"

He laughed. "Those words live in you. Look them up."

I watched him as he bounded up the steps. He moved with the grace of the swimmer that he was. There was no weight or worry in his step.

He turned around and waved, wearing that smile of his. I wondered if his smile would be enough.

God, let his smile be enough.

Four

I DIDN'T THINK I'D EVER FELT THIS TIRED. I FELL ON MY bed—but sleep didn't feel like paying me a visit.

Legs jumped up beside me and licked my face. She nudged closer when she heard the storm outside. I wondered what Legs made up in her head about thunder or if dogs even thought about things like that. But me, I was happy that for the thunder. This year, such wondrous storms, the most wondrous storms I'd ever known. I must have nodded off to sleep because, when I woke, it was pouring outside.

I decided to have a cup of coffee. My mom was sitting at the kitchen table, cup of coffee in one hand, a letter in the other.

"Hi," I whispered.

"Hi," she said, that same smile on her face. "You got in late."

"Or early—if you think about it."

"For a mother, early is late."

"Were you worried?"

"It's in my nature to worry."

"So you're like Mrs. Quintana."

"It might surprise you to know that we have a lot of things in common."

"Yeah," I said, "you both think your sons are the most beautiful boys in the world. You don't get out much, do you, Mom?"

She reached over and combed my hair with her fingers. And then she had that look that was waiting for an explanation.

"Dante and I fell asleep in the back of my pickup. We didn't . . ." I stopped, and then I just shrugged. "We didn't do anything."

She nodded. "This is hard, isn't it?"

"Yes," I said. "Is it supposed to be hard, Mom?"

She nodded. "Love is easy and it's hard. It was that way with me and your father. I wanted him to touch me so much. And I was so afraid."

I nodded. "But at least—"

"At least I was a girl and he was a boy."

"Yeah." She just looked at me in that same kind of way that she had always looked at me. And I wondered if I could ever look at anybody like that, a look that held all the good things that existed in the known universe.

"Why, Mom? Why do I have to be this way? Maybe I'll change and then like girls like I'm supposed to like them? I mean, maybe what me and Dante feel—it's like a phase. I mean, I only feel this way about Dante. So what if I don't really like boys—I only like Dante because he's Dante."

She almost smiled. "Don't kid yourself, Ari. You can't think your way out of this one."

"How can you be so casual about this, Mom?"

"Casual? I'm anything but. I went through a lot of struggles with myself about your aunt Ophelia. But I loved her. I loved her more than I'd ever loved anyone outside of you and your sisters and your father." She paused. "And your brother."

12

"My brother, too?"

"Just because I don't talk about him doesn't mean that I don't think about him. My love for him is silent. There are a thousand things living in that silence."

I was going to have to give that some thought. I was beginning to see the world in a different way just by listening to her. To listen to her voice was to listen to her love.

"I guess you could say that this isn't my first time at bat." She had that fierce and stubborn look on her face. "You're my son. And your father and I have decided that silence is not an option. Look at what the silence regarding your brother has done to us—not just to you, but to all of us. We're not going to repeat that mistake."

"Does that mean I have to talk about everything?"

I could see the tears welling up in her eyes and hear the softness in her voice as she said, "Not everything. But I don't want you to feel that you're living in exile. There's a world out there that's going to make you feel like that you don't belong in this country—or any other country, for that matter. But in this house, Ari, there is only belonging. You belong to us. And we belong to you."

"But isn't it wrong to be gay? Everybody seems to think so."

"Not everybody. That's a cheap and mean morality. Your aunt Ophelia took the words *I don't belong* and wrote them on her heart. It took her a long to time to take those words and throw them out of her body. She threw out those words one letter at a time. She wanted to know why. She wanted to change—but she couldn't. She met a man. He loved her. Who wouldn't love a woman like Ophelia? But she couldn't do it, Ari. She wound up hurting him because she could never love him like she loved Franny. Her life was something of a secret. And that's sad, Ari. Your aunt Ophelia was a beautiful person. She taught me so much about what really matters."

"What am I gonna do, Mom?"

"Do you know what a cartographer is?"

"Of course I do. Dante taught me that word. It's someone who creates maps. I mean, they don't create what's there, they just map it out and, well, show people what's there."

"That's it, then," she said. "You and Dante are going to map out a new world."

"And we're going to get a lot of things wrong and we're going to have to keep it all a secret, aren't we?"

"I'm sorry that the world is what it is. But you'll learn how to survive—and you'll have to create a space where you're safe and learn to trust the right people. And you will find happiness. Even now, Ari, I see that Dante makes you happy. And that makes me happy—because I hate to see you be miserable. And you and Dante have us and Soledad and Sam. You have four people on your baseball team."

"Well, we need nine."

She laughed.

I wanted so much to lean into her and cry. Not because I was ashamed. But because I knew I was going to be a terrible cartographer.

And then I heard myself whisper, "Mom, why didn't anybody tell me that love hurts so much?"

"If I had told you, would it have changed anything?"

Five

THERE WASN'T MUCH LEFT OF THE SUMMER. THERE
seemed to be a few rainy days still to come before they went away
and left us in our usual drought. While I was lifting weights in the
basement, I wondered about picking up some kind of hobby. Maybe
something to make me a better person or to just get me out of my
head. I wasn't good at anything, not really. Not like Dante, who was
good at everything. I realized I didn't have any hobbies. My hobby
was thinking about Dante. My hobby was feeling my whole body
tremble when I thought of him.

Maybe my real hobby would be having to keep my whole life a
secret. Was that a hobby? Millions of boys in the world would want
to kill me, *would* kill me if they knew what lived inside me. Knowing
how to fight—that was no hobby. It was a gift I just might need to
survive.

I took a shower and decided to make a list of things I wanted to do:

~~- Learn to play the guitar~~

I crossed out *Learn to play the guitar* because I knew I would
never be good at it. I wasn't cut out to be Andrés Segovia. Or Jimi
Hendrix. So I just got on with my list.

- Apply for college
- Read more
- Listen to more music
- Go on a trip (maybe at least go camping—with Dante?)
- Write in a journal every day (try anyway)
- Write a poem (stupid)
- ~~Make love to Dante~~

I crossed that out. But I couldn't cross it out of my mind. You couldn't cross out desire when it lived in your body.

Six

I GOT TO THINKING ABOUT DANTE AND HOW HE MUST have been so afraid when those assholes jumped him and left him there on the ground, bleeding. What if he had died? They wouldn't have given a damn. And I wasn't there to protect him. I should have been there. I couldn't forgive myself for not being there.

Seven

I FELL ASLEEP READING A BOOK. LEGS WAS LYING NEXT to me when my mother woke me. "Dante's on the phone."

"What's that smile?" I said.

"What smile?"

"Mom, just knock it off."

She shook her head and raised her shoulders in that *What?* kind of body talk.

I walked into the living room and grabbed the receiver. "Hi."

"What are you doing?"

"I fell asleep reading a book."

"What book?"

"*The Sun Also Rises.*"

"I never actually finished that."

"What?!"

"You're making fun of me."

"Yes. But it's that kind of making fun that you only get to do if you like someone."

"Oh, so you like me."

"You're fishing."

"Yup." I could picture him smiling. "So, aren't you going to ask me what *I'm* doing?"

"I was getting to that."

"Well, I was just hanging out with my dad. He's such a dork. He was telling me about all the famous homosexuals in history."

"What?"

Yup, we were both cracking up.

"He's trying to be all cool about this gay thing. It's, like, totally sweet."

"That would be the word," I said.

"He said I should read Oscar Wilde."

"Who's he?"

"He was this English guy. Or Irish. I don't know. Famous writer in the Victorian age. Dad said he was ahead of his time."

"And your dad reads him?"

"Sure. He's a literature guy."

"It doesn't bother him—this—you know—this—"

"I don't think the idea of someone being gay bothers my father. I think he might be a little sad—because he knows it's not gonna be so easy for me. And he's curious about everything, and he's not afraid of ideas. *Ideas won't kill you.* He likes to say that a lot."

I wondered about my own dad. Wondered what he thought. Wondered if he was sad for me, wondered if he was confused.

"I like your dad," I said.

"He likes you too." He was quiet for a moment. "So, you wanna hang out? Any minute now, school's gonna start again."

"Ah, the cycle of life."

"You hate school, don't you?"

"I kinda do."

"Don't you learn anything?"

"I didn't say I don't learn anything. It's just that, you know, I'm ready to move on. I'm over hallways and lockers and assholes and, you know, I guess I just never fit in. And now, well, I'm *really* not gonna to fit in. Shit!"

Dante didn't say anything on the other end of the telephone. And then finally he said, "Do you hate all this, Ari?" I could hear that hurt thing in his voice.

"Look, I'll be right over. We'll hang out."

Dante was sitting on the front steps of his house. Barefoot.

"Hi." He waved. "Are you mad?"

"Why? Because you're not wearing shoes? I don't care."

"No one cares about that except my mother—she likes to tell me what to do."

"That's what mothers do. And why? Because she loves you."

"*Correcto*. Isn't that how you would say it in Spanish?"

"Well, that's how a gringo would say it."

He rolled his eyes. "And how would a real Mexican say it? Not that you're a real Mexican."

"We've had this discussion before, haven't we?"

"We'll always come back to this topic because we live in this topic, a fucking no-man's-land of American identity."

"Well, we *are* Americans. I mean, you don't look like a Mexican at all."

"And you do. But that doesn't make you more Mexican either.

20

We both have giveaway last names, names that mean some people will never consider us real Americans."

"Well, who wants to be?"

"I'm with you on that, babe." He sort of smiled.

"Are you trying that out, the 'babe' thing?"

"I've been trying to work it into the conversation so, you know, so you wouldn't notice."

"I noticed." I didn't exactly roll my eyes. I just gave him that look that said I was rolling my eyes.

"What do you think?"

"I mean, I'm a babe," I said, "but 'babe'?"

"Just cuz you're a babe doesn't mean you have to get cocky." He had this tone when he was amused but also annoyed. "So, 'babe' doesn't work for you. What am I supposed to call you?"

"How about *Ari*?"

"How about 'darling'?" I knew he was just kidding.

"Oh, fuck no."

"How about '*mi amor*'?"

"Better, but that's what my mom says to my dad."

"Yeah, same with my mom."

"Do we really want to sound like our mothers?"

"Oh, hell no," Dante said. I loved that he brought so much laughter into what was once the pathetic-melancholy-boy thing I used to do all the time. And I wanted to kiss him.

"You know, Ari, we're screwed."

"Yup, we're screwed."

"We'll never be Mexican enough. We'll never be American

enough. And we'll never be straight enough."

"Yup," I said, "and you can bet your ass that, somewhere down the road, we won't be gay enough."

"We're screwed."

"Yeah, we are," I said. "Gay men are dying of a disease that doesn't have a cure. And I think that makes most people afraid of us—afraid that somehow we'll pass the disease on to them. And they're finding out that there are so damned many of us. They see millions of us marching on the streets in New York and San Francisco and London and Paris and every other city in the whole world. And there's a whole lot of people that wouldn't mind if we all just died. This is serious shit, Dante. And you and I, we're screwed. I mean. We. Are. Really. Screwed."

Dante nodded. "We really are, aren't we?"

We were both sitting there getting sad. Too sad.

But Dante took us both out of our sadness when he said, "So, if we're screwed, do you think that sometime, we could, like, screw?"

"There's a thought. It's not like we can get pregnant." I played that line very casually. All I could think about was making love to him. But I wasn't going to tell him that I was going fucking crazy. We were boys. And all boys were like this, whether they were gay or whether they were straight—or if they were whatever.

"But if one of us *did* get pregnant, then they'd not only let us get married—they'd *make* us get married."

"That is the smartest dumb thing you've ever said."

And, man, did I want to kiss that guy. I mean, I wanted to kiss him.

Eight

"LET'S GO WATCH A MOVIE."

"Sure," I said. "What?"

"There's this movie, *Stand by Me*. I wanna see it. They say it's good."

"What's it about?"

"A bunch of kids who go looking for a dead body."

"Sounds like fun," I said.

"You're being sarcastic."

"Yup."

"It's good."

"You haven't even seen it."

"But I promise you, you'll like it."

"And if I don't?"

"I'll give you your money back."

It was the middle of the week and it was late afternoon and there weren't many people in the theater. We sat near the very top row and there wasn't anybody sitting close to us. There was a young couple, looked like college students, and they were kissing. I wondered what that was like, to be able to kiss someone you liked any time you wanted. In front of everybody. I would never know what that would be like. Not ever.

But it was really nice to be sitting in a dark movie theater next to Dante. I smiled when we sat down because the first thing he did was take off his tennis shoes. We shared a large popcorn. Sometimes we both reached for the popcorn and our hands would touch.

As I watched the movie, I could feel his glances. I wondered what he saw, who he was making up when he looked at me. "I want to kiss you," he whispered.

"Watch the movie," I said.

He saw me smile.

And then he kissed me.

In a dark theater, where no one could see us, a boy kissed me. A boy who tasted like popcorn. And I kissed him back.

Nine

AS I WAS DRIVING BACK TO DANTE'S HOUSE, HE PLACED his feet on the dashboard of my truck.

I shook my head. "Guess what?"

"What's so funny?

"You forgot your tennis shoes at the movie theater."

"Shit."

"Should I turn around?"

"Who cares?"

"Your mom might."

"She'll never know."

"You wanna bet?"

Ten

DANTE'S PARENTS WERE SITTING ON THE FRONT PORCH when we got back from the movies. Dante and I walked up the stairs.

"Where are your shoes, Dante?"

"You're not supposed to be sitting on the front porch waiting for me to get home. It's called entrapment."

Mr. Quintana was shaking his head. "Maybe you should give up the art thing and become an attorney. And if you're hoping I forgot that you didn't answer my question, think again."

"Why do you like to say *think again*?"

Mrs. Quintana just gave him that look.

"I took them off at the movie theater. I forgot them."

Mr. Quintana didn't laugh, but I could tell he wanted to. "We're not making any progress here, are we, Dante?"

"Dad, who gets to define 'progress'?"

"I do. I'm the dad."

"You know, Dad, when you get all adult on me, it doesn't really work for me."

Mrs. Quintana wasn't going to laugh.

And then Dante had to keep going. He couldn't help himself. "Look at it this way. Some guy will find them and like them and take them home. And he'll have a new pair of tennis shoes. And maybe his parents can't afford to buy him a new pair of tennis shoes. So it all works out."

I *did* want to kiss that guy. Dante didn't know he was funny. He didn't say things to make people laugh. He was too damned sincere for that.

Dante's father just shook his head. "Dante, do you really believe all the things you say?"

"I think so. Yes."

"I was afraid of that."

Mr. Quintana and Dante kept playing their game of verbal chess, and I just stood there and watched them. I couldn't help but notice that Mrs. Quintana was beginning to look very pregnant. Well, maybe not *very*. But, you know, pregnant. What a strange word. Maybe there should be a more beautiful word for a woman who was going to have a baby. When they settled down, Mrs. Quintana looked at me and asked, "How was the movie?"

"It was really good. I think you'd like it."

Mr. Quintana squeezed Mrs. Quintana's hand. "Soledad doesn't like to go to movies. She'd rather work."

She gave her husband one of her smirks. "That's not true," she said. "It's just that I'd rather read a book."

"Yeah. Preferably a book on the latest theories of human psychological development—or the latest theories of how behavioral changes really happen."

She laughed. "Do you find me criticizing your tastes in postmodern poetry?"

I liked how they got along. They had a nice easy way of playing with each other that was really sweet. There was so much affection in Dante's household. Maybe Mrs. Quintana was harder than Mr. Quintana. But she was nice. She was tough *and* she was nice.

Dante looked at his mother. "Have you thought of a name yet?"

"Not yet, Dante." The way she said it was as if she was both annoyed and amused by Dante's new hobby. "We still have four months to decide."

"It's gonna be a boy, you know."

"I don't care. A boy. A girl." She looked at Mr. Quintana. "No offense, but I hope the baby turns out to be more like the mother."

Mr. Quintana looked at her. "Really?"

"Don't give me that *Really?* thing, Sam. I'm outnumbered. Dante takes after you. I live with two boys. We need another adult in this family."

That made me smile. That really made me smile.

"You wanna hear the list I have?"

"List?"

"You know, the names I've picked out for my baby brother." He was lying on his bed, and I was sitting on his chair. He was studying me. "You're laughing at me."

"No, I'm not. Do you hear me laughing?"

"You're laughing on the inside. I can tell."

"Yeah, I'm laughing on the inside. You're relentless."

"I taught you that word."

"Yeah, you did."

"And now you're using it against me."

"Looks that way." I shot him a look. "Don't your parents get a say in this?"

"Not if I can help it."

He walked up to his desk and took out a yellow legal pad. He threw himself back on the bed. "These are the names I have so far: Rafael—"

"Nice."

"Michelangelo."

"That's nuts!"

"This from a boy named Aristotle."

"Shut up."

"I don't do 'shut up.'"

"Like I hadn't noticed."

"Ari, are you gonna hear me out? Or are you gonna editorialize?"

"I thought this was a conversation. You always tell me I don't know how to talk. So I'm talking. But I'll shut up. Unlike you, I know how to do that."

"Yeah, yeah," he said.

"Yeah, yeah," I said.

"Look, just listen to the list, and then you can throw in your irony and sarcasm after I'm done."

"I don't do irony."

"Like hell you don't."

God, I wanted to kiss him. And kiss him and kiss him and kiss him. I was going fucking nuts. Did people lose their minds when they loved someone? Who was I? I didn't know myself anymore. Shit.

"Okay," I said. "I'll shut up. Read the list."

"Octavio. Javier. Juan Carlos. Oliver. Felipe or Philip. Constantine. Cesar. Nicholas. Benjamin. Not Ben, but Benjamin. Adam. Santiago. Joaquin. Francis. Noel. Edgar. That's what I have so far. I've eliminated all the ordinary names."

"Ordinary names?"

"John, Joe, Michael, Edward, etc. What do you think?"

"You do know a lot of those names sound very Mexican."

"What's your point?"

"I'm just saying."

"Look, Ari, *I want him to be Mexican*. I want him to be all the things that I'm not. I want him to know Spanish. I want him to be good at math."

"And you want him to be straight."

"Yes," he whispered. I couldn't stand to see the tears running down his face. "Yes, Ari, I want him to be straight." He sat up on his bed, covered his face with his hands—and cried. Dante and tears.

I sat next to him and pulled him close to me. I didn't say anything. I just let him sob into my shoulder.

Eleven

ALL NIGHT I DREAMED OF DANTE. OF HIM AND ME.

I dreamed his lips. I dreamed his touch. I dreamed his body.

What is this thing called desire?

Twelve

I WAS DOING MY HOMEWORK AT THE KITCHEN TABLE when my dad came in, looking tired and sweaty. He shot me a smile—and just then he looked young again.

"How was work?"

"Neither snow nor rain nor heat nor gloom of night—"

I interrupted him and finished his sentence: "—stays these couriers from the swift completion of their appointed rounds."

My father looked at me. "So you've memorized our motto?"

"Of course I have. I memorized it when I was seven."

It seemed like he was on the edge of tears. I was almost certain that my father had felt like crying many times in his life—it's just that he kept his tears to himself. I was a lot like him. Sometimes we couldn't see what was right in front of us. Things had changed between us. I thought I hated him—but that had never been true. And I thought he didn't give a damn about me. But I knew now that he'd thought about me, worried about me, loved me in ways that I would never fully understand.

Maybe he'd never kiss my cheek, like Dante's father did. But that didn't mean he didn't love me.

"I'm gonna take my shower."

I smiled at him and nodded. His ritual shower. He did that every day when he came back from work. And then he poured himself a glass of wine and went outside and smoked a couple of cigarettes.

When he came back into the kitchen, I had already poured him a glass of wine. "Is it okay if I sit with you in the backyard? Or is that kind of your private time?"

He walked toward the refrigerator and grabbed a can of Dr Pepper. He handed it to me. "Come and have a drink with your father."

My father. My father, my father, my father.

Thirteen

LEGS AND I WENT FOR A RUN IN THE MORNING. AND then I bathed her—and then I took a shower. I got to wondering about bodies and, well, I don't know, I got myself all worked up. See, this love thing, it's not just a heart thing, it's a body thing too. And I wasn't all that comfortable with the heart thing and I wasn't all that comfortable with the body thing either. So I was screwed.

I thought about Dante all the damned time. And it was making me crazy and I wondered if he thought about me all the damned time too. Not that I was going to ask him. I. WAS. NOT. GOING. TO. ASK. HIM.

"Wanna go swimming?"

"Sure."

"How'd you sleep, Ari?"

"That's a funny question."

"That's not an answer."

"I slept fine, Dante."

"I didn't."

I didn't want to have this conversation. "Well, you'll sleep better tomorrow. I'll send Legs over. You can sleep with her. I always sleep better when she's next to me."

"Sounds good," he said. There was a hint of disappointment in his voice. And I thought maybe he would rather have me sleeping next to him than Legs. I mean, did guys go over and sleep with their girlfriends right under their parents' noses? Nope. They didn't. Sleeping next to Dante in his parents' house? Not going to happen. In my house? No. Hell no. Shit!

People say that love is like a kind of heaven. I was beginning to think that love is a kind of hell.

My mom was drinking a cup of coffee and looking over some notes.

"Writing a new syllabus?"

"I don't like teaching the same class in the same way over and over." She looked right at me. "You were dreaming last night."

"Well, I'm like that."

"You're fighting a lot of battles, Ari." She got up and poured me a cup of coffee. "You hungry?"

"Not really."

"You really love that boy, don't you?"

"That was a pretty direct question."

"Since when have you known me to be indirect?"

I sipped my coffee. My mom knew to how make good coffee—but her questions were impossible. There was no escaping her and her questions. "Yeah, Mom, I guess I do love that boy." I didn't like the tears that were running down my face. "Sometimes I don't know who I am, Mom, and I don't know what to do."

"No one's an expert at living. Not even Jesus knew everything. You ever read the Bible?"

"You know I don't."

"You should. There are different versions of the story about his crucifixion. In one version he dies saying, 'I thirst.' In another version, he dies saying, 'My God, my God, why have you forsaken me?' That gives me hope."

"That gives you hope?"

"Yes, Ari, it does."

"I'll think about that." I looked at her. "Does God hate me? Me and Dante?"

"Of course not. I've never read anything in the Bible that indicates that God hates. Hate isn't in his job description."

"You sound so sure, Mom. Maybe you're not such a good Catholic."

"Maybe some people would say I'm not. But I don't need anybody to tell me how to live my faith."

"But me, I'm a sin, right?"

"No, you're not a sin. You're a young man. You're a human being." And then she smiled at me. "And you're my son."

We just sat there for a moment, quiet as the still morning light. I hadn't realized before that I had my mother's eyes. I looked like my father—but I had her eyes.

"Your father and I were talking last night when you were whispering Dante's name."

"It must have been a loud whisper. So what were you talking about?"

"Just that we don't know what to do. We don't know how to help you. We have to learn how to be cartographers too, Ari. And we love you so much."

"I know that, Mom."

"You're not such a boy anymore. You're on the edge of manhood."

"It feels like I'm at the edge of a cliff."

"Manhood is a strange country, Ari. And you *will* enter that country. Very, very soon. But you'll never be alone. Just remember that."

I smiled at her. "Dante's waiting."

She nodded.

I walked toward the front door—but as I reached for the doorknob, I turned around and walked back into the kitchen. I kissed my mom on the cheek. "Have a good day," I said.

Fourteen

I WANTED TO GO AWAY WITH HIM. MAYBE WE COULD go camping. And we would be alone, lost among the trees. Just me and Dante. But wouldn't our parents know what we were up to? I didn't want to be ashamed. And yet, the word "shame" was still a word loitering in my body. It was a word that clung to me, a word that didn't leave easily.

Fifteen

MRS. QUINTANA WAS SITTING ON THE FRONT STEPS when I walked up the sidewalk. "Hi," I said.

"Hi, Ari," she said.

"No work today?"

"I took the day off," she said. "I have an appointment with the doctor."

"Everything okay?"

"Prenatal care."

I nodded.

"Here," she said, "help me up." It was strange and beautiful to feel her hand grasp mine and help pull her onto her feet. It made me feel strong and necessary. To feel necessary, that was—wow—something I'd never thought of before.

"Let's take a walk," she said. "I need to walk."

We walked across the street—and as soon as we reached the park, the green grass beneath us, she took off her shoes.

"Now I know where Dante gets that shoeless thing from."

She shook her head. "I don't like to go barefoot. It's just that my feet get swollen. It's the pregnancy."

"You and Dante spend a lot of time in this park, don't you?"

It was strange to be walking through a park with an adult. Not an ordinary occurrence in my life. I asked a question I didn't really want to ask—especially because I knew the answer already. "Do you think Dante and I will change? I mean. You know what I mean." God, I was really stupid.

"No, Ari, I don't think you will. That's not a problem for me or for Sam or for your parents. But there is this problem—I don't think most people understand boys like you and Dante. And they don't want to understand."

"I'm glad you're not like most people."

She smiled at me. "Me too, Ari. I don't want to be like most people."

I smiled back at her. "I used to think Dante was more like Mr. Quintana than he was like you. I think maybe I was wrong."

"You really are a sweet kid."

"I don't know you well enough to argue with you."

"You really are a smart aleck."

"Yeah, I am."

"I suppose you're wondering if there was something I wanted to talk to you about?"

I nodded.

"When we came back from Chicago, that first day, when you came over. You looked at me and it was as if something passed between us. It seemed to me that it was something very intimate—and I don't mean that there was anything inappropriate about it. But you noticed something about me."

"I did," I said.

"Did you know I was going to have a baby?"

"Maybe. I mean, yes. I thought about it, and, well, yes. Yes, I did know. There was something different about you."

"How do you mean?"

"I don't know. Like you glowed. I know that sounds stupid. But it was like there was so much life—I don't know how to explain it. It's not as if I have ESP—nothing like that. Stupid, really."

"Stupid? Is that your favorite word?"

"I guess today it is."

She grinned. "It doesn't sound stupid, Ari, that you noticed something about me that day. You don't have to have ESP to have a very acute sense of perception. You read people. It's a gift. And I just wanted you to know that there's a lot more going on with you than the fact that you like boys."

We stopped under the shade of an old tree.

"I love this tree," she said.

I smiled. "So does Dante."

"I don't know why, but that doesn't surprise me." She touched the tree and whispered his name.

We started walking back toward her house. And suddenly, she took one of her shoes, which had been dangling from her left hand, and threw it as hard as she could. She laughed, and then took the other shoe and it landed right next to the first. "It's not such a bad game that Dante invented."

All I could do was smile.

Everything was so new. It felt as if I had just been born. This life that I was living now, it was like diving into an ocean when all I had known was a swimming pool. There were no storms in a swimming pool. Storms, they were born in the oceans of the world.

And then there was that cartographer thing. Mapping out a new world was complicated—because the map wasn't just for me. It had to include people like Mrs. Quintana. And Mr. Quintana too. And my mom and dad, and Dante.

Dante.

Sixteen

I WAS WATCHING THE NEWS WITH MY MOM AND DAD. The daily report on the AIDS pandemic came on the screen. Thousands of people were marching through the streets of New York City. A sea of candles in the night. The camera focused on a woman who had tears in her eyes. And a younger woman carried a sign:

MY SON'S NAME WAS JOSHUA.

HE DIED IN THE HALLWAY OF A HOSPITAL.

A man, trying his best to keep his composure, was speaking into the microphone of a news reporter. "We don't need health care in this country. Why have health care when we can just let people die?"

A group of people were carrying a banner that read: ONE AIDS DEATH EVERY 12 MINUTES.

And another carried a banner that read: IT'S NOT THAT WE HATE OUR COUNTRY—IT'S THAT OUR COUNTRY HATES US.

The camera moved away—and cut to the next story.

"Mom, when will it ever end?"

"I think most people think it will just disappear. It's amazing the capacity we have to lie to ourselves."

Seventeen

I WAS WATCHING DANTE SWIM. I THOUGHT OF THE DAY
I met him. It was an accidental meeting, unplanned. I wasn't the
kind of guy who made plans. Things just happened. Or, really, nothing ever happened. Until I met Dante. It was a summer day just
like today. Strangers meet strangers every day—and generally those
strangers remain strangers. I thought of the sound of his voice the
very first time I heard it. I didn't know that voice was going to change
my life. I thought he was only going to teach me how to swim in the
waters of this swimming pool. Instead, he taught me how to dive
into the waters of life.

I want to say the universe brought us together. And maybe it did.
Maybe I just wanted to believe that. I didn't know much about the
universe or God. But I did know this: It was as if I'd known him all
my life. Dante said he'd been waiting for me. Dante was a romantic,
and I admired him for that. It's as if he refused to let go of his innocence. But I wasn't Dante.

I watched him—so graceful in the water. Like it was a kind of
home for him. Maybe he loved the water as much as I loved the
desert. I was happy just to sit on the side of the pool and watch him

swim lap after lap. It was all so effortless for him. So many things were effortless for him. It was as if home was everywhere he went—except that he loved me. And that meant that maybe he'd never have a home ever again.

I felt a splash of water. "Hey! Where are you?"

"Here?" I said.

"You were in your head again."

"I'm always in my head."

"Sometimes I wish I knew everything you were thinking."

"Not a good idea."

He smiled and pulled me into the pool and we got into a splashing fight and we laughed and played at drowning each other. We swam and he taught me more things about swimming. I'd gotten better at the swimming thing. But I'd never be a real swimmer. Not that it mattered all that much to me. Just being in the water with him was enough. Sometimes I thought that Dante *was* the water.

I watched him as he climbed up the ladder and walked toward the edge of the diving board. He waved at me. He planted his feet firmly, then he went up on his toes—then he took a breath and he held this incredible look of serenity. He carried a certainty about himself that I had never had. And then calmly, fearlessly, he leapt up as if his arms were reaching for heaven, then reached downward, making a perfect arch, and twisted his body, a full circle, and then reached the water with hardly a splash. His perfect dive took my breath away.

I not only loved him. I admired him.

• • •

When we were walking home, Dante looked at me and said, "I quit the swimming team."

"Why? That's crazy."

"It takes up too much time. They already started practicing, and I told the coach that I just didn't want to be on the team anymore."

"But why?"

"Like I said, it takes up too much time. And, anyway, I missed last year, so they really won't miss me. And I'd have to try out again, anyway."

"Like you wouldn't make the team. Really?"

"And then there's the small matter that I don't really like a lot of guys on the team. They're such assholes. They're always talking about girls and saying stupid things about their tits. What is this thing about tits that so many guys have? I don't like stupid people. So I just quit."

"No, Dante, you shouldn't do that. You're too good. You can't quit."

"Yes, I can."

"Don't, Dante." I was thinking that he just wanted to spend more time with me—especially because we didn't go to the same school. I didn't want to be responsible for Dante holding himself back. "You're too fucking good to quit."

"So what? It's not as if I'm going to the Olympics or anything."

"But you love swimming."

"I'm not giving up swimming. I'm just leaving the swim team."

"What did your parents say?"

"My dad was okay with it. My mom, well, she wasn't very happy.

There was yelling involved. But look at it this way—this gives us more time to be together."

"Dante, we spend plenty of time together."

He didn't say anything. I could tell he was upset. Then he whispered, "I even told my mom I wanted to go to Austin High School. Just so we could spend more time together. I guess you don't feel the same way." He was trying to hold back his tears. Sometimes I wished he wouldn't cry so damned much.

"It's not that. It's just—"

"Don't you think it would be a lot more fun if we went to the same school?"

I didn't say anything.

"You agree with my mother, don't you?"

"Dante—"

"Ari, don't talk. Just don't talk. I'm too angry with you right now."

"We can't be together all the time."

"Ari, I said, 'don't talk.'"

As we walked toward his house in the silence of Dante's anger, a silence that I was not allowed to break, I wondered why Dante was so unreasonable. But I knew the answer already. Dante may have had a brilliant mind, but emotions ruled him. And he was stubborn as hell. I didn't know how to deal with that. I guess I would have to learn.

We reached his house—and we both stood there, saying nothing.

Dante didn't say bye; he didn't even face me. I watched him walk into his house and slam the door behind him.

Eighteen

AS I WAS WALKING HOME, I WAS AS CONFUSED AS I
had ever been. I was in over my head in this relationship with
Dante. Relationship. That was a vague term if ever there was one.
It could describe just about anything. I mean, Legs and I had a
relationship.

I loved Dante. But I didn't really know what that meant. Where
was love supposed take you?

And besides, we were beginning our last year of high school. And
then what? I knew that Dante and I weren't going to go to the same
college. I hadn't thought about college very much, and I knew Dante
was always thinking about it. Not that we'd talked about it much.
But there was this school that he'd talked about when I met him.
Oberlin. It was in Ohio, and it was, according to Dante, just the kind
of college he'd like to go to.

And me? I knew I wasn't going to go to some private school.
That was for sure. Not in the cards for a guy like me. I was thinking
maybe UT. Mom said Austin would be a good place for me to go
to college. My grades were good enough, I guess. Not that the good
grades came easy. Hell no. I had to work hard. I didn't have Dante's

giant brain. I was a workhorse. Dante was a thoroughbred. Not that I knew anything about horses.

Dante really was my only friend. It was complicated to be in love with your only friend. And now there was an anger from him that I hadn't expected—that I didn't even know was there. I had always assumed that there was no anger in him. But I was wrong. Not that anger was such a bad thing. I mean, it could be a bad thing. Oh hell, talking to yourself was no good. You just went around in circles.

What did "Aristotle and Dante" mean?

I was depressing myself. I was good at that. I had always been good at that.

Nineteen

THE FRONT DOOR WAS OPEN WHEN I GOT HOME. MY dad had put in a new screen door, and my mom liked to keep the door open. Even when the air conditioner was on. "It airs the house out." My dad was always shaking his head and muttering, "Yeah, we're trying to cool off the entire neighborhood." My dad, he liked to mutter. Maybe that's where I got it from.

When I walked into the house I heard two voices talking. The voices were coming from the kitchen. I stopped and realized that I heard Mrs. Quintana's voice. I froze. I don't know why. And then I heard my mom saying, "I'm scared for them. I'm scared the world will beat the decency out of them. I'm scared and I'm angry."

"Anger's not going to do us any good."

"Aren't you angry, Soledad?"

"I am a little angry. People don't understand homosexuality. I'm not sure I understand it either. But you know, I don't have to understand someone to love them—especially if that someone is my son. I'm a therapist. I have gay clients and gay friends. None of this is new to me. But it *is* new to me because now we're talking about my son. And I have no idea what's in store for him. And for Ari."

Then there was quiet, and I heard my mom's voice. "Ari, he's so full of self-doubt already. And now this."

"Aren't all boys his age full of self-doubt?"

"Dante doesn't seem to suffer from that."

"It's just that Dante's a happy boy. He's always been that way. He gets that from his father. But believe me, Lilly, he has his moments—just like every boy."

There was another pause, and then I heard my mother's voice again. "How's Sam handling this?"

"With his usual optimism. He says all we have to do is love him."

"Well, he's right."

"That's about all we can do, isn't it?"

"I suppose so."

And then there was a long silence and Mrs. Quintana asked my mother, "How's Jaime handling it?"

"He surprises me. He said Ari's stronger than he thinks. I think Jaime feels closer to Ari now. He's carried a war inside him for a long time. And I think he identifies with Ari's inner battles."

"Maybe we all do."

Then I heard them laughing. "You're a smart lady, Soledad."

I felt stupid standing there, listening in on a conversation that wasn't meant for my ears. I felt like I was doing something very wrong. I didn't know what to do, so I snuck back out of the house.

I decided to walk back to Dante's house. Maybe he had calmed down. Maybe he wasn't mad anymore.

I was thinking about my dad and my mom and Mrs. Quintana and Mr. Quintana and I felt bad because Dante and I were making them worry. We were making them suffer, and I hated that. But then I thought, it was really a beautiful thing that our mothers could talk about all this. They needed that.

As I was walking, a couple of guys passed me walking in the opposite direction. I knew them from school. And as they passed me, one of them said, "You beat up one of my friends, fucker. Defending some fag. What is he, your fucking boyfriend?"

Before I even knew what I was doing I was grabbing him by the collar and shoving him to the ground. "You wanna mess with me? That's great. I'll fuck you up. Try me. You won't live to be eighteen." I really, really wanted to spit on him. But I didn't. I just kept walking. I was glad Dante wasn't around to watch me behave like a close relation to Cro-Magnon man.

A block away from Dante's house, I had to stop and sit on the curb. I was shaking. I sat there until the shaking stopped. I wondered about cigarettes. My dad said they helped calm his shaking. My mom said it was a myth. "And don't get any ideas." It was good to sit there and think about smoking. Better than thinking about the things I might have done to that kid.

When I got to Dante's house, I knocked on the door. Mr. Quintana answered, a book in his hand. "Hi, Ari."

"Hi, Mr. Quintana."

"Why don't you call me Sam? That's my name."

"I know that's your name. But I could never call you that."

"Oh yeah," he said. "Too disrespectful."

"Yup," I said.

He smiled and shook his head.

"Dante's mad at me," I said.

"I know."

I didn't know what to say. I just shrugged my shoulders.

"I guess you didn't know that the boy you liked so much had a temper."

"Yeah, I guess I didn't."

"Go on up. I'm sure he'll open the door if you knock."

As I started up the stairs, I heard Mr. Quintana's voice. "You're allowed to get mad at each other."

I turned around and looked at him—and nodded.

Dante's door was open. He was holding a piece of charcoal and staring at his sketch pad. "Hi," I said.

"Hi," he said.

"Are you still mad at me?"

"Usually, I stay mad for a couple of days. Sometimes even longer. But you must be special—because I'm not mad anymore."

"So I can talk now?"

"As long as you help me clean my room. And then kiss me."

"Ah, I see. There are consequences for my actions." I looked around his room. It really did look like there had been a storm in there. "How can you live in this room?"

"Not everybody lives like a monk, Ari."

"What does that have to do with you being so messy?"

"I like messy."

"I don't. Your room looks like my brain."

Dante smiled at me. "Maybe that's why I love your brain."

"I don't think you love my brain."

"How do you know?"

We spent the afternoon cleaning his room and listening to records of the Beatles. And when the room was clean, Dante threw himself on his bed and I sat on his big leather chair. And Dante asked me what I was thinking. And so I said, "Our parents, Dante. They really, really love us."

"I know. But if we think about them too much, we're never, ever going to have sex. Because our mothers will be right in the same room as we are. And that is really messed up. So let's not bring our mothers into the bedroom—even though Freud says they're there anyway."

"Freud. I wrote a paper on him once. Thanks for reminding me."

"Yup. In Freud's world, whenever we sleep within anyone, it's a very crowded bed."

I noticed a big canvas on his easel, covered with a sheet. It had to be the painting he'd been working on. He'd been working on it for a long time. "When can I see it?"

"It's a surprise. You'll see it when it's time."

"When will that be?"

"When I say so."

I felt Dante's hand on my back.

I turned around. Slowly. Slowly. And I let him kiss me. Yeah, I guess you could say I kissed him back.

Twenty

I KEEP THINKING ABOUT DANTE AND THE CARTOGRA-
pher thing. Making a map of the new world. Wouldn't that be something fantastically, amazingly beautiful? The world according to Ari
and Dante. Dante and me walking through a world, a world nobody
had ever seen, and mapping out all the rivers and valleys and creating paths so that those who came after us wouldn't have to be
afraid—and they wouldn't get lost. How beautiful was that?

Yeah, Dante was wearing off on me.

But, hey, all I have is a journal that I'm going to write in.
That's about as fantastic and beautiful as it's going to get for me.
I can live with that. It's funny, I've had this leather-bound journal
for a long time. It was just sitting there on my bookshelf with a
note from my aunt Ophelia that said: *One day you're going to fill
these pages with words that come from you. I have a feeling that you
will have a long relationship with words. Who knows? They might
even save you.*

So now I'm sitting in the kitchen and I'm staring at the blank
page and I'm thinking of Aunt Ophelia's note and I've been staring at the blank page for a long time as if I were facing down an

enemy. I want to write something, and I want to say something that matters—not something that matters to the whole fucking world, because the whole fucking world doesn't give a damn about me or about Dante. In fact, when I think about the story of the world, I think whoever wrote that story wouldn't include us. But I don't want to write for the world—I just want to write what I'm thinking and the things that matter *to me*.

I've thought about this all day: me kissing Dante on a starry night in the desert. It was like someone lit me like a firecracker and I felt like I was about to explode and light the whole desert sky. How can my own words save me? I wish my aunt Ophelia were with me right now. She's not. But me, Ari, he's here. I think I'm going to begin like this: *Dear Dante*. And I'm going to pretend I'm talking to him. Though really, I'm doing what I always do—yeah, talking to myself. Talking to myself is the only thing I'm good at. I'll just pretend I'm talking to Dante and make myself believe that I'm talking to someone who's worth talking to.

Mom says I have to learn how to love myself—which is a strange thought. Loving yourself seems like a really weird goal. But, hell, what do I know?

Last year, Mr. Blocker said we could find ourselves in our own writing. All I could think was this: Sounds like a good place to get lost. Yeah, I think I might get lost a hundred times, a thousand times, before I find out who I am and where I'm going.

But if I carry Dante's name with me, he will be the torch to light my way in the darkness that is Aristotle Mendoza.

Dear Dante,

*I don't like it when you get mad at me. It makes me feel bad.
I don't know what else to say about this. I have to think
about this some more. You getting angry isn't part of the way I
thought of you. But you shouldn't have to fit in my definition of
you. I don't want you to live in the prison of my thoughts. I'm
the only one who should be living there.*

*The problem is this: I think about you all the time, about how
it might feel to watch you stand in front of me and you would
take your clothes off and say:* This is me. *And I would take my
clothes off and say:* This is me.

*And we would touch. And it would feel like I'd never touched
anybody or anything, like I'd never really known what touch
was until I felt your hands on my skin.*

*I keep picturing my finger running over your lips over and over
again.*

*I try not to think about these things. I don't want to think
about them.*

*But the thoughts are so incredibly beautiful to me. And
I'm asking myself why the entire world believes that these
thoughts—my thoughts—are so ugly. I know you don't*

have the answers to my questions. But I think you ask those questions too.

I just keep picturing you in a hospital room, your smile almost hidden by the bruises those guys left on you. They thought you were just an animal they could kick around and even kill. But I think it was them—they were the animals.

When will we all get to be human, Dante?

Twenty-One

LEGS AND I WENT FOR A RUN. I LOVED THE MORNING and the desert air, and it seemed as if Legs and I were the only living things in the world.

I never knew how far I ran. I would just run. I wasn't really into measuring things. I just ran and listened to my breathing and to the rhythms of my body just like Dante listened to his body in the water.

I always ran past Dante's house.

There he was, sitting on the steps of his house, barefoot, wearing the ratty T-shirt that was so worn you could see through it and still carrying the sleep in his eyes. He waved. I stopped, unleashed Legs, who ran up to Dante and licked his face. I never really let Legs lick my face, but Dante was all about getting kisses from Legs.

I watched them. I liked watching them. And then I heard Dante's voice. "You like watching, don't you?"

"Guess so," I said. "Maybe I'm like my dad."

I made my way up the steps and sat next to him. He and Legs were busy loving on each other. I wanted to lay my head on his shoulder—but I didn't. I was too sweaty, and I smelled bad.

"You want to go somewhere today?"

"Sure," I said. "We could take a long ride in the truck, you know, before school starts."

"School. Ugh."

"I thought you liked school."

"I know all I'm ever gonna learn in high school."

That made me laugh. "So there's nothing left to learn?"

"Well, not a whole year's worth. We should go straight to college and live together."

"Is that the plan?"

"Of course that's the plan."

"What if we kill each other—as roommates?"

"We won't kill each other. And we'll be more than roommates."

"I get that," I said. I so didn't want to have this conversation. "I'm going home to take a shower."

"Take one here. I'll shower with you."

That made me laugh. "I'm not sure your mother would be big on that idea."

"Yeah, well, parents sometimes get in the way of all the fun."

On the way home, I pictured Dante and me in the shower together.

A part of me wanted to run away from all the complications of being in love with Dante. Maybe Ari plus Dante equaled love, but it also equaled complicated. It also equaled playing hide-and-seek with the world. But there was a difference between the art of running and the art of running away.

Twenty-Two

DANTE AND I WENT SWIMMING LATER THAT DAY. WE got into a splashing war, and I thought that the only reason we did that was because we got to accidentally touch each other. On the short walk back to his house, Dante made a face.

"What was that?" I said.

"I was thinking about school. And that bullshit of looking up at your teachers as if you really believe they're smarter than you are is a little bit annoying."

"Annoying?" I laughed. "Annoying" was definitely a Dante word.

"Is that funny?"

"No. You like to say the word 'annoying.'"

"What? It's not a word you know?"

"It's not that—it's just that it's not a word I use."

"Well, what do you say when something annoys you?"

"I say it pisses me off."

All of a sudden Dante got this great look on his face. "That's awesome," he said. "That's fucking awesome." He leaned into me and nudged me with his shoulder.

"You're interesting, Dante. You love words like 'interminable,' as in 'I'm interminably bored,' and words like 'liminal'—"

"Did you look the word up?"

"I did. I can even use it in a sentence: Aristotle and Dante reside in a liminal space."

"Fucking awesome."

"See, that's why you're interesting. You're a walking dictionary and you love to cuss."

"That's what makes me interesting?"

"Yes."

"Is it better to be interesting or it to be handsome?"

"Are you fishing for a compliment, Dante?"

He smiled.

"Being interesting and being handsome aren't mutually exclusive." I looked at him, looked straight into his big, clear brown eyes and grinned. "Mutually exclusive. God, I'm starting to talk like you."

"Talking like you have a brain isn't such a bad thing."

"No, it isn't. But using your vocabulary as a tool to remind everybody that you're a superior being is—"

"You're starting to piss me off."

"And now you're talking like me." I laughed. He didn't. "You *are* a superior being," I said. "And you're interesting and you're handsome, and . . ." I rolled my eyes. "And you're charming." And then we both cracked up laughing, because "charming" was his mother's word. Every time he got into trouble, his mother would say, "Dante Quintana, you're not nearly as charming as you think you are." But he *was* that word "charming." I was thinking that Dante could charm the pants right off of me. And my underwear, too.

God, I had a dirty mind. I was going straight to hell.

Twenty-three

Dear Dante,

When I was helping you clean your room, I got to wondering
why you like to be so messy when everything in your mind
seems to be so organized. The sketch of the vinyl records you
did and of the record player is amazing. When you took it out
from under your bed and showed it to me, I couldn't even talk.
I saw that you had tons of sketches under your bed. Someday
I'd like to sneak into your room and take them all out and run
my hand over every sketch. It would be like touching you.

I live in a confusion called love. I see you take a perfect dive
and I think of how perfect you are. And then you get angry
with me because I don't want to spend all my time with you.
But a part of me does want to spend all my time with you.
And I know that's not possible—and it isn't even a good idea.
It isn't logical to think that I don't love you just because I think
it's not a good idea to go to the same school. And then you
want me to talk more and then suddenly you tell me not to
talk. You're so not logical. You're not logical at all. I guess that's

part of the reason I love you. But it's also the reason that you make me crazy.

I had a dream last night about my brother again. It's the same dream. I don't really understand my dreams and why they're inside me and what they do. He's always standing on the other side of the river. I'm in the United States. He's in Mexico. I mean, we live in different countries—I guess that's true enough. But I want so much to talk to him. He might be a nicer guy than people give him credit for—yeah, fucked-up and stuff, but maybe not completely corrupt. No one is completely corrupt. Am I right about that? Or maybe he's just a miserable fucking asshole and his life is a complete fucking tragedy. Either way, I'd like to know. So that I wouldn't spend the rest of my life wondering about a brother whose vague memory resides inside me like a splinter in your hand that can't be removed. That's how it feels. Dante, if your mom has a boy—if you get that brother you've always wanted—love him. Be good to him. So when he grows up, he won't be haunted by bad dreams.

My mother walked into the room as I was writing in my journal. "I think that's a great idea," she said, "to keep a journal." And then she noticed the journal I was writing in. "Ophelia gave that to you, didn't she?"

I nodded. I thought she was going to cry. She started to say something—then changed her mind. But then she said, "Why don't you and Dante go camping for a few days before school starts? You used to love to go camping."

Now it was me who was going to cry. But I didn't. I didn't. I wanted to hug her. I wanted to hug her and hug her.

We just sort of smiled at each other—and I wanted to tell her how much I loved her, but I just couldn't. I just, I don't know. Sometimes I had beautiful words living inside of me and I just couldn't push those words out so that other people could see they were there.

"So, what do you think about the camping idea?"

I didn't want to show her how damned excited I was, so I very calmly said, "Mom, I think you're brilliant." She knew. She knew how to read that grin I was wearing.

"I just made your day, didn't I?"

I looked at her with that wiseass look on my face that said *I'm not going to go there*.

And she looked back at me with that kind of sweet but self-satisfied look that said, *I did. I did make your day*. And then she laughed. I liked the way we could sometimes talk to each other without using words.

And then she dropped this bomb: "Oh, by the way, I almost forgot. Your sisters want to take you to lunch."

"Lunch? Mom . . ."

"You know, you're not such a boy anymore—and when you get close to being an adult, you start doing what adults do—go to lunch with family, with friends."

"You told them, didn't you?"

"I did tell them, Ari."

"Shit! Mom, I—"

"They're your sisters, Ari, and they love you. They want to be supportive. What's so bad about that?"

"But did you have to tell them?"

"Well, *you* weren't going to tell them. And they shouldn't be the last to know; they'd be hurt."

"Well, I'm hurt that you told them without my permission."

"I'm your mother. I don't need your permission. I get to tell my children what I think they need to know."

"But they're so bossy. They don't even think I'm a person. They used to dress me as if I was some kind of doll when I was little. And they were always telling me what to do. *And don't touch this, and don't touch that either cuz I'll kill you.* Ugh."

"My, how you've suffered, Angel Aristotle Mendoza."

"That's pretty snarky, Mom."

"Don't be mad at me."

"I am mad at you."

"I'm sure you'll get over it soon."

"Yup," I said. "Are they going to interview me? Are they going to ask me all kinds of questions I won't be able to answer?"

"They're not journalists, Ari—they're your sisters."

"Can I invite Dante to come along?"

"No."

"Why not?"

"You know why not. For the very reason you want to invite him to come along. He'll do all the talking and you'll just sit there and watch the whole thing play out. I love Dante, and I won't have you use him as a front man just because you don't want to talk about things that make you uncomfortable."

"Which is most things."

"Yup."

"I talk to you, Mom, don't I?"

"A very recent development."

"But a step in the right direction," I said. I had this stupid grin on my face.

My mother smiled—and then she broke into a very soft laugh. She ran her fingers through my hair. "Oh, Ari, let your sisters love you. Let yourself be loved. For all you know, there's a long line of people wanting you to let them in."

Twenty-Four

SO THERE I SAT AT THE HOUSE OF PIZZA, IN A BOOTH across from my twin sisters, Emilia, who looked exactly like a younger version of our mother, and Elvira, who was a younger version of my aunt Ophelia. Emmy and Vera.

Emmy, Madam Take-Charge, ordered a large pepperoni, sausage, and mushroom pizza. And she ordered me a Coke.

"I don't drink Coke so much anymore."

"You used to love Coke."

"Things change."

"Well, have one for old times' sake."

"Well, since you've already ordered it for me."

She smiled at me. God, I wish she didn't look so damned much like our mother.

Vera rolled her eyes. "She's pushy. She was born a whole three minutes and thirty-three seconds ahead of me and she's been my big sister ever since. You don't stand a chance, Ari."

I had my elbows on the table and rested my head in between the palms of my hand. "I've never stood a chance with either of you. I was the little brother you could push around."

Emmy gave me one of her famous grins. "You were sweet when you were little. We gave you a little teddy bear. You named him Tito. You used to take Tito everywhere you went. You were adorable. And then you hit ten and turned into a brat. And that's the truth. Mom and Dad spoiled you like crazy."

"Ahh, sibling resentments."

Emmy reached over and gently pulled my arm toward her. She kissed my knuckle. "Ari, whether you know it or not, I adore you."

Vera nodded. "Of course, I always adored you more."

"And you've always just blown us off."

"Yeah, well, I'm an asshole. But you already know that."

"You're not an asshole, Ari." Vera looked like she was about to cry. In our family, she was the queen of tears. "You're so hard on yourself."

And Emmy chimed in right on cue. "You really are. Ever since you were a kid. Once, you brought home your report card and as you handed it to Mom, you kept saying, 'I'm sorry.' You started hitting your head with your knuckles. Mom gently took your arm and sat you down. You were beating yourself up over one lousy C. All As, one B, and one C. And you were always saying things like 'It's my fault.' Everything wasn't your fault."

Vera nodded. "When Bernardo went away, you asked Mom, 'Did I make him mad? Is that why he went away?' That broke my heart, Ari. You loved him so much. When Bernardo didn't come back, you changed. You became quieter—and kept to yourself. Always blaming yourself for everything."

"I don't remember any of that."

"It's okay to not remember," Emmy said.

Vera looked at me. She had this look that was kind but firm. "Just try not to take responsibility for things you're not responsible for."

"You mean like me being gay?"

"Exactly."

And they both said it at the same time as if they'd practiced or something. "It's okay if you like guys."

Emmy laughed. "I mean, we like guys too, so we have no room to talk."

"You're supposed to like guys," I told them. "I'm not. And I'm going to wind up being the gay uncle that your kids whisper about. The uncle who's not all that much older than they are."

"I don't think they'll care. They worship you."

"I don't spend much time with them."

"That's true. But when you do spend time with them, you're awesome. You make them laugh and you tell them dumb stories right out of thin air. That's a rare gift, by the way. And you used to sing to them."

I hated the tears that were falling down my face. What the hell was happening to me? "Thanks," I whispered. "I'm not very good at loving people. And Mom said I should let myself be loved."

Vera flicked my knuckle with her finger. "She's right. And you know, Ari, it's not that difficult to love you."

"I think I'm pretty difficult to love."

"Well, it's time to stop believing everything you think."

"Where have I heard that before?"

"You may have heard that a thousand times, but you've never

actually listened. Time to start listening, dude." Emmy was all about the lessons of life. Somehow her advice came out sounding like a command. I wondered if her two children found her annoying.

"Ari, we've always loved you—even when you didn't want us to." There was a lot of tenderness in Vera's voice. "You can't tell other people who to love."

"I guess I'm supposed to love you back."

"It's not a requirement—but that would be nice."

"I'll work on it."

"You really are a wiseass, Ari, you know that?"

"Yeah, I know. Dante says it's part of my charm."

There was a silence between us for a moment. I stared at the floor and then I looked up at them—and I saw that look that my mom wore, the kind of look that just killed you because it didn't just say *I love you*. It said *I will always love you*.

"I guess it wouldn't kill me if I told you both that I love you."

"Well, you just said it—and you didn't die. You do realize you've never said that to us."

Emmy nodded.

"I really have been a jerk, haven't I?"

The pizza arrived before Emmy or Vera could answer.

Twenty-Five

ARI, WE ONLY WANT ONE THING FOR YOU—TO BE HAPPY.
I could still hear my sisters' voices in my head. Happiness. What the
hell did that mean? It had to be more than the absence of sadness.
And that word, "want." That word was related to the word "desire."
I rewrote what they said to me in my head. *Our one desire for you,
Ari, is for you to be happy.*

I heard Dante's voice in my head. *I see a longing in you . . . a
yearning . . . Those words live in you.*

Desire. A body thing. A heart thing. The body and the heart.

I used to live in a world that was made up of the things I thought.
I didn't know how small that world was. I was suffocating in my
own thoughts. It was like living in a world of make-believe. And the
world I lived in now was getting bigger and bigger.

For one thing, there was a sky in the world I lived in now. And
it was blue and it was large and it was beautiful. But where on my
map was I going to put the word "happy"? Where on my map was I
going to put "desire"?

And then this thought entered my head: "Happy" and "desire"
didn't go together. Those words didn't go together at all. Desire
didn't make you happy—it made you miserable.

Twenty-Six

IN THE WORLD I WAS MAPPING OUT, THERE WERE CER-
tain roads that went to certain places. There would be a road that led
to the desert, and I would name the desert Arid because it contained
my name and I would take that road and I would stand there, in
the desert named Arid, and I would see a summer storm coming in,
and I would breathe in, and understand that the smell of that storm
was the smell of God. And I would map out a path that led to a hill
where there was a mesquite tree and a huge boulder. I would sit on
that boulder and watch the storm coming straight at where I was
sitting—and the thunder and the lightning came closer and closer.
But the storm was not threatening me because the storm did not
exist as a bully, but as something that was coming to welcome me
into the world, and to remind me that I was a part of the desert and
all things beautiful. And when the rain arrived, it would pour down
on me, and *I would become a part of it*. I imagined Dante kissing me
in the rain. And we would not be afraid of the storm. And he and I
would sit there until we learned the language of the rain.

And on my map, I would name that place Lugar de los Milagros.
The Place of Miracles.

Twenty-Seven

DANTE PICKED UP THE PHONE ON THE SECOND RING. "Is there one Mr. Dante Quintana available? I will only take up a few minutes of his time."

"Yes, this would be Mr. Quintana. May I ask who I am speaking to and what products you're offering today—and what company you represent?"

"Why, of course. My name is Mr. Art Angel, and I represent a small vacation and tour company—Jaime, Lilly & Ari Incorporated, with offices in San Antonio, Houston, Dallas, Albuquerque, and our new office in El Paso. We specialize in affordable getaway vacations because we believe everybody deserves a vacation."

"I find that philosophy quite laudable."

"Laudable?"

"Yes, yes, laudable. Quite."

"Now, as I was saying, Mr. Quintana, this is your lucky day. You have been selected to take advantage of our end-of-summer vacation package. This offer includes two and a half days of camping in Cloudcroft, New Mexico, with a stop at the fabulous White Sands National Park. The white dunes are composed of gypsum crystals, which never heat up even on the hottest summer days and create an ideal hiking environment for a comfortable barefoot experience, perfect for individuals who have an antipathy for shoes."

"Antipathy? Do they teach you those words at sales conferences?"

"You must have a mistaken impression of the educational level of our sales force."

"Well—"

"As I was saying, the white dunes offer the opportunity for a perfect barefoot experience. From the dunes, the scenery all the way to Cloudcroft is nothing short of spectacular, and you need not have any camping experience in order to accept our offer. Transportation and all expenses will be completely covered by our company."

All of a sudden there was a silence on the other end of the phone.

"Dante? Are you there?"

And then I heard him whisper, "Are you serious, Ari? For real?"

I nodded into the phone.

"Don't cry."

"I wasn't going to cry."

"Yes, you were."

"And if I want to cry, I'll cry. You can't tell me what to do." And then I heard him crying. And then he controlled himself. "Don't I have to be twenty-one to accept your company's more-than-generous offer?"

"No," I said. "All our company needs is a signed statement from a parent or legal guardian."

There was quiet again on the other end of the phone. "And we'll spend all that time alone?"

"Yes," I whispered.

"You are the most incredible human being who ever walked on planet Earth."

I smiled into the receiver. "You might not think so after spending three days with me. Maybe that's the antidote for falling for a guy like me."

"I don't need an antidote. I don't happen to have a sickness."

I do, I thought. *I'm as love-sick as you can get.*

Twenty-Eight

Dear Dante,

I went down to the basement to check out the camping gear. My dad has it all perfectly organized. After every camping trip, he airs everything out before he puts it all away. And he makes sure all the gear is clean and ready to go for the next time—except we haven't gone camping in a long time. I had a good look at all the gear: a tent, two kerosene lanterns, sleeping bags, a small propane camping stove, an empty propane tank, and a couple of tarps. Everything neatly stacked on a shelf he built himself. I remember helping build the shelves when I was in fifth or sixth grade. I didn't actually help very much. I mostly just stood there and watched him. The only thing I really remember about building the shelves was my father's quiet lecture on having respect for saws. "If you like having fingers, you better pay attention and stay focused." Of course, he really didn't teach me how to use the saw. He didn't ever let me come too close when he was cutting the wood. I think that maybe my mother gave my father a lecture of her own regarding me and the saw.

When I think about it now, I think my mother has always been a little too overprotective of me. I used to think she was just bossy. But now I don't think she's bossy at all. I think she's always been afraid of losing me. I think that fear comes from her experiences with my older brother.

I remember you telling me that you were always analyzing your parents. And now I'm beginning to analyze mine. When did we get our degrees in psychology?

I shut my journal and looked down at Legs, who was lying down at my feet. "Legs, do you remember your parents?" Legs looked up at me and put her head on my lap. "Course you don't. Me, I'm your dad. And I'm a good dad too, aren't I?" Why the hell did we talk to dogs as if they understood the stupid things we were saying to them? I lifted her head and kissed her on her dog forehead.

My mother walked into the kitchen and shook her head. "It's sweet that some people kiss their dogs. But me, I love a dog by feeding it."

"Maybe it's because you like cats more than dogs."

"I like cats. I like dogs, too. But I don't like them in my bed—and I don't go around kissing them." And then she looked right at Legs. "And lucky for you that you have Ari as your master. Otherwise, you'd be sleeping out in the yard like any good old-fashioned self-respecting dog." She cut a piece of cheese, walked up to Legs—and fed it to her. "That's how you love a dog," she said.

"No, Mom, that's how you bribe a dog."

My dad and I looked over the camping supplies. "So, you and Dante are going camping?"

"What's that grin you're wearing?"

"It's just that I'm trying to picture Dante on a camping trip."

I couldn't help but laugh. "I have my work cut out for me. He'll do all right."

"We used to go camping all the time."

"Why did we stop?"

"I don't know. You loved going camping. You were always such a serious boy. But when you went camping, you seemed to loosen up. You laughed a lot and you were so in awe of everything around you. You'd pick up anything you could—and you'd turn it over and over in your hands as if you were trying to get to the bottom of its mystery.

"I remember the first time I lit a campfire with you. That look of wonder in your eyes. You were maybe four years old. And you grabbed your mother's hand and shouted, 'Mom! Look! Fire! Dad made fire!' It was easier for me when you were a little boy."

"Easier?"

"A man like me." He stopped. "A man like me can show a child his affection, but it's harder . . ." He stopped. "You get used to not talking. You get used to the silence. It's hard, you know, to break a silence that becomes a part of how you see yourself. Silence becomes a way of living. Ari . . ." He looked down at the floor—then looked back up at me.

I knew there were tears running down my face. I didn't even try to fight them off.

"It wasn't that I didn't love you. It's just that, well, you know."

"I know, Dad."

I understood what my father was trying to say. I leaned into him, and I was trembling. Trembling and trembling—and I found myself crying into my father's shoulder like a little boy. He put his arms around me and held me as I cried. I knew that something was happening between me and my father, something important—and there weren't any words for what was happening, and even though words were important, they weren't everything. A lot of things happened outside the world of words.

I didn't know if I was crying because of what my father had said. I think that was part of it. But, really, I think I was crying about a lot of things, about me and my desire for another boy's body, which was mysterious and terrifying and confusing. I was crying about my brother, whose ghost haunted me. I was crying because I realized how much I loved my father, who was becoming someone I knew. He wasn't a stranger anymore. I was crying because I had wasted so much time thinking shitty things about him, instead of seeing him as a quiet, kind man who had suffered through a hell called war and had survived.

That's why I was crying.

My mother had said that they were just people, she and my father. And she was right. Maybe that *was* a sign that I was starting to grow up, the knowledge that my parents were people and that they felt the same things that I felt—only they'd been feeling those things for a helluva lot longer than I had, and had learned what to do about those feelings.

I slowly pulled away from my father and nodded. He nodded

back. I wanted to memorize that soft smile he was wearing on his face and carry it with me everywhere I went. When I turned to walk back up the basement steps, I saw my mother standing at the foot of the stairs. Now I knew what people were talking about when they said somebody cried "tears of joy."

Twenty-Nine

Dear Dante,

I used to wonder about boys like you who cried—and now I've fucking turned into one of those boys. I'm not sure I like it. I mean, it's not that I'm crying for nothing, I mean, hell, I don't know what I mean. I'm changing. And it's as if the changes are all coming at me all at once. And the changes, they're not bad. I mean, they're good. They're good changes.

I didn't used to like who I was.

And now I just don't know who I am. Well, I do know who I am. But mostly I'm becoming someone I don't know. I don't know who I'm going to become.

But I'm better, Dante. I'm a better person—though that may not be saying much.

When I met you, I remember you telling me that you were

crazy about your parents. And I thought it was the weirdest thing I'd ever heard coming out of another guy's mouth. You know, sometimes I don't know shit. I think I have always loved my father and my mother. Maybe I just didn't think that my love for them was really all that important. I mean, they were my parents, right? I always thought I was sort of invisible to them. But it was the other way around. It was they who were *invisible to* me.

Because I wasn't capable of seeing them.

I think I've been like this kitten, born with its eyes closed, walking around meowing because I couldn't see where I was going.

But, Dante, guess what? The kitten has fucking opened his eyes. I can see, Dante, I can see.

Thirty

THE NIGHT BEFORE WE WERE HEADING OUT FOR OUR
camping trip, the Quintanas invited me over for dinner. My mother
baked an apple pie. "It's not polite to arrive at someone's house empty-
handed." My father grinned at her and said, "Your mother often
engages in immigrant behavior. She can't help herself." I thought that
was pretty funny. So did my mother, actually.

"Sending over a pie isn't immigrant behavior."

"Oh yes, it is, Lilly. Just because you're not sending over tamales
and roasted chiles doesn't make it *not* immigrant behavior. You're
just wrapping it up in an American costume. Apple pie? It doesn't
get any more American than that."

My mother kissed him on the cheek. "Shut up, Jaime. *Estás
hablando puras tonterías.* Don't you have a cigarette to go smoke or
something?"

I normally walked to Dante's house, but I decided to take the truck.
I had this vision of me dropping the pie on the sidewalk, and I just
didn't want to be the center of all that drama. I was scarred for life
when I dropped a porcelain plate loaded with my mother's Christmas

cookies when I was seven. Until recently, that was the last time I cried. And it wasn't even that my mother was upset. In fact, she was consoling me for some reason—and that made it even worse.

I could tell my mom was in total agreement with my decision. "You're showing signs of wisdom," she said.

"Mom, maybe I'm just showing signs of being practical."

"Well, being wise and being practical aren't mutually exclusive."

I just nodded.

"You're getting pretty good at not rolling your eyes at me. It shows restraint." I could hear my father laughing from the other room.

"Mom," I said, "I don't think you're ever going to make a very good bullshitter."

She grinned at me and handed me the pie. "Have a good time. Give my love to Dante's parents."

"Mom, they don't need your love," I said as I headed out the door. "What they need is your apple pie."

I could hear my mother's laughter as I shut the door softly and headed toward Dante's house.

On the short drive to Dante's house, I was smiling—I was smiling.

Mrs. Quintana answered the door. I felt a little shy and a little stupid as I stood there, holding an apple pie. "Hi," I said. "My mom sends her love and this apple pie."

God, Mrs. Quintana could win a smiling contest.

She took the pie from my hands. And all I could think of was that I hadn't dropped the pie and it was safely in the hands of an experienced pie handler. I followed her into the dining room, where Mr. Quintana was placing a big plate loaded with tacos.

"I made my world-famous tacos." He grinned at me.

Dante walked into the room, wearing a pink shirt with a little alligator on it. I tried not to notice how the pink against his fair skin almost made him glow. God, he was handsome. Dante. Shit. God. "And I made the rice."

"You cook? Who knew."

"Well, I only know how to make rice and warm up leftovers."

That sweet look on his face. Dante could be humble.

I gotta say, Mr. Quintana can make some mean tacos. And Dante's Mexican rice was pretty much to die for. Not quite as fluffy as my mom's, but still. Dante and I had a whopping five tacos each, Mr. Quintana had four, and Mrs. Quintana apologized for eating three. "I generally only eat two, but I'm eating for two. And he's kicking up a storm."

Dante's eyes lit up. "Is he kicking right now?"

"He sure is." She motioned toward him. "Feel."

Dante was up in half a second and stood next to his mom. She took his hand and placed it on her belly. "See?"

Dante didn't utter a word—then, finally, he said, "Oh, Mom, that's incredible. Oh my God, that's, that's life. You have all that life inside you. Oh, Mom." After a while he pulled his hand away slowly and kissed his mother on the cheek. "You know, Mom, when I fight you, I don't really mean it."

"I know. Well, except the shoe thing."

"Yeah"—he smiled—"except the shoe thing."

"Speaking of which—Ari, I'm making you the shoe police. Dante's only allowed to go barefoot at White Sands."

"I think I can handle that."

"You're taking her side?"

"Don't answer that question," Mr. Quintana said. "There is no right answer."

Dante gave his dad a snarky look. "Dad thinks he's Switzerland. He's always going for neutrality."

"No. I'm going for survival."

That made me laugh.

"Well, I've waited long enough to have a slice of Lilly's apple pie. We'll eat some pie and we can talk about how both of you are going to behave during your camping trip."

Oh God, I thought I was going to die. She wasn't going to talk about sex. I mean, the truth was, that was all I was thinking about, which just goes to show that I was just like every other seventeen-year-old guy on the planet. I sat there frozen. Good thing Mrs. Quintana was busy cutting the apple pie and serving it up on plates. Otherwise she might have noticed the *I want to hide under the table* look on my face.

"No smoking pot and no drinking beer. You got that?"

I nodded. "Yes, ma'am, I understand."

"Oh, I'm not worried about you, Ari. This little lecture is mostly intended for my Dante."

"Mom, it's not as if I can score pot at the drop of a hat."

"I don't know about that, Dante; you're very resourceful."

"Oh, Mom, don't tell me you and Dad didn't ever smoke pot or drink beer when you were underage."

"What your father did and what I did when he and I were underage is, one, none of your business, and two, irrelevant to your situation. I'm a parent, and you may want to believe that all I want to do is control you, but you'd be wrong about that. I just don't want you two to get into any trouble. You have enough to deal with already. And you know what I mean, so let's not push it." She kissed Dante on the forehead as she placed a piece of pie in front of him.

Mr. Quintana blew a kiss at Mrs. Quintana.

"You see," Dante said. "See how he blew her a kiss. That means he's telling her *Good job, honey.* And then he wants to believe he's Switzerland." He made a face, then stuck his fork in his piece of pie and when he tasted it, before he'd even finished swallowing, his eyes opened as wide as I'd ever seen them. "Oh my God, this is the best fucking piece of apple pie I've ever tasted."

Mrs. Quintana put her head down and shook her head. "I am about to wash your mouth out with soap. I know you love that word, just as you know I hate it. You have an extensive vocabulary, and I'm sure you can find other words to replace it."

"I have looked for other words. They pale in comparison."

"Do you see my look of disapproval? I may not be able to stop you from using that word when you're not in my presence, but don't use that word in front of me. Ever."

"I'm sorry, Mom. Truly. I am." He pointed the fork toward his piece of pie. "Taste."

She shot Dante one of her famous looks, then tasted the apple pie. "Oh my God, Ari, where did your mother learn how to bake?"

"I don't know. She's always been amazing in the kitchen."

"Is she as good in the classroom as she is in the kitchen?"

"I have a feeling she is."

Mrs. Quintana nodded as she went for another bite. "I get that feeling too," she said. "And I can almost forgive you for using that word."

Dante had this victorious look on his face.

"Don't get cocky. I said 'almost.'"

And then I noticed Mr. Quintana was serving himself seconds of my mother's pie.

"Sam, did you even taste it? Or did you just inhale it?"

"Oh, I tasted it, all right. The rest of you can go ahead and talk. I'm busy bonding with Lilly's apple pie."

Dante smiled at me. "Thank God for your mom's pie. It took my mom out of lecture mode."

"You can't ever quit while you're ahead, can you, Dante?" Mrs. Quintana couldn't quite keep herself from laughing.

We did get another brief lecture from Mrs. Quintana—but I didn't mind. She cared. And it also helped me understand where Dante got his stubbornness. From his mother, of course. When she'd finished, she kissed us both on the cheek. Then she looked at me. "Dante will never stop trying to out-stubborn me. He'll never succeed. But that's not going to stop him from trying. And tell Lilly she's a genius—and I'll return her pie plate tomorrow." Which meant our mothers were going to discuss their sons while we were gone.

• • •

Dante and I sat on the front steps and stared out into the darkness. Dante took off his shoes. "When we were joking around on the phone, you didn't know what 'laudable' meant, did you?" I didn't even have to look at his face to know he was wearing that *I'm smarter than you are* look.

I decided to ignore that tone that I was becoming familiar with. "No, I don't think I'd ever heard that word. Didn't have a clue. But now I've added a new word to my lexicon."

"Lexicon?"

"Lexicon," I repeated. "Laudable. It means worthy of praise. From the Latin '*laude*.' To praise."

"Well, look at you, Aristotle Mendoza."

"Yeah, Look at me."

"You'll be talking like a dictionary in no time."

"No fucking way," I said. "No fucking way."

Dante walked me to my truck. "I'm kissing you right now."

"I'm kissing you back," I said—then drove away.

Thirty-One

Dear Dante,

All I can think of is you. All I can think of is what it will feel like sleeping next to you. Both of us naked. What you will feel like as I kiss you and kiss you and kiss you and kiss you. And I'm so scared. I don't know why I'm so scared. I've never been so excited or so happy or so scared.

Are you scared too, Dante?

Please tell me that you're scared.

Thirty-Two

I DIDN'T SLEEP ALL NIGHT. I COULDN'T. DANTE. DANTE. Dante.

When the dawn was breaking, I went out for a run. I could taste the salt of my own sweat as it ran down my face, and I thought about my own body. Maybe my body was like a country and if I was going to be a cartographer, the first thing I was going to have to do was map out my own body. And map out Dante's while I was at it.

When I was in the shower, I whispered his name. Dante.

Dante, Dante, Dante. He was like a heart that was beating in every pore of my body. His heart was beating in *my* heart. His heart was beating in my head. His heart was beating in my stomach. His heart was beating in my legs. His heart was beating in my arms, my hands, my fingers. His heart was beating in my tongue, my lips. No wonder I was trembling. Trembling, trembling, trembling.

Thirty-three

MY DAD'S TRUCK WAS ALL PACKED WITH ALL OUR
camping gear. Dad wasn't about to let me take my own truck. We'd
had a discussion when I'd gotten back from dinner at the Quintanas'
house. "That thing's fine for driving around town, but you need
something reliable."

"You're saying my truck's not reliable, Dad?"

"You're looking at me as if I just insulted you."

"Maybe you have."

"Don't overinvest your identity in that truck," my mother said.

"You sound like you've been hanging out with Mrs. Quintana."

"I'll take that as a compliment."

Me and Dante, neither one of us would ever succeed in out-
stubborning our mothers.

Mom handed me a paper bag filled with burritos she'd made while
I'd been out running. I looked in the bag and stared at the burritos
wrapped in foil. "What kind?

"Huevos con chorizo y papas."

I couldn't help but smile. She knew they were my favorite.

"Greatest mom ever," I said. She combed my hair with her fingers. "You and Dante be careful. Come back to me safe."

I nodded. "I promise, Mom, I'll be careful."

She kissed me—and made the sign of the cross on my forehead. "And have fun."

My dad handed me the keys to his truck. "Don't wreck my truck while I'm gone," I told him.

"Wise guy." He handed me some money.

"I have money, Dad."

"Take it."

I nodded. My father was giving me something. And it wasn't money he was giving me. It was a piece of himself.

They waved at me from the porch as I started up the truck. Legs was looking at me as if I'd betrayed her by not taking her with me on the camping trip. Yeah, well, she didn't look all that miserable as she sat between my parents. I mean, Dad loved that dog almost as much as I did.

I waved back at my parents.

They seemed so alive, my mom and dad. They seemed alive because they were alive, alive in a way that most people weren't.

Dante and his parents were sitting on the front porch as I drove up in front of his house. As soon as I pulled up, Dante bounded down the steps, backpack and all. His parents waved at me. "If you run into any trouble, just get to a phone and call us collect."

"I promise," I yelled back.

I noticed Mr. Quintana was hugging Mrs. Quintana and kissing her on the cheek. He was whispering something to her.

As Dante climbed into the truck, he yelled back to his parents, "I love you."

I liked that Dante's parents acted like they had just gotten married. There was something about them that made me think they would be forever young. Dante was like them. He, too, would be young forever. And me? I already acted like an old man.

I turned on the ignition, and I was smiling or grinning, I don't know which. Dante slipped off his tennis shoes, and he said, "I've been writing a poem for you. I haven't finished it yet—but I have the ending. 'You're every street I've ever walked. You're the tree outside my window, you're a sparrow as he flies. You're the book that I am reading. You're every poem I've ever loved.'"

I felt as though I were the center of the universe. Only Dante could make me feel like that. But I knew better—I would never be the center of the universe.

Thirty-Four

ONCE WE GOT ON THE ROAD, I POINTED AT THE BAG ON the seat. "There's some burritos in the bag. My mom made them."

"Your mom's awesome." He handed me a burrito and took one for himself. He pulled off the foil and grabbed a napkin from the bag. He took a bite and then another. "These are fucking brilliant."

"Yeah, they are," I said. "My mom made the tortillas last night."

"Homemade tortillas? Wow. Will she teach my mom?"

"What if she doesn't want to learn?"

"Why wouldn't she want to learn?"

"Because they're work. And once people get wind of the fact that you know how to make them, you're screwed. My sisters, they said, 'Oh, hell no.' They buy them."

Dante smiled. "Well, maybe your mom will teach *me* how to make them."

"Sounds great to me. You can make as many tortillas for me as you want."

"Ha, ha, ha, ha, ha. You think I'm going to be making tortillas for you all the time? Oh, hell no. You can buy yours at the store."

"You probably wouldn't be very good at making tortillas, anyway."

"Why do you say that?"

"Because learning how to make tortillas takes patience."

"Are you saying I'm not patient?"

"I'm saying what I'm saying."

"You keep talking like that and you're going to have to kiss me again."

"Patience, my good man, patience." We joked around all the way to White Sands. Being with Dante made me playful. And for some reason, we were both really hungry. By the time we got to White Sands, we'd eaten three burritos apiece. And we were still hungry.

Thirty-Five

THE SECOND I PARKED THE TRUCK AT THE FOOT OF A large gypsum dune, Dante swung open the door and made a dash for the ocean of white sand that stood before us. "Ari! This is amazing! It's fucking amazing!" Off went his shirt as he climbed to the top of the dune. "Oh my God!" I loved watching him, Dante uncensored, Dante unafraid to act like a little kid, Dante unafraid to act like a dork, unafraid to be himself, unafraid to be a part of everything around him. I watched as he spun himself and stretched out his arms. He would've taken in the entire landscape and held it in his arms if that had been possible. "Ari! Ari! Look! It goes on forever!"

I took off my shirt and grabbed the sunscreen from the glove compartment. I took my time climbing up the dune. The feel of the sand underneath my feet was soft and cool, the harsh elements unable to steal away the leftover innocence of the earth. I remembered the first time my mom and dad had brought me here. My sisters had buried me in the sand, and I'd held my mom's hand as we watched the sunset. We'd stayed for some night program, and I remembered my dad carrying me on his shoulders as we made our way to the car. "Ari? Are you in your head again?"

"Sorry."

"What were you thinking about?"

"You."

"Liar."

"You got me. I was thinking about the first time I came here with my mom and dad and my sisters. I must have been five years old."

Dante took the sunscreen from my hand and I felt the cool of the sunscreen and his hand on my back and my shoulders. I thought of the day he'd washed me with a sponge after the accident and the tears on his face and how I hated him because I should have been the one with tears on his face. His tears had said *You saved my life, Ari,* and I didn't want to think about that. I thought I hated him then without knowing why, and how impossible he had been to hate—especially because I loved him so much without even knowing it. "Turn around," he said—and I did as I was told. He rubbed the sunscreen into my chest and shoulders and stomach—and I laughed because it sort of tickled. "I love you, Aristotle Mendoza," he whispered.

I didn't say anything. I just looked into his clear brown eyes, and I guess I was smiling, because he said, "Killer smile." He handed me the sunscreen. As I rubbed the sunscreen on his chest and arms and back, all I could think of was how perfect he was, his swimmer's body, his skin. As we stood there, I felt my heart beating as if it wanted to jump out of my chest and leap into his and stay there forever.

"What are you thinking, Ari? Tell me."

"I'm thinking that if I died right now it would be okay with me."

"Nobody's ever said anything like that to me before. It's a lovely thing to say. Truly it is. Except it wouldn't be okay with me if we died right here and now."

"Why not?"

"Because you haven't made love to me yet."

That made me smile. That really made me smile.

"Did you know this used to be an ocean? Imagine all that water."

"I could have taught you to swim in that ocean."

"And you could have taught me to dive into those waters."

He nodded and smiled.

"On the other hand," I said, "we might have drowned in those waters."

"Really? Did you have to go there?" He took my hand.

We walked into the forever white sand dunes, and soon we were far away from all the people in the world. Everyone had disappeared from the universe except the young man whose hand I was holding, and everything that had ever been born and everything that had ever died existed where his hand touched mine. Everything—the blue of the sky, the rain in the clouds, the white of the sand, the water in the oceans, all the languages of all the nations, and all the broken hearts that had learned to beat in their brokenness.

We didn't talk. This was the quietest moment I had ever been in. Even my busy brain—it was quiet. So quiet that I felt that I was in a church. And the thought entered my head that my love for Dante was holy, not because I was holy but because what I felt for him was pure.

No, we didn't talk. We didn't need to talk. Because we were

discovering that the heart could make music. And we were listening to the music of the heart. We watched the lightning in the distance and heard the echo of the thunder. Dante leaned into me—and then I kissed him. He tasted of sweat and the hint of my mother's burritos. Time didn't exist, and whatever the world thought of us, we didn't live in anybody's world but our own at that very moment.

It seemed that we *had* actually become cartographers of a new world, had mapped out a country of our own, and it was ours and only ours, and though we both knew that country would disappear, almost as soon as it had appeared, we had full citizenship in that country and we were free to love each other. Ari loved Dante. Dante loved Ari.

I didn't feel lost as I kissed Dante. Not lost at all. I had found where I belonged.

Living in the Land of What Matters

There's a voice in the universe that holds the truth of all those who walk the earth. I believe that we are born for reasons we do not understand—and it is up to us to discover those reasons. That is your only task. If you are brave enough to sit and listen to the voice of the universe in the silence that lives within you, then you will always know what matters—and you will know too that you matter more to the universe than you will ever know.

One

THE COLOR OF THE EARTH CHANGES WITH THE LIGHT.
My father's voice in my head. The light in the desert was so different
from the light in the mountains that sifted its way through the trees.
The slant of light made everything seem pure and untouched and
soft. The light in the desert was harsh, and nothing in it was soft—
everything was hard because everything had to be hard if it wanted
to live. Maybe that's why I was hard—because I was like the desert
I loved, and Dante wasn't hard because he came from a softer place,
where there was water and tender leaves that filtered the light just
enough to keep your heart from becoming a stone.

"How many miles have we traveled?"

I smiled. "Is that your version of *Are we there yet?*"

Dante shot me one of those *I'm not going to roll my eyes* looks.

"A little over eighty miles. I'd say we're about twenty-five miles
or so till we get to a camping spot."

"Camp. Do you know origins of that word?"

"Why do you like to know where words come from?"

"I don't know. I fell in love with dictionaries when I was six. My
mom thought it might be a better idea if I played with my Legos.

But, somehow, my parents knew I didn't really like toys. So they stopped trying to turn me into someone I wasn't."

"That's what makes them good parents."

"Yeah, I think that's true. When I was eight, they gave me the *Compact Edition of the Oxford English Dictionary*. Best Christmas present ever."

"When I was eight, I got a bicycle. Best Christmas present ever."

Dante smiled. "See, we're exactly alike."

"So," I said, "you were going to tell me about the word 'camp.'"

"Not that you really care."

"Tell me anyway. You can't begin a thought without finishing it."

"Is that a new rule?"

"Yup."

"You're gonna have a much harder time keeping that rule than me."

"No doubt in my mind that you'll call me on it."

"Bet your ass."

"A very Ari response."

"You're rubbing off on me."

"You are in deep fucking trouble."

"Maybe you're just the kind of trouble I was looking for."

I'd never had that kind of fun with anyone except with Dante. "So, the word 'camp.'"

"'Camp.' It means an open field. It was a term to describe a level geographical place used for military exercises. But it also has a slang meaning for the tacky ways homosexual men behave—mostly when they're playing around."

That made me laugh. But I wasn't sure I was quite getting it. Dante could read the puzzled look on my face.

"You know, if a guy acts, like, you know, super gay on purpose or if someone—that's like they're camping it up. And anyone who has really horrible taste—that's . . ." And then he stopped. I could tell he'd thought of something. "The Village People—they're camp. They're all about camp."

I was smiling. "The Village People? The fucking Village People."

And then Dante started singing "Macho Man." He got all into it. And he was laughing at himself. And then he said, "Do you think I act gay?" And all of a sudden, with that one question, he went from clowning around to being pensive and serious.

"What does that mean? I mean, you're gay, aren't you? And I'm gay too. Wow, it feels funny to be saying that. You know, that time I was at your house and you told me that your mom was inscrutable? I didn't really know what that word meant, so I went home and looked it up. And then I got to know that word and it began to live inside me. And then that word was different because it was mine. The word 'gay' is like that. I guess it will take a while before it lives inside me."

I could tell Dante was thinking. And then he said, "There are no words in the English language that could describe you, Ari Mendoza. There are no words in any language."

"So now we're a fucking mutual admiration society."

"Don't be a shit. I just said something really great about you. Just say thank you." And then he began humming "YMCA," a song I hated but everybody else seemed to like. His face lit up with a smile that reminded me of the light in the desert just before the sun went down.

"You know, Ari, it doesn't seem like you're the kind of guy that would like other guys."

"Whatever the hell that means."

"You know what I'm saying."

"I *do* know what you're saying. No, I don't think you act gay—I mean, if you'd tried out to be one of the Village People, I don't think you'd have made the cut. And anyway, does liking other guys mean you act a certain way?"

"For some guys, I think."

"Do you think about this a lot, Dante?"

"I guess I do. You?"

"No. Mostly I think about you."

"Good answer."

"Damn straight."

"We should train ourselves to avoid using that word whenever possible."

"Is there a handbook for gay guys?"

"We should write one."

"We don't know shit about being gay."

"Is there a class we can take?"

I shot him a look.

He ran his fingers through his hair. "What if the whole world knew?"

"Lucky for us the fucking world doesn't give a damn about us. It's not as if we're important enough to be investigated by the FBI or anything."

"Yeah, I guess you're right. Maybe it's a good idea not to go for camp."

"Well, for now, we're all about the level-field thing and not the tacky-horrible-taste thing."

"You'll never be camp, Ari."

"How do you know that?"

"You don't have it in you."

"I don't really know what I have in me. Nobody knows what they're going to become. But you? You, Dante, are going to be a well-known artist. You *are* an artist. Art is not just what you do—it's who you are."

He had a serious and fierce look on his face. "That's what I really want. I want to be an artist. And I don't care if I get famous. And I don't care if I ever make any money. I have dreamed of being an artist all my life. What about you, Ari?"

I thought about the list I'd made—of the things I wanted to do. I thought of the two things I had crossed out: *Learn to play the guitar* and *Make love to Dante*. If I wasn't any good at music, maybe I could be good at making love to Dante. But how could I be good at it if I'd never done it before? And there wasn't anything on my list that was long-term. I had no plans for my life.

"Well, I'm keeping a journal. I think that might help me in my quest to become a cartographer. And maybe I won't ever find some great passion for something like you have. But when I'm old, I don't want to be asking myself if my life mattered. Because if I was just a decent guy, if I had just been a good man, then my life would have been a good life. I guess that doesn't sound very ambitious."

"You have something I'll never have. You have humility. And that word lives inside you. And you don't even know it."

I think his idea of me was a little generous. "I'm not humble. I like to fight."

"Maybe that's your way of protecting people."

"Which doesn't really make me very humble at all, now does it?"

"You want to know what I think? I think I have impeccable taste in men."

"Well, I'm not exactly a man—but, hey, if you need me as an excuse to give yourself a compliment, well, what's it gonna cost me to play along?"

He shook his head. "Ari, I think you know that I just gave you an indirect compliment. When someone says something nice about you, say thank you."

"But—" He didn't let me finish.

"Thank you. That's all you have to say."

"But—" And he stopped me again.

"Just because you don't think that you're anything special doesn't mean I agree with you."

Two

"TREES!" DANTE YELLED, LIKE A BOY WHO'D NEVER seen an apple tree or a pine tree. He hung his head out the window, the wind blowing through his hair. He closed his eyes and took in the fresh air, breathing in and out. It was a natural thing for him to make himself become a part of the landscape. Maybe that's why he didn't like shoes. I wondered if I would ever belong to the earth like Dante did.

"Even the shape of the earth," he said. "It's like it's changing."

Maybe the shape of the heart changed along with the shape of the earth. I didn't know anything about physics or geometry or geography or the shape of things and why that somehow mattered so much.

"Gravity," he said.

"Gravity?"

"You're gravity," he said.

I had no idea what he was talking about.

We fell silent again.

We had traveled away from a city built around a desert mountain, and moved to walking on white sand dunes in our bare feet—and now as I slowly drove my dad's pickup and climbed up the curving road, I realized my truck would never have been able to take this trip. I was glad I'd listened to my dad. It occurred to me that Dante was always asking me what I was thinking and I hardly ever asked him that question, so I just asked, "What are you thinking?"

"I was thinking that people are very complicated. And people don't have logical conversations. Well, because people aren't logical. I mean, people aren't all that consistent, if you think about it. They jump around from here to there to there because, well, like I said, people don't think in straight lines, and that's okay, it's what makes people interesting, and maybe it's what makes the world go 'round. And 'round and 'round and 'round—going nowhere, getting nowhere—and a lot of people don't know how to think at all—they just know how to feel—"

"Like you."

"That's not where I was going. Yeah, but . . . so, yeah, I feel. Maybe I feel too much. Not that there's anything wrong with that. *But I also know how to think.*"

"Ever the intellectual."

"You're one too, Ari—so shut the fuck up."

"I never claimed to be one," I said.

"You read. And you think. And you don't buy everybody's bullshit."

"Well, except for yours."

"I'm going to ignore that."

I had to grin.

"It's not such a good thing to feel if you don't know how to think.

So, my question is why do so many White people hate Black people when they're the ones that brought them here in chains?"

"Because, well, because they feel guilty, I guess."

"Exactly. And that doesn't have anything to do with thinking. See, they don't let themselves *feel* guilty, but they *do* feel guilty because they *should* feel guilty. They just bury all that crap inside, but they bury it alive and it's all running around in there—and it gets all screwed up in their emotions and it comes out as hate. And that's fucking crazy."

"You come up with that theory all by yourself?"

"Nope. Wish I could take the credit. That's my mother's theory."

I smiled. "Ah, the therapist."

"Yup. She's brilliant."

"I think so too."

"She's a big fan of yours."

"Yeah, well, that's because . . ." I stopped myself from saying it. I don't even know why that thought entered my mind.

"That's because you saved my life."

"I didn't."

"Yes, you did."

"Let's not talk about it."

Dante was quiet for a long time. "You jumped in front of a car so that car wouldn't run me over—and because you did that, you saved my life. That. Is. A. Fact. And, Ari, that fucking fact isn't ever going to go away."

I didn't say anything. Then I just said, "Is that why you love me?"

"Is that what you think?"

"Sometimes."

"Well, that doesn't happen to be true. Ari, I loved you from the first time I saw you floating on the water."

"The desert disappeared," Dante said. "Or maybe it's us who disappeared."

Sometimes I wondered what it was about him that made me want to get close to him and stay close. Not that he was ever far away anymore, because when I wasn't with him, I carried him around, and I wondered if that was a normal thing. I didn't really know what love was supposed to be like. I only knew what it was like for me. And when he said things like that, I knew why.

"Things that disappear always reappear again," I said, "like Susie and Gina."

Dante gave me this look. He had a question that was hovering over his eyes. "Why do they bug you so much? They're nice."

"I've known them since kindergarten. Maybe I take them for granted. But they try too hard. They've been gone most of the summer. Otherwise they would have been badgering me. And they'd have talked you into being their friend. And I never said they weren't nice. They're good girls who think they want to be bad girls, but they don't have it in them to be bad girls."

"What's so bad about that? And what's wrong with them wanting to be my friend? I think that's awesome. And they're both really pretty,"

"What's that got to do with it?" I smiled. I knew why I was smiling. "I have a suspicion that I like pretty boys more than I like pretty girls. I can't believe I just said that."

"I'm glad you said that. Because it means you're beginning to understand who you are."

"I don't think I'll ever understand who I am."

"Well, if you ever want to know more, just ask me."

I shook my head and kept driving through mountain roads with pine trees crowding and bumping into one another on the slopes. I laughed to myself as I remembered the day when my dad drove us through this same road on my first camping trip.

"What's so funny?" Dante, he was always studying me as if it was somehow possible to learn everything about me. Unknowable me.

Three

WE STOPPED OFF IN CLOUDCROFT, A SMALL TOWN
that was crowded with shops and a few galleries and a couple of
saloons. Dante began wandering around as I put gas in the truck.

He waved at me, signaling for me to follow him into one of the
galleries. There wasn't anyone in the gallery except a woman who
had a calm, friendly, and sophisticated look about her. Dante liked
the word "sophisticated." I took the word to mean a rich person who
knew how to be nice to people who weren't as rich as they were.
Maybe I was wrong about that. But she *did* seem like a rich woman
who also happened to be nice.

I was standing next to Dante as he stared at a painting, and I
wanted to touch him, put my hand on his shoulder. But I didn't. Of
course I didn't.

The woman smiled at us. "Nice-looking young men," she said softly.

Dante smiled at her. "Are you flirting with us?"

She had a soft laugh, and the wrinkles around her eyes somehow
made her seem a little bit sad. I liked her black eyes, which looked
even blacker against her pale white skin.

I realized I'd been staring at her. And when our eyes met, I felt like I'd been caught doing something wrong. I looked away.

"I like this one," Dante said. The painting was nothing but a wash of blue, and it was hard to tell if it was the sky or a body of water. Maybe the ocean. And there was one eye that was peering out with something that resembled tears falling from it, only the tears weren't tears, but a straight line of little arrows falling downward. And on the edges of the painting there was some kind of writing, though the words were almost impossible to make out. "It's incredible."

I didn't think that the painting was incredible. But I liked it. And I liked that the artist was trying to say something—even though I didn't know what he was trying to say. But it made me want to stop and study it, so maybe that's what Dante meant by "incredible."

"Do you like it, Ari?"

I nodded. Somehow I knew he knew I didn't share his enthusiasm. I always thought he knew what I was thinking—even when I knew that wasn't always true.

"That's one of my son's paintings. These are all my son's paintings."

"Wow. He's very gifted."

"Yes, he was."

"Was?"

"He died recently."

We both nodded.

"I'm sorry," I said.

"He was young. He was so young." And then she pulled back, as if she was willing away the sadness. She smiled at Dante. "I'm glad you like the painting."

"What does the writing say?" I asked.

"It's a poem he wrote. It's taped to the back of the painting in an envelope."

"May we read it?"

"Yes, of course."

She walked up to where we were standing—then took the painting off the wall. "Take the envelope," she said.

Dante carefully untaped the envelope from the back of the painting. The woman placed the painting back on the wall.

Dante held the envelope as if it were something very fragile. He stared at it. I could see it said, *What is it that makes things matter?* He took out a sheet of paper from the envelope and unfolded it. He stared at the handwriting. He looked up at the woman, who had returned to her seat behind the antique desk where she had been sitting when we'd walked in. She seemed perfect and broken all the same time.

"My name's Dante."

"What a lovely name. I'm Emma."

I thought she looked like an Emma. I'm not sure why I thought that. "I'm Ari," I said.

"Ari?"

"It's short for Aristotle."

She had a super-beautiful smile. "Aristotle and Dante," she said. "How lovely. The names suit you. Dante the poet, and Aristotle the philosopher."

"Dante's a poet, that's for sure. But I don't think I qualify as a philosopher. Now or ever."

"Hmm," she said. "You don't strike me as being a shallow young man. Do you do a lot of thinking?"

"He's always thinking." I'd been wondering when Dante was going to dive in and give his opinion. "He thinks about everything all the time. And I mean everything."

"I think too much," I said.

"There's no such thing as thinking too much. The world would be a better place if everyone did more thinking and less talking. There might be a lot less hatred." She looked at both of us as if she was trying to see who we really were. "So, Ari, you just might be the philosopher you think you aren't. Humility is a fine quality. Hang on to it."

Dante pointed at the poem he was holding in his hand and then toward her. "Will you read it to us?"

"No, I don't think I can." Her refusal wasn't all harsh—it was soft, and I thought that I could hear a brokenness in her voice and I knew that she lived with a hurt inside her. "Why don't *you* read it to us, Dante?"

He stared at the poem. "I'm not sure I can do it justice."

"A poet knows how to read a poem."

"What if I ruin it?"

"I'm sure you won't," she said. "Just read it as if you wrote it. That's the trick."

Dante nodded. He stared at the writing—and began to read, his soft and sure voice filling the empty gallery:

> "*This is not a painting. And this is not a poem.*
> *This is not the ocean. And this is not a sky. Words*
> *do not belong in a painting. Words of an art teacher*

who told me I would never be an artist. Poems do not belong on a painting. And I do not belong in this world. This is not a painting. And that is not my eye that cries in the night for a lover I never knew. This is not about my pain, nor about the loneliness of nights I endured in the solitude of my own prison.

"'I am going blind and soon I will no longer be able to see. But what I saw and what I felt never mattered and the eye that looks out at you will be gone. My eyes and my poems and my art do not matter—not in a world where nothing can matter.

"'My mother taught me that love was the only thing that mattered—and her love lives in my heart and it is not something that can be bought or sold and it is here in this painting and in this poem and that is why this thing we call art matters.

"'A man who loves another man does not matter because he is not a man—and his paintings and his poems and whatever he thinks or says or feels do not matter. That is what people believe. But those are lies, and I do not believe any of those lies. So I became an artist and a poet so I could paint and write the things that mattered—even if they only mattered to me. And that is the only thing that matters.'"

I saw the quiet tears running down Emma's face, and I thought of the word "dignified," which was the only word I could reach for to describe her. My mother had worn that same look at my aunt Ophelia's funeral. Emma looked at Dante and said quietly, "You read like a poet. That was lovely."

Dante smiled. "Well, perhaps not as lovely as your son."

Dante—he always knew what to say.

And she sat there, just sat, because she had nothing else to say. And Dante and I stood there, just stood, because we had nothing else to say. And there seemed to be a kind of peace in that small gallery surrounded by the work of man who was dead and whom we did not know and surrounded too by a mother's love, and I had never thought about those things before, and now that I was thinking them, I didn't know if I liked thinking about how much mothers loved, because it hurt to know that. And I didn't want to live in hurt. But it was much better than self-hatred, which was just a stupid way to live.

I smiled at Emma. And she smiled back. Dante leaned into me, and I let him lean. The silence in the room was almost like a song. And Emma and Dante and me—we were singing the song of silence. Sometimes silence was the only song worth singing.

There are moments in your life that you will always remember. My mother's voice in my head. It made me happy that her voice lived inside me. I knew I would always remember this moment, and this woman named Emma whom I knew and didn't know. But I knew this one thing: She was a person who mattered. And that was all I needed to know.

It's funny, I didn't ever pay much attention to adults because, well, because I just didn't think about them and the fact that they had lives like I had a life. I guess I just thought they were in charge and they liked to tell you what to do. I hadn't really thought about anything except what I felt. Damn, I'd lived in a pretty small fucking world.

And this world I was living in now, it was complicated and confusing—and it sort of hurt to know that other people hurt. Adults. They hurt. And it was a good thing to know that. It was a better world that I was living in now. It was better. *And I was better now.* It was like I'd been ill. And I was recovering from an illness. But maybe that wasn't true. I'd just been a stupid kid. And selfish.

Maybe this is what being a man was. Okay, so maybe I wasn't a man just yet. But maybe I was getting closer.

I wasn't a boy anymore, that was for sure.

Four

I WAS DRIVING THROUGH A PATH IN THE FOREST LOOK-
ing for a place to camp. Dante was lost in thought and, anyway, I
wasn't exactly relying on him to find a place. There was a small fork
in the road, and I could see that it led to a small clearing that was
the perfect spot. It seemed later than it was because of all the shade.
But I knew we didn't have a long time before it got dark.

"Let's get to work."

"Just tell me what to do."

"That's a first."

We grinned at each other.

There were rocks in a circle where the last campfire had been. Dante
and I took out the logs I'd brought from home. I placed a few logs where
there were still some ashes and a half-burned log that had been put out.
I carried a tin bucket I'd brought filled with twigs and kindling.

"How come you brought all that stuff from home when we could
have gathered it all here?"

I grabbed some soil and held it in my fist. "Everything's damp.
Dad said you should come prepared with everything. Because you
never know." I smiled and threw the fistful of dirt so that it hit Dante
right in the chest.

"Hey!" But Dante didn't miss a beat, and we were having a damp soil kind of snowball fight and running around the pickup until we finally got tired.

"Didn't take us long to get dirty, did it?"

I shrugged. "We came to have fun." Dante brushed some soil from my face. Then he reached over and kissed me.

We stood there and kissed for a long time. I felt my whole body trembling. I pulled him closer and we kept kissing. And finally I said, "We need to finish setting up camp. Before it gets dark."

Dante bowed his head and bumped my shoulder. We both looked up at the gathering clouds and listened to the distant thunder. "Let's get to it." There it was, that sense of enthusiasm that was rarely absent in the way he spoke. But there was something else in his voice. Something urgent and alive.

We were sitting around the campfire. We had our coats on, and the cold breeze was threatening to break out into a wind. "It looks like it's going to storm," Dante said.

"You think the tent will hold up?"

I nodded. "Oh, Dante, ye of little faith. It'll hold up."

"I have a surprise."

"A surprise?"

He went into the tent and came back holding a bottle of liquor. He was smiling and looking very proud of himself. "I stole it from my dad's liquor cabinet."

"You crazy boy. You crazy, crazy boy."

"They'll never find out."

"Like hell."

"Well, I figured if I'd asked they might have said yes."

"Really?"

"They might have."

I shot him a look.

"And you know what they say, *It's better to ask for forgiveness than to ask for permission.*"

"Really?" I shook my head and smiled. "How do you get away with—"

"With all the things I get away with? I'm Dante."

"Oh, that's the answer? Talk about cocky."

"So I'm a little cocky sometimes."

"You stole your dad's bourbon."

"Petty theft does not make me a thief—it makes me a rebel."

"You're overthrowing your father's government?"

"No, I'm taking from the rich and giving to the poor. He's bourbon rich and we're bourbon poor."

"That's because we're underage. And your mother's going to massacre you."

"'Massacre' is such a strong word."

"I can't believe you stole a whole bottle of bourbon from your dad. Is it because you enjoy the drama?"

"I dislike drama. It's just that I want to feel alive and push the limits and reach for the sky."

"Yeah, well, if you drink enough bourbon you'll be kneeling on the ground and tossing your cookies."

"Okay, I'm done with this conversation. The man I love does not support me."

"What was that you said about not liking drama?"

He ignored my question. "I'm pouring myself a drink. If you don't want to partake in downing some stolen liquor, then I'll happily drink alone."

I reached for a plastic cup and held it toward him. "Pour."

We were sitting on folding chairs right next to each other. We'd kiss, then we'd talk. We were, of course, having our very adult drink of bourbon and Coke. Though I wasn't sure if adults actually drank their bourbon with Coke. And, really, I didn't give a damn. I was just happy listening to Dante talk and having him lean into me and then kissing him. There was only me and him and the darkness around us and the threat of a storm and there was a campfire and it made Dante seem like he was appearing out of the darkness, his face shining in the light of the fire. I had never felt this alive and I thought that I would never love anyone or anything as much as I loved Dante in this very moment. He was the map of the world and everything that mattered.

And then our kissing started getting serious. I mean, it was seriously serious. It was so seriously serious that my whole body was trembling. And I didn't want to stop, and I found myself moaning and Dante was moaning too and it was so strange and so beautiful and so weird, and I liked the moaning. And then there was a bolt of lightning and we both jumped back and laughed. And it started raining and we ran into the tent.

We heard the rain pelt the tent, but it was secure—and somehow, the storm made us feel safe and then we were kissing and we were taking each other's clothes off and the feel of Dante's skin against mine and the storm and the lightning and thunder seemed as if they were coming from inside me and I had never felt as alive, my entire body reaching for him and his taste and his smell and I had never known this, this body thing, this love thing, this thing called desire that was a hunger and I never wanted it to end and then there was this electricity that shot through me and I thought that maybe it was like a death and I couldn't breathe and I fell back into Dante's arms and he kept whispering my name—Ari, Ari, Ari—and I wanted to whisper his name, but there were no words in me.

And I held him.

And I whispered his name.

And I fell asleep holding him.

It was dawn when I woke.

I could sense the calmness of the day.

I could hear the steady breathing of the boy sleeping next to me. But he seemed more like a man to me just then. And my own body didn't seem to be a body that belonged to a boy. Not anymore. I *do* think that there are moments that change you, moments that tell you that you can never go back to where you started and you don't want to go back to whoever you used to be because you have become someone else. I stared at Dante. Studied his face, his neck, his shoulders.

I covered him and moved away slowly. I didn't want to wake him.

I unzipped the tent and the air was cold and I walked out into the sunlight, naked. The cold breeze hit my body and I shivered. But I didn't mind. I had never noticed my own body, not like this. And it was so new, and I felt like that baby that made a noise and then suddenly knew he had a voice. It was like that. It was a kind of thrill I'd never known, and I knew I might not ever know again. I just stood there. Not smiling, not laughing, just standing there as still as I could.

I took a breath. And then another.

And then I heard a laughter coming from inside me that I had never heard. And I felt strong. And for a moment, I felt that nobody in the world could ever hurt me.

And yes, I was happy. But it was more than just happiness. And I thought that this must be the thing that my mother called joy.

That is what it was. Joy.

Another word that was growing inside me.

When Dante woke, I was lying right beside him. And he smiled at me and I ran my thumb across his face. "Hello," I whispered.

"Hello," he whispered back. I don't know how long we lay there, staring at each other, not wanting to speak because anything that we said would be wrong—wrong because any word we used would spoil the silence and the beauty of it. Yes, it was true that words could lead to understanding. But they could lead to misunderstandings, too. Words were imperfect.

This silence between me and Dante, this silence was perfect. But the silence had to be broken sometime. And just as I was about to say something, Dante said, "Let's go for a walk."

I watched him get dressed in the tent and I didn't care that he noticed. "You like watching me?"

"Nope. I just don't have anything better to do." I tossed him a smile.

"That was such an Ari thing to say."

"Was it?"

He finished tying his tennis shoes and then he leaned over and kissed me.

We straightened out the sleeping bags and the blankets and Dante's pillow. "I have to have my pillow." I liked his pillow. It smelled like him.

We washed up and brushed our teeth and combed our hair using the side mirrors on the truck. Dante spent a lot of time combing his hair with his fingers even though it looked like he never combed it. It was like the breeze was always dancing in his hair.

I sometimes felt like I'd been asleep for a long time—and when I met Dante, I began to wake up, and I began seeing not only him but the mean and terrible and awesome world I lived in. The world was a scary place to live in, and it would always be scary—but you could learn not to be afraid. I guess I had to decide what was more real, the scary things or—or Dante. Dante, he was the most real thing in my world.

I was leaning against the truck, and Dante was waving his hand in front of my eyes. "Hey, Ari, where are you?"

His question was soft and kind and I pressed my head to his. "In my head."

"What were you thinking?"

"I was actually thinking about your parents."

"Wow. That's kinda nice."

"Well, your mom and dad are kinda nice."

He smiled, and he seemed so alive and bright in the sun. I thought of one of Dante's vinyl albums and I didn't remember the name of the song and I could hear her clear voice that was full of melancholy and there was some line about the flowers and how they were leaning out for love and how they'd lean that way forever. That was Dante. He was leaning out for love. And I was leaning out for him. But I didn't know about that forever thing.

What was forever?

Dante took my hand and we walked along a path, and everything was quiet and we could hear a stream in the distance. "I like it here," Dante said. "It's so people-less."

"I don't think that's a word."

"I don't think so either. But you get the message."

"Yeah," I said.

I don't think we were really looking at the landscape, and I don't think either of us cared where we were going, and it didn't matter. We were just walking down a quiet, lonely path that we had never walked before, and even though it was lonely, it didn't seem lonely— and it didn't seem to matter that there was nothing familiar about the path because I wasn't afraid. Maybe I should have been afraid, but I wasn't. But I was thinking that Dante just might be afraid, so I asked him, "Are you afraid of getting lost?"

"No," he said.

"I don't know where the hell we're headed."

"Do you care?"

"Not really."

"I don't really care either. And besides, it's impossible to be lost when I'm with you."

"No. It just means that if I'm lost, you're lost too."

"So, if I'm lost with you, I don't feel lost—so I'm not lost." He laughed. His laugh, just then, reminded me of the sound of the leaves as the wind blew right past them. "See, we shouldn't be afraid of getting lost because it isn't possible to be lost because: We. Are. Holding. Hands."

I just grinned. Yeah, we were holding hands, and he was discovering hands, my hands, and he was discovering a country that was named Ari, and I was discovering a country that was Dante. And everything seemed so serene. That was the word.

I remembered Dante on his bed, and me sitting on his big chair as he read the definition for that word from his well-worn dictionary: *Calm, peaceful, untroubled, tranquil*. "We're done for, Ari," he'd said. "Neither one of us are any of those things."

He was right. Neither he nor I was serene by nature. Me, my head was always cluttered with too many things, and Dante, his head was always creating some kind of art. His eyes were like cameras that took pictures and remembered everything.

We followed the stream, which formed a small pond, and we both looked at each other and then we laughed. And it was as if we were having a contest to see who could strip their clothes off first. Dante jumped in and yelled, "Fuck! It's cold."

I came in after. And it *was* cold. But I didn't scream anything. "Ah," I said. "You call this cold?"

We started splashing each other, and then I found myself holding him as he shivered. "Maybe this wasn't such a good idea," he said. He leaned into me.

The sun was shining through the small clearing, and I pointed to a big stone at the side of the pond. "Let's dry off over there."

We lay on the warm stone until we were dry. And Dante stopped shivering. I lay there, my eyes closed. And then I heard Dante laughing. "Well, here we are, two naked boys. I wonder what my mother would say."

I opened my eyes and looked over at him. I took him in my arms, and I kissed him. "You're thinking about your mother? That wasn't what I was thinking." And then I kissed him again.

And I kissed him and kissed him. And kissed him.

We didn't say a word as we found our way back to our campground. I found myself wondering what he was thinking. And I think he was wondering what I was thinking. But sometimes, you just didn't have to know these things.

I think Dante wanted to know everything about me. I was glad that today, he didn't want to know everything.

He took my hand. And he looked at me.

I knew what he was saying. He was saying, *I love your hand*.

Yeah, words could be super overrated.

When we got back to camp, it was still early afternoon. And it seemed like maybe there would be an afternoon thunderstorm. After we ate, Dante asked me what I was thinking. "I was thinking maybe we should take a nap."

"I was thinking the same thing."

As I was lying there holding Dante, I found myself whispering, "I miss Legs."

"Me too. I wish she could have come. You think she'll be all right?"

"Yeah. She's a tough dog. Maybe she'll learn to make her peace with cats."

"That's a hard one."

"You know, sometimes I think that dog saved my life."

"Like you saved mine."

"Really?"

"Sorry."

"I mean, I felt so alone. I mean, more alone than I'd ever felt. And I was running in front of your house. And there she was, Legs, and she followed me home. And I needed that dog. I really needed her. And she's an amazing dog. Loyal and smart and friendly. I mean, even my mom loves her."

"Your mom doesn't like dogs?"

"Oh, she likes dogs. She just doesn't like them in the house. But somehow, she just let it all happen. Sometimes I think my mom loves that dog more than I do. But she doesn't let on."

"Moms can be like that." He was mumbling. I knew he was falling asleep. And then I nodded off too.

I don't know how long I'd been sleeping. I was having a dream, and I must have been screaming, because Dante was shaking me awake. "It's only a dream, Ari. It's only a dream." I leaned into him. "It was about my brother. I've had that dream before. It's like it doesn't want to leave me alone."

"You want to talk about it?"

"No. I don't—I can't—I can't talk about it."

I let him hold me. Even though I didn't want to be held.

"It's getting dark," I said.

"I already started the fire."

I looked at him.

"I'm a quick study."

"Look at you. Dante, the Boy Scout."

"Shut up."

We roasted hot dogs over the fire. We didn't talk about anything important—which meant we were talking about school, about what schools we might want to go to. Dante wanted to go to Columbia or to that college in Ohio, Oberlin. And then we got quiet. Maybe we didn't want to think that probably we weren't going to be living in the same town for the rest of our lives and we wouldn't be together and that whatever Ari and Dante meant, Ari and Dante didn't mean forever. And then we got real quiet. Dante got two plastic cups and he poured us each a drink, bourbon and Coke. The drinks were a little strong, and I think I was feeling a little bit, well, a little drunk.

"I think I'll go to UT." He smiled at me when he said it.

I smiled back and we toasted. "Here's to us and UT," he said.

"I'll drink to that."

I don't think either of us believed that that Ari and Dante and

UT would ever happen. Yeah, whistling in the dark. People loved to whistle in the dark.

We weren't paying attention to the weather. And all of a sudden there was a crack of thunder and the lightning lit up the dark. Then the downpour. We ran for the tent and laughed. I lit a candle and the soft light made everything soft, but there seemed to be shadows all around us.

Dante reached for me. He kissed me. "Do you mind if I undress you?"

It reminded me too much of the time he'd washed me with a sponge when I couldn't move my arms or legs. But I didn't want to live in that time or in that moment, so I found myself saying, "No, I don't mind."

I felt him unbuttoning my shirt.

I felt his fingers on my skin.

I felt his kisses. And I let go. I just let go.

Five

FOR SOME REASON, WE BOTH WOKE UP IN A PLAYFUL
mood. Maybe we woke to the sound of a singing heart. The thought
of a singing heart had never entered my head before this moment.
Dante was trying to tickle me—which I hated, but it was somehow
fun, and when I got the upper hand and was tickling *him*, he was
laughing and yelling, "Stop! Stop!" and then we were sort of making
out and I didn't think it was such a bad way to start the day.

We broke up camp, wiping as much of the rain off the tent as we
could and folding it back. We packed everything into the back of the
pickup. I drove slowly through all the mud, hoping we wouldn't get
stuck, and I kept shifting the truck down and then up. Slowly, slowly,
we got back onto a wider road that wasn't muddy, and then we got
to the main road.

"Wanna stop in Cloudcroft for breakfast?"

"Yeah, and then we can see Emma on our way out."

Dante ordered strawberry pancakes. I ordered bacon and eggs and
wheat toast. Salsa on the side. He drank a glass of orange juice, and
I had two cups of coffee.

"I don't really like coffee."

That didn't surprise me. "I like coffee. I like it quite a bit, actually."

Dante made a face. "And you drink it black? Ugh. It's bitter."

"I don't mind bitter."

"You wouldn't."

"Everything in the world can't be sweet."

"Like me?"

"You're really pushing it."

He gave me this dopey smile.

"You're a dork."

"So what's your point?"

I reached for my wallet when the check came.

"Put your money away," Dante said. "This one's on me."

"Big man. Where'd you get all that money?"

"Sam."

"Sam? Your dad?"

"He said I should pay for something—since I didn't put any-thing in."

"Well, you put in his liquor."

"Ha. Ha." He took out some bills and paid the waitress. "Keep the change," he said, like a rich man.

I just shook my head and smiled.

We walked out of the restaurant toward the gallery. "You know something, Ari? It's hard for me to walk beside you and keep from wanting to hold your hand."

"Pretend you're holding it in your head."

"It's not fair. Look," he said, pointing his chin at a boy and a girl who were walking ahead of us holding hands. We watched them as they stopped and kissed, smiled at each other, then continued walking, hand in hand. "It's not fucking fair."

I didn't know what to say. He was right—and so what? Most of the rest of the world didn't see things the way we did. The world would look at that boy and that girl and smile and think, *How sweet*. If the world saw me and Dante doing the same thing, the world would grimace and think, *Disgusting*.

Dante and I stood in the doorway of the gallery. The door was open, an invitation for visitors to walk in and take a look at the art. Emma was lost in thought as she was reading the *New York Times*. I could see the headline: "Facing the Emotional Anguish of AIDS."

She looked up and smiled. "Aristotle and Dante," she said. "Well, it certainly looks like you've been camping. Have fun?"

"Yeah," Dante said. "I'd never been camping before."

"Never?"

"I'm not exactly an outdoors kind of guy."

"I see. You're a nose-in-a-book kind of guy."

"Something like that."

"So Ari's the outdoorsman."

"Well, I guess you could say that," I said. "We used to go camping two or three times a year when I was a kid. I really loved camping. El Paso's so hot in the summer. And it's so cool up here."

"You like to fish?"

"Not really. But I used to go with my dad. I think we both read more than we fished. My mom was the real fisherman in the family."

There was something about her. It was hurt, I think, her hurt about losing her son. She seemed to wear that hurt—but it didn't make her look weak. Somehow I felt like she was strong—and stubborn. She reminded me of my mom—that hurt she still carried over my brother. He wasn't dead, but she'd lost him.

"I'm glad you stopped by. I have something for you." It was the painting. She'd wrapped it up. "I wanted you to have this." She handed it to Dante.

"I can't take this. It's your son's work. And—"

"I have the work of his I treasure most in my home. The rest is in this gallery. I want you to have it. But it's for both of you."

"How does that work?"

"Well, one of you keeps it for a year. And the next year, it goes to the other. Back and forth like that." She smiled. "You can share it for your whole lives."

Dante smiled. "I like that."

I liked that too.

We talked for a while. Dante asked her if she had a husband.

"I had one of those at one time in my life. I loved him. Not everyone you love is meant to stay in your life forever. I don't have any regrets. A lot of people live their lives in their mistakes. I'm not one of those people."

I thought about that. I was thinking that maybe I was the kind of guy who just might live his life in the mistakes he made. But maybe not. I guess I'd be finding out soon enough.

She and Dante talked about a lot of things, but I mostly listened.

I wasn't really listening to what they were saying—not really. I was listening to the sound of their voices. I was trying to hear what they were feeling. I was trying to learn what it meant to really listen, because I hadn't ever been a very good listener. I was too in love with what I was thinking. Way too in love with that.

Before we left, she told us to always remember the things that matter, and that it was up to us to decide what mattered and what didn't. She hugged us both. "And remember that you matter more to the universe than you will ever know."

Six

AS WE WERE DRIVING BACK DOWN FROM THE MOUN-tains, back into the desert, Dante had a long yellow legal pad on his lap. He was writing down more suggestions for his brother's name to give to his mother.

"Do you think she even reads that list?"

"Of course she reads it."

"How much influence do you think you really have?"

"Well, I'm sure I'm about to find out. What do you think of these names: Rodrigo, Maximo, Sebastian, Sergio, Agustin, or Salvador?"

"I like Rodrigo."

"Me too."

"She might be a girl. Why don't you want a sister?"

"I don't know. I just want a brother."

"A heterosexual brother."

"Yes. Exactly."

"You think your parents will love him more than they love you?"

"Of course not. But he'll give them grandchildren."

"How do you know he'll want kids? How do you know your parents want grandchildren?"

"*Everyone* wants to have kids. And *everyone* wants to have grandchildren."

"I don't think that's true," I said.

"It's mostly true." Dante had this *I'm certain* look on his face.

"I'm not sure I'd ever want to be a dad."

"Why not?"

"I don't picture me as a father. Not that I really think about it much."

"Too busy thinking about me?" He was smirking.

"Yeah, that must be it, Dante."

"No, I mean, seriously, Ari? You wouldn't want to be a dad?"

"No, I don't think so. Does that disappoint you?"

"No. Yes. No, it's just that—"

"It's just that you think there's something wrong with someone who doesn't wanna have kids."

Dante didn't say anything.

I knew it was no big deal. But I realized Dante could be judgmental. I hadn't noticed that about him before. Not that I was above being judgmental. Everybody was—especially the people who claimed that they weren't. I guess I thought Dante was above that. He was a mere mortal like everyone else. Hey, he wasn't perfect. He didn't need to be. I sure as hell wasn't perfect. Not even close. And he loved me. Imperfect, fucked-up me. Nice. Sweet. Wow.

Seven

I WANTED TO ASK ARI WHAT HE KNEW ABOUT AIDS. I
wanted to ask him if he thought about it. More than four thousand
gay men had died of it. I'd watched the news with my parents, two
days before Dante and I had left to go camping. We saw images of
candlelight vigils in San Francisco and New York, and afterward, we
didn't talk about it. A part of me was glad that there hadn't been
some kind of discussion. And I knew that Dante knew something
about it because his parents talked about things that were happening in the world all the time.

I wondered if Dante and I just weren't ready to talk about something that was probably going to affect our lives. And why the hell
was I thinking about this just as we were on the outskirts of the city?

When I pulled up into the driveway, my mom and Legs were sitting
on the front steps, my mom reading a book.

Legs sat up and barked. I thought of the day I found her. I thought
of me, my legs in a cast. I sat next to her and kissed the top of her
head.

Dante reached down and hugged my mom.

"Nice," she said. "You both smell like smoke."

Dante smiled. "Ari turned me into a real camper." He sat on the front steps and started loving on Legs.

I rolled my eyes. "Yeah, I turned Dante into a regular Eagle Scout."

My dad came out of the house. "Back in one piece, I see." He looked over at Dante. "He wasn't too hard on you, was he?"

"No, sir. And I learned how to pitch a tent."

The wiseass in me almost wanted to say, *And we also learned how to have sex.* All of a sudden, I felt a little ashamed of myself. I almost felt myself blushing. Shame. Where did that word come from? For that one moment, I felt dirty. I felt like I'd done something really, really dirty.

It was so easy just to be with Dante. When we touched, it seemed like it was something pure. What wasn't easy was learning how to live in the world, with all of its judgments. Those judgments managed to make their way into my body. It was like swimming in a storm at sea. Any minute, you could drown. At least it felt like that. One minute the sea was calm. And then there was a storm. And the problem, with me, anyway, was that the storm lived inside me.

It was good to be back in my own truck. Dante started to take off his shoes. "Don't you think it would be better idea if you showed up wearing tennis shoes?"

Dante smiled. Then tied his shoelaces.

As I pulled up in front of his house, I glanced over at Dante. "Are you ready to face the music?"

"It's like I said, they probably didn't even notice."

I shrugged. "I guess we'll find out. Unless you want to go alone."

He shot me a look. "Oh, what the hell, come in and say hi to my mom and dad."

Mr. Quintana was sitting in his chair, reading a book, and Mrs. Quintana was reading a magazine. They both looked up and smiled at us when we walked in the door. "I can smell the smoke from here," Mrs. Quintana said.

"How was the camping trip?"

I looked at Mr. Quintana. "Dante's a quick study."

"That he is." The look on Mrs. Quintana's face told me she was about to drop a hammer. She didn't look angry. She just had this look, I don't know, like a cat about to catch a mouse. "Aren't you going to ask us about what we've been up to since you've been gone?"

"Well, to be honest, Mom, I wasn't." Dante knew it was coming. He had that *Oh shit, I've been found out* look on his face.

"Well, we had some friends over a couple of nights ago."

"Yes, we did," Mr. Quintana said. "And I'd bought a bottle of Maker's Mark just for the occasion. It's my friend's favorite bourbon." He glanced over at Mrs. Quintana.

"And when I went over to the liquor cabinet . . ." Mrs. Quintana paused. "We don't really need to go on with this story, do we, Dante?"

I had to give it to Dante. He might have felt like a rat caught in a trap, but he wasn't showing that face to his parents.

"Well, it's like this," Dante began. Mrs. Quintana was already rolling her eyes, and Mr. Quintana couldn't help himself—he was smiling and smiling. "I thought it would be nice if we had a little something to warm up because it gets cold up in the mountains, and I really didn't think that you'd mind—"

"Stop right there," Mrs. Quintana said. "I know exactly where you're going with this. You were about to say, *Well, and if you did mind, it's better to ask for forgiveness than to ask for permission.*"

Dante had this *Oh, shit* look on his face.

"Dante, I know you inside and out. I know your virtues and I know your vices. And one of the vices you need to work on is that you think you can talk your way out of anything. That's a terrible quality, Dante, and not one you got from either of us."

Dante was about to say something.

"I'm not finished yet. And we have already spoken about the use of mood-altering substances, alcohol included, and you know the rules. I know you don't like rules—and I don't know of too many boys your age who do—but you not liking the rules is not a compelling reason for you to break them."

Dante took out the bottle from his backpack. "See, we hardly drank any."

"You want credit for that, Dante? You stole your father's bourbon. And you're underage. So, technically, you broke two laws."

"Mom, you're kidding, right?"

Dante looked over at his dad.

Then Mr. Quintana said, "Dante, you should see the look on your face." And then he busted out laughing—and Mrs. Quintana busted out laughing—and then I busted out laughing.

"Very funny. Ha. Ha. Ha." And then he looked at me. "That's why you wanted to come in, isn't it? To see if there'd be any fireworks. Ha! Ha!" He picked up his backpack and marched himself upstairs. I was about to follow him up. But Mrs. Quintana stopped me. "Let him be, Ari."

"Weren't we a little mean? By laughing?"

"No, we weren't a little mean. Dante plays practical jokes on us all the time. He expects everyone to be a good sport. And he's generally a good sport too, but not always. And sometimes, he likes to spice up our lives with a little drama. This isn't any big deal, and I think he knows it. And, speaking as his mother, Dante needs to learn that he doesn't make the rules. Dante likes to be in charge. I don't want him to turn into the kind of man who thinks he can do anything he likes. I don't want him to ever believe he's the center of the universe."

I nodded.

"Go on up, if you like. Just don't be hurt if he doesn't open the door if you knock."

"Can I put a note under his door?"

Mrs. Quintana nodded. "That would be just fine."

Mr. Quintana handed me a pen and a yellow note pad. "We'll give you a little privacy."

"You're nice people," I said. It wasn't a very Ari thing to say. Still, the words had come out of my mouth.

"You're nice people too, Ari," Mrs. Quintana said. Yeah, she was something.

I sat there in Dante's father's office, wondering what to write. And then finally, I just wrote: *Dante, you gave me the best three days of my life. I don't deserve you. I don't. Love, Ari.* I walked up the stairs, pushed the note under his door, then let myself out. As I drove home, I thought of Dante, how I'd felt all that thunder and lightning shoot through my body as I'd kissed him and pressed against him and how strange and beautiful my body had felt and how my heart had felt so alive and I had heard talk about miracles and never knew a damn thing about miracles and I thought how now I felt I knew everything about them. And I thought about how life was like the weather, it could change, and how Dante had moods that were as pure as a blue sky and sometimes they were dark like a storm and that maybe, in some ways, he was just like me, and maybe that wasn't such a good thing—but maybe it wasn't such a bad thing either. People were complicated. I was complicated. Dante, he was complicated, too. People—they were included in the mysteries of the universe. What mattered is that he was an original. That he was beautiful and human and real and I loved him—and I didn't think anything would ever change that.

Eight

WHEN I WALKED INTO THE HOUSE, MY MOTHER SMILED at me. She was holding the phone and pointing it toward me. I took the phone. I knew it was Dante. "Hi," I said.

"I just wanted to say—I just wanted to say that I love you." And neither one of us said anything, we just listened to the silence on the other end of the phone. And then he said, "And I know you love me too. And even though I'm not in such a good mood, that doesn't matter very much because a mood is just a mood." Then he hung up the phone.

I felt my mother's eyes on me.

"What?" I said.

"You look so handsome just right now."

I shook my head. "What I need is a shower."

"That too."

I noticed my mom looked a little pensive, almost sad. "Is there something wrong, Mom?"

"No, nothing."

"Mom?"

"I'm just a little sad."

"What happened?"

"Your sisters are moving."

"What? Why?"

"Ricardo and Roberto have been working on some project. And they got transferred to Tucson."

"Isn't it weird that my sisters married men that work together?"

"It's not weird. I suppose it's unusual in that something like that doesn't happen very often. But they're good friends, and that works for your sisters. They're inseparable. And this job is a big opportunity. And they're chemists, and what they do isn't just a job for them."

I nodded. "So they're like you."

She looked at me.

"I mean, teaching's not just a job for you."

"Of course not. Teaching is a profession—but there are some people who don't happen to agree. That's why we're so well paid."

I liked my mother's sarcasm. Well, I didn't like it so much when it was pointed in my direction. "When are they leaving?"

"They're leaving in three days."

"Three days? That's kind of fast."

"Things happen fast sometimes. Too fast. I guess I just wasn't expecting this. I'll miss them. I'll miss the kids. You know, life throws you some curve balls. I guess I'm not much of a batter. Never quite learned how to hit a curve."

I didn't know what to say. I didn't want to say anything stupid like *They won't be that far away*. Besides, there wasn't anything wrong with being sad. It was okay to be sad about some things. And sometimes there wasn't anything to say—but I hated to see her so sad. Being sad wasn't something my mother did very often. I thought of the poem that she had framed in her bathroom. And I found myself repeating the poem to her. "Some children leave, some children stay. Some children never find their way."

She looked at me, almost smiling, almost on the verge of tears. "You're something special, Ari."

"My sisters, they're the ones who are leaving. My brother, he's the one who never found his way. And, Mom, I guess I'm the one who stays."

I saw my mother's tears falling down her face. She put her hand on my cheek. "Ari," she whispered, "I have never loved you more than I do right now."

I took a long hot shower, and when I washed my body, I thought of Dante. I didn't think of him on purpose. He was just there, in my head. Legs was lying at the foot of my bed. She couldn't jump anymore. So I picked her up and put her on my bed. She put her head on my stomach and I told her, "You're the best dog in the world, Legs. The best dog ever." She licked my hand. And we both went to sleep.

I had a dream about my brother—and my sisters—and me. And we were all sitting around the kitchen table and we were talking and laughing, and we all looked so happy. When I woke up, I was smiling. But I knew it was just a dream, and I knew that dream would never happen. Life wasn't a nightmare—but it wasn't a good dream either. Life wasn't a dream at all—it was something we all had to live. How was I going to live my life? And Dante, what would my life look like without him in it?

I woke up early and Legs walked into the kitchen, following me. I put on some coffee, drank some orange juice, and took out my journal:

Dear Dante,

I don't know why I didn't want to talk about this with you—even though we both understood that Emma's son had died of AIDS. I don't know much about that disease, but I know it's how gay men are dying, and I do watch the news at night with my parents and none of us ever talk. Your mom probably knows a lot about it. I don't know if you saw the headline in the New York Times *that Emma was reading that said: "Facing the Emotional Anguish of AIDS." And I heard my dad tell my mom that four thousand men had died from the disease. And my mother said it was more than that. Forty thousand gay men, Dante. I think Emma's sadness and the graceful way she dealt with her grief really moved me. And yesterday, when we got back, we got lost in our little dramas and we forgot about the painting she'd given us. I think we should put it up in your room today.*

The world is not a safe place for us. There are cartographers who came and made a map of the world as they saw it. They did not leave a place for us to write our names on that map. But here we are, we're in it, this world that does not want us, a world that will never love us, a world that would choose to destroy us rather than make a space for us even though there is more than enough room. There is no room for us because it has already been decided that exile is our only choice. I have been reading the definition for that world and I don't want that word to live inside me. We came into the world because our parents wanted us. And I have thought about this and I know in my heart that our parents brought us into this world for the purest of reasons. But no matter how much they love us, their love will never move the world one inch closer to welcoming us. The world is full of people who are stupid and mean and cruel and violent and ugly. I think that there is such a thing as truth in the world that we live in, but I sure as hell don't know what it is. And there's a shitload of assholes who think it's okay to hate anybody they want to hate.

You're the center of my world—and that scares me because I don't want to lose myself in you. I know I'm never going to tell you any of these things because, well, because there are things that I just need to keep. The men who are dying of AIDS have a poster that says SILENCE = DEATH. I think I know what that means. But for a guy like me, silence can be a place where I am free of words. Do you understand that, Dante? Before I met you, I didn't think anything about words. They were invisible to me. But now that words are visible, I think that they're much too strong for me.

Now my head is cluttered with words and cluttered with love and cluttered with too many thoughts. I wonder if people like me ever get to know what peace is like.

I shut the journal and finished my coffee. I changed into my running clothes. Legs had a sad look on her face.

I looked up and noticed my mom had been watching me.

"Talking to your dog again?"

"Yup."

"I've read that people who talk to their dogs are more compassionate people." She combed my hair with her fingers. "Have a good run."

I wanted to kiss her on the cheek. But I didn't.

I ran. I ran liked I'd never run before. I ran, maybe out of anger or maybe out of love. Or maybe because running wasn't always bad. You could run and run—so long as you came back home again.

Nine

I WAS WATCHING THE NEWS WITH MY DAD.

It was a way of spending time with him.

And what he was watching on the news really set him off. I'd never really seen my father's anger, and I was glad he wasn't angry with me. They'd interviewed a veteran who was going off on all the protesters that were marching on the streets of San Francisco. The man said he didn't fight a war just so all those perverts could get their chance to disrespect their own government and trash up the streets. "Let them move to China."

And my dad said, "I wish I could sit that asshole down, right here in this living room, and talk to him man to man, vet to vet, and he wouldn't talk like such a superior asshole. And I'd make him read the Constitution and the Bill of Rights aloud just so I knew he was getting it. Because apparently, he's never read the damned things."

He got up from his chair and sat down again. Then he got up again. Then he sat down again.

"It pisses me off when people act like experts just because they fought in a war. They appoint themselves to speak for all of us. And now this asshole thinks he has the right to invite people to move to China. I'll tell you something about a lot of us vets—we love to complain about our government. I guess only vets have earned the right to do that—which is bullshit."

I'd forgotten how much my father liked to cuss.

"Those people marching in San Francisco aren't perverts, they're citizens, and their own are dying in an epidemic that's killed more people than were killed in the war he and I fought in. And the government isn't lifting a finger to help. Why? Because they're gay and I guess to some that means they're not people. But when we got in a war, they told us that we were fighting to defend the freedoms that we have. They didn't tell us we were only fighting for the people who agreed with whatever the hell our politics were.

"You know, I saw a lot of young men die in that war. I held more than a few young men who were dying in my arms. And some of them were not much older than you. They died, their blood soaking into my uniform, their lips chattering in the hot rain of the jungle. They didn't get to die in their own country. They died on a soil that wasn't theirs. And they died with a question in their eyes. They'd been men no more than an hour, and they'd died in the arms of another soldier who was the only family they had. Hell, they should have been home playing basketball or kissing their girlfriends or their boyfriends, kissing anybody they loved. I know a lot of us who've fought in our country's wars are looked on as heroes. But I know who I am—and I'm no hero. I don't need to be a hero to be a man."

My father was crying. And he was talking through his trembling lips. "You know what I learned, Ari?" He looked at me. And I could see all his hurt, and I knew he was remembering all the men who died there. And he carried them with him because that's the kind of man he was. And I understood now that he lived with that hurt every day of his life.

"I learned that life is sacred, Ari. A life, anyone's life, *everyone's life* is sacred. And that asshole goes on television telling the entire world that he didn't fight for them because they didn't deserve it. Well, that's exactly who he was fighting for. He was fighting for their right to be heard. And his life is no more sacred than theirs."

Anything I had to say would sound cheap. And I didn't have anything to say that could heal his hurt and his disappointment. I didn't know anything about anything.

He wiped the tears off his face with the sleeve of his shirt. "I guess you didn't think your father could talk this much."

"I like it when you talk."

"Your mother's better at it than I am."

"Yeah, but it's missing something that you have and she doesn't."

"What's that?"

"She doesn't like to cuss."

He let loose a smile that was better than a laugh. "Your mother believes we should be more disciplined with the words we use. She doesn't believe in violence—in any form. She thinks cussing is a form of violence. And she can't stand for people to lie to her for any reason. She thinks that lies are the worst kind of violence."

"Did you ever lie to her about anything?"

"I never lied to her about anything that mattered. And besides, why would anybody want to lie to a woman like your mother? She would see right through you."

Ten

"IS THAT YOU, ARI?"

I looked up and saw Mrs. Alvidrez. "Hi," I said. "It's me."

"You've grown up to be as handsome as your father."

Of all my mother's friends, Mrs. Alvidrez was my least favorite. I always thought she was kind of fake. She gave out a lot of compliments, but I didn't think she meant any of them. She put something overly sweet in her voice, and there was no reason to do that—except, of course, if you weren't sweet at all. I guess I just didn't think she was a very sincere person, but what the hell did I know? She was one of my mom's church-lady friends, and they did good things like clothing drives and Christmas toy drives and the food bank. She couldn't have been that bad. But sometimes you just got a bad feeling about someone—and you couldn't shake it.

"Is your mother home?"

"Yes, ma'am," I said, pulling myself up from sitting on the steps. "Come on in. I'll go get Mom." I held the door open for her.

"You have very good manners."

"Thank you," I said. But somehow, the way she said that—it didn't sound like a compliment. It sounded more like she was surprised.

"Mo-om," I yelled, "Mrs. Alvidrez came to visit you."

"I'm in the bedroom," she yelled back. "I'll be right out."

I pointed at the couch and offered Mrs. Alvidrez a seat. I excused myself and walked into the kitchen to grab a glass of water.

I heard my mom as she greeted Mrs. Alvidrez. "Lola, this is a surprise. I thought you were upset with me."

"Well, it doesn't matter. It was a small thing."

"It was, wasn't it?"

There was a brief silence between them. I think maybe she was looking to get an apology from my mom for whatever that small thing was. But my mom didn't take the bait. And then I heard my mother's voice breaking what I took to be an uncomfortable silence. "Would you like a cup of coffee?"

They both came into the kitchen, where I was about to begin writing in my journal. I smiled at them. My mom put on a fresh pot of coffee, then turned to Mrs. Alvidrez. "Lola, I'm sure you didn't come over just to have a cup of coffee." I could tell that my mother didn't consider Mrs. Alvidrez to be one of her closest friends. There was an impatience in her voice that I rarely heard. It wasn't the same voice she used with me when she was annoyed. It was the tone of voice she took with my father because he refused to give up smoking.

"Well, I would prefer to speak with you in private."

That was my cue to leave the room. I started to get up—but my mother stopped me. "There isn't anything you have to say to me that you can't say in front of my son." I could tell that my mother *really* didn't like Mrs. Alvidrez and for whatever reason she resented her presence in her house. I'd never really seen my mother act like this. When someone dropped in unexpectedly, she stopped everything she was doing and made them feel welcome. But I wasn't getting the welcoming vibe from my mother.

"I really *do not* wish to have this discussion in front of children. It just isn't appropriate."

"Ari isn't a child. He's almost a man. I'm sure he can handle it."

"I thought you were a more discreet mother."

"Lola, in all the years I've known you, this is only the second time you've walked through my front door. The first time was to comfort me when my older son's name appeared in the newspaper. Only you didn't come to comfort me. You came to condemn me for the kind of mother I was. You said, and I remember every word, *All of this might not have happened if you'd been the kind of mother that God expected you to be.* You'll forgive me if I tell you that I don't give a damn about your opinions on the kind of mother I am."

"I suppose some people just don't take constructive criticism very well."

My mother was biting her lip. "Constructive? You and I have differing views on what that word means."

"You've never liked me."

"I've never treated you with anything but respect—even if you didn't earn it. And there was a time I liked you very much. But it's been a long time since you've given me a reason to like you."

I was starting to like this little discussion my mom and Mrs. Alvidrez had going on. If this was going to be a fight, I already knew Mrs. Alvidrez was going to be on the losing end. She didn't have a prayer. I kept my head down. I didn't want them to notice I was smiling.

"I speak my mind. When I know something to be wrong, my faith demands that I speak regardless of what others may think."

"Really, you're going to drag your faith into this? Whatever it is you have to say, Lola, say it—and try to leave God out of it."

"God accompanies me everywhere I go."

"He accompanies all of us everywhere we go, Lola. That's what makes him God."

"Yes, but some of us are more aware of his presence than others."

I'd never seen that look on my mother's face. And I knew her well enough to know that she wasn't about to say most of the things she was thinking. "Now that we've established that God is on your side, Lola, get to the point."

Mrs. Alvidrez looked straight into my mother's eyes and said, "Lina's son has died of that disease."

"What disease?"

"That disease that all those men in New York and San Francisco are dying of."

"What are you saying?"

"I'm saying that Diego, who apparently chose a lifestyle contrary to everything our faith stands for, has died of AIDS. And I understand that the obituary will say he died of cancer. I do not approve of that lie. And I do not believe that he should have a funeral in the Catholic church. And I thought that a group of us should approach Father Armendariz and ask that he do the right thing."

I could tell my mother was trying to take a couple of breaths before she said anything. Finally, she said in a voice that was quiet but firm as a fist about to punch her lights out, "I want you to listen to me, Lola, so that you clearly understand my perspective. Has it even occurred to you how painful all of this must be for Lina? Have you any idea or have you even considered what she must be going through right now? She's a good and decent woman. She's generous and she's kind. In a word, she possesses all the virtues that you lack. I have no idea why you think our faith is centered around condemning people. Lina and her family must not only be in a great deal of pain, I'm sure they're also feeling a great deal of shame. A funeral for her son from the church she has attended all her life is a consolation no one is entitled to refuse."

She wasn't finished, but she paused and looked right into Mrs. Alvidrez's eyes.

Mrs. Alvidrez was about to say something, but my mother stopped her. "Lola, get out of my house. Get out and don't ever think of ever entering my house again for any reason. In all my years of walking God's good earth, I have never refused my hospitality to anyone for any reason. But there's a first time for everything. *So get out of my house.* And if you think that you're taking God with you as you leave, you had better think again."

Mrs. Alvidrez didn't seem to be the least bit hurt by my mother, though it was clear that she was pissed and dying to have the last word. But the fierce look on my mother's face stopped her dead in her tracks. She quietly walked out of the kitchen and slammed the front door behind her.

My mother looked at me. "I swear I could choke that woman. I could choke her and go in front of a judge, and in all honesty and sincerity, I would plead justifiable homicide. And I am absolutely certain I'd get an acquittal." She moved slowly toward one of the chairs at the kitchen table and sat down. There were tears running down her face. "I'm sorry, Ari. I'm sorry. I'm not quite as good a person as I set out to be." She kept shaking her head. I reached my hand across the table and she took it.

"Mom, you want to know what I think? I think I'm a really lucky guy to have you as a mom. Seriously lucky. And I'm starting to find out that you just might be one of the most decent human beings I will ever meet."

I loved the way she was smiling at me right then. She whispered, "You really are becoming a man." She got up from the table and moved behind me and gave me a kiss on the cheek. "I'm going to help your sisters pack. And when I come back tonight, I'm going to sit down and think about what I'd like to take to Lina and her family when I go to visit them. And I'm going to send Lina flowers. Not something for the funeral home, but something for her."

If the word "feisty" hadn't already been invented, it would have been invented just to describe my mother.

I heard my mother leave and then I felt Legs's head on my lap. I petted her for a long time. And then I talked to her—even though I knew she didn't understand. "How come people aren't as sincere as dogs? Tell me. What's your secret?" She looked at me intently with her dark, dark eyes, and I knew that even though dogs didn't understand the language of human beings, they did understand the language of love.

. . .

I took out my journal, and I wasn't sure what to write. I don't know why I suddenly had this thing with writing. I mean, sometimes I'm thinking something, and I just want to write it down. I want to see what I'm thinking, maybe because if I see what I'm thinking in words, then I can know if what I'm thinking is true or not. How can you ever know what's true? I guess people can make you believe something is true if they use beautiful words, and it may sound beautiful, but that doesn't mean it really is beautiful. I guess I don't have to worry about that because I don't think that anything I write will ever be close to being beautiful or, as Dante would say, "lovely." But why the hell should that stop me? I'm not a writer. I'm not going for art. I have things inside me that I have to say, and they are things I need to say to myself. To figure things out for myself. If I don't say the things I need to say, it's going to kill me.

Dear Dante,

My mom is a good person. I don't mean that like she's my mom. I mean like she's a person. Dante, I used to think that I was invisible. I used to think that my mom and dad didn't know a damn thing about me and what I felt and who I was. And I thought that they didn't much care one way or the other. Especially my dad. I thought he was just this sad guy who didn't see anything or anyone around me. And I wanted him to love me and I hated him because he didn't love me. And I was always getting mad at Mom because she was always getting into my business and I thought she just wanted to run my life and tell me what I could and couldn't do. And when she wanted to talk to me, I just thought she wanted to lecture me or teach me something she felt I needed to know and I would say to myself, Yeah, yeah, my mom the schoolteacher, and I'm stuck in her class the rest of my life.

I'm not like you, Dante. You have always understood that your parents loved you. And you loved them back. You never thought it was cool to look down on your parents. You've never cared what other people thought because you've always known who you were. You're kind and you're sensitive (and yeah, a little bit moody, and you get hurt maybe a little bit too easily). But you feel. You feel and you're brave. I used to think maybe you needed me around to protect you. But you don't need protecting. Because you have a special kind of courage that most people don't have and will never have. I'll never have the kind of goodness you have living inside you. But you've taught me a lot of things. All those things I thought about my parents, well, they were mostly lies, and I believed my own lies. My dad noticed, even before I did, that I loved you. And not only that, he didn't judge me for it. And I'm beginning to realize that he really loves me. And yeah, he loves me because I'm his son, but he also didn't judge me for loving another boy. And that's because he's a good person. God, Dante, I never saw them as people. Not really. You know, I've been a piece of shit for a long time. I don't want to be a piece of shit anymore.

And my mom, she's a little like you. She knows who she is and she knows what she thinks because she's actually the kind of person who sits down with herself and gives things some thought.

And Dante, my mom, she is one fine, fantastic, feisty lady. And if my life is going to be a war because I love you, which means I like guys, then I'm one lucky guy to have my mom fighting that war right beside me.

We're lucky, Dante. Not just because our parents love us but also because they're good people.

I had never thought about that until today.

I love you, Dante. And that has changed everything in my life—and that matters. But I don't really know what that's going to mean for the life that I am going to live. There are so many things I don't know. So many things I will never know.

Eleven

I HEARD DANTE'S VOICE ON THE TELEPHONE. "HI," HE said.

"Hi," I said.

"I'm such an asshole. I—I mean—I mean, I acted like a five-year-old last night. I don't know what's wrong with me sometimes. Sometimes I think that I'm nothing but a lot of emotions all tangled up in my body and I don't know how to untangle them."

"You really are a poet," I said. "You talk like one. You think like one. And there's nothing wrong with you, Dante. Your parents were messing with your head, and maybe they were making a point—but they were also being playful."

"I know, and I just, I don't know. I know they didn't mean to hurt my feelings—and you didn't either. I know I have a good sense of humor, but sometimes that sense of humor abandons me. And you think I'm some kind of saint. But I'm not, Ari. I'm not."

"I don't think you're a saint. I don't think saints make love to other boys. But sometimes I do think you're some kind of angel."

"Angels don't make love to other boys either."

"Well, maybe some of them do."

"I'm not an angel and I'm not a saint. I'm just Dante."

"That works for me. Can I come over? I think I'll put Legs in the truck and take her over."

"That is one brilliant idea."

"Does the word 'brilliant' live inside of me? If it does, I didn't get the memo."

I hung up the phone. I had to pick Legs up and put her in the front seat. She kept licking my face as I drove to Dante's house. One of the mysteries of the universe is why dogs are always trying to lick your lips.

Twelve

WHEN I GOT TO DANTE'S HOUSE, I LIFTED LEGS FROM the seat of the truck and placed her on the sidewalk. She climbed up the steps without a problem—and licked Dante's face as he sat there.

"My mother read me the riot act this morning. I mean, that woman can lecture like no one else in the entire Western Hemisphere. 'And it's my job to remind you that there are consequences for the things you do, however small or big those actions are. I will not let you charm your way through life, because charming your way through life is cheating. There are no shortcuts in a life that is worth living.' You know, Ari, she's like this flame in the night and it doesn't matter if a wind or a storm comes along, because no storm is strong enough to snuff out the flame that is my mother."

I wanted to say something important to him, but I didn't know how to say important things. So I just whispered, "Dante, one day you'll be that flame. Maybe you are that flame already."

"Maybe you see what you want to see."

"Is that a sin?"

"It might be, Aristotle Quintana. It just might be."

Thirteen

WHEN I GOT HOME, MY MOTHER WAS IN THE KITCHEN making an enchilada casserole. Two enchilada casseroles. One red, one green. "What's up with all the food, Mom?"

"I'm taking it over to the Ortegas' house and offering my condolences to Lina."

"Why do people take food over when someone dies? Where did that come from?"

"Your father would call it immigrant behavior."

"What does that even mean?"

"Most people who came to this country didn't come here because they were making it in their home countries. People were poor. When someone died, a lot of people dropped by and families didn't have anything to offer them. People have their pride. So people would stop by and drop off food, and there's nothing like sharing food, eating with people. And it turns a funeral into a kind of celebration."

"How do you know all these things?"

"It's called living, Ari."

And I was thinking that my mother had always talked to me and told me things and I don't think I ever listened to a damn thing she said. At that moment, I was ashamed of myself. I'd always wanted to escape her presence as if I were some kind of prisoner. I was always wanting to leave the house, not because I had anywhere to go, but because I just wanted to go.

As I watched my mother place aluminum foil to cover the casseroles she had made, I thought how easy it was now to be around her. She was intelligent and interesting and she had a sense of humor and things that didn't matter didn't upset her or ruin her day. I used to think that she wanted me to be someone else. But it wasn't her who wanted me to be someone else—it was me. She pushed and challenged me. And I didn't like it. But it wasn't because she wanted to ruin my day. She was, in some ways, like Dante's mother. They both expected their sons to be decent human beings—and they were going to do everything they could to make that happen. And they sure as hell let us know when we weren't getting it.

I had homework to do, but I decided to go with my mother to give the Ortegas our condolences. "Why tonight, when the funeral isn't until tomorrow?"

"Because," she said, "it's our tradition that we surround the mourners with our love. Our presence gives them consolation when they feel inconsolable. That matters."

As my father drove us to the Ortegas', he said he had a theory about the importance of attending funerals. "Funerals," he said, "are much more important than weddings. People won't remember if you went to their son's wedding—but they *will* remember if you weren't at their mother's funeral. Deep down, they'll feel the hurt that you did not stand beside them when they needed you most. And it's good to remember that we not only mourn the dead when we go to a funeral, we celebrate their lives."

I was sitting in the back seat, and my mother turned her head and winked at me. "Your father has a poor attendance record when it comes to weddings. But when it comes to funerals, his attendance is perfect."

My father let out something that resembled a laugh. "Liliana, did anyone ever tell you that you talk like a schoolteacher?"

"Maybe it's because I am one. My husband, on the other hand, has been retired from the military for eighteen years, and he still cusses like he's a grunt in the army."

"I don't cuss all that much, Lilly."

"Only because you don't talk that much."

They were being playful—just like Dante and I were sometimes playful when we talked.

"The thing you don't understand is that cussing is just as much fun for me as I've grown older as it was when I was Ari's age. It's the only part of me that's still a kid. There's way too much adult in me. Vietnam killed most of the boy I had inside. But I still have a little piece of that boy living somewhere in me, and that boy likes to cuss."

"That has one of the most moving justifications for cussing that I have ever heard." There were tears in her eyes. "You never talk about the war. You should do it more often. If not for yourself, then for me."

"I'm trying, Lilly. I'm trying real hard. And you know, even before the war, I wasn't much of a talker. But I do know how to listen."

"Yes, you do," she said. She wiped the tears from her eyes. "Just when I think I know all there is to know about you, you manage to surprise me. And I think it's very manipulative. You make me fall in love with you all over again."

I couldn't see my father's face, but I knew he was grinning.

One small car ride and you find out something about your parents that you knew *but that you didn't really know*. That they had managed to stay in love with each other for thirty-five years. I always heard that one person in a marriage loves the other more than the other loves them. How could you really know that? Well, I guess that in a lot of marriages it was obvious that one of them cared and the other didn't give a damn. But in the case of my mom and dad, I'd call it a toss-up.

And what was it about human beings that wanted to measure love as if it were something that could be measured?

In the Country of Friendship

Every human being—each of us—is a like a country. You can build walls around yourself to protect yourself, to keep others out, never letting anybody visit you, never letting anybody in, never letting anybody see the beauty of the treasures you carry within. Building walls can lead to a sad and lonely existence. But we can also decide to give people visas and let them in so they can see for themselves all the wealth you have to offer. You can decide to let those who visit you see your pain and the courage it has taken you to survive. Letting other people in—letting them see your country—this is the key to happiness.

One

WHEN I WAS A LITTLE BOY AND I'D WALK INTO A ROOM full of people, I would count them. I would count them and recount them—and I never knew why I did that. I wasted a lot of time counting people, and the counting had no purpose to it. Maybe I didn't see the people as people but just as numbers. I didn't understand people—and even though I was a people too, I lived far away from them. For no reason, I thought of that when we arrived at the Ortegas' house. I knew that the house would be full of people and those people were people and not numbers—and that they were people who had hearts. It was their hearts that had brought them there.

I was holding one of the casserole dishes, and my father was holding the other. I think we both had this look on our faces that said *Just don't drop it.*

When Mrs. Ortega answered the front door, it was obvious that she really liked my mother. She hugged my mother and burst out crying on her shoulder. "I'm sorry," she said.

"What have you got to be sorry about?" my mother said. "This isn't a New Year's party—you've just lost a son."

She smiled and tried to pull herself together. "Thank you for the flowers, Lilly, it was very thoughtful. You've always been so thoughtful. And I'm glad you came." We followed her into the living room and Mrs. Ortega made room so we could set my mother's casseroles on the dining room table. Mrs. Ortega looked at me and shook her head. "I know you hate it when your mother's friends give you compliments. But I have to say that you are a very handsome young man." A lot of adults had to say something about my looks, which I always found interesting. I didn't have anything to do with the face I was born with. And it didn't mean that I was a good guy. And it didn't mean that I was a bad guy either.

"And I look just like my father," I said.

"And you look just like your father," she said. "Only you have your mother's eyes."

I felt awkward, and I didn't know what to say next, so I just opened my mouth and said, "I'm sorry that you're hurting."

She started crying again. And I felt bad because I'd made her start crying again. "I didn't mean to—I mean, I'm always saying the wrong things."

She stopped crying. And she shook her head and smiled at me. "Oh, Ari, don't be so hard on yourself. You didn't say anything wrong." She kissed me on the cheek. "You're as thoughtful as your mother."

Nobody there was my age. There were a lot of little kids running around, and they made me smile because they seemed like they were happy. Two of the Ortega girls were there too—and they were older. Not that much older, but old enough to be disinterested in me. Just like I was disinterested in them. And then there was Cassandra. She was the youngest. She was my age, and you could say we went to school together, but "together" wasn't really a word that applied in this instance.

Cassandra pretty much hated me. And I pretty much hated her right back. It was a mutual dis-admiration society, even though I don't think "dis-admiration" is a word. And I hoped I would manage to avoid running into her and seeing that look of outright disdain on her face. Her looks only added to her sense of superiority. I was relieved that Cassandra was nowhere in sight.

After a while, I was tired of my mother's friends' question, "Ari, when did you turn into a man?" I was a good sport about it, but about the fifth time I heard that question, the wiseass in me wanted to say, *Yesterday. Yes, I think it was yesterday. I woke up and looked into the mirror, and there I was, a man!* I was getting a little bored of listening to conversations of people who were talking about other people—in a nice way—I didn't know. I piled some food on a paper plate, and I was looking for a place to sit where I could make myself invisible. That's when Mrs. Ortega came up to me.

"Cassandra's out on the patio. Maybe she could use some company." I was thinking that Cassandra probably *could* use some company, but I thought that she'd prefer the company of a rat—even a really big rat, even a really big rat that was disease-infested, to being in my presence. I felt like I was going into battle with a rifle that wasn't loaded—something of a suicide mission. Mrs. Ortega couldn't help but see the look on my face. "Ari, I know you two don't like each other very much. But I hate to see her out there all alone. And maybe you'll distract her from all that sadness."

"What if she hits me?" I said. God, I really said that.

At least I made Mrs. Ortega laugh. "If she hits you, I'll pay for your medical bills." She was still laughing—and making someone laugh was better than making someone cry. She gently pointed me in the direction of the back door.

I stepped out onto the patio, which was more like an outdoor living room, with plants and furniture and lamps. I saw Cassandra sitting there. She resembled a character in a tragic novel, a solitary figure who had been condemned to live in a sea of sadness.

There was a chair with cushions that looked pretty comfortable next to the outdoor couch where Cassandra was sitting. She was intimidatingly beautiful. She had hazel eyes that could stare you down and make you feel like a *cucaracha* crawling around in her house and she was about to step on you and rid you of your miserable life. "Mind if I sit?"

She came back from wherever she was and gave me that look, the one I just described. "What. The. Hell. Are. YOU. Doing here?"

"I tagged along with my parents."

"Well, when you're as friendless as you are, I guess you have to settle for hanging out with your parents."

"I like hanging out with my parents. They're smart and they're interesting—which is more than I can say about most of the assholes that go to Austin High School."

"Well, aren't you one of those assholes? I guess not all assholes like one another." She may have been a superior being—but that was no reason to make other people feel like they should apologize for breathing. "What's that smug look on your face?"

"I should have just acknowledged the fact that you hate me—and left it at that."

"You want me to apologize for hating you?"

"You don't owe me any apology. And I don't owe you one either."

She looked away from me. It seemed like a studied pose to me. And I felt as though she was something of an actress. Which didn't make me believe that what she felt about me wasn't real. It was real as hell.

"You're a little boy. I don't like little boys. I prefer adults."

"I forgot, you've been an adult since you were twelve. Maybe that's why you lack compassion. You just can't relate."

"Thank you, Dr. Freud. Tell me, when did you start your psychiatric practice? I've got a few observations of my own. You get into fights because it makes you feel like a man. And you have a high opinion of your own intelligence."

"I don't think I'm all that smart."

"Well, you certainly don't qualify as being thoughtful. You hurt people. You hurt Gina and Susie, who really like you. They try to be friends with you, and you don't give a damn. Susie has a theory. She says you're not arrogant at all. You just hate yourself."

"Well, maybe I do."

"There's a lot to hate. I can hand you some reasons to put on your list."

"Don't put yourself out. For someone who doesn't know me, you seem to know all about me."

"You don't have to interact with someone to know them. Do you know that you've never, ever said hi to me in the hall?"

"You're not exactly Ms. Congeniality. You look at me as if you're one second away from slapping me from here to hell. But then again, you look at everyone that way."

"You think you can walk into my house and insult me? Fuck you."

I held back my own *Fuck you too, Cassandra.* "When you let people put you down, then you're a dead man. You know what you are, Cassandra? You're a killer. You use your looks as a weapon. You're a loaded gun disguised as girl."

"You don't know *one* thing about me. You don't know anything about what it means to lose. I just lost a brother, and he didn't die of cancer. He died of AIDS, and a lot of people already know that, courtesy of Mrs. Alvidrez. The last time I saw him was at a hospital in San Francisco. I didn't even recognize him. He was already dead. He always made me feel like I was worth something." She was crying—not just crying, but sobbing—and her tears were tears of loss and they were tears of anger and they were tears of hurt and they were tears that said *I'm not going to let anybody hurt me again. Not ever.*

"Do you know what it's like to be helpless in the face of a dying brother? He was brilliant, and brave—and he was gay, which meant he wasn't a man. And not even human. Let them die. Guys like you don't care. You don't know anything about what a man like my brother went through just because he was born. You'll never know his kind of courage."

"How do you know that?"

"Because straight little boys are callous dicks."

I didn't know I was going to say what I said, but it just came out. "How do you know I'm straight?"

She looked at me. She kept studying me with a look of confusion, and she didn't say anything, couldn't say anything, but there was that question on her face.

"How do you know that I'm not gay?" I'd said it, and a part of me was glad and another part of me regretted it. "Cassandra, I'm gay. I'm seventeen years old—and I'm scared." The silence between us seemed to last an eternity. "I'm sorry," I said. "I didn't mean to tell you. It just came out. I'm sorry, I—"

"Shhh," she whispered. It was as if all the hardness in her had just vanished. And then she looked at me with a softness in her that I had never seen. And she whispered, "Well, maybe you shouldn't have told me. Because you only say things like that to people you trust, and you have no reason to trust me. But you said it. And I heard it And I can't unhear it." I think she was trying to find the right thing to say—but there wasn't a right thing. "I guess that explains a lot of things," she said. "Oh God," she said. "Oh God, I'm such an asshole." And she was crying again, and she was really fucking crying. "Ari, I'm, oh God, I am such an asshole. I'm—"

"Hey, hey, listen to me. Don't. Don't say that. You're not an asshole. You're not. You're really not. There's only a handful of people who know. Five people. You make six. And now that I've told you, I feel like I've given you just one more burden you have to carry. And I don't want that. I don't. I know that all the gay activists are saying that silence equals death, but my silence, at least right now, equals my survival."

She just kept looking at me. She was studying me. She wasn't crying anymore. She tried to smile—and then she said, "Stand up."

"What?"

"I said stand up."

I looked at her with that almost cynical question on my face. "Okay, if you so say so." So I stood up—and she hugged me. And she cried into my shoulder. And I just held her and let her cry. I don't know how long she cried, and as far as I was concerned, she could have cried on my shoulder forever—if forever was what it took for her to let out the hurt she held inside.

When she stopped crying, she kissed me on the cheek. And then she sat down and she looked at my plate loaded with food, and she said, "Are you gonna eat that?"

"You can have it."

She grabbed the plate. "I'm starving," she said.

And I gotta say she really dug in. And I couldn't help it, I just started laughing.

"What? What's so funny?"

"Such a pretty girl, wolfing down food like a guy."

She gave me a kind of dismissive look, almost kind of playful. "I can do a lot of things like a guy. I can throw a baseball as well as any boy, and I bet I'm a better batter than you are."

"Well, being that I don't play baseball, that's a pretty low bar."

She smiled. "I have an idea."

"What's that?"

184

"Why don't you be a gentleman and—"

"I thought we'd established I wasn't a gentleman." Yup, I was smiling.

She returned that smug smile of mine. "That's true. But apparently the rules of the game have changed, and I see now that you have real potential. This calls for new strategies."

"New strategies?" That really made me smile.

"Exactly. So, as I was saying, why don't you be a gentleman and grab us another couple of plates of food?"

I shook my head and headed toward the house. As I opened the back door, I turned around and asked her, "Are you always this bossy?"

"Always," she said. "It's one of the things I'm best at."

"Well, the more we practice a virtue, the better we get at it."

I could hear her laughing as I stepped into the house.

Cassandra and I talked for a long time. She told me about her abusive father and how he'd beaten her brother when he'd come out to him—and how that had ended her parents' marriage. She was twelve years old when he left.

She laughed when she told me that her mother had been able to take him to the cleaners, courtesy of some information that he was having an affair. The information had come from none other than Mrs. Alvidrez.

She'd had a lonely life. But as I listened to her, there wasn't any hint of self-pity. She hadn't wasted her time feeling sorry for herself. Me, that was all I'd ever done.

• • •

"So you have a boyfriend named Dante."

"I do. That word, 'boyfriend,' still sounds so strange. But I don't know what else to call him."

"You love him?"

"I'm crazy about him. I've figured out that falling in love with someone is a form of insanity. Have you ever been in love?"

"Almost. I almost fell over the cliff."

"What happened?"

"He was older. He was in college. I saw myself as a woman. He thought of me as a girl. He thought of himself as a man. I thought of him as a boy. I knew I was headed for disaster, so I told him to lose my number."

"Good for you, Cassandra Ortega. Good for you."

As we were leaving the Ortegas' house, Mrs. Ortega and Cassandra walked us out to the car. My parents were talking about some last-minute details about the funeral, and I took it that my mother was involved. Cassandra and I followed behind.

"Cassandra, do you have a good memory?"

"Nearly photographic."

"I had to ask, didn't I? Then I'll give you my number and you can write it on your photographic brain." As I gave her my number, I traced it in the air with my finger. She repeated the number.

"Got it," she said.

I could see that my father had gotten into the car, but my mother and Mrs. Ortega were still talking.

"I take it you haven't said anything to Gina or Susie."

"No, I haven't."

"Ari, you should tell them." There was a real pleading in her voice. "They would never betray you. And they care about you. And I get that you're a private person and you don't think you need to tell anybody—for your own survival. But I promise you, Susie and Gina—and me, too—we'll help you. Sorry, that sounded condescending. It's a habit of mine. Gina and Susie, they're loyal, you know. You should trust them."

I nodded.

"I will. I mean, it's like we've made a game of them bugging me and me being annoyed and we've all sort of gotten used to playing that game. They always kinda knew that they didn't bug me half as much as I made out. But I honestly don't know what to do or say when I'm around them."

"Time to learn." She kissed me on the cheek. "It's time to learn, Aristotle Mendoza." She just kept shaking her head. And then she turned away. I watched her walk back toward the sidewalk that led to her front door. And I whispered her name. "Cassandra Ortega." Whatever that name had meant to me, now it meant something completely different. Her name had meant something frightening. Now it sounded like an invitation to visit a new world.

Two

BEFORE I WENT TO BED, I WANTED TO WRITE SOME-
thing in my journal. So I took it out and grabbed a pen and thought
a moment. I wasn't quite sure what I needed to write down—but I
knew I needed to write something. Maybe it was a way of becoming
a cartographer. I was mapping out my own journey.

Dear Dante,

*When my mother told me that my sisters were moving, she said
they were moving in three days. And she said that sometimes
life turns on a dime. I know what that expression means,
though I don't know where that expression came from and
I don't remember when and where I learned what it means.
It means a sudden turn. One moment you are going in one
direction and another moment you are suddenly going in
another direction. Something you never expected happens and
suddenly everything has changed and you find yourself going
somewhere that you never intended to go.*

Dante, you changed my life and changed its direction. But that change wasn't sudden. I had a conversation with Cassandra Ortega tonight, and I don't remember if I've ever talked about her with you before. Because I hated her with a hatred that was almost pure. But tonight, a part of my life turned on a dime. And suddenly, a girl I hated became a girl I admire. A girl who was a true enemy became a true friend. No one in my life has ever become an instant friend. But just like that, she has become important to me.

And I feel that I'm a little different—but I don't know how exactly.

I once thought that you could find all the secrets of the universe in someone's hand.

And I think that's true. I did find all the secrets of the universe in your hand. Your hand, Dante.

But I also think that you can find all the secrets of the universe when a girl who is more a woman than she is a girl cries all her hurt into your shoulder. And you can also discover all the hurt that exists in the world in your own tears—if you listen to the song your tears are singing.

If we're lucky. If we're very lucky, the universe will send us the people we need to survive.

Three

A WEEK. SCHOOL WAS STARTING IN A WEEK. THAT word, "school," was hovering over us like vultures over a dead carcass. It was a Saturday. Not that Saturdays meant all that much during the summer. I went for a run. I always liked the sweat that poured out of me after a run.

Afterward, I sat on the porch steps thinking. I laughed to myself. *Ari, and you thought you didn't have any hobbies.*

My mom came out and sat next to me. "Don't get too close, Mom. I'm pretty smelly."

She just laughed. "I used to change your diapers."

"Ugh. That's disgusting."

That made her shake her head. "There are certain things that sons may never understand."

I nodded, and then this idea ran through my head. "Mom, do you have plans today?"

"No," she said, "but I feel like cooking."

"That's perfect."

"Why? Do you feel like eating?"

"And you wonder where I get my smart-ass attitude." I just

jumped into my idea. "Mom, do you think I can have my friends over for lunch?"

My mom had this great look on her face. "I think that would be wonderful. But who are you? And what did you do with my son?"

"Ha! Ha! Well, I think I need to tell Susie and Gina about me— and I thought having them over for lunch and, you know—"

"Susie and Gina, the girls you're always complaining about because they won't leave you alone? The girls you've always pushed away for having the nerve to want you as a friend?"

"You've made your point, Mom." I felt like an asshole. "I guess I'm starting to get it. This may sound strange. But they're the closest I've had to friends ever since I was in first grade. I don't want to shut them out anymore. And it's like you said, I'm going to need some friends. Dante and I can't go at this alone."

"Ari," she whispered. "I'd all but given up hope that you'd open up your eyes and see how much those girls cared about you. I'm proud of you."

"It only took me twelve years."

"Better late than never." She blew me a kiss. "You're right. You're pretty smelly. Take a shower. I'll cook up something special."

I called Dante and asked him what he was doing for lunch.

"Nothing. Are you planning on taking me out on a real date?"

"My mom's making lunch. She feels like cooking. And when she feels like cooking, it means a feast."

"Sounds great! Do you still love me?"

"That's a stupid question."

"It's not a stupid question. A stupid question is when you're walking down the street with a friend and it's raining, and your friend asks, *Do you think it's going to rain today?* A stupid question is if my mom walks into the room looking convincingly pregnant and for me to ask her, *Mom, you're thirty-seven. You're not really pregnant, are you?* That would be a stupid question."

"Okay, not a stupid question. This is what I should have said: *Keep asking me questions that you know the answers to—and I'll—*" I had no idea where I was going with this.

"You'll what?"

"I'll kiss you. But I'll kiss you like I don't mean it."

"I don't think you'll be able to pull that off."

"What makes you so sure?"

"Because it's me." He had the over-the-top tone he took when he was joking around. "Because once you place your lips on mine, you will be unable to control the passion that I have aroused in you."

"I'll say one thing for you, Dante: You just might have a future writing cheap romance novels."

"You really think so? I'll dedicate them to you."

"See you soon. And please bring the smart Dante with you and leave the airhead I've been talking to on the phone at home."

"Fine, I'll leave the airhead here all alone to die of a broken heart."

I hung up the phone. He was a riot, that Dante. And I admired the ability he had to make fun of himself. I hadn't yet acquired that art.

And maybe I would never acquire it.

Four

I TOOK A DEEP BREATH—AND DECIDED TO MAKE THE
call. The dreaded call, that's what I called it in my head. You know,
there have been lots of things I've dreaded. Right before I met Dante,
I dreaded waking up in the morning. That's some serious dreading.
Cassandra was right. I owed it to Susie and Gina to tell them that I
was gay. It was so fucking weird. I mean, I actually practiced saying
that in the mirror. I'd look in the mirror and point at the me in the
mirror and say, "Ari, you're gay. Now, repeat after me: *I'm gay.*" It was
stupid, I know, but maybe it wasn't so stupid. And I wasn't normally
the kind of guy who did silly things like that because I didn't particularly like silly, and I didn't even like the word. Dante said that
every word deserved to be respected. I thought that was admirable.
But sometimes we had too much respect for certain words. Like the
word "fuck." I didn't particularly want to lose my respect for that
word. Or maybe I didn't have to respect that word in order to use it.
I know which side of this argument my dad would take. And I didn't
have to guess what my mother would think.

I knew I was sitting around thinking all these things because I
was delaying the dreaded call. *Ari, you should tell them.* Cassandra's

voice in my head. Great, just fucking great. Another voice living in my head.

I looked up Susie's number in the phone book. I heard the phone ringing, and then I heard Susie's voice on the other end. "Susie? This is Ari."

"Ari? Aristotle Mendoza is calling Susie Byrd? Well, push me into the swimming pool wearing a wedding gown."

"Knock it off. This isn't such a big deal. I've known you since the first grade."

"Well, that's a good point. You have known me since we were in the first grade. And not once have I heard your voice on the other end of the telephone line."

"And what's ever stopped you from picking up the phone?"

"You, Ari. That's what's stopped me. *Oh, I think I'll give Ari a call, see what he's up to?*"

"Okay, okay, I get it." And then the smart-ass in me kicked in and I said, "So, Susie, what have you been up to?"

"Oh, nothing. I was just sitting around waiting for a phone call from my friend Ari, hoping against hope that today was the day that he would finally call." And then she started laughing, a little overly amused with herself.

"Susie, you're starting to piss me off."

"I wish I had a nickel for every time you said that to me."

"You want me to apologize for waiting twelve years to call you on the phone?" *Oh shit*, I thought. I wasn't exactly making myself look good. I was thinking that maybe an apology might not be such a bad idea.

There was a brief silence on the other end of the phone. "Ari, did you hear what you just said to me?"

"Unfortunately, after I said it, I did hear it." And then I knew what the right thing to say was. "I'm sorry, Susie. Being friends with people isn't my strong suit. And I haven't had a lot of practice. And I knew you and Gina weren't just bugging the shit out of me for the fun of it. I wasn't invisible to you and Gina—and I liked being invisible. I wanted to be left alone. And you didn't accept that. And I'm glad, I am, that you and Gina took the time to see me."

I knew it was coming. She was crying. I mean, that's what she did. Her tears were part of the way she lived in the world. I waited for her to stop crying.

"Your loneliness made me sad, Ari. And there's something about you. I mean, people are like countries, and me and Gina, and your friend Dante, we're all countries—and maybe you've given your friend Dante a visa. But even if you have, that's just one person. And one person isn't enough. Having friends is like traveling. Gina and I have offered you a visa to travel to our countries whenever you want. So, Ari, when are *you* going to give *us* a visa? We want so much to visit you. We want so much for you to show us around your beautiful country." And she was crying again.

Her tears used to bug me. But I was thinking that it was really pretty sweet—to be so sensitive.

And then I said, "Well, that's exactly what I was calling about. I wanted to inform you that all the paperwork has been processed and your visa has been approved to enter into the country of Ari. But you're entering at your own risk."

I knew she was smiling. And it made me happy that I had made that phone call. It was hard—but change was a difficult thing. And I was starting to discover that change didn't just happen—I had to make it happen.

"Listen, I was going to ask you and Gina to come over for lunch today. I know it's sort of a last-minute thing, and I know you're probably busy and—"

She stopped me right there. "We'll be there," she said. "Damn straight we'll be there." I wished she hadn't used that word.

"But you haven't talked to Gina yet. How do you know she's not busy?"

"Believe me, she'll get unbusy." And then she paused and said, "I don't mean to question your sincerity, Ari, but I can't help but feel you're up to something."

"Well, maybe I am up to something. But it isn't anything nefarious."

"Nefarious. I love that word."

"I know you do. It was you who introduced me to that word."

She laughed.

"Twelve o'clock. You know where I live."

I hung up the phone. And I noticed I was trembling. I didn't know what I was doing. The Ari I used to be would never behave like this. But the Ari I used to be was disappearing, though I knew he would leave parts of him behind. And the Ari I was becoming hadn't quite arrived just yet. I couldn't stop trembling. I was afraid. I didn't know how to go about any of this. For a moment, a kind of panic took over me, and I couldn't breathe. I felt sick—and I ran to the bathroom and threw up.

I took a deep breath. And then another. And then another. And I just kept telling myself that everything was going to be okay.

I was doing the right thing. I didn't like placing my life in other people's hands. It didn't have anything to do with Cassandra or Susie or Gina. But deep down I already knew that my whole life was going to be in other people's hands. And I felt an anger in me, and then I felt myself trembling again and I wondered if this was what the earth felt like during an earthquake, but then I thought, *No, no, this is what a volcano feels like when it's about to explode.* I felt dizzy and sick, and I found myself retching whatever was left in my stomach into the toilet bowl. I don't know why, but I was crying and I couldn't stop and didn't want to stop.

And then I didn't feel anything and I wanted to feel something, so I whispered Dante's name and I started to feel something again. For an instant I wanted to be someone else or some other version of me, one who liked girls, and feel what it was like to be a part of the world and not just living in its corners. But if I was that guy, I wouldn't love Dante the way I loved him, and that love was the most painful and beautiful thing I had ever felt and I never wanted to live without it.

And I didn't give a shit that I was young, and I had just turned seventeen and I didn't give a shit if anyone thought I was too young to feel the things that I felt. Too young? Tell that to my fucking heart.

Five

LEGS AND I WERE SITTING ON THE STEPS OF THE FRONT porch, and she just wasn't a puppy anymore. She moved toward Dante as he walked up the sidewalk. He knelt down and hugged her. I smiled when he kept telling Legs how much he loved her.

He sat next to me and he looked up and down the street, and when he saw that the street was empty, he kissed me on the cheek.

"I have a story to tell you." And then I told him everything that had happened between Cassandra and me. And I didn't leave anything out that was important, and I told him that Cassandra was right about telling Gina and Susie and that I'd invited them to lunch but I had no fucking clue how I was going to begin the conversation or the revelation or the coming out or whatever the hell you wanted to call it. And I watched him as he listened to me, never taking his eyes off me.

And when I finished, he said, "Sometimes loving you makes me miserable. And sometimes loving you makes me very, very happy." And I was glad that he'd told me that sometimes loving him made him miserable because sometimes loving him made me miserable too. Knowing that made me feel like I wasn't a complete piece of shit. And I also knew that I had just made him happy.

"And you know, now you can stop being in love with hating Cassandra. All the time it was Cassandra this and Cassandra that."

"I don't remember talking about her that much."

"Well, I was exaggerating. But I do remember telling you that I'd like to meet this Cassandra and you said, *Oh no, you don't.*"

Just then, Gina Navarro's Volkswagen pulled in front of the house. As she and Susie walked up the sidewalk, Dante got up and gave them each a hug. Was this how it was going to roll? Shit. Dante was already setting the bar for a behavior that just wasn't the way I showed my affection, but yeah, yeah, I got up and hugged them both.

And then Gina said, "Were you abducted by a UFO? Did they mess you up and change you into someone else, a nicer version of who you used to be?"

And then she looked at Dante and said, "Dante, fess up, where did you put the real Ari that Susie and I loved to hate?"

And I looked at Gina straight in the eye and said, "That's not true. You never hated me."

"You're right. But I wanted to. Doesn't that count?"

"Nope," I said.

"Well, you hated us."

"I wanted to, but I didn't."

And Gina laughed and looked at me. "And that does count."

"That's not fair. How does that work? What kind of math is that?"

"If you haven't learned by now, girls do math very differently from boys. We grow up faster. Boys' math is the very basic, one plus one equals two. Girls' math is theoretical math—the kind of math you get a PhD in."

I watched Dante, and he wasn't saying anything in my defense. So I nudged him to say something. "Aren't you going to at least comment on Gina's rather overstated claims?"

"No," he said, "today I'm a cultural anthropologist, and I'm observing behaviors of young men and women who have known one another for almost twelve years and, having been stuck in a kind of emotional stasis, are attempting to examine their behaviors in order to deepen their interpersonal skills that support and promote emotional stability. In order for me to maintain my role as a social scientist, I must maintain my objectivity."

Gina and Susie looked at each other, and Gina said, "I like this guy."

And I looked at Dante. "Objectivity? You walked up to Gina and Susie and greeted them by hugging them. And then set up the expectation that I, too, would greet them with a hug. And there I was, hugging Susie and Gina."

Susie just shook her head. "Hugging people isn't going to kill you."

"Well, don't expect the hugging thing in the future. Dante can hug you if he wants. He's an indiscriminate hugger. I reserve hugging for special occasions, apart from spontaneous outbursts, which may or may not happen every now and again."

"What do you call consider special occasions?" Susie was crossing her arms.

"Birthdays, Thanksgiving, Christmas, New Year's, Valentine's Day, which is a fake holiday, but yeah, Valentine's Day, and very sad days—bad moods don't count—and very happy days when something happens that calls for a celebration. Labor Day, the Fourth of July, and Memorial Day are not hug days."

"I get the picture." Gina had that tone that insisted everything I had just said was wrong and she had no intention of following any of my rules because they were ridiculous.

"Do you really get the picture, Gina? You can't make me be somebody else."

"Ditto, Ari."

"Are we fighting?" Susie was wearing her *I'm not happy* face. "Since you invited us to lunch, I think you should be more gracious. We'll be gracious guests and you'll be a gracious host."

"Objectively speaking, I have to agree with Susie."

"Observing cultural anthropologists don't get to talk."

"Oh, that's not true."

"And objectively speaking? Really? You're allergic to objectivity."

He thought a moment. "You're right. And I was only messing with your head. I'd make a terrible cultural anthropologist. But you, sir, would make a very good one."

I wanted to kiss him. I was always wanting to kiss that guy.

Just then, I heard my mother's voice. "Anybody hungry?"

Of course my mother hugged Gina and Susie. I mean, she'd known them forever, even though she didn't really know them. But she liked them, and sometimes women had a solidarity between them that men didn't have—maybe because they needed it and men didn't. I watched them, and they seemed to have an affection for each other that was honest and natural. Maybe it was that mothers felt a kind of love for all the children in the neighborhood. And my mother knew Gina's and Susie's parents—from school board meetings and church and neighborhood association meetings. On the walks she took with my dad, she stopped and spoke with them and asked about their lives. My mother was a good neighbor, and I think, for her, that was a way of loving people.

I used to think of love as only something intimate that happened between two people. I was wrong about that.

My mother filled our plates with her tacos and *sopa de arroz* and chiles rellenos. After she'd served us all, she said, "I don't want to get in the way of the things you need to talk about." She looked at me. "I'll eat with your father when he gets back."

Susie shook her head. "You have to stay and eat with us. We want you to."

"I don't want to feel like I'm in the way. I don't want you to feel censored."

"Mom, I want you to be here." I think she saw something in the look on my face and she understood that I really wanted—and needed—her to stay and eat with us.

She smiled, served herself a plate, and sat in the empty chair right between Susie and Dante.

"On my God!" Gina had just put a forkful of chile relleno in her mouth. "This is amazing!" By then, we were all digging in.

"Mrs. Mendoza, you have to give these recipes to my mom."

"Dante, I'm sure your mother already has these recipes."

"No, she doesn't. Her food doesn't taste like this." Then he looked at her. "But don't tell her I said that. Just invite her over and start cooking. You know, so she can watch."

"I would never insult your mother with such an obvious tactic. I'm sure she's a fine cook."

"There's a difference between a fine cook and a chef." Dante was very proud of what he'd said.

My mother couldn't help but rub his hair. "You are a charmer, Dante. There's no room for doubt on that one."

I thought that, since everybody was eating and focusing on my mother's food, I'd just jump in and, you know, begin the dreaded coming-out conversation and get it over with. I turned to Susie and Gina. "Susie, remember how you told me you thought I was up to something? Well, I am up to something." And I got that feeling in the pit of my stomach and there was a part of myself that was fighting against another part of myself and part of me wanted to speak and another part of me wanted to forget all the words I had ever known and live in a silence that I would not be able to break. I cleared my throat. "I have an announcement to make." My heartbeat was slowing down. "Susie. Gina." And then the words were caught in my throat.

Susie kept looking at me. "I don't like that serious look on your face, Ari."

"Just give me a sec." I felt my mother's hand on my shoulder—and just having her hand there made me feel better.

Susie had that big question mark on her face. "Are you sure you're okay, Ari?"

"Yeah," I said. "I did have ulterior motives for having you come over today. What I have to say may not be a big deal for you, but apparently, it's a bigger deal for me than I ever thought." And then I began talking to myself out loud. "Shut up, Ari. Spit it out."

I saw Susie laughing and shaking her head.

"Susie? Gina? I'd like to introduce you to Dante Quintana. He's my boyfriend, and I love him. I know I don't know much about love—but what I know about love, my mother and Dante taught me."

Susie Byrd had turned on her faucet of tears. I'd expected that.

But Gina wasn't crying, and she said, "I have two things to say. The first thing is that I don't think that what you said is any big deal because I don't think being gay is any big deal—but I do know that for you, it's a very big deal, and I've just witnessed just how much you're suffering over this, and so, in my eyes, you're very brave. And the second thing I want to say is that you have better taste in men than I do."

Which made my mother burst out into the kind of laughter I had rarely, if ever, seen or heard—which made the rest of burst out laughing.

Susie looked at my mom. "Well, you seem to be taking this pretty well, Mrs. Mendoza."

"He's my son, Susie. Jaime and I have always believed that a parent holds a sacred office. And we will never abdicate or resign from that office just because things get difficult.

"My sister, Ophelia, was a lesbian. My family abandoned her. But Jaime and I loved her. I happen to know that Jaime loved Ophelia more than he loved any of his siblings. And except for my husband

and my children, I've never loved anyone as much as I loved her."

She smiled. I'd watched her teach a class or two, and I'd seen that smile. I knew she was about to step into her role of teacher. Fully composed and alert and in charge, she said, "Gina? Susie? I'm going to tell you something that I have never, ever told anybody. I have a confession to make: I AM A HETEROSEXUAL WOMAN."

Gina and Susie looked at my mother and then each other—then cracked up laughing. "Mrs. Mendoza, you're a hoot."

Even though she herself was laughing, she said, "Why is that funny? Because what I just said sounds ridiculous. But what I told you is absolutely true. I have never uttered those words. And do you know why? I've never had any reason to utter those words. Because no one has ever asked me. But now that I've said something to you that I've never told anybody else, what do you know about me?"

"Nothing," Susie said.

Gina nodded. "Nothing."

"That's exactly what you know about me. Nothing. But the world we live in doesn't play fair. If everybody knew that Ari and Dante were gay, then there's a whole lot of people who would feel as if they knew all they needed to know, in order to hate them. There isn't much I can do about what the world thinks. I'm sure I'd be judged for encouraging a behavior that some say shouldn't be encouraged—but I've never lived my life according to what other people thought of me. And I'm not going to start now."

The conversation made a turn and took a lighter tone, almost as if all of us just needed to chill out. Dante had remained mostly quiet, but it didn't take long before Susie and Gina began to interview Dante about how our relationship began. Dante was more than happy to be interviewed. Dante loves talking about himself—and I don't mean that in a bad way.

I enjoyed listening to them. All three of them could be funny as hell. And somewhere along the line, the interviews became an actual conversation. Mostly I watched my mother. And I knew from the expression on her face that there was a lot of happiness living inside her—even if that happiness was living there only for a moment.

My father appeared at the entrance to the kitchen. He was sweaty, and his mailman uniform looked a little tired on him. He was uncharacteristically verbal. "Well. I don't believe I've seen anything quite like this in Lilly's kitchen." He seemed to get a kick out of what he was seeing. "Susie, how are your folks?"

"They're fine, Mr. Mendoza. They're still recovering hippies, but they're moving along."

"Well, I think being a recovering hippie is a far easier task than being a recovering Catholic."

My mother shot him a look. So he decided to amend what he'd just said. "But, you know, there's nothing wrong with being a hippie, just as there's nothing wrong with being a Catholic. So, recovering or not—it's all good." He gave my mother a look, and I knew that look was asking, *Have I redeemed myself?*

"Oh, Susie, would you do me the favor of returning the books I borrowed from your father?"

"Sure thing. He said he wanted to talk to you about some novel that you both read. But I don't remember what it was."

"I think I know the one he's talking about."

My mother asked him if he was hungry, but he said he wasn't. "I'm going to take a shower and change and just relax for a moment."

My father disappeared down the hallway. I looked at Susie. "Your father talks books with my father?"

"All the time."

"And you never told me?

"Why would I tell you something that I thought you already knew?"

I sat there and asked myself how many more things I didn't know. Not that I had anyone to blame. It's like my mother once told me. When you open up the yearbook, and you know that you didn't show up to take your photograph, why would you be surprised to find that there's a little cartoon that says GONE FISHING in the place of your picture? I guess I'd been gone fishing for a long time.

Mom got up and started clearing the table.

"Mom, I'll get that."

"Aristotle Mendoza, in the seventeen years that you have lived in this house, I have never heard you offer to do the dishes."

I heard Gina's harsh condemnation: "You've never washed the dishes?"

Susie's judgment was even harsher: "You're a spoiled brat."

And I thought I might as well go with it. "Does anyone want to add any more remarks, commentaries, editorials, before I get on with this?"

"It's not that hard to put the dishes in the dishwasher."

"We don't have a dishwasher." My mother shrugged her shoulders. "I've never liked them. Jaime and I are the dishwashers."

Gina and Susie looked at my mother like *Oh, wow*. Susie wasn't very convincing when she said, "Well, washing dishes the old-fashioned way is better, anyway. Way better."

Sometimes the way you say something doesn't convince anyone—not even the person who said it. Susie and Gina gave themselves away with that look that said, *You really don't have a dishwasher?*

My mom stepped in. "Ari, do you even know how to wash dishes?"

"How hard can it be?"

"It's not hard at all," Dante said. "I know how to wash dishes. I can show Ari the ropes."

I actually couldn't quite believe that Dante knew anything about washing dishes. "You know how to wash dishes?"

"Yup. When I was eight, my mother told me it was time for me to learn. She said dinner could be broken down into three parts: the cooking, the eating, and the cleaning up. She said that I was now responsible for part three. I told her that I liked part two. I got the look. I asked if I was going to be paid, and I knew in two seconds that I'd asked the wrong question. All she said was that she didn't get paid for cooking and neither did my father—and that I wasn't going to get one penny for cleaning up. After a while, my mom got tired of seeing me be all mopey and pouty while I did the dishes. So, one day, she put on some music, and she made me dance with her and we sang and we did the dishes together. And we had a real nice time. After that, every time I did the dishes, I put on some music and danced. It kinda worked out."

Dante and I were talking as we gathered up the all the dishes. My mother took off her apron. "Your mother is a brilliant woman, Dante."

As my mother walked out of the kitchen, I said, "Mom, you know, this washing-dishes thing isn't such a big deal."

"Good," my mother said. "Then you can start doing the dishes after dinner from now on."

I could hear her laughing all the way down the hall. I liked my mother when she behaved like something in between the good schoolteacher that she was, and the little girl that still lived inside her.

Six

AFTER LUNCH, LEGS AND I WERE SITTING ON THE STEPS of the front porch. Gina and Susie whisked Dante away. They were all too ready to give him a ride home and get more information about how Ari and Dante came to be Ari and Dante. They certainly weren't going to get any information out of me—and they knew it. But I didn't really mind. I already knew that Dante was going to be one of Susie and Gina's favorite people. I was discovering that I wasn't the jealous type.

Legs looked up at me in the way that dogs do. "I love you, Legs," I whispered. It's easy to tell a dog you love her. It's not so easy to say those words to the people around you.

Seven

DANTE ASKED IF IT WAS OKAY IF HE WENT TO Cassandra's brother's funeral with me. "I know that I don't really know Cassandra—and I didn't know her brother. But I feel like I should show a little solidarity. Does that make sense to you?"

"It makes sense, Dante. It makes perfect sense. I'm sure Cassandra wouldn't mind."

My mother told me she would be wearing a white dress to the funeral—which seemed odd to me. She explained that all the Catholic Daughters were going to march in procession wearing white dresses. "For resurrection," she said. My father and I were wearing white shirts, black ties, and black suits. We were on the porch, waiting for my mother—and my father kept looking at his watch impatiently.

I don't know why my dad got impatient at moments like these. Our Lady of Guadalupe Catholic Church was close, and it didn't take but five minutes to get there. "I'm going to go pick up Dante," I said. "I'll meet you at the church."

Just then, my mother walked through the front door. I saw a look on my dad's face I'd never seen before. Or maybe that look had been present many times before—it was just that I hadn't noticed. My mother could still take my father's breath away.

Dante and I were sitting next to my father. The priest was about to bless the casket at the entrance to the church. Susie and Gina sat right next to us. We nodded at one another. I leaned over to Susie and whispered, "I didn't think you were Catholic."

"Don't be stupid. You don't have to have to be Catholic to go to a Catholic funeral," she whispered back.

"You look pretty," I whispered.

"At least you're learning how to make up for saying stupid things," she whispered back.

"Shhh," Gina said.

My father nodded and whispered, "I'm with Gina."

The opening hymn began, and the voices of the choir sang out. The Catholic Daughters filed in, two by two, in a slow and respectful procession. There were maybe sixty of them, perhaps a few more. These women knew something about solidarity. I saw a look of grief on many of their faces, including my mother's. Mrs. Ortega's grief was their grief. I'd always thought those ladies were a little bored with their lives and they themselves were a little boring—and that was the reason they'd become Catholic Daughters. Yet another thing I'd been wrong about. They had far better reasons. I'd never found it difficult to keep my mouth shut—but maybe I should think about keeping my mind shut when it came to judging the things other people did that I didn't understand.

The Mass was a typical funeral Mass—except it was bigger than most. And there were a lot of young men there who were about Diego's age, men in their twenties, and they all sat in the back of church and there was a lot of sadness in their eyes and they had this look as if they knew they weren't welcome, and it made me angry that they'd been made to feel that way. Anger, there it was again, and I think I was beginning to understand that it was never going to go away and that I'd better get used to it.

Dante and I got in my truck, and we became a part of the procession leading to the cemetery. I thought about my parents. I agreed with my dad and his thoughts about the religion they were raised in—and the religion I was raised in. And I knew somewhere inside him, my father still considered himself a Catholic. My mother was every bit the good Catholic woman she made herself out be. She didn't have a difficult time forgiving her church for its failings.

Eight

DANTE AND I DIDN'T SAY MUCH AS WE FOLLOWED THE long line of cars toward the cemetery. I thought of the enlarged photograph of Diego that had been placed on an easel in the front of the church. He was a handsome man with a clean-cut beard and clear dark eyes that were almost as black as his hair, the same eyes Cassandra had. He was laughing, and it must have been a candid shot because the wind seemed to be playing with his thick hair. I tried to imagine the day it was taken, before the virus entered his body and stole it from the world. I tried to imagine the thousands of men who had died, who had names and families and had known people who loved them and had known people who hated them.

They had been alive once, and they had known something about what it was to love and be loved. They weren't just numbers that someone kept count of. Dante asked me what I was thinking. And I said, "My dad told me that during the Vietnam War, there was a body count. He said that the country was counting bodies when they should have been studying the faces of the young men who had been killed. I was thinking that the same thing is happening with the AIDS epidemic."

"That's exactly what's happening," Dante said. "We'd rather see a number than a life. And I asked my mom why so many of the newspapers and the media referred AIDS as an epidemic when it was actually a pandemic that's spreading all over the world. She said that my question was very astute, and she said that she was happy to know that I was looking at the world with open eyes. Her feeling was that maybe they didn't want to give AIDS that kind of importance. That most people wanted to minimize the disease. What do you think, Ari?"

"I think your mother's right about almost everything."

I had only glimpsed Cassandra as she'd walked down the aisle with her mother at the end of Mass. I was looking for her and finally spotted her standing at the edge of the crowd circled around her brother's casket. She was wearing a black dress and she'd draped a Mexican gold silk scarf around her shoulders. As she stood there, she looked like the sad, solitary figure I'd seen when I'd first stepped into her backyard. Only this was different. Despite her sadness, there was something else, something more. She wasn't hanging her head in any kind of shame. The afternoon sunlight seemed like it was shining on her and her alone. And she had a look of defiance. She wasn't broken, and she wasn't going to break.

I motioned at Susie and Gina. And they saw her, and we all nodded to each other. So we moved toward her and stood next to her. Gina was standing right next to her on one side, and I was standing on the other. She kept her eyes focused on the casket as the pallbearers carried it out of the hearse. It didn't even seem like she was aware of the fact that we were there. But then I felt her take my hand and hold it tight. And I noticed she was holding tight to Gina's hand. "When you are standing all alone," she whispered, "the people who notice—those are the people who stand by your side. Those are the people who love you."

She kissed each one of us on the cheek—and she did it with the grace of a woman.

Nine

Dear Dante,

Before every school year begins, I feel like crawling under my bed and staying there. I don't know what it is about the whole school thing that makes me feel anxious. I always feel like I've thrown my summers away—well, until I met you.

And this summer has been amazing. Touching you and feeling your touch. Summer will always be Dante Season.

I don't know what the hell I'm trying to say. I don't.

But one thing is for certain. This will be the last year of my schooling season. And then the college seasons will begin.

I guess I don't want my Dante season to end.

And I'm afraid.

Maybe this season will be the season that will change
everything. I am almost excited. But mostly I'm afraid.

Let's map out the year, Dante. Let's write our names and chart
out some paths. And go see what we have never seen. And be
what we have never been.

The night before the first day of school, Dante called me on the phone. He didn't even say hi. "Did you know that our word for 'school' comes from the Greek word meaning 'leisure'?"

"No, I didn't know that. And that doesn't make any sense, does it? And hi, Dante. How are you? Fine? I'm fine too, by the way."

"I was going to ask."

"Sure you were. And I was just kidding."

"Sure you were. And leisure does make sense if you lived in Ancient Greece. If you have leisure time, what do you do with your leisure time?"

"I think about you."

"Nice answer, Aristotle. What's the real answer?"

"Well, other than spend time with you, I run, I read, I write in my journal."

"I'm not leisure time."

"You're right. You're a lot of work."

"Wrong. For your information, I fall under the category of pleasure."

"I knew that."

"Sure you did. Now back to your answer. You run, but that falls in the category of exercise—and that's not leisure time. But reading and writing do come under things that you do with your leisure time. So that is exactly what the Greeks thought. If they had leisure time, they used that time to think, and to have what might today be called 'educational purpose.' So, if we looked at school as leisure time, then maybe we'd have a different attitude about it. And we would be all the happier."

And I said, "'The world is so full of a number of things, I'm sure we should all be as happy as kings.'"

"Are you mocking me? You're mocking me."

"I'm not mocking you. I'm just remembering. And I happen to be smiling, and it's not an *I'm mocking you* kind of smile."

"Then I have another thought to make you smile. Tomorrow, the very first day of school, is the very last first day of high school that we will ever have. And after this, there will be no more first days of school for Aristotle Mendoza at Austin High School and no more first days of school for Dante Quintana at Cathedral High School. It is the last first day of school, and every event that has anything to do with school, we can now say with smiles on our faces that it is the last time we do whatever the hell it is we're doing at that event. And that should ease our burdens."

I started laughing. "I don't hate school that much—and neither do you."

"Well, I like the learning, and you have finally admitted to yourself that you like the learning too. But the rest of it sucks the big one."

"You're funny. One minute you're talking as if you're so fucking sophisticated that, if you lived in London, you'd be speaking BBC English. And the next minute you're speaking like a ninth grader."

"What's wrong with ninth graders? You don't like ninth graders?"

"Are you on something?"

"Yes, most definitely. I'm high. I'm high and on top of the world because I am deeply, profoundly, ecstatically, entirely, and most emphatically in love with a guy named Aristotle Mendoza. You know him?"

"I don't think so, no. I used to know him. But he's changed into someone else. And I don't think I know him. Lucky guy, though—I mean, all that love that's deep, profound, ecstatic, entire, and emphatic, well, that's some kind of love aimed at that Aristotle guy."

"Oh, I'm lucky too. I have it on good authority that this Aristotle Mendoza that you claim not to know has the purest and sincerest form of love for me. And, if you see him, tell him—well, no, you won't see him because if you do see him, you won't recognize him. Because you used to know him, and now you don't know him—so it isn't any use to ask you to convey a message to him."

"Well, you never know, I might run into him at school and there's a chance I might recognize him, and if that happens, I will be more than happy to convey your message to him—only I don't know what that message is."

"Well, if by chance you should be lucky enough to run into him, tell him Dante Quintana used to be a boy who didn't have any real friends. Not that having no real friends made him unhappy, because he was happy. He loved his parents and he loved reading and listening to vinyl records and art. He loved to draw—and he was liked well enough at school, so yes, he was happy." And then there was silence on the other end of the phone. "But, Ari, I wasn't happy-happy. I was just happy. I didn't really know happy-happy until the day you kissed me. Not the first time. That first time I wasn't happy-happy. I wasn't even happy. I was miserable. But the second time you kissed me, I knew what it was to be happy-happy. And I guess I just wanted to thank you for adding that extra happy to my happy."

"Well, I had an extra happy lying around, so I decided to give it to you."

Everybody went to school early on the first day of school. Just to have time to feel things out. As I was about to enter the front doors, who did I see? Cassandra. And Gina. And Susie.

I got their attention with that old catcall whistle that no one used anymore but that my mom and dad laughed about.

"Is that whistle supposed to sexually objectify us?"

"I don't do the sexually objectifying thing. I'm not even sure I know what it means."

"The hell you don't."

Of course, I wasn't sexually objectifying them. I was gay. But it was a good game to play, and people would overhear us. And we'd sort of argue because the whole school knew that Susie was a feminist—even though that seemed like such a dated word, but Susie had set me straight about that one when we were sophomores—and I really do have to stop using that expression, *set me straight*, even if I was just thinking it.

I looked at Cassandra. "Did you feel sexually objectified by my catcall whistle?"

"No, not really. More than anything, I'm embarrassed for you." God, did she ever have a killer smile.

"Thank you for doing for me what I am incapable of doing for myself."

"You shouldn't thank people when you don't mean it."

"How do you know I don't mean it?"

"I know insincerity when I see it."

"And I know a beautiful woman when I see her."

"Now, that was sincere."

"Was it? How's that?"

"Sincerity clothed as insincerity. Now, that's sincere."

"Cassandra, you're crazy."

"You are as crazy as I am. In fact, you're crazier. You're a male, and even the best representatives of your gender are crazier than any female."

"Because?"

"Do you like having a penis?"

"What kind of crazy question is that?"

Gina hadn't said a word, but she figured that moment was as good a time as any to join the conversation. "Answer the question. Do. You. Like. Having. A. Penis?"

"Well, well. Well, yes."

"Well, yes?" Susie wouldn't be left out.

"Hell yes! Yes, I like having a penis. Am I supposed to apologize for that?"

"Well, I don't know about Gina and Susie, but I'd say yes. I think apologies for liking having a penis might be in order."

"Do you think you should apologize for liking having a, I mean, for having a, for having a—"

"Vagina? Is that the word you're looking for?" I liked that smug look on Cassandra's face.

"Exactly. That's the word."

"You can't even say it. You see, here's the thing: Women don't think that having a vagina qualifies them to be in charge of the world. In fact, it disqualifies us from being in charge of the world. For our part, no apologies are necessary."

I knew where she was going with this. I was way ahead of her. I took out a pad and pencil and wrote six words on them, tore the page off, and folded it in half while she was talking.

"Men, on the other hand, think that having penises does qualify them to run the world. And that's truly fucked up. Which is why the world is fucked up. Which is why we have so many damned wars. There's a lot of women making noise that they want to be soldiers just like men. Not me. Human beings with penises start those wars. And human beings with penises can die in them. So yes, you should apologize for liking having a penis."

I handed her the note. She unfolded it and read my six words. *You're right. But I am gay.*

She took a pen from her purse. *But you still have a penis.*

She handed me the note. And I wrote, *Penis or not, I'm still disqualified from running the world. But at least it also disqualifies me from joining the military and getting killed in a war started by the human beings who have penises.* She smiled as she read the note. She showed the notes to Gina and Susie, who nodded and kept looking at each other.

"Well," Gina said, "Cassandra's not going to say it, but someone has to. Congratulations, Ari! You've just won round one of a year-long debate that will have God knows how many rounds, and Susie and I will be keeping track. And may the best human win, penis or no penis. And just so we're clear, there will be no extra points given for having a penis—and—"

Cassandra interrupted her. "Yes, I know—and no extra points for having a vagina. And it should not be *may the best human win*. It should be *may the greatest intellect win*."

The girls—or should I say the two almost-women and the woman who was already a woman—handed one another smiles as if they were giving one another medals.

Cassandra gave me a kiss on the cheek. "The outcome is not in doubt. I have fallen in love with you, Aristotle Mendoza—but I am going to shred you like I'm going to shred this note." She put it in her purse.

"Hey, that's mine."

The first bell rang. We had ten minutes to get to class. Cassandra grabbed my arm. "You keep this note, you'll lose it. Someone may find it and maybe figure something out that they have no right to be figuring out. In my possession, it's safe. Like I said, I'll shred it like I'm going to shred you."

"Bullshit. You're not going to shred it. You're going to save it."

"Yes, I'm so fucking sentimental."

"Sincerity clothed in insincerity. Now, that's sincerity."

"I really should slap that smile off your face."

"You shouldn't say things you don't mean."

She gave me a look I couldn't quite read. I really didn't know what she was feeling and why. "For the first time in my four years at Austin High School, I actually believe that it might approach being a great year."

She turned left, and Gina, Susie, and I turned right—and headed to Mr. Blocker's English class. My school days would start on a good note—a note I'd written to win the first round. I was going to get trounced. It would give me a good excuse to run to Dante. He would console me by kissing me. That didn't sound so bad to me. Not bad at all.

Ten

I DIDN'T GET INTO A FIGHT ON THE FIRST DAY OF school. I saved that for the second day. I didn't start it. And I'm not saying that to make myself feel better. I've lied to myself about a lot of things, but I've never lied to myself about the fights I've gotten into.

When I drove into the parking lot, there were five guys surrounding a little guy. I knew who that little guy was. Yeah, he was effeminate, a word Dante taught me. He was a nice guy, smart, nerdy, and with a lot of lilt in the way he spoke. But he didn't bother anyone. He hung with a crowd, each one of them misfits in one way or another. He was in the same class as I was, though he didn't seem to be any older than fourteen. His name was Rico and I'd heard his friends call him Rica but as if it was a joke, and it was their joke.

The guys had him surrounded and they were calling him all the predictable names those guys used to refer to guys like Rico. *Joto, maricón, pinche vieja,* faggot, queer. They thought the whole thing was funny. Yeah, hilarious. I didn't know exactly what was going to happen, but when one of then kicked him in the groin and he fell to the ground, I was in the middle of it before I even knew I'd gone there. One of the guys tried to punch me, and it didn't take but a couple of punches before he was kissing the asphalt—then the other guys came at me. Out of fucking nowhere, some tough guy with tattoos jumped in on my side. That guy was small, but he had muscles and he knew how to fight. He could have given me lessons. He was standing right beside me and he laughed. "It's two to one, baby. They fuckin' think the odds are in their favor. That's what makes them losers." And the fight didn't last more than five minutes when this tattooed badass and I had them all face-to-face with the tires of the parked cars.

"I'm Danny," he said. I couldn't help but notice he was a good-looking guy. "Danny Anchondo."

"I'm Ari Mendoza."

"You're probably not related to the Mendozas I know. And the Mendozas I know aren't related to one another. But I gotta say, *vato*, I never met a guy with that last name that didn't know how to fight. These fuckers here only pick fights with guys like Rico."

One of the guys lying on the ground was trying to pick himself up. Danny put his foot on his back. "Don't even try it. Relax. Chill."

"But I'm fuckin' gonna be late to class."

Danny threw his own words back at him. "Late to class. Next time I see you, or my friend Ari sees you, picking on Rico or any of his friends, you're not gonna be able to find your own ass, cuz I'm gonna own it."

Danny walked over and helped Rico get up from where he was lying. "You okay, Rico?"

"Yeah, I'm okay." He was crying, though he was trying not to.

Danny scolded him. "Don't let 'em see that. Don't ever show those fuckers the best part of yourself."

Rico wiped his tears and gave Danny a smile.

"Atta boy. That's it. Shake it off."

He nodded, and picked up his backpack. He started to walk away—and then he turned around and shouted, "Everybody says you guys are trouble. People don't know shit." His head down, he turned back around and headed for his first class.

I turned to Danny and said, "How do you know Rico?"

"My sister hangs with him. She's not into guys. She's got attitude. She likes to give the world the finger. But she's always helping people out. She's cool." And then he looked at me, like he knew something about me. "I know who you are. You fucked up one of my buddies."

"Sorry."

"Sorry? For what? He and a couple guys caught one of your buds kissing some other guy. They put 'im in the hospital. He okay?"

"Yeah, he's good."

"You did the right thing. A friend who doesn't stick up for a friend ain't no goddamned friend. And besides, it's pretty fuckin' chickenshit to put someone in the hospital for kissin' another dude. You don't wanna kiss a guy, don't kiss 'em. What's the fuckin' problem? People are always askin' me why I go around beatin' the crap outta people. It's cuz the world's full of assholes, that's why."

That just made me laugh. I couldn't help myself.

"Why you laughin'?"

"Because sometimes, you run into someone who knows what the

truth is. So you laugh. You laugh because somebody made you happy."

"I sure as hell don't make a lot of people happy."

"Well, like you said, the world's full of assholes. What you did for Rico, Danny, that was a beautiful thing."

"Yeah, but Rico's my friend. And you don't even know him. You fucker, now that's a beautiful thing."

Danny, there's another one that could break the world's heart with his smile.

We gave each other a knuckle.

"See you around, Mendoza."

"See you around, Danny."

It was funny. I didn't even know Danny—but I did know something about him that made me feel that I could trust him. It made me sad to think that people didn't see the most obvious thing about him—that he had a noble heart. I had a funny feeling that I would always think of him as a friend. And I also had a feeling that it wasn't the last time I'd see him.

The way the world judged and misjudged certain people—and threw them away, erased their names from the map of the world—that was the way that the whole system worked. Maybe Danny's sister knew exactly what to do in the face of all the judgments aimed in her direction—help people out when you can and give the world the finger.

I didn't know why I hadn't known this about myself before. There was something of a rebel in me. For once, I discovered a trait in me that I didn't think needed changing.

Eleven

MR. BLOCKER KEPT ME AFTER CLASS. "WHAT HAPPENED
to your knuckles? They're bleeding."

"They ran into a couple of guys."

"Why do you do these things to yourself?"

"I didn't do anything to myself. But I think those guys think I did
something to them."

He gave me a look. "What we do to others—"

I finished his sentence. "We do to ourselves. I've heard that before.
I don't think you understand that—"

"That what, Ari?"

"That you understand a lot of things."

"Like why you get into fights when you have a mind and imagination that are far better gifts than your fists?"

"What makes you think that I don't use my intelligence and my
imagination when I get into a fight?"

Mr. Blocker didn't say anything. Then he said, "I know you think
that I don't understand anything about what you're going through.
But you would be wrong about that."

He saw something in my face. "You have the look of a young man who wants to punch my lights out because you don't really believe I understand anything about you. And that pisses you off."

"Something like that," I said.

"I grew up in Albuquerque. I lived in a neighborhood that was a tough place for a little gringo to grow up in. I'm not complaining. The kids I grew up with had a tougher time than I ever did—and my mother was smart enough to point that out to me. When I was thirteen, I decided I wanted to be a boxer. I joined Golden Gloves. You know what that is?"

"Of course I know what that is."

"Of course you do. When I was eighteen years old, I was a Golden Gloves champion boxer. Just so you know that you're not the only guy in this world who turns to his fists to get him through the hard times."

Just at the moment I hated Mr. Blocker, he said something to make me like him again. I hated that.

Twelve

I HANDED MR. BLOCKER'S NOTE TO THE NURSE, MRS. Ortiz. "He's a nice man, isn't he, Mr. Blocker? Bet he's a good teacher." She put my fists into a small tub she'd filled with ice. She worked on me as she talked.

"Yeah," I said, "he is. I had him last year, too. Sometimes he gets a little pushy, though. I don't like that." I knew I had a pained look on my face.

"The ice hurts. But leave your fists in there. I'll tell you when you can pull them out." It really hurt. "Don't be such a big baby. You can handle getting yourself into fights, you can handle a little ice." She was looking for some gauze, and I knew she was gonna wrap my fists up. And everybody was gonna be asking, *What happened to you, Ari?*

"Oh God," she said, "I just realized who you are. You're Liliana's son. As soon as I saw you, I thought there was something familiar about you. You look just like your father." And then I said to myself, *but you have your mother's eyes*. And that's just what she said. "But you have your mother's eyes. I was your mother's best friend in grade school. We've been friends ever since."

She liked to talk. Did she ever like to talk.

"Just relax and I'll fix you right up and you'll be golden, Mr. Aristotle Mendoza." She was smiling from ear to ear. "Liliana Mendoza. What a wonderful woman."

Thirteen

I WAS SITTING BY MYSELF AT LUNCH, AND THEN I SAW them headed toward me: Cassandra, Susie, and Gina. They sat down, surrounding me. And somehow, I felt trapped. I knew what was coming. "Spit it out," Susie said. "Everyone's asking Gina, 'So what happened to Ari? He got into another fight, didn't he?' And Gina comes up to me in the hallway and says, 'Ari got into another fight.' And so I go to my next class and there's a guy named Kiko who has a black eye. And not that we're friends, but you know me, I had to ask—and he says, 'Ask your friend Ari.'"

"And nobody asked me anything. Nobody knows we're friends yet. I'd like to say let's keep it that way." I couldn't tell if Cassandra was annoyed or not. "But I did hear a group of *vatos* saying that some guys got into a fight in the parking lot and one of them wound up in the hospital with a few broken ribs. That your handiwork, Ari?"

"Could be. Or it could be the work of my colleague, one Danny Anchondo."

Cassandra. "Danny. He's a year behind us. He's one of the few guys in this school who actually talks to me. And he's one of the few guys I respect. Totally sweet guy."

"We agree," Susie said. "Gina went out with him once."

"Yeah, it didn't go well. But we sort of became friends. He's not easy to hate."

I looked at Cassandra. "We took on five guys. That totally sweet guy is a born street fighter."

"You took on five guys?"

"Well, I took care of one of them before Danny arrived on the scene. Then I took two and Danny took two. If you're going to pick a fight, you better know what the hell you're doing—or you could wind up in the hospital with a few broken ribs."

Susie was looking at me. "I know you like to fight. But I can't picture you fighting."

"Actually," Gina said, "I can't quite picture it either."

"I can," Cassandra said. And she said it with conviction. "Speaking of which," Cassandra said, "just ahead of me and to the left, Amanda Alvidrez. She's as bad as her mother. And she has just spotted us. Don't look, Gina. We do not notice her. She's invisible to us, although she might as well be taking a picture. So, Ari, I want you to show me your wrapped hands and I'm going to kiss them."

"You're serious, aren't you?"

"Dead serious."

"I was afraid you were going to say that."

I showed Cassandra my wrapped hands, and she kissed both the palms of my hands in a moment of tenderness. Of course, there wasn't actually anything tender about that moment, but that's not what everyone else around us saw. She managed to keep her composure— but I know she wanted to bust out laughing.

"Cassandra, you're awful."

"I'm not awful, Susie, I'm giving the gossip columnist over there something to print in her column. I have to practice being the actress I'm going to become."

I had to smile at that. "You're already that actress."

"Yeah, but I'd like to get paid for it someday."

"What? Our friendship isn't enough payment?"

"Not by a long shot, Mr. Mendoza. But I'm sure you'll find a way to repay me for having made you the center of attention at second-period lunch."

"Just what I wanted to be—the center of attention."

"Oh, you've always attracted attention," Gina said. "Just because you liked to sit by yourself in the corner didn't mean you weren't getting attention."

Susie laughed. "Ari, did you actually think you were making yourself invisible?"

"Well, yeah, I guess I did."

Susie shook her head. "For such a smart boy, you can actually be pretty stupid."

I wanted to tell her that the same thought had crossed my mind—more than once.

Fourteen

HIGH SCHOOL.

Teachers.

Students.

Some students would have preferred to have no teachers. Some teachers would have preferred to have no students. But it didn't work that way. Somewhere along the line, high schools were born. That was the place where the country of teachers and the country of students met, where the two countries embraced, collided, clashed, crashed into each other, fought each other, and, through the efforts of the citizens of both countries, something happened called learning. I thought about these things a lot, maybe because my mother was a teacher.

I think that because my mother was a teacher, I was a better student. Or maybe that wasn't true. But I do know that because my mother was a teacher, I looked at my teachers with a different perspective. I saw them as people. And I don't know if a lot of my classmates saw them that way.

I think mostly what we learned in high school was about people, about who they were and what made them change or refuse to change or incapable of change. That was the best part of high school. And teachers were people too. And they were the best and worst of people. The best teachers, and the worst ones, they taught you as much about people as the students in the hallway.

The country of teachers.

The country of students.

The country of high school.

The country of learning.

Just because everybody had visas to enter into those countries, didn't mean that everybody would use them.

One of my teachers was fresh out of college. This was her first teaching gig. Her name was Mrs. Flores, and she was amazingly smart. Some teachers were alive with a kind of intellectual energy. I thought Mrs. Flores was a kind of angel. And she was smart, in and out of the classroom. She had a look at my bandaged hands and she knew exactly what she was seeing. But she couldn't help but ask, "Ari, do you happen to be accident prone?" She had a seating chart, and I didn't doubt that she'd already memorized all our names.

"Yes, I think so. Sometimes my hands clench up and they seem to belong to someone else—and they accidentally run into things."

"And even when your hands clench up and seem to belong to someone else, you do have an understanding that your hands belong to you and only to you, right? And that you are responsible for whatever they do? If you remember that, then maybe your hands won't be so prone to having so many accidents."

"Well, I don't have that many."

"One accident is one too many, don't you agree, Ari?"

"You know what they say: Accidents do happen."

"They do. That's why paying attention is important. People who are prone to accidents aren't paying attention."

"Maybe they're paying attention to more important things."

"Or less important things." She smiled. "Ari, let me ask you a question. Do your fists run into things? Or people?"

"Who said anything about fists?"

"We're both smart enough to know what a clenched hand is. Your fists, do they run into things or people?"

"Sometimes the two are indistinguishable."

Everybody in the class started laughing—including Mrs. Flores.

"Ari, do you have a reputation for being the class smart aleck?"

"No."

"Why don't I believe you?"

A hand went up. "Yes? Elena." She *had* memorized her seating charts.

"You should believe him. For the past three years, I've been in the same classes with him, and in most of those classes he never said a word."

She looked around the room. "Anybody else want to chime in here?" She saw a hand go up. "Marcos, do you wish to add to the discussion?"

"Well, first of all, it's freaking me out how you know our names."

She had this great smile on her face. "When you came in, I had you sit at the desk with your name on it. I have a seating chart. And I memorized my seating chart. Simple."

"So when you called on me by name, you didn't actually know who I was."

"Of course not. But believe me, Marcos, pretty soon, I'll know who you are." The way she said that, with the fun in her voice—that is what Dante would call a sincere seriousness—I was going to love this class.

And then Marcos said, "And you should believe Ari when he said he wasn't the class smart-ass. That would be me. I didn't even know what Ari's voice sounded like."

"Well, apparently, some changes have occurred in you, Ari. Let's discover if those changes are for the good or for the bad. And, Marcos, it seems that you're going to have some competition. And I'm not just talking about Ari. I'm talking about me."

Marcos shot right back. "Is this a competition?"

"No, Marcos. You and Ari don't have a prayer. Fun is fun—but don't push it." She looked around the room. "Why don't you help me put some humanity behind your names? Yvonne, let's begin with you."

She liked us. She didn't like us in the sense that she knew us and we were her friends. She liked us because she enjoyed her students in the same way that Mr. Blocker enjoyed his students. They were both playful and serious—and always, as if by instinct, they could take a discussion, even if it occurred spontaneously, and point it in the direction where real learning began. In classes like this one, you didn't just learn something about chemistry or English or economics or how a bill became a law, you learned something about yourself.

After Mrs. Flores's class, three of my classmates came up to me together. One guy asked, "Hey, Ari, what happened to you?"

I looked at him blankly.

"I mean, what happened to the old Ari? The one who sat there, socially disengaged?"

"Socially disengaged?" I didn't remember any of their names—I did know Elena's name, but only because she'd testified on my behalf in class. And I had no idea how they remembered mine.

"I'm Hector, by the way." He stuck out his hand for a handshake, which was a little strange to me. He kept talking. "Socially disengaged as in: the Ari who always seemed to connect with the material but had no idea that classrooms were social settings."

"Elena, why do I feel as if I'm being attacked?"

"I have no idea why you feel the things you feel."

"You're screwing with my head."

"That's an easy art around guys."

I took it that Elena was one of those nice people who always had to tell the truth. "You seem like you may have learned to do the lighten-up thing," she said. "Or is that the wrong assumption? The old Ari didn't know that that the phrase *lighten up* existed."

"The new Ari does do 'lighten up.' He's no expert. Yet."

Elena gave me that *I'm not really all that patient with guys because guys are generally out to lunch* look. "We're here to welcome you to the world of high school. Filled with students. Who are people."

"So you're the welcoming committee?"

"Exactly! Self-appointed. Welcome to Austin High School,

Aristotle Mendoza." She looked at me up and down and said, "Even on your worst days, you at least provide the landscape with some eye candy. But you're an idiot."

"Elena, there are a lot of reasons why someone might refer to me as an idiot."

"You want my reasons? You were so completely oblivious to the fact that people liked you, and you seemed not to care. Ari, last year, you were elected junior class prince at Homecoming. And you didn't even bother to show up."

"I know this sounds fucked up, Elena, but I found that whole thing humiliating. Everybody always wanted me to be something I wasn't. I would've just fucking died standing up in front of everybody. How could I be someone's friend when I didn't know how to be one? It's not that I was trying to make any of you invisible. I was trying to make *me* invisible."

"That's heartbreaking. And anyway, it's just not possible to make yourself invisible. You have superpowers—or what?"

I looked into the eyes of the boy who'd spoken those words. His eyes didn't look all that different from mine. "I've had you in some of my classes for three years," I said. "And I don't even know your name." I looked at Elena and I said, "Add another reason to your list of why I'm an idiot."

"You're not an idiot. Well, at least no more than the rest of us." He reached out his hand. "I'm Julio."

A handshake. My second handshake. And I was suddenly in awe of such a simple gesture. Boys didn't engage in those gestures. Only men did. "I'm Ari," I said.

"I know. Everyone knows who you are."

I guess you could say I was a failure at turning myself into the invisible man.

One of our teachers, Mrs. Hendrix, had moved up in the world. She'd been my ninth-grade math teacher, and now she was teaching a senior-level course in biochemistry. Not exactly my favorite subject. I wasn't much of a science guy. She'd taken me to the principal's office once because I had what she referred to as an altercation with another guy in the hallway after school. I thought "altercation" was a pretty big word for saying that I'd popped Sergio Alarcon right in the kisser because he'd referred to a girl I liked (or apparently a girl I thought I liked) as a prostitute. Actually, he'd used the Spanish word "*puta*." Mrs. Hendrix was sympathetic, but she was one of those people who didn't believe that there could be any justification for giving another guy a bloody nose.

When I walked into her classroom, she smiled in that kind of way that was half-natural and half-forced. "Well, Mr. Mendoza, welcome to my class." She had the habit of calling all her students by their last names, adding Mr. or Ms. as suffixes. She explained that she meant to honor her students by addressing them as though they had already become adults or to remind them that adulthood was a goal. If she'd had any powers of observation, she would have realized that most of us did not consider adulthood a goal worthy of pursuing.

I don't know how some teachers manage to go to almost extraordinary efforts to teach you something while at the same time succeeding in making their students hate them. That takes real talent.

She would have liked us to believe that we were never going to succeed at anything without her help.

It was to our credit that we never believed her.

Mrs. Ardovino looked like an older rich woman right out of the movies. She seemed like she had a lot of class, and there was something very formal about the way she carried herself. Her white hair was in a bun and her dress looked like it cost a lot of money and she knew how to wear makeup. When she saw my bandaged hands, she asked me if I was able to take notes. I shrugged.

"Not really," I said.

"Perhaps I will allow you to use a tape recorder until you've recovered."

I couldn't see myself lying on my bed, listening to that voice that had a hint of a British accent.

"No, that's fine. I won't need a recorder," I said. "It's not serious. The bandages will be off by tomorrow."

"Is it a burn? Because if it *is* a burn, it may be far more serious than you think." She had zero street smarts. Not good for any teacher. And it wasn't going to be good for us, either. For all the formality of her voice, I already thought she was an idiot.

"No, it's not a burn."

"Have you seen a doctor?"

"I went to see the school nurse. She took care of it."

"Nurses are not doctors." Really? Who was this fucking lady? "And was it the nurse who said it wasn't necessary to see a doctor?"

"We both agreed."

"Some school nurses are quite competent. Others are not."

Was this teacher, if that's what she was, using delay tactics because she wasn't prepared for class?

"This nurse is a real pro," I said.

"How can you be so sure of your own judgment?"

I heard the guy behind me whisper, "Jesus fucking Christ."

And Mrs. Ardovino had to have heard that half the class was beginning to fall into a contagious laughter that threatened to engulf the entire room. Or maybe she was just oblivious.

"Mrs. Ardovino, the nurse was fine. I'm fine. It's all fine."

"Well, if you're quite sure."

She was going to drive me fucking insane.

"I'm quite sure." I didn't mean it say it that loudly.

Some of my classmates found the whole interchange between me and Mrs. Ardovino to be hilarious. And though I did sort of want to laugh, I couldn't. I was embarrassed for her. I felt a Dante-like compassion for her.

The guy behind me whispered so half the class could hear, "This is what fucking purgatory is like."

And people were starting to laugh again.

"Mrs. Ardovino," I said, "I got into a fight. I punched someone. Several someones. And if there had been more someones present, I would have punched them, too. My knuckles were bleeding and my hands were swollen. And they're still throbbing right now. But tomorrow, I will be fine."

"I see," she said. "I'm sorry about the throbbing. Perhaps you've learned that when you think you've come up with a solution to your problem by punching someone, several someones, that you have not only not solved your problem, but you have created another."

"That's exactly what I've learned."

"Excellent."

"Excellent," I said.

The guy behind me was laughing his ass off.

And the girl who was sitting in one of the desks at the very front of the room was trying to laugh as silently as she could and I could see that she had her hands over her mouth and her back was shaking.

And there was still some quiet laughter in the room, but when Mrs. Ardovino seemed to acknowledge it, the laughter died down completely. She said, "I don't know why, when a teacher shows concern for a student, some of his classmates find this a matter of entertainment and respond not with a sense of compassion, but instead with a barbaric laughter."

I honestly was embarrassed for her. She made for a comic figure that was almost tragic. And it made me a little angry that someone had given her a teaching position when she wasn't equipped to do the job.

"Well," she said, "perhaps it's best to adjourn for the day. Perhaps tomorrow, we'll all do a little better." My classmates filed out, and you could hear their laughter down the hall. And, if Mrs. Ardovino didn't want to cry, I did. I was the only one left in the classroom. "I'm sorry," I said, "this was all my fault."

"No, it wasn't, Mr.—"

"Mendoza. My name is Aristotle Mendoza. My friends call me Ari." I could say that now without lying. I actually had some friends.

"What a lovely name. And, no, this wasn't your fault. I'm not very good at reading social situations and how to respond to them."

And then she started giggling. And the giggling gave way to laughter. And then she really got going and her laughter grew louder and louder. She laughed and laughed and laughed. And then she said, "And I kept digging myself deeper and deeper and I just couldn't stop. And you looked so exasperated. And I just kept right on going."

And she was laughing just as hard as the students had been laughing. And then she stopped—and tried to compose herself. "And when the young man behind you whispered, 'This is what fucking purgatory is like,' well, I almost lost it too. And I saw the look on your face and you thought I was about to cry—but I do have a little discipline: I wasn't about to cry. I was about to join in the laugher. And I'm sorry I exerted so much self-control when I should have let her rip." And she was laughing again.

"You're a very interesting lady."

"I am. I am an interesting lady. But I don't belong in the classroom. At least not anymore. I retired two years ago. The teacher who actually teaches this class is on maternity leave. They asked me, rather last minute, if I would take this class. And I said I was interested—but I thought they would at least interview me. If they had, I wouldn't be sitting here.

"My husband said, 'Ofelia, you're going to make a fool of yourself.' And I did." I thought she was going to start laughing again. "I can't wait to get home this evening and tell him about my day. We're going to have ourselves a good laugh."

I was blown away. Completely. I'd never run into anybody quite like this lady. And I liked that she shared my aunt's name.

"Why didn't you join the fun, Mr. Aristotle Mendoza?"

"I don't know. I thought it was hilarious—and then I didn't."

"Well, I know why you didn't laugh—even if you don't. You didn't laugh, not because you didn't find the entire scene ridiculous, but because you would have been ashamed of yourself if you had laughed at an old woman whose heart you thought might break if you joined in the merriment of it all. You thought I was in trouble— and that wasn't funny to you. Either your mother or your father, one of them or both, must be lovely, lovely people. But frankly, I embarrassed myself in front of all of you. And I'm glad I made a fool of myself today. Happy. That's a better word."

"How can you be happy about that?"

"We have to be honest about our own limitations, Aristotle. I knew from the moment I began to teach my first class here that I'd made a mistake. I didn't have the courage to say, *You're going to have to find someone else because I can't do this*. I would have lived a lie for an entire year because I couldn't or wouldn't do the honest thing. When you know you've made a mistake, don't live in it."

She got up and gathered her purse and sweater. "Most young men who are as astonishingly handsome as you are, grow up to be men who use the world as their personal toilet. You don't have that kind of indecency in you."

She walked out the door, and I could hear her laughing down the hall. I sat in the quiet classroom and thought, *This has been a very interesting day*. But if I had more days like this, I was going to be a fucking mess.

Fifteen

I WAS WALKING TOWARD MY TRUCK—AND EVEN though the throbbing was almost gone, my hands were still swollen. I must have hit those guys pretty damned hard. I smiled at Mrs. Ardovino's remark about how by solving one problem you create another. Mrs. Ardovino. What a trip. I wondered what she had been like when she was Mrs. Ortiz's age.

This was going to be quite a year. For once, I wasn't happy about the fact that Dante and I attended different high schools. There were moments I found myself thinking about him—and missing him.

I shouldn't have been surprised to find Susie and Gina and Cassandra standing beside my truck. They were talking about everything that happened at school that day. Finally, I said, "What are we doing here?"

"We're carping on our teachers."

"No, I mean here beside my truck."

Cassandra smiled. "Take a guess."

"You think I can't drive myself home."

"The word 'think' does not belong in that sentence. I'm driving you home. Gina's following in her car. I'll drop you off, and they'll pick me up and take me home. And we'll all be safe and sound doing our homework. Gimme the keys."

"Don't I have a say in any of this?"

"You've already had your say. That's why you can't drive."

"Cassandra, why do you—"

"Shut up, Ari. This is not subject to debate. Hand me the keys."

"Well, I—"

"Ari," she said, and then she cocked her head and did that *I'm a bull about to gore you* thing.

"I can't reach my keys in my pocket. My hands are too swollen. That's what I've been trying to tell you."

"Why didn't you say something?"

"Because you were preventing me from saying something."

"Well, you have to learn to be more assertive."

Gina and Susie walked away laughing. "We'll see you at Ari's."

She gave me that play-sexy look. "Which pocket? Or do you want me to search around?"

I pointed to my pocket on the right side.

She reached for them.

"That tickles."

"Does it? Hasn't Dante ever felt you up?"

"Knock it off."

"That embarrasses you, doesn't it? You shouldn't be embarrassed by that."

She laughed.

"Just be quiet," I said. "Don't talk. Just drive me home."

Sixteen

CASSANDRA PULLED THE TRUCK INTO THE DRIVEWAY. "How'd I do?"

"You're really going to make me tell you that you're a good driver?"

"Only if it's true."

"You're a good driver."

"You don't think girls are good drivers, do you?"

"It's not something that I've ever thought about. Guys don't go around thinking about how good girls are at driving, or doing anything else, for that matter."

"Yes, they do."

"Well, I don't."

"Well, that's because you're—"

"Let me finish your sentence. That's because I'm gay."

I don't know. Maybe it was too many things happening in one day, but I just sat there, and the fucking tears started rolling down my face.

"Aw, Ari. I'm sorry. Don't . . ." And then she was crying too. "I know I'm hard. I need to be a little softer. It kills me to think that I hurt you."

Seventeen

"ARI, WHY DID YOU THINK IT WAS A GOOD IDEA TO return to that kind of behavior?"

"Mom, why don't you ask me what happened?"

"I don't need to know the facts. A fight is a fight is a fight. And I won't ever find that kind of behavior acceptable."

"I know," I said. "But, Mom, I can't make all of my decisions based on whether you approve or disapprove. I'm not a kid anymore. I've earned the right to be wrong."

"No one has the right to be wrong with intent."

"Can we talk about something else?"

"The sun rose today at five fifty-seven a.m. in El Paso, Texas."

"Nice, Mom, nice."

"I learned those smart-ass tactics from you."

"I didn't teach you those tactics with intent."

"Okay, we don't have to talk about this now. But *we are* going to finish this conversation."

"You mean this lecture."

"Lecture. There's a word. You may think that term has negative connotations, but usually when someone attends a lecture, they learn something."

Eighteen

WE WERE HANGING OUT AT DANTE'S PLACE—AND FOR once his room was clean. Well, more or less.

"You think Cassandra became a woman much too soon?"

"What's too soon, Dante? I think she decided not be anybody's victim. I think her father's emotional abuse explains some of it—but not all of it."

"You really like her, don't you?"

"Dante, I do. I really do. I have a connection with her that I've never had with anyone. And I think she feels it too."

Dante was quiet.

"Does that bother you, Dante?"

"No, not really. That's not true. It does bother me. You have something with her that you don't have with me."

"So?"

Dante didn't say anything.

"There's no reason to feel threatened by her, Dante."

"Can I ask you a question?"

"Yes. You can ask me anything."

"Do you think you might be bisexual?"

"I don't think so."

"*I don't think so* isn't very reassuring."

"What I feel for Cassandra isn't sexual. I'm not attracted to girls in that way. But I am discovering that I like girls. That I like women. They can be so honest and vulnerable. And I think that women are a helluva lot nicer than guys."

He nodded. "I guess you're right. It's just that, well . . . let's just talk about something else."

Nineteen

SOMETIMES I WOULD GO TO THE CHARCOALER ALL BY myself. Just to grab a bite to eat. I don't know why. Part of it was the nostalgia of having worked there. And I still picked up a shift when they needed me. But nostalgia was only a part of it. I had this deep need to be alone sometimes. And I didn't always have time to drive out into the desert. So I just came to the Charcoaler and got a burger, some onion rings, and a Dr Pepper. I just sat in my truck and ate and listened to the radio.

That Sunday afternoon when I drove up to the drive-in window to get my order, I noticed Gina Navarro's blue Volkswagen parked in the lot. So I pulled up next to her and said, "Hey, you!"

And she said, "Ari! What are you doing here?"

"Same thing you're doing. Came to eat a burger."

"By yourself?"

"Oh yeah, well, I don't exactly see a carful of people in your Bug."

Gina laughed. "It's actually one of my favorite things to do. Come here and be by myself and listen to music. I don't always want to be around other people. Sometimes I just want to be. Just to be. You know?"

"Yeah, I do know."

We were both smiling.

"I won't tell anyone," she said.

"I won't tell anyone either."

We stopped talking. I let her be. And she let me be.

I was lost in my own thoughts and the taste of my onion rings when I heard the beep of Gina's Volkswagen. She waved at me as she drove away. I waved back.

And we were both smiling.

That's the thing about friends. Each one of them is different. And each friend knows something about you that your other friends don't know. I guess a part of being friends is that you share a secret with each one of them. The secret doesn't have to be a big secret. It could just be a little one. But sharing that secret is one of things that makes you friends. I thought that was pretty amazing.

I was learning a lot of things about living in the country of friendship. I liked living in that country. I liked it very much.

Between the Living and the Dying Is the Loving

No one asks to be born. And no one wants to die. We don't bring ourselves into the world, and when it's time for us to leave, the decision will not be ours to make. But what we do with the time in between the day we are born and the day we die, that is what constitutes a human life. You will have to make choices—and those choices will map out the shape and course of your life. We are all cartographers—all of us. We all want to write our names on the map of the world.

One

DANTE AND I WERE REDISCOVERING THE WORD "friend." You learn a word and you know it and it's yours—and then you learn the word again and get to know it again, but in a different way. "Friend" was a word that contained an entire universe, and Dante and I were just beginning to explore that universe.

"Friend. We throw that word around too casually," Dante said.

"I don't. That's why I don't have any."

"That's not true. You have as many as you can handle. And I wasn't talking about you. I'm talking about most people."

"Well, most people don't respect words as much as you do. Just like most people don't respect the water that they swim in like you respect it. It's something deep inside you."

"Words are deep inside you, too, Ari."

"Not deep enough. Not by a long shot. It's like when you read a poem to me. You read it like you wrote it."

"Maybe I'm just a frustrated actor."

"You're not acting. You're being yourself."

"Yeah, well, I can be a drama queen."

That made me laugh. "You're very sincere about that, too."

"I'm not perfect, Ari. You always tell me you struggle with your demons. I have my own demons. I know that love is difficult for you—and yet you love me. But love is difficult for me, too—it's just that our difficulties are different."

"But I think we're doing great."

"Yeah, we are, Ari. But it's more work than I thought it would be."

I nodded. "Yeah, but I'm thinking of a camping trip—and nothing about that trip seemed like work to me."

Dante smiled. "Let's go back there." His eyes were crazy, alive at that moment. And then he said, "When are you going to make love to me again?"

"We'll find a way."

Dante and I were students. That's something we had in common. We wanted to learn. We were both learning words and their meanings, and we were learning that the word "friendship" wasn't completely separate from the word "love."

I wondered where Dante and I would wind up. I think he wondered too. Would we wind up as friends? Would we wind up as lovers? Or would the differences between us turn us into enemies? I wanted us to be lovers because I liked that word. It was a word that appeared in some books I'd read. But seventeen-year-olds didn't have lovers—because we weren't adults, and only adults had lovers. Seventeen-year-olds only had sex that they weren't supposed to be having—but it didn't have anything to do with love, because that's what we were told—because we didn't know anything about love. But I didn't believe that.

Nobody was going to tell me that I didn't love Dante. Not anybody.

I never knew I could feel all the things I felt for Dante. I didn't know I had it in me. But what in the hell was I supposed to do with that knowledge? If Dante were a girl and I were not gay, I would be imagining a future for us. But there was no imagining a future. Because the world we lived in censored our imaginations and limited what was possible and what wasn't possible. There was no future for Ari and Dante.

To imagine a future for Ari and Dante was a fantasy.

I didn't want to live my life in a fantasy.

The world I wanted to live in didn't exist. And I was struggling to love the world I *did* live in. I wondered if I was strong enough or good enough to love a world that hated me.

Maybe I just worried too much. What Dante and I had was *now*. Dante said our love was forever. But what if it wasn't forever? And what was forever? No one had forever. My mom says we live our lives one day at a time, one moment at a time. *Now is the only thing that's real. Tomorrow is just an idea.* My mom's voice forever in my head.

Two

Dear Dante,

In my dream, we were walking along a riverbank. We were holding hands as we walked and there were dark clouds in the sky and you said, "I'm afraid." And I didn't answer because I couldn't talk. And then I saw my brother on the other side of the riverbank. And he was yelling something at us.

And for some reason I could see his face as if I were standing close to him. And he spit into my face and then I was standing next to you again and I was afraid because you were afraid and when I turned to look at you, you were gaunt and I knew you were dying and I also knew you were dying from AIDS. And I heard what my brother was yelling: "Faggots! Faggots!" And there were thousands of marchers moving toward us and then you were gone. And as the marchers moved past me, I could see that they were holding your dead body up and carrying it with them to wherever they were going. And I was yelling, "Dante! Dante!"

The marchers kept marching. And they took you with them. And I knew I couldn't follow.

And then I was alone. I was cold and the sky was nothing more than dark clouds—and when the rain fell, the drops felt like bullets on my body. And I kept yelling, "Dante!"

I woke up yelling your name and I was soaked in sweat.

My mother was sitting on my bed. She looked like an angel. And she whispered, "It's only a dream, Ari. I'm here. Dreams can't hurt you."

Dante, do you ever have bad dreams?

And why do bad dreams follow you for days? And what are they trying to tell you? Does your mother know how to interpret dreams?

The next day, at school, I walked down the hallway. I felt as if I was alone again—as alone as I had been before I met you. I wondered if one day you and I would die from AIDS.

Maybe all of us would die from AIDS. All the faggots would be gone.

The world would go on without us in it. Finally, the world would get what it wanted.

Three

"WHY DO THEY CALL MRS. LIVERMORE 'MRS. MORE Liver'?"

"Gina made up a story about her. She said she was just the kind of mean mother who served her children liver on special occasions because she knew her children hated it. She didn't believe in happy children. So she'd serve them all a plate of liver and sautéed onions and when they'd all finally managed to get it all down, she was back up, standing in front of their empty plates, asking, 'More liver?' Like the wicked witch in Snow White, offering her an apple. And then she'd serve them a second helping and they all just wanted to barf. And she made sure they ate every bite of their second helping. And if one of her children had made her unhappy, she'd stand before that child a third time, and smile. 'More liver, dear?' And she'd plop another piece of liver on the plate. And then she'd smile and say to herself, *That will teach them.*"

"Wow, but she's not that evil. I mean, I'm sure she's a nice mother."

"I don't think she's a nice mother at all. I don't think she's a nice anything. And if you think about it," Susie said, "that's what she does to us in class. Every damn day she serves us more liver. I can't stand that woman. Ari Mendoza, you're going to tell me that Livermore doesn't get under your skin?"

"Well, she kinda does, but look, we need the class to graduate, and I guess I'm just going to push on through. I don't let her ruin my day."

"Don't you think that deep down she hates Mexicans?"

"She doesn't hate us. She just thinks we're inferior." I grinned at Susie.

She didn't laugh.

"It was supposed to be a joke."

She pretty much tore me up with that look of hers.

"Yeah, yeah," I said. "Look, it's pretty obvious she's a racist. I mean, she told Chuy that she was happy that there was a nickname for Jesus because *it just wasn't right that any person should be named after the Lord*. She just thinks shit like that, Susie. Who cares? She's just not all that smart."

"Well, let her think like that if she wants to—but does she have to say it? You're a little too laid-back about this, Ari. I mean, what was that bullshit when she walked into class one day and asked why Hispanics didn't read the Bible? And she didn't even get the joke when Chuy shouted out, 'Catholics don't like the Bible. We just worship Jesus and Our Lady of Guadalupe.'"

"Give her some credit, Susie. Maybe she did get his sarcasm when she shot back, 'Biblical literacy is foundational for any person who claims to be educated.'"

"How does she get away with that shit?" And then on the day

she was talking about our judicial system, she just had to say"—and then Susie did an impersonation of her—"'It's very important that you listen closely because in Mexico, where you come from, there is no judicial system.' Why the hell does she have to say crap like that? And then Chuy shot back, 'Well, they do have a judicial system in Mexico—though I'm not from there. I'm from here. Mexico does have a judicial system—it's just that it's corrupt. You know, like in Alabama, where you're from.' Chuy may seem like he's been smoking too much pot—but he doesn't take any crap."

"Well, you gotta admit the class can get pretty entertaining."

"To quote Mr. Blocker, 'You don't come to school to get entertained—you come to learn.' And if you're not careful, Ari Mendoza, you're going to grow up and be a sellout." And she gave me a disapproving look that rivaled Cassandra Ortega. "One of these days I'm going to walk into her class when I'm in a bad mood. And all hell's going break loose."

Four

CASSANDRA AND I WERE SITTING ON MY FRONT STEPS.

"It's either music or acting," she said.

"You're into music?"

"I play the piano. I'm good at it. Not great. Not brilliant. But good. I have time to get better. And I'm into singing. You sing?"

"I sing okay—but it's not something that interests me very much."

"Doesn't interest you?"

"I love music. But I'm no musician."

"I get that." She offered me a hand and pulled me up. Damn, she was strong.

"Which way should we go?" I asked.

"That way," she said. "I'm dying for a candy bar."

"I like PayDays."

"I *love* PayDays."

We passed a house where a woman was clipping her roses. Cassandra greeted her, "Hello, Mrs. Rico."

"Cassandra, you're as pretty as ever. And how are you, Ari?"

"I'm just fine, Mrs. Rico."

"And don't you two make a lovely couple."

"Yes, we do," Cassandra said.

As we moved down the street, I looked at her. "Lovely couple? Every time someone says something like that, I feel like a total fraud. I feel like an impostor."

"Well, you're not lying to anyone. Don't own other people's assumptions. And we *do* make a lovely couple."

That made me laugh. "Yeah, we do. And who was that lady?"

"You called her Mrs. Rico, and she knew your name. I thought you knew her."

"I called her Mrs. Rico because you called her that."

"Well, she's another Catholic Daughter. She runs her own CPA firm."

"Those Catholic Daughters—they sure as hell have contacts. It seems like they know everybody."

"They do. One of the ladies is one of the national all-time best saleswomen for Mary Kay products—and she drives a pink Cadillac to prove it. You should see it. She loves to pretend she's Jackie Kennedy Onassis. She gets a big kick out of making fun of herself.

"You know, we need to do what Ms. Mary Kay did. She made a place for herself in the business world. She didn't give a shit if the men around her snickered. She makes more money than most of the assholes put together. And she came by that money honestly. She put her name on the map."

"That's awesome. And that's what the Catholic Daughters have managed to do—write their names on the map of the world. They don't need anybody's permission to just dive in. And you know something, Ari, neither do we."

We walked into the 7-Eleven. "My treat," Cassandra said, as she reached for a Coke.

"No, I'll get it."

"No, you won't. You know why guys like to pay? Because they have to be in charge. And when I say I'll pay, you're not supposed to get in an argument with me, you're just supposed to say 'thank you.'"

"Thank you," I said.

"That's a start. Next time say it with conviction." We sat on the curb and smiled at each other.

"We're loitering," I said.

"Well, it's a loitering kind of day." She took a drink from her Coke.

"You know, we not only have to be smart enough to be cartographers—we also have to be brave enough to dive into waters that may not be very friendly."

She looked me—to make sure I was listening. "We can do this. One of these days the world is going to be very surprised by the things we accomplish. But we won't be. We won't be surprised at all. Because we will have learned by then what we have in us."

Cassandra Ortega's voice was just what I needed in my life.

We were back at my house sitting on the front porch. Legs was sleeping between us.

"I think I'll go for a run. You need a ride home?"

"What a great idea, Ari. What. A. Great. Idea."

That's the day Cassandra Ortega became my running partner.

I missed Legs running right beside me. That dog had wandered into my life at a time when I felt I was more or less alone in the world. Somehow she sensed my sadness and gave me her heart. People couldn't give you the things a dog could give you—and I didn't have the language to translate the love that lived in Legs, the love she gave me, the love that made me want to live again.

I'm not sure exactly why I let Cassandra into the private, silent world of running. But from that first morning, it seemed like it was right, like we fit. She was naturally athletic. And she was like me— she didn't like to talk, not when she ran. She just wanted to run. Somehow the silence we kept as we ran brought us closer together.

In some ways, we were both lost. It's funny, there were so many moments where I felt I had found myself or was finding myself. And then I felt lost again. For no reason. I just felt lost. Maybe it was that way for Cassandra, too. And we both found something we needed in the running.

I loved her silent presence in those moments. And they were sacred to me. I was starting to believe that we lived in different ways with each person that we loved.

Five

MY LIFE TOOK ON A KIND OF RHYTHM, THE GOING TO
school, the talking to school friends that I'd never had before. School
friends were good because you could leave them at school. That
sounds mean, I know, but for me, my life was really crowded. I don't
think I could have handled one more take-home friend.

I had never really felt a part of this place called school. Now I *did*
feel like I was a part of it. But then there was this thing that I was—
this thing called gay. When did we start using that word? "Gay" was a
word whose original meaning was associated with the word "happy."
I wondered how many gay men were actually happy. I wondered
if someday, I would look in the mirror and say: *Ari, I'm happy that
you're gay.* I didn't think that would ever happen. It might happen
to Dante, but not to me. That made me feel as if I never could or
would truly be a part of the country of high school. Dante called it
"exile." It was the perfect word. He gave me a note one day as he was
leaving my house. "Oh, I forgot. I've been carrying this around," he
said. He put the folded note in the palm of my hand. When he left,
I unfolded the note:

My mom said that we will always live between exile and belonging.

Sometimes you'll feel the loneliness of exile. And sometimes you'll feel the happiness of belonging. I don't know where my mom learned all the things she knows. And when I hear your mom's words, and listen to the things she says, I swear they went to the same school for moms. They went to graduate school at Mom University—and it's like they got their PhDs. P.S. I wrote this note in my history class. Only Brother Michael could make the Civil War sound boring.

I guess I was happy. Or at least I was happier than I'd ever been. And though there was a lot of confusion inside me, at least I wasn't miserable. I went to school. I did my homework. Most of the time, Dante, Susie, Gina, and Cassandra came over and we studied at my kitchen table. I knew that made my mom happy—even though that wasn't why we were studying together. Sometimes, we studied at Cassandra's.

Tuesday nights, Dante and I studied together, just him and me. He would read his homework assignments or do his math problems and I would read and take notes or work on a paper. Somehow just being in the same room with Dante made everything seem a lot easier. I liked sensing his presence in the room. I liked listening to his voice when he talked to himself.

I noticed that Dante often took a break from studying his books—and studied me. I thought I was his favorite book. Which scared me. Sometimes, when he looked at me, it was like electricity shot right through me. And I wanted him. And there were times that my desire for him was insatiable. It wasn't that we had a lot of sex. We didn't. We couldn't. There wasn't the time or the opportunity, and we both refused to have sex in either of our parents' houses because we felt it was disrespectful. But my want was beyond desire. Because what I felt transcended my own body.

What we had was safe. We made each other feel safe.

But the problem was that love was never safe. Love took you to places you had always been afraid to go. What the hell did I know about love? Sometimes, when I was in Dante's presence, I felt that I knew everything there was to know about love. But, for me, to love was one thing. To let yourself be loved, well, that was the most difficult thing of all.

Six

Dante,

I've been thinking about my brother. When I went to the food bank with my mom, I overheard two of the women talking. They were saying nice things about me. One of them said that they were happy for my mother because I was such a good kid, not like my brother, who had a severe and chronic allergy to goodness. "Some people are just born that way," she said.

I think my brother was and is a very violent man. That's why Mom and Dad got so upset with me when they found out I beat the crap out of the guy who put you in the hospital. I shouldn't have done that. I wasn't sorry then—but I'm sorry now. But it doesn't work both ways, of course: He wasn't sorry he'd put you in the hospital. And if he had half a chance, he'd do it again. Sometimes I see him in the hallway, and once his friend was next to me at the urinal in the bathroom and he said, "Did you wanna have a look?" and I said, "Did you want me to stuff your balls down your throat?" People do not leave people alone. They can't even live and let live. They just want to get rid of you.

You know, I've been wondering about the person my brother killed. She was a transgender woman. The newspaper story was pretty vague. They called her a transvestite prostitute. And how do they know she was a prostitute? I get the feeling they just put that article in the newspaper as another example of the Mexican lowlifes that live in the city, which includes my brother and the woman he killed. Sometimes I get the feeling that, even though we're the majority population in this town, Mexicans are still not wanted.

Seven

MRS. LIVERMORE HANDED BACK OUR TESTS.

"I want you all to know that I am on *your* side. I have started grading on a curve because I have come to understand that Hispanics are not comfortable in educational settings and I have made a note of that."

Susie's hand went up immediately—and it was like a flag flapping in the wind.

"Susie, did you want to say something?"

"Yes, I wanted to know where you got the information that Hispanics are uncomfortable in educational settings. I mean, did you read that somewhere? Does the KKK have an educational newsletter?"

"What does the KKK have to do with this conversation? I don't have anything to do with that horrible organization."

"They're not an organization. They're domestic terrorists."

"I'm not going to argue with someone who has such extreme views."

"*I'm* extreme?"

"To answer your question, I did not read an article. But I have had discussions with intelligent people who have given me insights in order to better serve my students. And I have observed that my students are indeed uncomfortable in educational settings. Does that answer your question?"

"It does." I knew Susie Byrd, and she was just getting started. "Well, using my own powers of observation, I think that your students are uncomfortable only in educational settings where you happen to be the teacher."

"I don't know why you have decided to attack me instead of—"

Susie interrupted her. "Mrs. Livermore, you do know that you're racist, don't you?"

"That is an unfair and unjust accusation. I have no idea where you got the notion that you were entitled to attack your teachers with such venomous slanders. If I am to maintain order, I cannot allow you to remain in this class without an apology. I don't know why you would be offended in any way, since you are not Hispanic and nothing I have said concerns you in the least."

Susie kept crossing her arms, then biting her lip and playing with her necklace. I knew Susie—and I knew she was pissed. I mean, she was *pissed*. "I don't have to be Hispanic to notice the condescending and downright insulting things you say. On the first day of class you said to José"—and then Susie began imitating the way she talked—"'In Iowa there's a brand of tortillas, Happy José tortillas, and he's throwing a sombrero in the air.' And then, if that wasn't bad enough, you asked him if he had a sombrero—"

Mrs. Livermore interrupted her. "I was being friendly, and I don't know why you think what I said is in any way derogatory."

Susie rolled her eyes. "And every time someone you think is stupid gets a good grade on a test, when you're passing them out, you always have to say shit like"—and again Susie imitated her voice—"'You must have studied very hard, or perhaps you had some help.' You are such a racist bitch!"

I wasn't gonna let Susie go down in flames all by herself, and I jumped in before Mrs. Livermore could respond. "I agree." And then I decided to add, "And on behalf of all your Hispanic students, and on behalf my mother, who is a schoolteacher, I am asking for an apology."

All the students were giving a thumbs-up, but Mrs. Livermore's anger and attention were focused on Susie and me.

"I'm afraid I misjudged you, Ari Mendoza. I thought you to be a cut above—"

I stopped her. "A cut above the rest of the Mexicans?"

"Do not put words in my mouth. But a self-appointed spokesman for an entire group of people should not be taken seriously." And then she put this growl in her voice. "Now, both of you follow me to the principal's office *right now*."

As she marched toward the door, Chuy Gomez couldn't help himself and shouted, "Hey, Mrs. Livermore!" She turned around and saw Chuy giving her the finger.

"You too! Join the rebels with no cause. You show the behavior of people who were raised by wolves. And you three are about to be thrown out of this educational institution."

"The educational institution we're so uncomfortable with?" Chuy moved toward the door. Susie broke out laughing, and I just tried to keep myself together. Mrs. Livermore marched ahead of us and we followed behind.

"They won't throw us out," Chuy said.

Susie rolled her eyes. "My mom and dad will be jumping down somebody's throat in a New York minute. My parents are former hippies. They don't put up with this crap."

"My dad's an activist," Chuy said. "This is bullshit."

"Well," I said, "I doubt my mom will let us hang out to dry."

Susie smiled. "Something tells me your mother would eat Mrs. Livermore for lunch."

So there we were in the principal's office. Mr. Robertson had a look about him that prevented him from appearing to be a professional despite the jacket and tie. He wasn't really much of a tough guy, but when he felt cornered, he could be a hard-ass. Mrs. Livermore was pulling on her pearl necklace and fingered each pearl as if she were praying a rosary. All of us were seated, but Mrs. Livermore decided to remain standing, hovering over the rest of us. She was doing all the talking, and she was more or less succeeding in sounding reasonable and thereby making herself appear to be the victim of her cruel students who had no discipline and behaved like barbarians.

"The just thing to do would be to suspend these students. I am not a punitive person, and I will not insist that they not be allowed to graduate. This, after all, is their last chance." Susie and I looked at each other. Mrs. Livermore clearly assumed we would not be attending college.

"But I cannot allow these students to return to my classroom.

They have not only disrespected me, but they have disrespected my profession."

Susie interrupted her. "No one disrespects your profession more than you do, Mrs. Livermore."

She pointed at Susie. "There. See for yourself how they give themselves the freedom to say whatever they feel like saying. They have no understanding of the consequences of their actions. These three barbarians apparently have no respect for my position as a teacher, and I will never accept what this"—she pointed at Susie—"this person, this, this—I will never accept her slanders. Tell him, tell him what you said to me."

Susie wasn't the least bit repentant. She looked at Mr. Robertson and said, "I called her a racist bitch."

Mr. Robertson winced.

"And it's not slander if it's true. I don't know which part is truer—the racist part or the bitch part."

"I could have you thrown out of this school for that."

"You could." Susie was still pissed. "But I'd like to see you try to throw out a student with my grade point average and my perfect attendance."

"I've had enough. I leave these ersatz human beings to you, Mr. Robertson. I don't care what you do with them so long as you do not return them to my classroom." And then she looked at me. "I really did think that you might amount to something." She turned her glare to Susie. "And you are the very worst."

Susie shot her a grin. "I must be living proof that White people aren't superior."

Her storming away seemed a bit much—but it had its effect on Mr. Robertson.

Chuy was laughing his ass off. "Susie Byrd, did you hear that? You're the worst. You're even worse than us Mexicans."

"Oh, Lord," Mr. Robertson said. "I don't think any of you realize how much trouble you're in. And, Ms. Byrd, did you have to refer to her with the b-word?"

"Mr. Robertson, you can't tell me you don't know she's a racist. And you can't tell me that you've never had any complaints about her. And as far as I'm concerned, if you're a woman and you're racist, well, then you're also a bitch. There's no getting around it."

"Can we please show some respect? If I hear one more bad word coming out of your lips, I'm suspending you."

He kept biting his lip and rubbing his hands. He needed a cigarette. I could smell it on him.

"You're all good students and you have spotless records. And all of you, as Ms. Byrd has pointed out, have nearly perfect attendance. Which does not excuse your behavior. Ari, what did you say to Mrs. Livermore that earned her anger?"

"I just voiced my agreement with Susie. And I followed up by speaking on behalf of all the Hispanic students and asked for an apology."

He put his hand over his face and laughed—though it sounded more like he wanted to cry.

"And you, Jesus?"

"Chuy," he said.

"Yes, yes, Chuy, what was your contribution to this little drama?"

"As they were walking out of the classroom, I yelled Mrs. Livermore's name. And I gave her the finger."

Mr. Robertson burst out laughing, but it really wasn't a happy laugh, more like an *I'm disgusted and can't help but laugh because if I don't laugh, I'll cry* kind of thing. "I'm going to call your parents and I'm going to discuss this matter with them. And you are to attend study hall. I will get a copy of Mrs. Livermore's syllabus. You will keep up with your schoolwork and you will turn in all your assignments in to me. And I will be responsible for grading them. You're getting off light—and you're welcome.

"And, Ms. Byrd, watch your language. It's simply not acceptable."

"But racist teachers *are* acceptable?"

"I'm giving you a break. Don't push it." He looked at Chuy. "Put that finger away. Use it to play the guitar or something. And, Mr. Mendoza, you just may have a future in politics. But don't practice your little speeches on my teachers."

Eight

"I GOT A CALL FROM MR. ROBERTSON. WE HAD A friendly chat."

"Friendly?'

"I used to teach across the hall from him."

"Why aren't you the principal instead of him?"

"Don't think that I haven't been asked. But I'm exactly where I belong—in the classroom." My mother looked at me. It wasn't the *I'm angry* look. It was more like an *I'm deciding what to say* kind of look.

"Am I going to get a lecture?"

"Not exactly a lecture. Let's call it a talk. You and Susie and your other friend—"

"Chuy."

"Chuy. You and Susie and Chuy are very brave. But—"

"I knew there'd be a 'but.'"

"But you didn't have to react that way. I met Mrs. Livermore on parents' night. I don't have a high opinion of her. But she *is* your teacher. And your teachers deserve respect. Being a teacher isn't a walk in the park. You might have gone about this another way."

"Like what other way?"

"You could've gone to Mr. Robertson with your concerns."

"He's kind of a bozo."

"Let me finish. You could have told him that you refused to sit in her class and told him why. If you didn't feel listened to, you could have come to me and your father and we could have stepped in."

I knew I was wearing a blank look.

"Ari, I don't disagree with your view of Mrs. Livermore. And when I said that you three were very brave, I meant it. But you could have been thrown out of school. And you should all take control of the language you use. It doesn't help your cause."

"Maybe you're right. We should have had a plan instead of just exploding in her classroom. We dealt with the situation the best we knew how. But running to our parents and having them step in—I don't think that's the answer. This is the way we grow up, Mom."

I thought my mother was going to push right back at that. But she didn't. "I'm open to the possibility that you may be right. But you dodged a bullet. And I'm going to tell you something you may not want to hear. One of the reasons Mr. Robertson didn't suspend any of you for a week or two was that we're friends. So, without wanting to, I *did* intervene."

"It's who you know—is that it, Mom?"

"I don't make the unwritten rules, Ari. Just like you, I live in a world with rules that have nothing to do with fairness. And just remember that I said that it was *only one* of the reasons. The other reason is that all three of you are very fine students. We have to have rules, Ari. Otherwise, there's nothing but chaos. But we always have to be able to break the rules if they do not serve the people they were meant to protect."

"I know you feel like you shouldn't have to put up with racist teachers. But all of us have some racism lodged in the way we think. That's what the world we inhabit teaches us from childhood. If Mrs. Livermore is a racist, it's because she was taught to be one. It's awfully hard to unlearn those kinds of terrible lessons, especially if you don't recognize that what you learned was wrong. A lot of White people—and I don't say all White people—think they're a little bit better, a little more American—and a lot of those people aren't bad people. They aren't even aware of the fact that they're a part of an entire system that is centered around them. It's complicated, Ari. I don't think I'm explaining this very well."

"I think you're explaining it just fine. You really are super smart. And I like it so much that you think about these things. Because these things really matter. I like that you work so hard to understand what's really happening. And you try even harder not to judge people. Is it okay if a guy wants to grow up to be like his mother?"

Nine

ONE NIGHT, WHEN I WAS READING A CHAPTER OF MY history textbook, I looked up and the whole world was blurry. My mother walked into the kitchen, and she must have seen a strange expression on my face. "Is there something wrong, Ari?"

"I don't know. I was reading and when I looked up, everything was blurry. I'm not sure what that means."

She smiled at me. "It means you need glasses. I'll make an appointment for you with my optometrist."

"Glasses? I'm not a glasses kind of guy."

"Well, you are now."

"I can't see me in glasses."

"You can't see without them."

"Shit."

She combed my hair with her fingers. "Ari, you'll look even more handsome wearing glasses."

"Can't I get contact lenses?"

"No."

"Why not."

"Because I said so. They're a lot of trouble. They're expensive.

And you shouldn't wear contacts until you get used to wearing regular glasses."

"'Because I said so'? Really?"

"Did you hear any of the words that followed 'because I said so'?"

"Aristotle Mendoza was not born to wear glasses."

"Apparently, Aristotle Mendoza's eyes do not agree."

I kept staring at myself in the mirror. The glasses were kind of cool. But still, they were glasses. And I felt like I was someone else. I had to admit, though, when I put them on for the first time, I was fucking amazed. The world was sharper. Like I could read street signs, and the words the teacher wrote on the board. And I could see Dante's face as he walked toward me. I hadn't realized I'd known it was him not because I could see his face clearly but because of his walk. I didn't know how long I'd been seeing things out of focus. That's what I'd been doing: looking at the world with eyes that were out of focus.

I liked that I could see now. It was a good thing. Beautiful, really.

"This is the new you, Ari." I pulled myself away from the mirror.

When Dante answered the doorbell, he took a long look at me. "This is the Ari of my dreams," he said.

"Oh, knock it off," I said.

"I want to kiss you."

"You're mocking me."

"I'm not. Now I'm going to want to kiss you all the time."

"You always want to kiss me all the time."

"Yeah, but now, it's like I want to tear your clothes off all the time."

"I can't believe you just said that."

"Oh well, I thought that honesty was the best policy."

"Honesty doesn't have to be verbally expressed."

"Silence equals death."

I couldn't help but shake my head and grin.

He took my hand and pulled me inside. "Mom! Dad! Come see Ari wearing his new glasses."

I felt like an animal at the zoo. I found myself standing before Mr. and Mrs. Quintana. "The look of an intellectual becomes you, Ari."

Mrs. Quintana nodded her approval. "Handsome as ever. And somehow it reflects the intelligence that you so love to hide."

"You think I like to hide my intelligence?"

"Of course you do, Ari. It doesn't fit the image you have of yourself."

I nodded as in *I see*. "It's three against one. It's hard to argue with a united front."

Mrs. Quintana smiled, and then all of a sudden, she bent over. She touched her side and sat down and took a deep breath. "Oh, this one's going to be a fighter. And I think he or she wants out."

She reached for Mr. Quintana's hand and placed it right where the baby was kicking.

I thought Mr. Quintana was going to cry. "Dante, put your hand right here."

When Dante felt his mother's belly, he got that incredible look on his face—it was as if he had become a sentence ending with an exclamation point. "That's amazing, Mom!"

"Ari," Mrs. Quintana said, "here. Put your hand right there."

I looked at her. "I don't—"

"Don't be shy. It's okay."

She took my hand and placed it on her belly. And I felt it, the baby. Maybe that's where the expression "alive and kicking" came from.

"Life, Ari. This is life."

Ten

HALLOWEEN. YES, I WAS THE SPOILSPORT. I REFUSED
to wear a costume to the party at Gina's house. Susie said I should
come as a wet blanket. Ha, ha.

"I'm going to uninvite you," Gina said.

"Okay, fine. Uninvite me. I'll just crash the party."

"Sometimes I hate you."

"You just hate that peer pressure doesn't work on a guy like me.
And besides, I'll be wearing my new pair of glasses."

"That doesn't count."

"So I won't wear them. I'll go as Ari, BG."

"Ari, BG?"

"Ari, before glasses."

"You're too much, you know that? Why can't you just let yourself play? 'Play' as in 'to have fun.' 'Play' as in 'you're in a play and
you can be anyone you want to be just for a night.'"

"I *am* in a play. It's called life, and I already play a role, Gina. I'm
a gay guy who plays a straight guy. And it's fucking wearing me out.
And it's not play, it's work. So, if you don't mind, I'll just wear the
false face I wear every day, the one that makes me feel like a fraud."

"You know, Ari, the same things that I hate about you are the things I love about you."

"Thank you, I think."

"You're impossible to hate."

"You're impossible to hate too."

"You're more stubborn than I am."

"Oh, I don't know about that one, Gina. I'd call that a toss-up."

"Do you really feel like a fraud?"

"I *am* a fraud."

"You're not. You're trying to make it out of high school alive. You don't owe anybody anything. Repeat after me: *I am not a fraud.*" She waited. "I don't hear you."

"I am not a fraud," I whispered.

"That's a start, Ari. We'll have to repeat this lesson often." Yeah, yeah, we both laughed.

Sometimes everybody was a comedian. And sometimes everybody was a teacher. And sometimes I just said too much. I had a running argument with that *silence = death* thing.

Cassandra went dressed as the goddess Athena. Dante went as William Shakespeare. They had the best costumes by far. Nobody came even close. Certainly, they were the most elaborate. But Susie's costume was the funniest, and maybe the most original. She was dressed as a ghost, which was pretty cliché—but on top of the ghost's head, there was a wrapped gift. And when people asked her who she was, she said, "I am the ghost of Christmas present." And people would laugh their asses off.

Susie Byrd was awesome.

You would have thought Dante went to school with all of us. He had a way of making himself fit in. Most people would have sat in a corner saying to themselves, *I don't know anybody here.* That's exactly what I would have done. But not Dante. Not Dante Quintana.

I smiled to myself as he talked to a girl who was obviously flirting with him.

Gina knew half the world. Or it seemed like she did. Mostly everyone wore a costume—but not everybody. And those of us who didn't were frowned upon—especially me. *I know you've changed, Ari. But you haven't changed that much. Too good to wear a costume, huh? You didn't wear a costume. Of course you didn't.* I got that one all night. It was the equivalent of *Look at you, Ari, you look just like your father.* I smiled and was a good sport about it.

Cassandra actually looked like a goddess. And I told her so.

"Was that a compliment?"

"I thought so."

"It didn't come out sounding like one."

"Well, maybe you won't be winning any more friends if you scare the hell out of people with those looks of yours."

"Like I'm interested in winning more friends. I've got the friends I need. Why get greedy?" She kissed me on the cheek.

I was onto her. Every time she thought she'd won another round of our yearlong debate, she'd kiss me on the cheek.

She pointed to one of our classmates. "Would you rather I'd come as the Wicked Witch of the West?"

"Well, maybe Glinda the Good Witch."

"I'll take the Wicked Witch any day. Or," she said, "what about her?" She pointed her chin at a girl who was dressed as Snow White.

"Somehow I don't picture you singing 'Someday My Prince Will Come.' You could've come dressed as a man."

"Better to come dressed as a prostitute."

"Better to be a prostitute than a man?"

Someone had turned up the music. "Why ask a question when you know the answer? Shut up and dance with me."

I didn't know how to dance. I danced anyway. Though I'm not sure bobbing my head up and down qualified as dancing. Cassandra, she could dance—and when she danced, nobody noticed if she even had a dance partner or not. That didn't bother me at all—but I was happy when Dante cut in. I retired to the corner of the room. Just as I made myself comfortable, Susie found me. "C'mon," she said, "we're going to dance the night away."

And that's what we did. We danced the night away. Between Susie and Cassandra and Gina, they began to teach me to do something that resembled dancing.

As I tried to make my body move with the music, I watched Dante and Cassandra dance. I had no idea where Dante had learned how to dance. Hell, he just knew how. So many things came so easily to him. I think every guy in the room envied Dante. If only they knew.

When the evening was winding down, the DJ put on a slow song, an oldie: "Hold Me, Thrill Me, Kiss Me." Cassandra grabbed me. "You haven't danced with me all night." Something about holding her in my arms felt right. Not like love, not like that. It just felt comfortable and intimate. Well, it *was* like love—not like the love I had for Dante, but the kind of love I couldn't put a name to.

I could sense Dante's eyes on us. Somehow I knew there was something going through his head—and I knew that wasn't a good thing. But when the song was over—the Village People saved the moment. Cassandra grabbed Dante and they led the way. And there we all were—making the *Y* and the *M* and the C and the *A*. Even I got in on the act.

Susie flung off her ghost outfit, and she and Gina, they looked so alive. I wondered what it would take for me to be as alive as they were.

Eleven

ON THE FIRST FRIDAY OF NOVEMBER, DANTE AND I
went out to the desert in my pickup. It was a little chilly. I think I
was a little peopled out. I needed some quiet. And I needed to be
with Dante. Just me and him. It had been a while since we'd gone
out there, to that spot where I kissed him for the first time. I'd put
some sleeping bags in the back of the truck. Dante was singing as we
drove, Christmas carols he was practicing for the concert. He had a
good voice. Strong.

"I like to hear you sing," I said, "but what I really enjoy doing is
kissing."

"Really? Where'd you learn? Who taught you?"

"Some guy. It wasn't that hard to learn."

"Some random guy?"

"Yeah."

"Where'd you meet him?"

"I met him at the swimming pool one summer day. He taught
me about the physics of water. He taught me that our bodies are
mostly water and that the Earth is seventy-one percent water. He
said if I didn't understand the beauty and the dangers of water, then

I would never understand the planet I lived on. He told me once that swimming was an intimate thing and that it was like making love to the Earth."

"Your random friend said that?"

"He did."

"How do you remember all those things I said to you, Ari?"

"Because you taught me how to listen to people who have something to say."

"I didn't teach you that. You learned that all by yourself." He kissed me. "Come and swim all the waters of the world with me."

I nodded. And all I could think was, *God, Dante, I wish I could. If only that were possible. If only we could become cartographers of the waters of the world.*

Just to hold him.

Just to kiss him.

Just to feel his body next to mine.

And feel that thing we call life running through me—that thing we call love. That thing we call "want" or "yearning" or "desire." And I looked up at the heavens as my breathing returned to normal. And the stars were as brilliant that night as I'd ever known them to be.

I heard Dante whispering a poem: "'Ah, love, let us be true to one another . . .'"

Sometimes it was so unnecessary to whisper the words "I love you."

Twelve

I WOKE UP IN THE MIDDLE OF THE NIGHT. I'D BEEN RUN-
ning down a dark street, and Bernardo was chasing me. And I was
scared. I was so scared. I don't why—but I thought if he caught me,
something bad was going to happen. Like he was going to hurt me.

I lay there in bed, catching my breath. Legs was licking me, so I
must have been talking or screaming in my sleep.

When will these dreams end? When will they end?

Thirteen

MY MOM AND DAD AND I WERE EATING DINNER—AND I was just picking at my food. My mom and dad were talking—but I was somewhere else. I'd had that dream about my brother, and it had stayed with me all day. I took off my glasses and studied them.

"Still can't get used to those things?"

"They're not so bad. I mean, I didn't know that my vision was off." And I knew that I couldn't wait anymore because I'd been wanting to ask for such a long, long, long, long time. "Dad, can I ask you to do me a favor?"

"What's that, Ari?"

"I want to see Bernardo. I want to go see him."

My mother didn't say anything. And I saw that my parents were looking at each other, not knowing what to say.

"I just need a rest from this big question mark that's been there for my whole life. I don't want to live with that question mark anymore."

"We don't want you to get hurt, Ari."

"Mom, it's hurt for a long time. You and Dad, you've made your peace. You've moved on with your lives. And I know that hasn't been easy. But what about me? It's like there's a hole in my life—and I don't want that hole to be there anymore."

"I went to see him once."

"I know, Dad."

"It wasn't pretty, Ari."

"I figured it wasn't. But did it help to settle things? For you and Mom?"

He nodded. "At first, I thought it had been a mistake. A very big mistake. It opened up some old wounds. But yes, in the end, I think it did help settle some very important things."

And I just busted out crying. And I couldn't stop. And I was talking through my sobs. And I didn't want to be sobbing, but sometimes the open wound just hurt too damned much. "There's so much crap in my life that I can't do anything about. I can't do anything about being gay. And I hate it. And I don't want to hate it—because it's me. I don't know, I just need to shut the door on this. I loved him. And I missed him. And then I stopped missing him. But I still dream about him. I don't want that dream anymore. I don't want it anymore, Mom."

I felt my mother sitting beside me. "Sometimes," she whispered, "when we want to protect the people we love, we wind up hurting them more." I felt her combing my hair with her fingers.

"I'm sorry, Mom. Dad? I'm sorry."

My mom and dad were looking at each other again. And I knew they were talking to each other in that language of silence they had learned.

"I think I can arrange a visit. Why don't we take a trip during the Christmas break? Will that work?"

I nodded. "I know this hurts you, Mom. I know—"

"Shhh," she whispered. "Shhh. I can't protect you from your own pain, Ari. And you can't protect me from mine. I think every parent has some moments when they say to themselves, *If I could take my child's pain away and make it mine, I would make it mine.* But I have no right to take your pain away, because it's yours."

I heard my father's voice. "You've stopped running, Ari. You're facing the things you need to face. That's what grown-ups do."

He reached his hand across the table.

And I took his hand—and I held on to it. Sometimes you did discover all the secrets of the universe in someone else's hand. Sometimes that hand belonged to your father.

Fourteen

IT WAS LATE NOVEMBER, AND I THINK THE SEMESTER was tiring us out. We were all starting to rebel a little. So, one Monday morning, this super-alternative girl named Summer came to school wearing a pair of very unusual earrings. We were sitting in class waiting for the bell to ring to signal the beginning of class, and some girl said to Summer, "Love your earrings." And Summer said, "They're gold-plated IUDs." The girls around her all started laughing.

I had no idea what an IUD was. But Mrs. Hendrix knew, and she'd been listening in on the conversation. "Summer, go the principal's office immediately."

"Why?"

"You're asking why?"

"That's what I'm asking."

"Do you think this is funny? Human sexuality is not a joke. Public statements about birth control are inappropriate for high school girls. And if you are announcing to the world that you are engaging in sexual activities and are publicly promoting birth control, then it is our job as teachers to intervene. Now go to the principal's office."

"I'm not doing anything wrong. And I can publicly promote birth control if I want to. It's a free country. And I'm not going to the principal's office."

"Come with me," she said.

Summer rolled her eyes.

"Ari," Mrs. Hendrix said. "Make sure the students read the next chapter in the textbook, and if there is mayhem in the class when I return, I'm going to hold you responsible."

I just looked at her.

"Do you understand me, young man?"

"Why me?"

"You are a paragon of responsibility."

"But—"

She gave me that *I don't have time for this crap* look. She was pissed. I wasn't going to say another word. "Summer, come with me. *Right now.*"

After they'd left for their little visit with Mr. Robertson, Sheila looked at me and said, "Go, go. Go and sit at the teacher's desk, you paragon of responsibility." Sheila had replaced Cassandra as the girl I loved to hate. She'd slapped me once in the eighth grade, and I always got the feeling that she was looking for another opportunity.

"Give me a break."

"You're such a kiss-ass."

"Kiss-ass?"

"What else do you call somebody who always comes to class prepared?"

"A student," I said.

"You little faggot."

"That's an ugly word used by ugly people." I think the look on my face told her something she hadn't expected.

She rolled her eyes. But she didn't say a word.

The stragglers were filing into the classroom just as the bell rang. I went to the blackboard and wrote, *Mrs. Hendrix took Summer to the office for some crime against the nation. We're supposed to read the next chapter in the book and be quiet.*

And of course, Sheila had to yell out, "Why don't you tell us all what it's like to be a paragon of responsibility?"

Everyone laughed.

I turned around and made sure she could read the anger written on my face. "Why don't you put your attitude in the toilet and flush it down?"

"'Paragon.' Is that another word for 'faggot'? We should get paragon here in trouble. Mrs. Hendrix told him if there was mayhem in this class when she returned, there would be hell to pay and that she'd hold the paragon responsible. I say let's raise hell."

And one of the guys yelled out, "Sheila, just shut the fuck up."

"You're all a bunch of sheep."

There was this chola-type of girl in the class. She kind of dressed like a guy. Her name was Gloria, and she didn't take any crap from anybody. "If I hear one more word out of your mouth, Sheila, I'm gonna take you outside and stuff your bra down your throat." And the room got real quiet. And everybody just took out their textbooks and started reading.

Fifteen

Dear Dante,

There was an incident in class today. I won't get into it. But the teacher, Mrs. Hendrix, said that human sexuality was not a joke. I don't think she was talking about homosexuality. I'm sure she wasn't. It was all about good old-fashioned heterosexuality.

Sheila, one of the girls in class, called me a little faggot. She didn't call me that because she thought I was gay. She called me that because she wanted to insult me. It's like the worst thing you can call someone is a faggot. Wow.

It's Thanksgiving week—and I got to thinking what I'm grateful for. The first thing I thought of was what I'm not grateful for. I'm not grateful for my sexual orientation. That's such a weird way to explain my unfortunate circumstances. Okay, I'm laughing at myself. I got that line from some old movie I was watching one night with my parents. And some evil guy tells this helpless young woman: Perhaps I can be of some help to free you of your unfortunate circumstances. *Yeah, I find myself in unfortunate circumstances.*

I'm not grateful that I'm gay.

Maybe that means that I hate myself.

And I'm wondering if I told you that, I'm wondering how you'd feel? How can I not want to be gay and love you at the same time? The thing I'm most grateful for is you. How does that work? The only thing I know about sexuality is you. Me and you. That's all I know. And the only word that comes to mind is "beautiful." Dante, there are so many things I don't get. There are so many things I'm still so confused about.

But the one thing that I'm not confused about is that I love you. I'm not a faggot. And neither are you. I won't label myself with an ugly word when what I feel for you is so fucking beautiful.

Oh, and there's one thing I want to ask you. Do you think I'm a paragon of responsibility? Just thought I'd ask.

Sixteen

DANTE CALLED ME ON THE PHONE AND MADE AN announcement. Dante loved to make announcements. "We're going to have Thanksgiving at my house."

"We are? Who's 'we'?"

"You and your mom and dad and Cassandra and her mom."

"How'd that happen?"

"My mom's been on a cooking spree. She calls it nesting."

"Nesting?"

"Yeah, she says a lot of women nest when they're pregnant. They want to cook and clean—you know, like birds building a nest. Our house is spotless. I mean, even my room is spotless right now. It gives me the creeps to walk in there. My mom's nesting is serious business. So she's all about the turkey and stuffing and the mashed potatoes and the gravy and the cranberries. And my dad's going to bake some bread. And Cassandra's mom is going to bring a couple of side dishes, and your mom's going to bake the pies."

"And I know nothing of this because?"

"Because you're Ari, and you don't pay attention. I mean, even though you're very nearly socialized—"

"Very nearly socialized?"

"You know, you can still be pretty socially distant, Ari."

"Socially distant? Is that like a new Dante concept? Never mind."

I could hear him laughing as I hung up the phone. I wasn't mad. More annoyed. Even people you loved could annoy you.

I decided to make my own contribution to Thanksgiving. I called a flower shop and told them I wanted to order something appropriate for a Thanksgiving dinner. "A nice centerpiece for the table, perhaps?" the lady said.

"Yes," I said.

"We can arrange that. Only you'll have to pick it up yourself. We're fully booked on deliveries."

"I can pick it up," I said.

So, on Wednesday after school, I drove to the flower shop, and paid the nice lady, and she had one of her employees open the door for me—and she even opened the truck door for me as I placed the centerpiece on the seat of the truck.

"I'd put it on the floor," she said. "That way if you make too quick a stop, it won't tip over."

These people knew their business.

I drove to the Quintanas' house, and I have to say I was feeling proud of myself. Maybe I was feeling a little *too* proud of myself.

I managed to get the centerpiece out of the truck and kick the door closed, and I walked up the steps very carefully. All I could think of was the cookies I'd once dropped on the floor. I managed to ring the doorbell and, all of a sudden, I felt like an idiot.

Mr. Quintana answered the door.

"I brought you something." I never knew when all that shyness living inside me was going to come out.

"I see that," Mr. Quintana said. "And you wonder why I'm always telling you and Dante how sweet you are."

"We don't have to go there, do we, Mr. Quintana?"

He was grinning ear to ear. "You know, Ari, that's an awfully adult thing you're doing there."

"Well, it happens to the best of us."

He cocked his head. "Right this way." He led me to the dining room table—which they never used. I placed the centerpiece in the middle of the table. "Soledad, come look at this."

Mrs. Quintana was wearing an apron and she looked like she'd been in the kitchen for a while. "From you, Ari?"

I just sort of shrugged my shoulders.

She kissed me on the cheek. "Someday," she said, and then she winked, "you're going to make some man very happy."

I didn't know if I was supposed to laugh—but I did. And then I said, like an idiot, "That was supposed to be a joke, right?"

Her smile. I think the word for it was "radiant." Maybe women who were about to have a baby had a halo around them. Somehow Mrs. Quintana's pregnancy had brought out the girl in her. It was nice. But I hoped the other Mrs. Quintana would come back.

I watched my mother as she was baking her pies. She already had an apple pie and a pecan pie in the oven. She always made a cherry pie for my father—because he didn't care for pumpkin pie. And everybody liked pecan pie. Me, I was all about pumpkin pie. I was all over it.

"How come you just don't order them from a bakery?"

"When have I ordered anything from a bakery? I don't even order birthday cakes from a bakery."

"It's a lot of work."

"Not if you like to bake. It's a part of the whole holiday thing."

"It's a thing?"

"Yes. A whole big thing. And you want to know who taught me how to bake the best pies?"

"Who? Your mom?"

"Nope."

"Aunt Ophelia?"

"Your aunt Ophelia once burned a frozen apple pie. She burned more than one, actually."

"Well, then who?"

"Mrs. Alvidrez."

"Mrs. Alvidrez? Her?"

"Yes, her."

"No kidding?"

"No kidding."

Dinner wasn't really dinner. We all gathered at the Quintanas' at one in the afternoon. When we arrived at their front door, Mrs. Quintana said, "I've been having contractions."

"Oh, no," my mother said. "We should cancel the dinner."

"Don't be silly—it's probably just false labor." She didn't look particularly worried. Then she had this pained look on her face and bent over a bit and took a deep breath, then another. My mother took her hand, then helped her into the living room and gently helped her sit down. And then Mrs. Quintana smiled. "It's gone. Much better."

"How long have you been having contractions?"

"Off and on most of the night. But they're irregular. And I expect it's not quite time." Mr. Quintana poured my parents a glass of wine. He and Mrs. Ortega had already been enjoying their red wine.

"I really think you're going to have that baby tonight." Mrs. Ortega seemed concerned.

"Let's enjoy our Thanksgiving," Mrs. Quintana said.

"She's bound and determined to have her Thanksgiving meal before she goes to the hospital. Dante and I have stopped trying to out-stubborn her." Mr. Quintana shook his head. "Sometimes Dante likes to beat his head against the wall."

Mrs. Quintana moaned in pain as she took a breath, then another, then another. And then she seemed to go back to normal. "Well, perhaps we may not make it to dinner after all." She laughed. "I was twenty years old when I had Dante. And seventeen years later, here I am."

And then her eyes opened wide and she held her stomach. Through her breathing, she whispered, "Sam, I think now would be a good time to drive me the hospital." And then she laughed. "Oh, Sam. You had that same look of panic on your face when Dante was about to be born."

"I'll drive," my father said.

Seventeen

ON THURSDAY, NOVEMBER 24, 1988, AT 10:43 P.M., Sophocles Bartholomew Quintana was born into the world at Providence Memorial Hospital in El Paso, Texas. The next morning, I watched his older brother hold him in his arms as he looked at me with tears in his eyes. "It's a boy, Ari. It's a boy." And I knew what he was thinking. *And he's going to be straight. And he's going to give my parents the grandchildren I will never be able to give them.*

Does being gay screw with our heads and our hearts?

"Here, Ari," Dante said. "Sophocles wants you to hold him."

"Oh, does he, now?" I said.

Dante handed his baby brother over to me—carefully. Mrs. Quintana said, "It's sweet that you're so careful with him. But, you know, he's not going to break. Just relax."

Dante rolled his eyes at his mother. "Now we have something new to fight about, Mom."

"Just wait till I show you how to change his diapers."

"I didn't sign up for that one."

"You don't have to sign up. You're going to get drafted."

I really did get a big kick out of how Dante and his mother got along. As I held Sophocles in my arms, I stared into his dark eyes. He seemed to be as wise as his name.

"You're a natural, Ari," Mrs. Quintana said.

I smiled—and then I laughed.

"What's so funny?"

"I was just thinking of a poem Dante taught me. 'The world is so full of a number of things, I'm sure we should all be as happy as kings.'"

"I taught that poem to Dante."

"You did?"

"I certainly did. I bet you thought his father taught him that poem."

"I guess I did."

"Did you know I used to write poetry?"

"Mom? Really?" Dante said.

"When I was in high school. It was terrible. Beyond awful. I kept them—and one day I was cleaning out the closets and I found a shoe box all tied up in a bow. I was going to throw them out. In fact, I did throw them out. But your father rescued them. He has them somewhere. I have no idea why he wanted to keep them."

"Because you wrote them," I said.

She smiled. "I suppose you're right."

"My mother, the poet. Can I read them?"

"Ask your father. I don't know where he put them."

"Where did the name Sophocles Bartholomew come from?"

"Bartholomew was our best friend in graduate school. He died of AIDS not so long ago. We wanted to honor him. And your father picked out Sophocles. He was one of the great Greek playwrights. He was known for his musical abilities, for his athleticism, and for his great charm."

"Is that true?" Dante asked.

"Everything I know about Sophocles, I learned from your father. Once, when he was drunk, he and Bartholomew started reading one of his plays aloud: *Oedipus the King*. They didn't get very far. I put a stop to it."

"Why, Mom?"

"I didn't believe that drunk graduate students, sincere though they may have been, were doing justice to a great playwright." She laughed. "Plus, I thought it was boring."

I handed Sophocles back to Mrs. Quintana. "Sophocles," she whispered and kissed him on the forehead.

"Well, it's a great name. Not very Mexican—but a great name. Sophocles Bartholomew Quintana. A truly great name. I mean, the name wasn't on my list—but still."

"We thought you'd like it, Dante."

"It's a big name for a little guy."

"He'll grow into it."

Eighteen

I WAS STARING AT THE PAINTING EMMA HAD GIVEN US. It was a strange and mesmerizing painting. I asked Dante to read me the poem again and I got lost in his voice, not really caring about the words he was reading, listening only to the stubborn softness in his voice. When he finished reading, he looked at me with a sadness in his eyes. "It's so sad, this poem. Do we all wind up in sadness, Ari? Is that how we'll all wind up?"

I didn't, couldn't say anything.

He put the poem back in the envelope and placed it back in his desk drawer. I noticed the college admissions applications on the top of his desk. "How many colleges are you looking at?"

"Well," he said, "about four or five. But I'm really only interested in one of them. It's a small liberal arts college in Oberlin, Ohio. And I'm also applying for an arts summer program in Paris." He didn't seem very enthusiastic. I could tell he didn't really want to talk about the college admissions thing or the Paris thing. "What about you?"

"I'm applying to UT. That about does it."

He nodded.

We were both sad.

There would be no Ari in Oberlin, Ohio.

There would be no Dante in Austin, Texas.

I don't think either of us liked quiet sadness in the room. But Dante didn't want to be sad so he changed the subject. "I was talking to Susie about art the other day and she informed me that *The Raft of the Medusa* was your favorite painting."

"It is my favorite painting."

"That's my favorite painting and you know it." He was trying to pick a fight with me—but he was just playing. I could always tell when he was playing. "I'm afraid you'll have to pick another favorite painting."

"No, I don't think I will."

"I guess you're not as original as I thought."

"I never claimed to be original."

And then he laughed.

And then I laughed.

And then he kissed me. And we weren't sad anymore.

Nineteen

A COUPLE OF DAYS AFTER SCHOOL ENDED, CASSANDRA and I went to Rico's funeral. We sat next to Danny in the back of the small church. It was small and simple.

My mom said that funerals were about resurrection.

Resurrection didn't seem to be present at this one. There was only the sadness of Rico's body in a casket. And his mother's quiet sobs.

Afterward, Cassandra and Danny and I went to the Charcoaler. I don't think Danny even tasted his food—he just wolfed it down. "Guess I was hungry," he said.

We sat in one of the outside benches and listened to the music coming from the radio in my truck. "Everybody Wants to Rule the World" came on and Danny and Cassandra smiled at each other. "Danny, this is our song, baby." She took him by the hand, and they danced in the parking lot. For an instant, Danny was happy.

It was just a small, quiet scene in the many scenes in the story that was my life. And I suppose this moment didn't seem all that important.

But it *was* important. It was important to Cassandra. And to Danny. And to me.

Twenty

"ARE YOU SCARED, ARI? TO SEE YOUR BROTHER?"

"Not scared. I have these butterflies in my stomach. My insides are a mess."

"I hope this doesn't hurt you too much."

"How much is too much?"

"I know you have to do this alone. And it's really great that you'll be spending time with your dad. But I wish I were going with you."

"You'll be with your parents and visiting your family in California. And that's a good thing."

"Yeah, but I don't fit in there. And everybody will be speaking Spanish and they'll be hating me because I don't speak it—and they'll all be thinking that I think I'm too good to speak Spanish and that's not true and—well, screw it."

"We both do what we have to do, Dante, Everything's not about us."

"Yeah, yeah. Sometimes you talk too much."

"I don't say enough—and then I say too much. Got it. It won't be such a long trip."

"I guess sometimes we have to go our own separate ways."

"But then we'll both come back. And I'll be here. And you'll be here. We'll both be back sitting where we are right now."

"And you'll kiss me, Ari?"

"Maybe."

"If you don't, I'll kill you."

"No, you won't."

"What makes you so sure?"

"Well, to begin with, dead boys can't kiss."

We were smiling at each other.

"Sometimes, Ari, when we're away from each other—it seems like forever."

"Why do we say the word 'forever' so much?"

"Because when you love someone, that's the word that comes to mind."

"When I think of the word 'love'—I think of the name Dante."

"You mean that?"

"No, I was just saying that for the hell of it."

We sat there for a long moment in a silence that wasn't quite comfortable. "Merry Christmas, Ari."

"Merry Christmas, Dante."

"Someday we'll spend Christmas together."

"Someday."

Twenty-One

BEFORE DANTE LEFT, HE HUNG THE PAINTING THAT
Emma had given us on a wall in my bedroom.

"It's like he spoke for me when he painted this. And when he
wrote his poem."

"He did speak for you, Dante. He spoke for all of us."

Dante nodded. "Sometimes we have to be able to speak for those
who can't. That takes a lot of courage. I'm not sure I have that kind
of courage in me. But you do. I envy your courage, Ari."

"How do you know I have courage?"

"Because you're brave enough to go see your brother even though
you may not like what you find."

"Maybe I'm not brave at all. Maybe I'm just tired of being afraid.
And maybe I'm just being selfish. I'm not sure I'm looking for my
brother anymore. Maybe I never was. I think I'm just trying to find
a piece of me that I lost."

Twenty-Two

DANTE LEFT FOUR DAYS BEFORE CHRISTMAS. IT WAS
as if Gina and Susie knew I was sad, because that's the day they
dropped off a Christmas gift for me. Cassandra and I were running,
so I wasn't home. They handed the gift to my mother.

"I made them stay, and we ate some of my *bizcochos* with some
hot chocolate." My mother was very proud of her hospitality.
"And I gave them some tamales to take home." Mom loved to
feed people.

On Christmas morning, I opened Gina and Susie's gift. It was a silver cross on a silver chain. They'd written me a card:

> *Dear Ari,*
>
> *We know you're not all that religious. Sometimes you believe*
> *in God and sometimes you don't. You say you're still deciding.*
> *We know that you think God hates you, and we don't believe*
> *that. We will never believe that. And we know that you think*
> *that God has better things to do than to hang around and*

protect you. But we got you this anyway, just to remind you
that you're not alone. And you shouldn't blame God for all the
stupid and mean things people say. And we're both pretty sure
God isn't homophobic.

Love, Susie and Gina

I put on the silver chain and looked at myself in the mirror. It felt strange to be wearing something around my neck. I'd never worn any kind of jewelry or anything like that. I stared at the simple silver cross hanging on my chest. I thought of Susie and Gina. They were determined to love and be loved. They loved their way into my heart, a heart that seemed to be determined not to be loved. And they made me understand what a beautiful thing it was to be a girl.

I knew I would never take off this silver chain with a cross hanging on it. I would wear it always. Maybe God would protect me. Maybe He wouldn't. But the memory of what Gina and Susie had given *would* protect me. And that was good enough for me.

Dear Dante,

I miss you. I know it's a good thing you went to visit your
parents' families in LA. And I'm sure they've all fallen in
love with Sophocles. I know I have. Babies make you want to
be more careful. I keep trying to picture all your cousins and
your uncles and aunts. I know you don't feel close to them. But

maybe something will happen—and you won't feel like such an outsider.

What the hell do I know.

It's Christmas day and I feel as stuffed as my mother's turkey. The sun is setting, and the house is quiet. My sisters and their husbands and my nephews and nieces have gone to spend the evening with their in-laws, and I like this quiet. I don't mind being alone. I used to be alone and I felt a loneliness living in me that I didn't understand, the kind of loneliness that made me miserable.

I don't feel that loneliness when I'm alone anymore. I'm a lot more comfortable spending time with the Ari I have become. He's not so bad. He's not so great. But he's not so bad.

There's always something new to learn about myself. There's always a part of me that will be a stranger to me. There will always be days when I look in the mirror and ask myself, "Ari, who are you?"

I was thinking about Danny and Rico. Rico never got to have a life. He was gay, and he wasn't like you and me—he couldn't pass. And he was born into a poor family. Danny told me the world doesn't want people like Rico in it. And the world doesn't want guys like me in it either. That's what he said.

And I keep thinking that I wished the world would understand people like you and me.

But we're not the only ones the world doesn't understand. I want people to care about me and care about you. But don't we have to care too? Don't we have to care about the Ricos and the Dannys? Don't we have to care about people who aren't treated like people? I have a lot to learn. I heard a guy in the hallway at school call some other guy the n-word. The guy he meant to insult was a white guy, and the whole thing was a little confusing, but it made me mad. I hate that word. And I didn't chase after the guy who said it and say, Listen here, you little fucker. *I should have chased him down the hall. I should have told him that he was acting as if he had no respect—not for other people and not for himself. I should have said something—but I didn't. And that is exactly what the gay rights movement is saying about the AIDS pandemic, yeah, Silence = Death.*

Dante, I have so many things going through my head sometimes. It's as if the whole world is in chaos and it's all living inside me. It's as if all the riots in San Francisco and New York and London and Chicago—all those riots, all the broken glass and the broken hearts, are cutting up my own heart. And I can't breathe. I just can't breathe. And I want to be alive and be happy. And sometimes I am. I'm going to write Rico's name in this journal.

Rico Rubio. Rico Rubio.

Rico Rubio was here. He was alive. And now he's dead. It wasn't drugs that killed him. It was that word "hate" that killed him. And that word is going to kill us all if we don't learn how to fight it. Loving you, Dante, helps me fight that word.

In another week, it will be a new year. And maybe in the new year, we'll do better. I'll do better. In another week, maybe the world will be new again. Like Sophocles. He makes the world new again, doesn't he, Dante?

A new year. A new world. A chance to start again. My dad and I will be going to see my brother. Well, my dad is taking me—but it's me who's going to visit him. My mom and dad, they've come to terms with the whole matter. But I haven't. I love my parents for respecting what I feel I have to do. What am I expecting when I see him? I don't know, Dante. I just don't know. Maybe something important. Maybe something that matters. Maybe I'll have some peace. "Peace" is not a word that lives inside me. The year ends with me and my brother.

You'll be back by then, and when the new year arrives, I'm going to kiss you. That's what everybody does when the new year arrives. We may have to be far away from the eyes of a watching world that disapproves, but I don't give a shit. I want to kiss you when the new year arrives. We should get to do what everybody else gets to do—even if we have to do it in secret.

I have felt a change in me that began the day I met you. And I don't even think I can put into words or map out the changes in me since that day. I make for a terrible cartographer. The way I think and the way I see the world—even the way I talk—have changed. It's as if I was walking in a pair of shoes that fit so tight on me because my feet had grown. And then it finally occurred to me that I needed a new pair of shoes—a pair of shoes that fit my feet. The first time I walked down the street wearing those shoes, I realized how much it had hurt, how much pain I had been in, when I did something as simple as walking. It doesn't hurt anymore to walk. That's what it feels like, Dante, to walk in the changes that have occurred in me since I met you. I may not fit the definition of a happy guy. But it doesn't hurt anymore to be me.

And all of this is because you looked at me one day at a swimming pool and said to yourself, I bet I can teach this guy how to swim. *You saw me and I wasn't invisible anymore. You taught me how to swim. And I didn't have to be afraid of the water anymore. And you gave me enough words to rename the universe I lived in.*

Twenty-Three

Dear Dante,

It's two days after Christmas and—

I stopped right there. I just didn't have anything to say. Actually, I think I was something of an emotional mess. I kept staring at my journal. My mom walked into the kitchen and watched me for a second. "You nervous?" she asked me.

"Yeah, well, maybe a little anxious."

"Tell your brother . . ." She shook her head. "No." She had a look that was unbearably sad. "It's broken. What was, no longer is. I know that. I have been through all this before. I know you think I'm a fixer. You don't say it, but you think it. And you would be right about that. But there are a lot of things that can't be fixed. I don't blame myself anymore. That took a long time. There is nothing left to be said."

I nodded. I wanted to say I understood. But I didn't. I would never be a mother and would never know what it was like to lose a son—to lose a son who was still living.

"I hope you find what you're looking for."

"I hope so too, Mom. I'm not going with a lot of expectations. Maybe I am. Maybe I'm just kidding myself. I just know I have to do this."

"I know you do."

I nodded. "It's time. 'Some children leave, some children stay. Some children never find their way.'"

I always wondered why sometimes, when we smiled, the smile didn't make the sadness disappear.

My mother hugged me. "I'm going to Tucson for a couple of days to see your sisters. I'll tell them you send your love."

"Tell them I still have Tito. He's in a box in the basement."

"Tito." My mother laughed. "You loved that bear."

"I used to talk to him. He never talked back. I think that's why I loved him."

Twenty-Four

WHEN I WOKE, MY MOTHER WAS SITTING ON MY BED.
"I'm off to Tucson. I just wanted to give you my blessing."

I sat up on the side of the bed.

I felt her thumb on my forehead as she made the sign of the
cross. And she whispered her blessing. "Father of all nations, look
upon my son Ari. Watch and protect him and fill his heart with the
peace that only you can give."

She crossed herself.

And I crossed myself too—and tried to remember the last time
I had done that.

She kissed me on the forehead.

And after a moment of silence, she left the room.

I envied my mother for her faith.

I fell asleep again.

When I woke up again, I wondered if I'd been dreaming.

I reached to pet Legs—but I'd forgotten my mom had taken her
to Tucson. I remembered the day she followed me home. When I sat
down on the front steps to slow down my breathing, she licked me
and wouldn't stop. And then she put her head on my lap. It was as if

she'd loved me from the moment she saw me. And I loved her too. I loved her because I was lost and she was lost, and a lost boy and a lost dog equals love.

When I took a shower, I looked at the cross hanging on my chest. I thought about God. I wondered why everyone thought about God so much and I tried not to think of him at all. Because so many people had decided he didn't love me. I wondered why people felt they could speak for God.

Had my brother ever loved me like I'd loved him? But why did that matter? Maybe it wasn't true that I had no expectations. Maybe I wanted to know that there was still something left in my brother that was sacred. My father said that every human life was sacred— that's what fighting in Vietnam had taught him. I wanted to ask him about that. I wanted to know exactly what he meant.

And then I thought, *Well, if Jesus gets along with Mrs. Alvidrez, he can get along with anybody.*

God contained all the mysteries of the universe. Did he love the world and everyone in it?

I thought of Dante. One of the things we had in common was that we asked questions that no one knew the answers to. But that didn't stop us from asking.

My father had an interesting look on his face when I came into the kitchen. "I got a call from the Huntsville prison this morning. You were scheduled to spend tomorrow afternoon with your brother. Apparently, your brother isn't a model prisoner, and they weren't going to allow him any visitors. But since he doesn't ever get any visitors, you'll be allowed to see him for one hour and not out in the open, but behind a glass barrier and using a speaker."

I didn't say anything. What was there to say?

"You think driving seven hundred and forty-one miles is worth seeing your brother for an hour? That's an eleven-and-a-half-hour drive."

"Yes," I said. "I do think it's worth it."

My father smiled at me. "I think so too. It's a little less than three hours from Austin. We can stay the night in Austin and then head for Huntsville. You can see your brother at one o'clock."

"Something doesn't seem right. This all sounds a little unusual, doesn't it, Dad?"

"Well, I guess you've learned how to smell a fish. There's a guy who works for the Texas Bureau of Prisons. His name is Michael Justice." My dad laughed. "I'm not kidding you—that's really his name. I fought in 'Nam with him. If you want to know the truth, they called the whole thing off. I asked to speak to Mike. They asked me why I'd like to speak to him. And I told him what I told you— that I fought in 'Nam with him. That's all I had to say. He made it happen."

People always say it's who you know. And that isn't always such a bad thing.

I hadn't seen my brother since I was six years old. Eleven years had passed, and he had become nothing more than a memory. But he was more than that. Of course, he was much more than that. People aren't memories.

I kept thinking: What could you say in an hour? Maybe all of this had nothing to do with what you said. Or what he said. Or what anybody said.

Dante made me fall in love with words. And sometimes I hated them. Sometimes I had no use for them.

Sometimes words just took up space. I wondered if they were depleting the world's supply of oxygen.

You get to talking about a lot of things when you're on a seven-hundred-and-forty-one-mile drive. I don't know why but I started asking my dad if he agreed with Mom—about what Susie and Chuy and I referred to as the Livermore incident. "And I think Mr. Robertson is a dick."

My father laughed. "You're seventeen years old. It's your job to think that." I could tell that my father wanted to say something more and that he was trying to measure his words. "You know, Ari, racism is something that's almost impossible to talk about. And so most of us don't talk about it. I think that we somehow know that we're all implicated. Racism is a finger that points at all of us, and every few years, there's an explosion—and we all talk about it for a little while. And everybody raises their hands and says, 'Racism? I'm against it.' We're all against it. And we feel a solidarity. We make a few changes here and there—but we don't make any real changes. It's like we buy a new car but keep driving in the same direction."

"But why?"

"Because we don't know how to talk about certain things. And we've never learned. We've never learned because we're not willing to change because we're afraid of what we might lose. I don't think that we want Black people to have what we have. And when it comes to Mexicans, this country loves us and hates us. We're a country of immigrants that hates immigrants. Only we pretend not to hate immigrants." He laughed. "I know a few guys who think Native Americans are immigrants." He shook his head. "Americans are not really very nice people. And I say that as an American."

"But, Dad, how do we change that?"

"That's what your generation is going to have to figure out."

"That's not fair."

My father gave me this look like what I'd just said was about the stupidest thing you could ever say. Then he said, "Sometimes the weather is fair. We're going to have a fair-weather day. And then somewhere else there's a tornado killing a hundred people. Across the globe, there are places where the weather isn't fair."

I knew what he was telling me. Saying things like "That's not fair" said nothing and did nothing. And maybe he was trying to tell me that only children fighting on a playground said things like that.

We didn't say anything for a while, and he was thinking, and I was thinking. I finally asked, "How many battles have you had to fight, Dad?"

"Only one that matters. I stole it from a writer named William Faulkner. I'm paraphrasing. The battle of my own human heart against itself."

"Did I ever tell you the story about the time someone let out a bunch of lizards into your mom's classroom?"

"That happened? Did Mom freak out?"

"Of course not. Your mother happens to like lizards."

"Seriously?"

"Oh, yeah. She said if you had lizards in your house, you wouldn't have a mosquito problem because they'd have them for dinner. She said that everyone in small villages welcomed lizards into their houses because they ate all those unwanted insects. She used to keep lizards in an aquarium until her mother made her get rid of them."

"Mom? My mom?"

"What makes you think your mother's a scared little girl? Why should she be afraid of lizards? They're harmless. So, anyway, your mother had this awful class one year and she was tearing her hair out. And some kid in that class lets loose about twenty lizards. The first thing your mother did was rush to the door and seal the cracks with cleaning rags to make sure the lizards couldn't get out, and the girls were screaming and some of the guys weren't all that thrilled either. Your mom managed to get ahold of one of the lizards and let it crawl on her, and she said, 'Does anybody know who this little guy belongs to?'

"She'd already figured out who the prankster was. 'Jackson, let's put them back in the box you brought them in and then let them out in the desert, where they belong. They're not interested in American government.'

"Your mother didn't run to the principal. Your mother took no punitive actions against any of those students—even though she knew they were all in on it. And your mother won twenty-seven admirers that day. Her worst class became her best class. Jackson was

333

an African American student. He lived with his grandmother. She couldn't come to parents' night, so Liliana started going to her—to talk about Jackson's progress. That was many years ago. Do you know what happened to Jackson? He's an attorney who works for the Department of Justice. He sends your mother a Christmas card every year without fail. He always writes a little note. And he signs the card, 'Lizard.'"

"Why doesn't Mom tell me all these stories?"

"Because she's not the kind of person who likes to go around trying to get her name in the newspaper every time she does something to change a kid's life."

Wow, I thought. *Wow.*

My father pulled the car over to the side of the road. There was a small town just ahead, but my dad liked parking on the side of the road. It was the loner in him. "I need a cigarette."

We both got out and stretched our legs. My dad liked to make noises when he stretched. I got a big kick out of that. He lit his cigarette and leaned against the car. I don't know why the words came out at that very moment. "I hate being gay."

"Well, they have these conversion therapy schools."

"Do they work?"

"We had a conversation about this with Soledad and Sam one night when we went to dinner. And the answer is no. No, they don't work. But people go to them anyway."

"So why do they go?"

"Well, most of the time it's because their parents send them there. Not my idea of love, but . . . And some people go on their own. Hoping it just may work. So they can live a normal life. Now, who in their right mind wants to live a normal life?"

"But you live a normal life."

He nodded. And then he tapped his head. "But I don't live a normal life up here." And he tapped his temple again. "One day, you will thank the universe that you were born the man you are."

I watched my father finish smoking his cigarette.

When you drove through Texas, you could see forever. The sky let you see what was ahead. Seeing was important. But once I couldn't see who my dad was.

And now I could see him. I could see who he was.

And I thought he was more beautiful than the Texas sky.

Twenty-Five

DAD SAID THAT THE ONLY THING YOU LEAVE ON THIS earth after you die that's worth anything at all is your name. I wanted my father to live forever. But that wasn't going to happen. And every time I entered a library, I was going to grab a book and write his name in it. So I could keep his name in this world.

Twenty-Six

WE CHECKED INTO A HOTEL IN AUSTIN. IT WAS CHILLY enough to wear jackets, but really it wasn't all that cold. We were walking around the state capital, and Dad was reading some historical marker. "Texas," he said. He shook his head. "Did you know that in 1856, there was a county in Texas that made every Mexican illegal?"

"How could they do that?"

"Well, you just made it a crime to be in the county. Matagorda County, Texas."

"So it was illegal for Mexicans to live there? All the Mexicans who lived in that county had to leave?"

"Or be incarcerated. But you know there are good things in the history of Texas too. In 1893, some untamable woman who probably wanted a divorce and couldn't get one founded an organization called the Association of Southern Women for the Prevention of Lynching."

I almost wanted to laugh. But it wasn't funny. "How do you know these things, Dad?"

He looked at me and smiled and shook his head. "There's this thing called a library. And in those libraries, there are books. And—"

"You're a wiseass, Dad. Now I know where I get it from."

"Oh, I don't know. I think your mother made a contribution to that too."

"Did they lynch homosexuals, Dad?"

"I'm not up on that. But in jolly old England, they didn't hang homosexuals—they burned them. Alive."

I should've left the question unasked.

"Ari, people love. Who they love and why they love, who knows how that happens? And people hate. Who and why they hate, who knows how that happens? I found the meaning of my life when I met your mother. That doesn't mean that there weren't a thousand questions left unanswered. I've tried to come up with my own answers. And very often, I have failed. I've learned not to punish myself for my failures. And I try—but do not always succeed—to greet the day with gratitude."

He messed up my hair with his hand. He hadn't done that since I was a boy.

"Don't ever let the hate rob you of the life you've been given."

I was lying in bed in the hotel room. I was thinking about my brother. All kinds of things were racing through my head. My father was lying in the bed next to mine. He was reading a book, *All the King's Men*. Then he shut the book and turned off the light.

"You okay, Ari?"

"Yeah, I'm okay."

"You're a brave kid."

"I'm not so sure about that."

"I don't know what's in your head about your brother, but he's lived there rent-free for too many years. I have to tell you something about him—he doesn't have an innocent bone in his body."

"But he's your son."

"Yes. And sometimes you have to let a son go. Because, for reasons I don't fully understand, your brother has lost his humanity. There are such people."

"Are you angry that I need to see him?"

"You're doing what you should be doing. You're discovering life—which includes your brother—on your own. Nobody should deny you that."

We were quiet for a long time. And then a thought entered my head and it made me smile. "Dad?"

"What?"

"I like you, Dad. I mean, I really like you."

My dad broke out into this great laugh. "Sometimes telling someone you like them is a helluva lot better than telling someone you love them."

Twenty-Seven

I WAS MET BY A GUARD WHO LET ME ENTER INTO THE prison. I wasn't afraid, and I'd thought I would be. I wasn't nervous, and I'd thought I would be. One of the prison guards, who looked like he'd been born bored, led me into a room with a row of windows. There was no one in there. "The one at the end." He pointed toward the last seat. "When you're done, you can just walk out and check out at the front desk before you leave. I'm the front desk," he said. And he half chuckled. A bored man with an almost sense of humor.

I waited in the cubicle no more than a minute. The man who was my brother was let into the room, and there I was, face-to-face with the brother I had only imagined for years, a thick piece of glass separating us. He had thick black wavy hair and a mustache. He looked older than a man in his late twenties. He was handsome in a very hard way, and his black eyes didn't have any friendliness or softness in them.

We stared at each other, not saying anything.

"So you're little Ari. Look at you. I bet you think you're something."

I ignored what he said. "I've been wanting to see you for a long time, Bernardo."

"What for?"

"You're my brother. When I was a kid I really loved you. I missed you when you were gone. Nobody would talk about you."

"That's very touching. I might have been a sensitive little crybaby like you once. I like me better this way."

"I take it you didn't really want to see me. You didn't have to say yes."

"No, no. I wanted to see you. I was curious. I mean, what the fuck. But if you were expecting a fucking Hallmark card, I'm not your guy. Sorry to disappoint you."

"I'm not disappointed. I didn't have expectations. I just wanted to meet you."

"Wanted to see for yourself."

"Why not?"

"Oh, so you wanted to come to the zoo."

"I don't happen to think you're an animal. And I've thought about you a lot."

"What a waste of time. I didn't think about you at all."

"Am I supposed to feel hurt?"

"Isn't that what sensitive boys do for a living—get their feelings hurt?"

"Not this one."

"You're not gonna cry? I'm disappointed."

"You should have lowered your expectations."

And he started laughing. I mean, he was really laughing. "What d'ya know—my baby brother can hang with the big boys. He knows just what to say." He had an awful grin. "You look a lot like the old man. That's too fucking bad. But that's not your fault." He was studying me. But it felt like he was searching. "So, you wanted to meet your big brother? To find out what? To interview him? To write a paper for your English class, 'My Visit with My Brother'? To make you feel like you're better than me? To make you feel good about yourself—*Look, everybody, I'm such a good guy, I went to see my brother who's murdered someone? Look at me, I'm such a decent guy?*"

And then it was like he decided to be nicer or to try to carry on a conversation. "So, you a junior? A senior?"

"A senior."

"President of the senior class?"

"No, not even close."

"Bet you're a good student."

"I do okay."

"Bet Mom likes that. She liked her children to be good students. It made her look good. I mean, a teacher whose kids get bad grades—that's just not cool."

"She's not like that."

"The hell she isn't. I bet you love her ass."

"Don't talk like that about my mom."

"Well, she happens to be my mom too. And I can talk about her any fuckin' way I want. Oh, I bet you're her little prince. A mama's boy."

"Are you really an asshole—or are you just putting on a show just for me?"

"I don't put on shows for pretty little boys. You know what

happens to pretty boys in places like this? Pretty little boys become pretty little girls. But you'll never get the chance to find out. Because you're a good boy who brings good girls home to Mama. I bet she approves of all your little girlfriends."

I looked at him. I could tell him, or I could not tell him. But I had another question for him. "Why'd you have to kill her?"

"It was a he."

"Well, 'he' sure fooled you. Didn't you believe she was a woman?"

I could see the rage written on his face. "Fuck you. He deserved to die."

"She," I said.

"Fuck you."

"Either way," I said. "She was a person. She was a human being."

"Oh, so you're a moralistic son of a bitch who came here to let me know he doesn't approve of me. Go fuck yourself. Go and run into the arms of one of your pretty girlfriends and let them coddle you."

Maybe because I already didn't care what a man like him thought of me, I decided to tell him. "I don't have girlfriends—I'm gay."

He laughed. He laughed. And he laughed. "A little faggot. That's what I got for a brother. So, you take it up the ass or what?"

I started to get up.

"What? You leaving already? We have a whole hour to have some fun. Can't you take it?"

"I can take it. I just can't think of a reason why I should."

"Fuck you! I'm nothing. You're nothing. Everybody in the whole fucking world is nothing. But little faggots are worse than nothing."

"What happened to you?"

"What happened to me? Take a good look. I'm a mirror to what the world is really like."

I stood and looked at him. "I don't think so. Whatever gets you through the day. Maybe I'm a mirror to what the world is really like."

"Dream on. The world doesn't look like a faggot."

I stared right at him. "I'm happy I came. I'm even happier I'm leaving."

I was already walking away as he tossed curse words at me like they were grenades.

I signed my name out where I'd signed my name in. I didn't really know what I felt. But one thing I didn't feel—I didn't feel like crying. And I didn't feel hurt. I didn't feel hate. A part of me was smiling. Sometimes a memory of the past keeps us in a prison, and we don't even know it's a prison. I had a memory of me and my brother and it represented a love that wasn't real. And I had to visit a prison to discover my own prison.

My brother, he was gone. He was not a man I wanted to know. I did not know how all of this had happened. And I didn't have to know.

Some children leave, some children stay.

Some children never find their way.

My brother's life was his.

And my life was mine.

As I walked out of that prison, I felt like a free man.

I was free. Free of a memory. Free.

Twenty-Eight

WE WERE DRIVING TOWARD FORT DAVIS, TEXAS. WE'D planned to camp there overnight. It was pretty damn cold, and my dad said we didn't have to camp out. But I wanted to. "What's a little cold night air?" My father smiled.

He had spent time there with his uncle as boy. He told me he'd loved his uncle more than he had ever loved his own father.

We hadn't said a word to each other since we'd left Huntsville. Two hundred miles and not one word. My father let me be. He didn't ask any questions. Finally, I said, "Thank you, Dad. Thank you for everything."

"You okay?"

"I'm better than okay."

I liked the look on his face. We returned to our comfortable silence. After a while, my father decided to introduce some music into our road trip and put on the radio. An old Beatles song came on. It reminded me of Dante—it was a song we listened to a lot: "The Long and Winding Road." And I found myself singing. I'd forgotten how good it felt to sing. And then my father began to sing along too.

How strange and how beautiful, to be sitting in a car and singing with your father.

Twenty-Nine

WE WERE EATING DINNER AT SOME DIVE DINER. "IT'S been here forever. My uncle sent me a picture he'd taken at the entrance of this place. He said I should keep it so I wouldn't forget. There was a sign that said NO MEXICANS, NO DOGS, NO BARE FEET." My father laughed. "At least we were the first on the list. And what did they have against dogs?"

I don't know how he could laugh about all these things. He could get super angry about the screwed-up world we lived in. But he could also be very patient with the world. He had a good dose of cynicism in him. But he wasn't a bitter man.

We didn't set up a camp or anything. We found a good spot and just laid out our sleeping bags on the ground. My dad made a fire and took out a pint of bourbon and lit a cigarette. "Not too cold for you?"

"I like it."

"Here," he said, "take a swig. We won't tell your mother." I took a swig and there was a little explosion. I must have made a face.

"You're not a drinker, are you?"

"I'm still in high school."

"That doesn't stop a lot of kids from drinking. You're a good kid. I shouldn't call you a kid. You're not a kid anymore." He was smoking his cigarette and the light of the fire made him look younger. We had been such strangers to each other, a father and a boy who had lived in different countries in the same house. He had been an unsolvable mystery. And though there were some mysteries about him that I would never solve, there was something intimate between us now. And he felt like home.

There were billions of stars in the sky. Billions. A part of me wished that Dante was here so I could hold him underneath these stars. Maybe he and I would come here someday. We were lying in our sleeping bags, silent, in awe of the stars.

"I brought your mother up here when I came back from 'Nam. Your mother and I think that's the night you were conceived."

"Really?" I loved the thought of that. "Is that really true?"

"It's a very good possibility. Maybe it isn't. But your mother and I would like to believe that. Because of those stars up there."

There was a long silence, but I knew my father felt like talking—and I felt like listening. "Your mother is the only woman I ever loved. I saw her on the first day of school at the university. She was the most beautiful girl I'd ever seen. She was walking and talking with a friend, and she seemed so incredibly alive. I followed her to class. It was a literature class. I went to the liberal arts office and got myself registered for the class.

"I sat in the back. It was a good place to watch. She was so smart. I think the professor called on her because she always had something interesting to say and it helped the discussion. The professor was a discussion-kind of guy. I sometimes saw her on campus and followed her from far behind so she wouldn't notice.

"I went to a Christmas party with a friend at the end of the semester. And she was there. Some guy, good-looking, was hitting on her. I just watched how she handled herself. She wasn't interested. But she seemed so comfortable and unbothered. Someone handed me a beer, and I went into the backyard to have a cigarette. There were plenty of people in the backyard, and it may have been December, but it wasn't all that cold outside. I just stood there and watched. And there was your mother standing next to me. 'So,' she said, 'are you ever going to talk to me, or do you just like stalking me?'

"I was so damned embarrassed. I just didn't know what to say. So that's what I said: 'I never know what to say.'

"'Let me help you out. I'm Liliana.' She stuck out her hand.

"I shook her hand and said, 'I'm Jaime.'

"She just looked at me. And she smiled. 'One of these days you're going to work up the courage to kiss me.' Then she walked away. I felt like an idiot. And I just stood there—and it dawned on me that I should have followed her. But when I searched for her, she'd already left. I was asking around to see if anybody knew some girl named Liliana. Some people knew her—but they didn't have her phone number. And then this girl walks up to me and hands me a folded piece of paper. 'This is her phone number. And if you don't call her, I'm going to find you and I'm going to kick your ass.' That girl turned out to be your mother's best friend, Carmela Ortiz."

"The nurse at my school."

"Yup. Pain in the ass. But she's grown on me over the years. Anyway, I finally called your mother. And on New Year's Eve, we went out on a date. And I kissed her that night. And I knew that I was going to marry her, and never kiss another woman again. Not that I'd kissed that many.

"I've always been a watcher. Always watching. If your mother and Carmela hadn't given me a shove, I might have never married her. And it wasn't just that I was a watcher. I thought your mother was way out of my league.

"You know, in 'Nam, they called me Trucha. It's the word for 'trout,' but it's slang for someone who's always watching, always alert. I'll never forget this Jewish kid. He was almost twenty. He got shot and he was bleeding real bad, and I took a towel I carried and pressed it against him to help stop the bleeding and I radioed for a medic, and they were coming—but I knew this kid wasn't going to make it. So I just held him, and he was cold and shaking and he said, "Tell my mom and dad. Tell them I'll see them next year in Jerusalem." And he was gone, that faraway stare the dead have after life leaves them. I closed his eyelids. He was a good man. He was a good soldier. When I got back, I delivered that message in person. Because he deserved that. Because his parents deserved that. I'll never forget the gratitude—and pain—written on his parents' faces.

"Don't ever let anybody tell you that war is something beautiful or heroic. When people say war is hell, *war is hell*. Cowards start wars, and the brave fight them."

My father fell into a silence.

I was happy to know how my parents fell in love. I was happy to know that my mother had found a way to move a quiet man who was standing still into action. I was happy that my father could talk about the war—though he only said very little about what had happened there. I understood that the war had left him with a pain that had found a home in his heart, the kind of pain that no one could heal and that would never go away.

Thirty

AS WE REACHED THE EL PASO CITY LIMITS, I ASKED MY
father, "If you could give me just one piece of advice that would help
me live my life, Dad, what would it be?"

"Why is it that sons ask their fathers such ambitious questions?"
He glanced at me as I drove. "Let me think about that one."

My mother arrived from Tucson about an hour after we'd gotten
back home. She looked at me. "Did you find what you were looking
for?"

"Yes," I said. "I wasn't looking for my brother. I was looking for a
piece of me that was missing. I found it." I loved that smile of hers.
"And you know what else? I found out that your husband can be a
talker. But he doesn't know how to make small talk."

"No, he doesn't."

"Mom," I said, "I have never been this happy."

The phone rang. I was hoping it was Dante. I heard his voice. "We
got back early this morning. Dad drove all night. I just woke up from
a nap."

"My dad and I drove in a couple of hours ago."

"And are you okay?"

"Yeah. I'll tell you all about it."

There was a kind of joy in the silence that followed. Yeah, joy.

My parents took my friends and me out for pizza—Dante and Gina and Susie and Cassandra. We were having a good time. Gina and Susie noticed I was wearing their Christmas gift.

"What's that chain around your neck?" Gina asked.

"Jesus."

"Jesus?"

"Yeah," I said. I took out the chain and showed it to her. "These girls I know gave it to me for Christmas. I guess they figured I need Jesus to protect me."

"That was sweet of them," Susie said.

"Well, they're sweet girls—when they're not busy pushing people around."

My dad was getting a big kick out of watching us.

Everybody was having a good time making fun of one another. And Susie had a new theory. She had a mind that was always trying to figure out things—especially gender things. "So, I go out with this guy. I don't know why I said yes. There's something about him that isn't right. And he sees an old girlfriend and he starts telling me what a B—you know the word—she was. And he went on and on about all his old girlfriends and what a bunch of Bs they were. And I thought, *This guy is a misogynist.*

"He tried to make a move on me. So I slapped him. He wasn't

like forcing himself on me or anything like that—but still. But I figured something out. Most misogynists are married to women. They think that being married to a woman means they're not misogynists. Wrong. Think about all those women marching for the right to get the vote. Where were their husbands? They were fighting against the rights of women wanting to get the vote. Misogynists, all of them."

Cassandra nodded. "Well, you finally figured it out."

And Gina said, "You've saved me some research."

"I'm not a misogynist," Dante said.

"Well, neither is Ari. But you guys don't count."

"Why? Because we're gay?"

"Something like that," Cassandra said.

Dante gave her a look that was something like an arrow. "This merits further discussion." He pointed at my parents. "But not around the children." I'd never seen my father laugh so hard.

"That's a nice laugh you got there, Mr. Mendoza." He looked around the room. "So, does anyone have any New Year's resolutions?"

I rolled my eyes. "I hate New Year's resolutions. Nobody keeps them."

"So what?"

"I have one," Susie said. "I'm going to be dating someone by the end of the new year. Someone really nice."

"Oh," Cassandra said, "so you'll be dating a gay guy?"

"Stop it. There are nice straight boys out there."

"Let me know when you find one."

"I have a resolution for you, Cassandra. You're going to stop being so cynical."

"I have a better one," Cassandra said. "I'm going to be a nicer person."

"You *are* a nice person."

"Yeah, but I'm going to let people know."

"I'll be watching you," I said.

"And I'm going to stop giving my mom such a hard time," Dante said.

"That will last until a day after New Year's," I said. "And why ruin a good thing? It's how you get along."

"People can change."

"Let sleeping dogs lie," Susie said.

My mom was getting a big kick out of us. "Well, I'm going to stop working so hard." She said it with conviction.

My dad shook his head. "Lilly, that resolution won't last more than an hour."

My mother looked at my father and said, "You have no idea what a determined woman is capable of."

"Yes, I do. And I still say that your resolution will last about an hour."

She gave my father a look and decided to change the subject. She looked at all of us and said, "Did you know that Jaime and I went on our first date on New Year's Eve? He kissed me. I made the mistake of kissing him back." I loved the look on both my parents' faces. It was true. My parents were still in love.

Dante and I sat on his porch and we talked. And we talked. And we talked. I told him all about the trip and everything that had happened.

He asked me questions and I answered them and didn't hold back. I don't know how long we sat out there on his steps. Sometimes, when I was with Dante, time didn't exist—and I liked that.

He kissed me. It felt strange sometimes to feel another man's lips on mine. But kissing Dante made me happy.

"Happy" was a word that was alive in me now.

"Ari, it's going to be the best year of our lives."

"You think so?"

"Yes, I absolutely think so."

Thirty-One

IT WAS THE SECOND TO LAST DAY OF THE YEAR, AND IT was a beauty of a day. Even if the breeze was cold, the sun was warm, and as I ran, I thought the entire world was blazing with life. The year was ending, and a kind of order seemed to be filling up the chaos in my life. It was as if everything good was converging and everything seemed to make some kind of sense. My brother was gone from my thoughts, and if he ever returned, I would never again suffer from the pain of having loved him as a boy. He would no longer haunt my life or my dreams.

I felt as if the new year would be full of hope and the promise that something rare and beautiful awaited me.

I was happy.

I took a shower after my run and talked to Legs. She was getting old. But her eyes were still bright with life, and she still wagged her tail like a puppy.

I was drinking coffee with my mom, and Legs had her head on my lap. "Your friends are hilarious. Hilarious and wonderful. They're fine people. Behind all that laughing and all that humor, they have very serious young minds. I enjoy their company."

My mom and I talked for a while. She didn't ask about my brother. We had plenty of time to talk about that. Not today.

"I'm going to the grocery store. I want to make a nice New Year's roast. And, of course, menudo for New Year's Eve."

"Why don't you and Dad go dancing?"

"Your father's worst nightmare. The last time we danced was—I can't remember. When it comes to dancing, your father likes to watch. I like staying home. I don't know why, but I feel very close to your father on New Year's Eve. I think he feels the same way. It sounds boring, but we love New Year's Eve. We drink wine and listen to music and talk about the songs we're listening to and why they matter to us. When the clock strikes twelve, he kisses me. And I feel like a girl again."

And she did look like a girl again.

I thought of my mother and father kissing each other at the stroke of midnight as the old year ended and the new year began. I pictured them as two young people holding each other and the worries of the world going away. Just the two of them. Their whole lives still ahead of them.

The house was quiet.

My mother had left for the grocery store, and my father had slept late. I was writing in my journal at the kitchen table.

"Dad, what's wrong?"

He was standing in the doorway to the kitchen, and he was clutching at his chest and having a hard time breathing, and he looked at me, a look of panic on his face, and then fell to the floor.

"Dad! Dad!"

I was holding him, and he was looking up at me, and I didn't know what to do. And he whispered, "Ari," but he couldn't manage to say anything else and I wanted Mom to be here and I didn't know what to do and I wanted to call 911 but I didn't want to let him go as I held him and he hung on to me, he hung on to me and then he just smiled at me and he seemed to be at peace and he looked at me with such a calmness and he whispered, "Liliana." And he whispered her name again. "Liliana."

And I saw the life go out of him and he was motionless and his eyes, which had been so alive, went blank and so far away. And I rocked him in my arms, rocked and rocked him, and I knew I was crying out—but it felt like it was someone else. "No. No. No, no, no, no, no. Dad. Dad. This isn't happening. This isn't happening. No, Dad! Dad!"

Thirty-Two

I DON'T REMEMBER MY MOTHER AS SHE WALKED INTO the house and got down on her knees to kiss my father one last time. I don't remember her making the sign of the cross on his forehead. I don't remember her gently prying my arms away from my father. I don't remember that she took him in her arms and whispered, "*Amor, adios. Adios, amor de mi vida.*" I don't remember the coroner arriving and pronouncing my father dead. And I don't remember the hearse from the funeral home taking my father's body out of the house on a stretcher as I stood by my mother on the front porch and watched them drive away. I do remember thinking that the world had ended and wondering why I was still here, on this earth, in this world that had ended. I don't remember falling. I don't remember everything going dark. My mother recounted all of these things to me later. And she said, "Your father died in your arms. And the weight of it was too much to carry. And your body reacted by just shutting down."

What I remember is waking up on my bed and a man who seemed like he was a doctor was examining me, taking my vitals, a doctor

I later found out was the son of one of the Catholic Daughters. Everything is connected. And everyone seemed to be connected through the women who were members of the Catholic Daughters. He had a kind voice and he said, "You'll be okay. You fainted. Or you passed out. We call it syncope—it happens when your brain isn't getting enough oxygen. A trauma can cause that. For a moment, you simply couldn't breathe. Your father died in your arms. Your body will be fine." He tapped my heart. "But your heart is another matter."

"Did you know my father?"

"Yes. He used to take your older brother and me fishing."

"You were my brother's friend?"

"When we were small. It was just before your father joined the military. Your brother was nice. And then he could be very mean."

"But—but what happened?"

"I'm not sure exactly, but I think your brother had some pain inside him that he took out on other people. I'm sorry."

"It's okay. It's not your fault."

He nodded. He looked at his watch.

"I know you have to go. You didn't have to come."

"Well, your mother called my mother. She didn't really know if you should be taken to the hospital. And she called me—you know how it goes with those women."

We were both smiling. "Yeah, I know."

"They're maddening and annoying and wonderful. I took a break just to check on you."

"So you're a doctor?"

"Not yet. I'm doing an internship."

"What's your name?"

"Oh, I'm sorry. I didn't introduce myself. I'm Jaime."

"That was my father's name."

"I know. It's a great name, isn't it?" He laughed. He was kind. He was so kind. I knew that I felt vulnerable, like all of my emotions were jumping out of my skin. And somehow, I didn't even care. I just let the tears fall from my face.

He had that same look my mother had, that look that seemed to see your pain and respect it. He smiled. "But I gotta say you have the greatest name of them all. Aristotle. Are you as wise as your name?"

"Oh, hell no."

"Someday you will be, I think." He shook my hand. He got up to go. And then he said, "Your father may not exist as a man anymore, but he didn't die, Ari."

"You mean he went to heaven?"

"Oh, I don't know if he did or he didn't. I'm not a believer in the traditional sense. I was raised Catholic like you. But I call God the Great Creator. Science tells us that we are all energy and that we are all connected. And once energy is present in the universe, it doesn't just disappear. Life moves from one form of energy to another. Your father is still very much a part of the universe."

I thought of what Emma had told us in her gallery. *You matter more to the universe than you will ever know.*

"Thank you, Jaime. You're a good man. And you're going to make a fucking great doctor."

He laughed. "I love that word."

We nodded at each other. As he walked out the door, I couldn't help but feel that the universe had brought him to me. Because I'd needed to hear what he'd said.

As soon as Jaime walked out of the room, Dante appeared at the doorway—standing there like some kind of angel. I had always thought he was part angel. His signature tears were running down his face as if my pain was his. And I fell into his arms and I went from being almost calm to being a mess in less than a second. I wanted to tell him to make it all go away. But the only thing I could say through my tears was, "My dad. My dad."

And I felt his body, how strong it was, and how soft his voice was when he said, "If I could bring him back for you, I would. If I could be anybody right now, I'd be Jesus Christ and bring him back to life."

It was such a beautiful thing to say that it sent my tears away.

"Mom? How's Mom?"

"She's in the kitchen with my mom and dad."

I kissed Dante on the cheek. I was so numb. And there was so much chaos in my mind. Everywhere, there was chaos.

Mom and Mrs. Quintana were sitting at the kitchen table, and Mr. Quintana was rocking Sophocles in his arms. I looked at my mother and said, "I don't remember you walking into the house. When I was holding Dad, there was a look of panic, and then he was so calm. He was calm, Mom, like he knew and didn't mind letting go. And he looked at me and he whispered my name. And then he almost had this smile on his face. It was a smile—and he whispered, 'Liliana.' And then he whispered your name one more time—'Liliana.' He wasn't afraid. He let go. But I didn't. I didn't—and I still can't."

"I don't know how to thank you for that, Ari. To know he left this world in peace. To know he wasn't afraid when he died, to know he died in his son's arms, a son whom he loved with all his wounded heart, to know he died with a smile and my name on his lips.

"He was the only man I ever loved. And I was the only woman he ever wanted to love. I have always felt that our marriage was a miracle—maybe because it felt like a miracle, at least to me."

My mother had always had a sense of dignity about her. And though she carried that dignity with her always, it seemed at the moment to be the largest presence in the room. Her tears were quiet, and there was an absence of drama, an absence of self-pity, no asking the question *Why?* Why did he die so young? He was fifty-seven. Four years older than my mother—though my mother seemed ageless. War had aged my father, even as it left my mother untouched. But my mother's dignity could not erase the fact that grief would live in our house for a long time to come.

Dante's hand was on my shoulder. It was as if that hand was holding me up.

Mrs. Quintana was quiet.

"Thank you for bringing Dante over," I said.

She smiled. "I brought me over too," she said. "I brought my family to grieve with yours. I'm old-fashioned in that way."

Mrs. Quintana took my mother's hand, tears running down her

face. Everywhere, tears, tears of sorrow, of grief, of disbelief. Rivers, streams, and where did tears come from and why did people laugh and cry and feel pain and why did emotions come with having a mind and a body? It was all such a mystery, unsolvable and cruel, with a little kindness thrown into the mix. Pain and joy and anger and life and death—everything present all at once—everything reflected in the faces of the people in this room, people I had come to love even as I didn't understand love at all. I remembered reading one of the letters that my aunt Ophelia wrote to my mother, and she'd written: *God has no face but yours. God has no face but mine.* Were we all the face of God? I thought that was a beautiful thing—though I couldn't quite believe that anyone saw God when they looked at my face. Dante's face, yes. My face—not so much.

And Sophocles, his was the face of an innocent God. I smiled at Mr. Quintana. "You certainly know how to hold a baby, Sam."

He handed Sophocles to me. "He's asleep. Holding babies is good therapy." He mussed Dante's hair. "Only Dante doesn't think so."

Dante decided to mess his father's hair up too. That was totally sweet.

"By the way, Ari, you do realize you just referred to me as Sam."

"Oh, shit! I'm sor—"

"No, don't be. It just came out sounding perfectly natural. Not at all disrespectful. So I expect you'll be calling me Sam from now on. Or else—"

"Or else what?" I joked. "You gonna beat me up?"

"Oh, no," he said. "I'd never take it outside with you. You'd have me for lunch."

They were such good people, Dante's parents. Good-natured and they had a sense of fun—and their hearts were brilliant like their minds. Dante was so like them.

"You can call me Soledad, Ari. I wouldn't mind."

"Oh, that one I can't do. No way. But how about 'Mrs. Q'?"

"Mrs. Q." She laughed. "That's brilliant. Absolutely brilliant."

My mom and Mrs. Q went to the mortuary to make arrangements. Sam was walking back and forth, trying to get Sophocles to go to sleep. Dante and I were sitting on the couch and holding hands. It was kind of weird but kind of nice.

Of course, Dante wasn't going to leave it alone. "Is it weird for you to see us holding hands, Dad?"

"A lot of things you do are weird, Dante." He looked at us, then cocked his head to the right, then to the left—and I knew he was going to make a joke of it. "Hmm. I'm not sure you're doing it right. Am I going to have to give you lessons?"

He didn't laugh—but he had that little-boy look on his face.

"So, Professor Quintana, if you were to assign me a grade, what grade would I get?"

"Well, if I would have to assign each of you a grade, I'd give you a C, Dante. You're just trying too hard. Not at all relaxed. Ari gets a D. He looks like he's about to die of embarrassment." And he was right.

"I make jokes sometimes. I like to play around. But I don't want you to feel ashamed of who you are. Things can be awkward and uncomfortable, yes, so what? Two boys holding hands. One of them is my son. Is that a crime?" Where are the cops when you need them?

"Will you take the baby, Dante? I need to step outside and get a breath of fresh air." Dante took Sophocles in his arms and we both kind of doted on him.

Sam stepped outside.

"Your dad okay? He seems sad."

"He really loved your dad."

"I hadn't thought about that."

I decided to step outside to see if Sam was okay. He was sitting on the front steps and sobbing. I sat next to him. "Sorry," he said. "I just lost a good friend today. A very passionate and wise and good friend. I don't want to grieve in front of you. It seems disrespectful. What is my grief compared to yours?"

"You know what my father would have said?"

"Yeah, I think so. He would have said something like, *Sam, it's not a contest.*"

"Yup, that's what he would have said." We sat there for a moment.

"The world seems so quiet."

"It does, doesn't it?" I said. "Sam, I don't know how to say this. I guess I want to thank you for your grief. Maybe that's what I want to say. Because it means that you loved him. I don't have him anymore. But I have you."

"You're turning into one helluva man right before my eyes."

"I'm just a kid."

"No, you're not."

I don't know how long we sat there. "This feeling, this grief, this sorrow. It's a new thing. It seems like it owns me."

"It does own you, Ari. But it won't own you forever."

"That's good to know."

As we walked back inside, we heard Dante's voice. "Sophocles! You just pooped all over the map of the world."

Sam and I busted out laughing. "That's why we keep Dante around. He's always good for comic relief."

"Yeah, well, now I have to go change him."

"It's a rough life, Dante."

"Don't go there, Dad," he said, though he was smiling.

I watched Dante as he took off his baby brother's diaper. Mrs. Q had a service that delivered cloth diapers. Dante sang to him, *"The wheels on the bus go round and round.* Little man, you really made a mess this time." Dante grabbed a small plastic tub—and we both bathed Sophocles in the kitchen sink. He was squealing and gurgling and making noises. "Here," Dante said, "dry him off."

"You're kinda bossy."

"I get it from my mother. Take it up with her." He kissed me on the cheek and took Sophocles from my arms. He placed a soft folded towel on the kitchen table. He knew what he was doing. I'm sure Mrs. Q was a strict teacher.

He took Sophocles from my arms. "Look at you, all clean, Mr. Sophocles." I loved the way Sophocles looked up at him. He took a clean diaper out. "Sing to him, Ari. He likes people to sing to him."

"Let's see," I said. *"Hush, little baby, don't say a word. Mama's gonna get you a mockingbird"*—and then Dante was singing too. And we sang—and Dante held Sophocles in his arms, and we sang. And he had the most amazing look on his face. And I really wanted to ask him, *Sophocles, did you come into the world to comfort us? To give us hope?*

I noticed Sam standing in the doorway, and he was singing too. I thought of my dad, when we'd sung together along with Paul McCartney.

It's strange to wake up and then realize that there is sadness in the house. And there is sadness everywhere inside you. I knew that Jaime the almost doctor was right. That once the energy of something living enters the world, it never dies, and that we are, and always will be, connected. But my father didn't live in this house anymore. And I felt cheated. Just when my father had learned to be my father and I had learned to be his son, he left this world.

And I would never hear his voice again.

And I would never see him sitting in his chair reading a book, never see that pensive look on his face, not ever again.

And I would never see him walk in through the door wearing his mail carrier uniform, that look that said, *I've done my job today*.

And I would never smell the lingering scent of cigarettes in the room again.

And I would never see those looks that he and my mother passed between them.

I got up and took a shower. I knew my sisters would be coming from Tucson and that the house would be crowded, and I had no idea when they were arriving. For some strange reason, I felt so alone as I took a shower and I wished Dante was here. I had never taken a shower with him, and I wondered what that would be like. I supposed men and women did that all the time. And then I just said, *Stop, stop, stop with all this thinking.*

My mother was sitting at the kitchen table talking to someone on the phone and having a cup of coffee. I poured myself a cup and kissed her on the top of her head. When she hung up the phone, she said, "I know this may be a little rough for you, but will you write your father's obituary so we can have it to the newspaper by one o'clock? And will you hand it to the people at the front desk? They'll take it from there."

Like I was going to say no. I'd never written an obituary before.

My mother had written some notes on a notepad. "You might want to include this information." And she'd cut out several sample obituaries from the pile of newspapers she kept to recycle.

"Mom, you are the quintessential schoolteacher."

"Thank you—I think."

"And one more thing," she said. I could tell that what she was going to ask me to do next was going to be lot harder than writing an obituary. "Will you honor your father by giving his eulogy?"

I think we both wanted to start crying again—but we refused to do it out of sheer stubbornness.

"Oh, your father kept a journal sporadically. I have the others put away. Sometimes he wrote in it every day. Sometimes he'd go weeks without writing in it. But I want you read the last entry." She handed me the journal. I turned it to the last page that had writing on it.

Ari asked me if there was one piece of advice I could give him that would help him live his life. I thought it was a very ambitious question, but I have a very ambitious son. We had been so distant that I thought I would never hear my son ask me for any advice. But we've earned the love we have between us, I think. I see him and I think, How can a young man so rare and so sensitive and beautiful have come from me? The answer is easy: He came from Liliana. What advice would I give to Ari to help him live his life? I would tell him this: Never do anything to prove to anyone else, or even to prove to yourself, that you're a man. Because you are a man.

I kept staring at his words and at his handwriting. "Can I have this, Mom?"

She nodded. Neither one of us had anything to say. But I promised myself that I would live my life according to those words, because if I did, then I would always be able to look at myself in the mirror and call myself his son.

My mother was making a list, and I was writing a draft of my father's obituary on a legal pad of paper. I heard the doorbell ring. "I'll get it." And when I opened the door, there stood Mrs. Alvidrez, holding an apple pie.

"Hi," I said.

"I was very saddened to hear of your father's passing. He was an honorable man."

"Thank you," I said.

My mother had come to the door, and I stepped aside.

"I know I'm not welcome in your house, Liliana. You have your reasons, and I am not here to disrespect you or your house." I couldn't see, but I could hear what was happening and it seemed to me that Mrs. Alvidrez was fighting back tears. "Jaime was a good man. And I know that your grief must be a heavy weight. He loved my apple pies, so I thought I'd . . ." And then she stopped in midsentence. And I knew that she was struggling to hold back her tears. If she was anything, she was a fiercely proud woman.

"Come in, Lola. Come in and have a cup of coffee with me and we'll eat some apple pie and you can tell me what you remember of Jaime so that I will remember that part of him. I was angry the last time you were here. But you are always welcome in this house."

I was sitting on the couch in the living room. My mother took the pie from Mrs. Alvidrez and handed it to me. Then she hugged Mrs. Alvidrez and the two women wept into each other's shoulders. "Thank you for coming, Lola. Thank you."

When the tears were done, my mother took the pie from my hands and they both walked into the kitchen. I kept working on my draft of my father's obituary and then I shook my head. I heard laughter coming from the kitchen.

My mom and Mrs. Alvidrez—their connection mattered. And they respected that connection. It was true, adults were teachers. They taught you things by how they behaved. And just now, my mom and Mrs. Alvidrez taught me a word Cassandra had begun to teach me: "forgiveness." It was a word that needed to live inside me. I had a feeling that if that word didn't live inside me, the word "happiness" would never live inside me either.

My mom and Mrs. Alvidrez were in the kitchen—and they were laughing. They had lost something valuable. And that thing of great value had returned. Forgiveness.

Thirty-three

THE HOUSE WAS FULL OF PEOPLE. THE LIVING COMING to pay their tributes to the dead. Already I was tired of the tears and the sadness—even though I went into the backyard to cry off and on. Legs would follow me and lick my tears away, and I told her that she had better not ever die. This thing of losing your father was a kind of hell I didn't want to live in. But it wasn't as if I had a choice.

I knew that death didn't only happen to me. I knew that hundreds, if not thousands of people would die today, some of them in accidents, some of them killed for no reason, some of them from cancer.

I remembered the banner of the protesters: ONE AIDS DEATH EVERY 12 MINUTES. Who would go to their funerals? Who would give their eulogies? Who would praise their lives? Who would sing their names?

I was thinking that, somewhere, a man with AIDS died at the same hour as my father.

And maybe a woman's child died in a hospital in London, and maybe a wealthy man who was once a Nazi now hiding in Bogotá took his last breath.

And maybe seven people died in a terrible explosion in a country we know as Syria.

And there was a murder taking place in Grand Rapids, Michigan.

And a man and his wife died instantly in a terrible car accident.

And somewhere it was spring and a nest of tiny sparrows were singing for food. And Legs was sitting beside me in my truck as I drove to Dante's house to write a eulogy for my father, who just a few days before had told me the story of how he met and fell in love with my mother.

And Sophocles, not a month old, was already connected to the land of the living and the dying.

Thirty-Four

NEW YEAR'S EVE. MY MOTHER WOULD NOT BE KISSING my father. Dante and I would not be going to the party that Gina had invited us to—though it wasn't her party to be inviting people. I wasn't so hopeful about the new year anymore. My mother was talking to my sisters, and it seemed they were planning everything out. There was something very practical about all three of them. Maybe that's what made them all such good schoolteachers.

I was staring blankly at the Christmas tree, and I had gone downstairs to find Tito, the bear my sisters had given me when I was an infant and that I'd slept with until I was six.

I kept staring at him, and then I just held that bear and I didn't feel stupid. Tito seemed to give me comfort even though his soft fur was worn and not so soft anymore.

I heard the doorbell ring. I opened the door and saw Mrs. Ortega and Cassandra standing on our front porch. Mrs. Ortega was carrying a large pot, and I knew it was menudo by the smell. "Take this, will you, Ari? It's a little heavy for me." I took the pot of menudo as Cassandra handed her mother the big bag of *bolillos* she was carrying and held the door open. They followed me into the kitchen. "Mom, Mrs. Ortega brought some menudo." My mom shook her head, and her eyes rained tears again. The two women embraced.

"Ay, Liliana, como me puede. Era tan lindo, tu esposo."

Cassandra hugged my mother, and softly she said, "I'm so sorry, Mrs. Mendoza. He was a good man."

She knew how to behave like a woman, and she seemed perfectly at ease in what I would have found to be an awkward situation. Cassandra grabbed my hand and we went into the living room. "Dante and Susie and Gina are coming over. We wanted to spend New Year's Eve with you."

"I'm really not up for company. I'm sorry, that was rude. I'm just tired—hell, Cassandra, I'm just sad. I've never been this sad and I don't know what to do and I just want to fucking hide somewhere and not come out until it stops hurting."

"Ari, not a day goes by that I don't think of my brother. It will be a long time before it stops hurting. But you're not a possum. You can't play dead."

At that moment, I didn't feel as if I had any tears left in me. I just sat there wishing I were a chair or a couch or a cement floor—anything inanimate—anything that didn't feel.

"We're you're friends. We don't need to be entertained. And we're not here to cheer you up, either. We're just here to let you know we love you. So let us love you, Ari. It's a beautiful thing to let the people you love see your pain."

"It isn't pretty."

"You don't listen. I said it was beautiful."

"I have a choice?"

"Actually, you do."

Just then the doorbell rang—not that they waited for me to answer the door. The three of them just walked in. When I saw them, I wasn't mad. I thought I would be—but I wasn't. As Dante would have put it, they were such lovely people. I just stood there and started crying. Apparently, I did have some tears left in me. And each one of them just hugged me and they didn't say stupid things like *Don't cry* or *Be a man* and they didn't utter clichés like *He's in a better place*. They just held me. They just held me and respected my grief.

We sat around the Christmas tree, and we mostly were lying on the floor. I used Dante's stomach for a pillow. We heard the women's voices in the other room and sometimes their conversations grew serious and sometimes we heard laughter. Cassandra saw Tito lying on the couch. "Who is this?"

"That's Tito," I said. "He was my bear when I was a baby, and I slept with him until I was six."

"Who would have ever guessed?"

"Are you gonna make fun of me? I mean, everybody had a Tito or someone like him."

"I think it's totally sweet. But me, I never liked stuffed animals."

"Me neither," Dante said.

"You didn't?" I was really surprised. "Wow. So much for Mr. Sensitive."

"What did you hug, Dante? A dictionary?" Susie was wearing that smug smile of hers.

Everybody laughed. Even Dante.

"I had a doll," Gina said, "but, you know, I wasn't all that attached to her. One day when I was mad, I decapitated her."

I needed that. A good laugh.

"I had a rag doll named Lizzie. I tried to teach her to call me Susie. She never learned. I used to pull her hair out. I got mad at her one day and made her sleep under the bed."

"Seriously? Of all the people sitting in this room, I'm the un-nicest, and I'm the one who's sentimental about a stuffed bear?"

"Excuse me," Cassandra said, "but I'm the un-nicest person here. Don't try to move in on my turf."

"You're plenty nice."

"Well, yeah, we all know that. But I have a reputation to live up to—and we can't let the word get out."

Dante held Tito by the shoulders. "Sorry, dude, but I'm Ari's Tito now."

"And I'm your Tito," Susie said.

"Me too," Gina said.

"And me," Cassandra said. "We're all your Tito. And we're going to see you through this, Ari. We promise."

And right then I knew that they would all be my friends forever. I knew they would always be in my life. I knew that I would always love them. Until the day I died.

• • •

We were all gathered in the kitchen at midnight, eating menudo. Even Dante was eating menudo. "Someday you're going to be a real Mexican."

"But will I ever be a real American? That's the question. It used to be my last name that was an impediment. But now I think it's the fact that I'm gay that's the real impediment to being a fully enfranchised American citizen. See, a gay man is not a real man, and if I'm not a real man, then I can't really be an American. I think there are people all over this nation who are invoking Scotty's name."

"Scotty?"

"Yeah, Scotty from *Star Trek*. They're begging for Scotty to beam me up, beam me up and leave me off on the planet Klingon."

"They'll have to beam me up with you."

"I was hoping you'd say that. You'll come in handy if we have to fight off one of the Klingons."

Dante looked at his watch—then his eyes met Susie's.

"Tonight I'm Dick Clark, and it's time for the New Year's count-down . . . ten, nine, eight, seven, six, five, four, three, two, one, HAPPY NEW YEAR!"

Susie found a radio and "Auld Lang Syne" was playing. I hugged my mother first, and whispered, "I know I'm not much of a stand-in for Dad."

"I don't need a stand-in," she whispered. "I have what I need to get me through—and that means you." She kissed me on the cheek and combed my hair with her fingers. "Happy New Year, Ari."

Not even her grief could rob her of that smile.

Dante kissed me. We didn't say anything to each other. We just looked into each other's eyes with a kind of wonder.

My sisters hugged me, kissed me, both of them telling me how glad they were that I looked like our father.

There may not have been a lot of happiness in the kitchen that night. But there was a lot of love.

And maybe that was even better.

Thirty-Five

NEW YEAR'S DAY 1989. SUNDAY.

I went to Mass with my mom and my sisters and their husbands and my nephews and nieces.

I felt numb. There was something dead in me. It was hard for me to talk. After Mass, the priest spoke to my mother. So many people knew my mother. People hugged her, and there was a kind of beauty in the words they used when they spoke to her.

I wanted to be anywhere but there.

I wanted to go home and find my father sitting on the front porch, waiting for us.

I just wanted the day to be over.

And then Monday would come.

And then Tuesday would come and the final semester of my senior year would begin—but I would not be going to school. I would be going to my father's funeral.

Thirty-Six

Dear Dante,

I keep repeating to myself, my father is dead my father is dead my father is dead. *I write and rewrite my father's eulogy—* my father is dead my father is dead my father is dead. *I look out the window to see if he is in the backyard smoking a cigarette—*my father is dead my father is dead my father is dead. *He is sitting across from me at the kitchen table and I hear him telling me what I know but refuse to accept: "The problem is not that Dante is in love with you. The problem is that you're in love with Dante."* My father is dead my father is dead my father is dead.

Dante, I'm so sad. My heart hurts. It hurts. I don't know what to do.

Thirty-Seven

DANTE COMES OVER IN THE AFTERNOON. HE TELLS ME
it looks like I've been crying. I tell him I'm tired. We escape to my
room and we lie down on my bed and I fall asleep as he holds me. I
keep repeating, *My father is dead my father is dead my father is dead.*

Thirty-Eight

I'D ATTACHED MY FATHER'S DOG TAGS TO THE CROSS Gina and Susie had given me. When I got out of the shower, I put them on. I stared at myself. I shaved. My father had taught me how to do that. When I was a small boy, I would watch him in wonder. I got dressed and looked at myself in the mirror as I tied my tie. My father had taught me how to tie a tie the day before I made my First Communion. I tied my shoelaces. My father had taught me how to do that, too. I was surrounded by him, my father.

It was strange to follow my father's casket as the eight pallbearers walked beside it, four on each side. Sam Quintana was one of my father's pallbearers, and Susie's father was too. Over many years they had discussed books, a fact I had only recently become aware of because I had paid so little attention to my father's life. The rest of the pallbearers were mail carriers. My mother and I walked down the aisle arm in arm. My sisters and their husbands followed behind.

I tried to pay attention to the Mass, but I was too distracted. I was nervous about giving my father's eulogy and the church was full, all of the Catholic Daughters dressed in white and sitting together—including Mrs. Alvidrez.

Dante and Mrs. Q and Sophocles were sitting behind us. I wasn't paying attention to the priest when he began his sermon. I could see the priest's lips moving—but it seemed as though I had lost my hearing.

After communion, the priest motioned to me. My mother squeezed my hand. I felt Dante's hand on my shoulder. I rose from the pew and made my way to the pulpit. I reached in my pocket and unfolded the eulogy that I'd written for my father. My heart was racing. I had never spoken in front of a church full of people. I froze. I closed my eyes and thought of my father. I wanted him to be proud of me. I opened my eyes. I looked out at the sea of people. I saw my sisters and my mother clothed in their grief. I looked at the words I'd written—and began:

"My father worked for the US Postal Service. He was a mail carrier, and he was proud of what he did. He was proud to be a public servant, and he was far prouder of his service to this country as a mail carrier than his service to his country as a soldier.

"My father fought in a war, and he brought a piece of that war with him when he came back home. He was a silent man for many years but, a little at a time, he broke that silence. He told me that one lesson he learned in Vietnam was that every human life is sacred. But later he told me, people say that all lives are sacred but they're lying to themselves. My father hated a few things; racism was one of them. He said he worked hard to rid himself of his own racism. And that is what made my father a great man. He didn't blame other people for the problems of the world. He pointed to the problems of the world within himself and fought a battle to rid himself of them.

"My mother gave me the journal my father was keeping. My father filled the pages of several journals over the years, and I was going through them as I was trying to figure out what I wanted to say. Reading a passage was like sitting inside his brain. When I was thirteen and fourteen and fifteen, I longed to know what my father was thinking, this silent man who seemed to be living in the memory of a war that left his heart and mind wounded. But he was far more present than I imagined him to be. I had no idea who my father was. And so I made him up. Which brings me to this entry he wrote when I was fourteen years old:

"'America is the country of invention. We are a people who constantly invent and reinvent ourselves. Mostly our inventions of who we are are fictions. We invent who Black people are and make them out to be violent and criminal. But our inventions are about us and not about them. We invent who Mexicans are, and we become nothing more than a people who eat tacos and break piñatas. We invent reasons to fight wars because war is what we know, and we make those wars into heroic marches toward peace, when there is nothing heroic about war. Men are killed in wars. Young men. We tell ourselves they died to protect our freedoms—even when we know that is a lie. I find it a tragedy that such an inventive people cannot bring themselves to invent peace.

"'My son Ari and I are fighting a war. We are fighting a war with ourselves and with each other. We have resorted to inventing each other. My son dislikes me—but he is disliking his own invention.

And I am doing the same. I wonder if we will ever find a way out of this war. I wonder if we will ever be brave enough to call a truce, imagine peace, and finally see each other for who we are and stop this nonsense of inventing.'

"My father and I did finally manage to stop the war we were fighting. I stopped inventing him and finally saw him for who he was. And he saw me.

"My father cared about the world he lived in. He thought we could do a lot better, and I think he was right, and I loved that he cared about things that were bigger than the smaller world he lived in. In one journal entry he wrote: 'There are no reasons to hate other people—especially other kinds of people. We make up reasons why other people are less human than we are. We make up reasons and then we believe those reasons and then those reasons become true and they are true because now we believe they are facts and we even forget where it all started—with a reason we made up.'

"My father wasn't just my father. He was a man. He was a man aware of the larger world around him. He loved art and read books about art. He had several books on architecture, and he read them. He had a curious mind and he wanted to know things and he didn't think he was the center of the universe and he didn't think that what he thought and what he felt were the only things that mattered. And that made him a humble man. And I'm going to quote him here. He said, 'Humility is in short supply in this country, and it would be a good thing if we went in search of it.'

"My father not only went in search of humility, he found it. When he died, he died of a heart attack—and he died in my arms whispering my name and whispering the name of my mother. I thought of a story he once recounted to me of a young soldier who died in his arms. The young soldier asked my father to hold him. He had been a man barely an hour, my father said. And the young soldier, who was Jewish, asked my father as he died, 'Tell my mom and dad. Tell them I'll see them next year in Jerusalem.'

"My father went to Los Angeles for the purpose of delivering that message to his parents. Now, some people would think that only a special kind of man would do such a thing. But he would quote my mother, the schoolteacher who is as proud of what she does as my father was proud of what he did, saying, 'You don't get extra credit for doing what you're supposed to do.'

"My mom and dad and I traveled to Washington, DC, one summer. I was about nine or ten. My father wanted to see the Vietnam Memorial. More than fifty-eight thousand soldiers died in Vietnam. He said, 'Now they are not just numbers. They were human beings who had names. And now, at least, we have written their names on the map of the world.' He found the names of the men who had been killed in Vietnam who had fought alongside him. He traced each name with his finger. It was the first time I ever saw my father cry.

"My father traced his name on my heart. And his name will remain there. And because his name lives in me, I will be a better man for it. My name is Aristotle Mendoza, and if today you ask me who I am, I will look you in the eye and say to you: I am my father's son."

• • •

I looked into my mother's eyes as I finished. Tears were running down her face, and she was standing, and she was clapping, applauding, proud. And I saw my sisters and Dante, standing, applauding. And then I realized that all of the people gathered in that church were standing, applauding. All of those people—their applause, I knew it wasn't for me. It was for the man they had come to honor. And I was proud.

Thirty-Nine

IT WAS A MILITARY FUNERAL. AND THE TRUMPETER played out taps, the solitary notes disappearing into the clear blue desert sky, and the seven soldiers pointed their guns up to that same blue sky and shot off a round of bullets—and those shots echoed in my ears. Then another round of shots and then another. And the soldiers folded the flag in that careful ceremonial way they had learned—and one of the soldiers handed the flag to my mother and whispered, "From a grateful nation," but I did not think those words were true, and I did not think that my father would have thought those words were true either. My father loved his country. Sometimes I think he loved it more than he could bear. But he was a man who sought the truth, and I knew he did not believe those words were honest.

The priest gave my mother the crucifix and then hugged her and then he stood in front of me and said to me in a whisper as he shook my hand: "The words you spoke today—those were not the words of a boy—those were the words of a man." I know he meant what he said—but I knew better. I was not a man.

$\bullet \quad \bullet \quad \bullet$

My sisters and my mother made their way back to the black funeral limousines. But I stayed behind. And I stood there alone, wanting to say good-bye even though I'd said good-bye already—but no, that wasn't true. I knew I would be saying good-bye for a long time to come. I didn't want any of this to be true, and I didn't know how to let go. I stared at his casket, and I thought of his tears as he knelt at the Vietnam memorial. I thought of it in the cold as we looked up at the stars and how soft it was when he told me the story of how he met my mother and how he'd loved her from the start.

"Dad," I whispered, "next year in Jerusalem." What I felt—it was an awful pain. I didn't know that I'd fallen to my knees. There didn't seem to be anything but darkness all around me.

And then I found myself surrounded by Dante and Susie and Gina and Cassandra, and I felt Dante pulling me and holding me up. And my friends, they were all as silent as I was, but I knew they were saying that they loved me and that they were reminding me that we were all connected. They stood with me. And then I heard Cassandra singing "Bridge Over Troubled Water" and then Dante joined his voice to hers and then Susie and Gina. And at that moment, they sounded like a choir of angels—and I never thought I could love this much or hurt this much.

And even though a part of me felt like it had died, another part of me felt alive.

Dante walked me to my car and whispered, "I'll see you back at the reception." When I approached the limousine, I could see my mother was standing outside the car and she was talking to a man.

As I got closer, I saw who the man was. "Mr. Blocker?"

"Ari," he said.

"Aren't you supposed to be teaching?"

"I had something more important to do today."

"You came. You came to my father's funeral."

"I did." He looked at me and nodded. "I was just telling your mother that I was very moved by what you wrote. Well done, Ari. I was sitting next to a woman and her husband, and after all that applause died down, I said to them, 'He's my student.' I was proud. I was, and am, very proud of you." He shook my hand. He looked into my eyes and nodded. He turned to my mother and hugged her and said, "He may be his father's son. But he is very much your son too, Liliana." He turned and slowly walked away.

"He's a fine man," my mother said.

"Yes, he is," I said.

"It says something about his character that he came to Jaime's funeral. And it also says something about yours." I opened the car door for her. "And I want a copy of the eulogy you wrote for your father."

"I'll just give it you."

"I'll give it back to you when I die."

"I hope you never die."

"We can't live forever."

"I know. I was thinking that the world won't mourn for guys like me and Dante when we die. The world doesn't want us in it."

"I don't give a damn what the world thinks or wants," she said. "I don't want to live in a world without you or Dante in it."

Forty

WHEN I GOT HOME, I CHANGED INTO SOME OLD JEANS
and a T-shirt. I sat in the living room and tried to have a conversation with my sisters. But it was like I couldn't hear. And I couldn't talk. I guess my mother was watching me. She took me by the hand and led me to my room. "Get some sleep. All you need right now is sleep."

"No," I said, "all I need right now is Dad."

She combed my hair with her fingers. "Get some rest."

"'But I have promises to keep.'"

"'And miles to go before I sleep.'"

We smiled at each other, and our smiles were sad. And then I said, "Some children leave, some children stay, but, Mom, I'll never go away."

"You will someday."

"No. Never."

"Sleep."

Forty-One

WHEN I WOKE UP, IT WAS LATE, ALMOST NOON. LEGS was still asleep. She was sleeping more and more. She was getting old. But she was still a great sleeping companion. I petted her. "Let's get up." She barked softly. "Mom will make us breakfast." I wondered when this strange sadness would lift.

I put on my jeans, slipped on a T-shirt, and headed for the kitchen to have a cup of coffee.

The house was quiet—except for my mom's voice and the voices of my sisters.

"Morning," I said.

"It's afternoon."

"What's your point?" I gave Emmy a crooked smile. "I need coffee."

Vera kept looking at me. "You really look like a grown-up."

"Don't judge a book by its cover." I poured myself a cup of coffee. I sat down next to Mom. "How come it's so quiet?"

"The husbands took the kids to see their grandparents. My in-laws were very impressed by you, Ari."

"They're nice people."

"Still don't know how to take compliments." Emmy was looking more and more like Mom.

"Compliments are nice. But, well, what am I supposed to say? I don't like getting all that attention."

"You're just like Dad," Vera said.

"I wish I were."

"Ari, it makes us happy to know that you and dad stopped fighting with each other."

"Me too, Emmy. But just when we'd gotten so close—it doesn't seem fair." I sort of laughed. "Dad hated the *That's not fair* thing."

"I didn't know that."

"I know exactly what your father thought when people said *It's not fair*. But I decline to enter this conversation you're having with your sisters."

"Why? Because they never happen?"

My two sisters nodded.

I looked at them. "Since I have taken steps to try to not hate myself anymore, I will not blame myself for the lack of communication among the three of us. I will only take one-third of the blame."

"Well, we were older," Vera said. "Maybe you should take only one-fourth of the blame. And I can take one-fourth of the blame— and Emmy will take half of the blame. She's the oldest, and she likes being in charge."

"Because I'm the bigger person—" Emmy began, which made us all laugh, which even made her join in the laughter. "Okay, since I'm so bossy, it's one-third everybody's fault that we two haven't made all that big of an effort to reach out to you, Ari. Let's make a better effort."

"Well," I said, "in Dad's universe, when people say it's not fair, they're not really talking about fairness."

"What's it about, then?"

"He said all we're doing is letting the world know how selfish we are. We're making an assumption and also making an accusation. It's all in one of his journal entries. Would you like to read them? When I finish reading them, I'll send them to you, so you can read them too. And if you don't send them back to me, I'll have to drive to Tucson and steal them back."

"I'd like that," said Vera.

"Well, will you look at that," Emmy said. "Little Ari has learned to share."

I looked at Emmy and nodded. "Nice. And you were doing so well. But you had to screw it up."

"I like this pretend fighting more than I liked the other kind of fighting."

Vera was always the kindhearted peacemaker. She was so nice. Both of my sisters were nice.

"I want to say I'm jealous," Vera said, "of what you and Dad had. But I'm not. It makes me really happy that you fought your way toward each other. All that quiet living inside Dad and all that stubbornness living inside you, Ari—but you made it happen."

"You *did* make it happen." Emmy was nodding and smiling. "It's like that passage from Dad's journal you read in your eulogy. We do invent who other people are. And we invent ourselves. And we can have very unpretty and very ungenerous imaginations."

Mom laughed. "It's true." She reached over and took my hand

in hers. "As sad as I am about your father's death, right now, in this moment, I'm happy. And all of my children are here."

And Emmy whispered, "Except Bernardo."

"Oh, he's here," my mother said. She tapped her heart. "He has never left. He will always be here."

I had no idea how my mother had learned to bear all her losses.

Happiness. Sorrow. Emotions were fickle things. Sadness, joy, anger, love. How did the universe think to invent emotions and insert them into human beings? My father, I suppose, would call them gifts. But maybe our emotions were part of the problem. Maybe our love would save us. Or maybe our hate would destroy the earth and everybody in it. *Ari. Ari, Ari, Ari, can't you ever just give it a rest from thinking and thinking and thinking?*

What was I feeling right now? I didn't know. I just didn't know. How did I explain not knowing what it was I felt?

When my sisters left to visit their in-laws, I went to my room. I was reading one of my father's journals, and I could hear his voice in them—and it didn't feel like he was dead. It felt like he was in the room, sitting in my rocking chair and reading to me.

I decided I'd take the journal I was reading and sit on the front steps. It was cool outside, but the sun seemed to break through the unusually cold day. I headed for the front steps of the house. I don't know why, but it was one of my favorite spots. It was one of my mother's favorite spots too.

I found the place where I'd left off, and just as I started reading, my mother came out and sat right next to me. "Read me the part you're reading."

"He copied his favorite passage from the Bible."

"Read it to me."

"'For everything there is a season, and a time for every purpose under heaven: a time to be born, and a time to die . . .'

"And then Dad writes: 'I have refrained from embracing for too long—now it is time for me to embrace. My time for silence has passed—now it is my time to speak. I have had my time to weep—now it is my time to laugh. My time to hate has passed. And now it is my time to love. I'm going to ask Liliana to marry me.'"

She leaned into my shoulder. "He never let me read them."

"We can read them together now, Mom. How did he ask you to marry him?"

"I'd just gotten out of a night class. We went for a walk. 'What's different about me?' he asked. I kept looking at him. 'Are you better-looking today than you were yesterday?' He shook his head. 'You got a haircut.' He shook his head. And then on the street corner of Oregon and Boston, your father put my hand on his heart. 'Do you feel my heartbeat?' I nodded. 'That's what's different. Today, when I woke up, my heart was stronger.' He put his hand on my cheek. 'Will you be poor with me?' And I said, 'I won't ever be poor as long as you love me.' And then I kissed him and said, 'Yes.'"

I remembered Dante telling me that he could never run away from home. *I'm crazy about my parents.* It had taken me a lot longer to be crazy about mine.

My mother and I sat in our own silence for a while, and the cool wind blew on our faces and it made me feel alive. There were clouds in the distance, and I could smell the rain. It was like my father was sending me what I loved most. Or maybe it was the universe that was sending me the rain. Or maybe it was God. Maybe it didn't matter. Everything was connected.

The living were connected to the dead. And the dead were connected to the living. And the living and the dead were all connected to the universe.

The World, the Universe, and Aristotle and Dante

There have been explosions in the universe for billions of years—explosions that give birth to a world breathing with new life. The universe creates.

We live on a planet that is a part of that universe. And though we are only a speck, a tiny particle, we, too, are a part of that universe. Everything is connected and everything belongs. Everything that is alive carries the breath of the universe. Once something is born—a dog, a tree, a lizard, a human being—it becomes essential to the universe and never dies.

The earth does not know the word "exile." Violence begins in the dark and stubborn riots of the human heart. The human heart is the source of all our hate—and all our love. We must tame our wild hearts—or we will never understand the spark of the universe that lives within us all.

To live and never to understand the strange and beautiful mysteries of the human heart is to make a tragedy of our lives.

One

DANTE CAME OVER. I WAS STARING AT MY JOURNAL. But I didn't have any words living in me just then. Sometimes words ran away just when you needed them to stay.

"I'm going back to school tomorrow."

He nodded. "Ari, you look so sad. And all this love I have for you, it can't make you un-sad. I wish I could take all your pain away."

"But the pain is mine, Dante. And you can't have it. If you took it away, I would miss it."

I walked Dante home in the cold. We took the backstreets and I held his hand and there was a silence between us that felt better than a conversation. I kissed him in front of his house, and he combed my hair with his fingers like my mother did. And that made me smile.

As I walked back home, I looked up at the stars and whispered, "Dad, which one are you?"

Two

I WENT BACK TO SCHOOL ON THURSDAY. MY LAST
semester of high school. I felt far away. A little empty. A little numb.
I felt like crying. But I knew I wasn't going to cry. Mr. Blocker asked
me how I was doing. I shrugged. "I'm not sure."

"I'm going to say something stupid. It will get better over time."

"I guess so."

"I'm going to stop talking now."

He made me smile.

The students seemed to flood into the classroom.

Susie and Gina walked up to me as I sat at my desk. They both
kissed me on the cheek.

"Nice," Chuy yelled from the back of the room.

Mr. Blocker shook his head and smiled.

"For the next three weeks we're going to take a crack at poetry."

There were groans.

"It gets better," he said. "You're going to have the opportunity to
write a poem."

It was good to be back at school. I was going to make an attempt—
at getting back to normal.

I don't remember what went on in class.

I honestly don't remember anything about that day—except for listening to Cassandra's voice as she gave Susie and Gina a lecture on her theories about male privilege. And I remember saying, "Stop! My balls are shrinking."

I felt that I was living in the land of the dead. But I knew that I had to return to the land of the living—that's where I belonged.

My father was dead. But I wasn't.

Three

I WOKE UP TO THE SOUND OF MY MOTHER SOBBING. I
knew her sadness was much greater than mine. She had loved my
dad for a long, long time. They had slept in the same bed, listened to
each other's problems, cared for each other. And now he was gone.
And I lay there in my bed, sad and paralyzed. *Oh, Mom, I'm sorry.
What can I do?* But I knew there was nothing I could do. Her pain
was hers alone. Just as mine was mine alone. No one could heal it.
The wound would have to heal itself.

I didn't know if I should go to her or just let her grieve. And then
there was silence. I waited for her sobs to start again.

She must have fallen back asleep. And then my own sobs filled
the room. I don't remember how long it took before I cried myself
to sleep.

Four

I WAS HAVING COFFEE WITH MY MOM. "I HEARD YOUR
pain last night."

"I heard yours," she said.

I don't know why, but we smiled at each other.

Five

DANTE WAS ON THE PHONE. AND HE WAS TALKING AND talking. Sometimes he talked too much and it was a little annoying. But sometimes I loved that he talked so much. "We're almost done, Ari. We're kicking ass."

"Is this Dante pretending to be Ari?"

"You know, I sometimes do talk like everybody else that passes you in the hallway."

"Well, that's too bad."

"Just be quiet. I'm talking about how we are almost done with this thing called high school and I'm just fuckin' excited about it. Good-bye, all-boys Catholic school."

"And this coming from a guy who likes guys."

"Not the guys from Cathedral. I like this guy who goes to Austin High."

"Tell me about him."

"Nope. I don't kiss and tell."

"I'm going to hang up now."

"I'm crazy about you."

"Yeah, yeah, you're just plain crazy."

Really, it was me who was crazy. I was crazy for him. Or like some of the women in the movies. They're mad about the guy they're in love with. Madly in love. Yeah. That was an expression I think I understood. See, love wasn't about thinking, it was a kind of state that affected the entire body with this thing called desire. Or want. Or whatever the hell you wanted to call it. And it made you mad with desire. Or just mad. Or just plain crazy. I was crazy. I was. I admit it.

And another thing, I was also mad with grief. I know that sounded like a badly written line from a telenovela. But it was the fucking truth. Yeah. I woke every day thinking about my father. So being madly in love gave me some stability. That's really crazy.

Six

AFTER SCHOOL, AS I WAS APPROACHING MY TRUCK IN
the parking lot, I saw Susie and Gina and Cassandra waiting for me.

"No loitering," I said.

"Call the cops," Susie said.

"I just might."

"What's the big occasion?"

"You're going away again," Gina said.

"I'm not. I promise. I'm just sad."

"Okay," Cassandra said, "we get that. But isolating yourself from
the world won't heal your hurt."

"I know."

"Good. It's Friday, what do you say we visit your old stomping
grounds and get us some burgers at the Charcoaler?"

"Sure," I said.

"You're not even faking enthusiasm."

"One day at a time," I said.

"Fair enough."

"So we're on?"

"Yeah, I'm down."

And then they did what I knew they were going to do. They kissed me on the cheek and hugged me. One by one.

"I'm going to die from too many kisses and too many hugs."

"Well, if we were going to kill you, we'd just choke you."

"It's more direct," I said.

"Affection never killed anybody."

"For all you know." I could see they weren't going to let me wallow in my own sorrow. Just then I almost hated them for that. I jumped into my truck. "See you this evening," I said. And I waved. And as soon as I took off, I felt the tears and I thought, *Will somebody please turn off this faucet?*

Seven

AS SOON MY THREE FRIENDS LEFT ME ALONE, I TURNED on the ignition and started to drive. I found myself driving into the desert. It didn't feel like I was driving. It was more like my truck was taking me there.

I parked the truck in the same spot I'd always parked it. I just sat there. I was picturing my dad as he smoked a cigarette. I was imagining his voice as he told me to stop punishing myself. I was picturing the look in his eyes right before he died. So much love in those eyes that I'd never see again. I don't know how long I sat there. But it was dark now. The sun was long gone.

"Dad, Dad. Why did God take you when it was me who needed you? Tell me why. I don't understand. I hate, I hate the fucking universe. And the universe hates me. Hates me, hates me, hates me."

I could hear myself saying those words and saying other words.

It was as if I had left my body and someone else was living there, in my body. But then I'd come back—and then leave again. I got out of the truck and sat on the desert floor and leaned against the bumper.

There was lightning and thunder in the desert skies and it started to rain. It started to pour. The rain mixed in with my salty tears. I got up to get back into the truck—but I felt myself drop to my knees. *Dad, Dad.*

I was all alone in the world.

Nothing but me and the desert rain.

And my broken heart.

"Ari! Ari!" I knew that voice. I knew that voice. It was a better voice than mine.

"Dante?" I whispered.

"Ari!"

I felt him pick me and carry me in his arms.

I heard voices I knew. Girls' voices. Women's voices. And they kept saying my name over and over and there was love everywhere. Everywhere there was love. And I wanted to reach out and grab it. But I couldn't move.

Eight

I FELT DANTE HOLDING ME AS THE HOT WATER OF THE shower hit my skin. I looked at him. I don't know what kind of look I was wearing. He just kept whispering my name. And I know that I was smiling.

Nine

I WOKE UP AND SAW THE SUN STREAMING THROUGH
the window. I thought of that morning, that summer morning when
I'd met Dante. The sun had been streaming through that same window and I'd tapped my feet on the wood floor as I listened to "La
Bamba." It felt as if that day had happened in another life. To another
boy who had the same name. And in some ways, it *had* happened
to another boy. I was different now. I'd left that boy behind. I'd said
good-bye to him. And I was still saying hello to the young man I'd
become.

But the young man I'd become didn't have a father. No, that
wasn't true. I'd always have a father. I'd just have to look for him
where he lived now. Inside my heart.

Ten

MY MOM WALKED INTO THE ROOM. SHE SAT ON MY BED. "I know you're sad. I know your heart is broken. But there are moments when you have to think of others, Ari. You have to overcome your own hurts and think of other people. You can drown in your own bitter tears or you can look up at the sky. Dante and the girls—you scared them. They're so afraid of losing you. And me, too, Ari. Do you know what it would do to me if I lost you, if you gave in to your own grief? You loved your father? Then learn to live again."

She reached over and combed my hair with her fingers.

She got up and walked out of my room.

Eleven

I FOUND MY MOM IN HER BEDROOM. SHE WAS GOING through my father's things. She looked up at me when I walked in. "I'm giving some of his things away to people who loved him. You get first choice."

She sat on the bed and fought the tears. I sat next to her and held her. Then I said, "You want to hear a dirty joke?"

And we both started laughing. She gently slapped my arm. "What is wrong with you?"

We spent the entire day going through my father's belongings. These are the things I chose:

- His mailman uniform
- His wedding band
- His army uniform
- The flag we'd received at his funeral
- A picture of my mother he'd taken in a photography class
- The letters my father and mother had sent to each other when he was in Vietnam (but I had to promise to let my sisters read them)
- His favorite shirt

- A pair of his dress shoes (we wore the same size)

- His last pack of cigarettes

- His watch

- A picture of my father holding me the day they brought me home

- A picture of me smiling at the camera, my front teeth missing, and holding Tito

After everything was packed and sorted, my mom looked around the room. "I thought about getting a new bed. I thought about moving into the spare bedroom. But then I thought, *Well, that's just running away*. I don't want to run away from the memories of the man who loved me. So I'm staying put. But I am going to buy some new bedding. It's a little too masculine for my taste."

I kept nodding. "We're going to be all right, aren't we, Mom?"

"Yes, Ari, we are. Your father once told me, 'If anything ever happens to me, please don't become my widow. Become yourself. Fall in love again.' Hmm. Fall in love again, my ass. The only man I ever needed was your father. The rest of the men on the planet, I can live without."

"Well, there's me, Mom."

"You don't count."

"Why? Because I'm gay?"

"For all of your intelligence, you can be downright silly. No, not because you're gay. Because you're my son."

Twelve

I CALLED DANTE. "HEY, I'M SORRY I SCARED YOU."

"It's okay, Ari."

"And thanks. Shit, I finally get to take a shower with you, and my head is somewhere else."

"Well, we can try it again."

"You can always make me smile."

There was silence over the phone.

And then Dante's soft voice. "Are you sure you're going to be okay?"

"Yes, I'm sure. And I say we go to the Charcoaler tonight and do some hanging out. I'll call the girls."

Dante was sitting on his front porch when I picked him up. He leapt off the porch and smiled when he saw my mom. "Mrs. Mendoza! You gonna hang with us?" Some days Dante reverted to talking like the hipster he'd never be.

My mom smiled at him. "I hope you don't mind."

"Why would I mind? I mean, sometimes you're a lot more fun than Ari."

"Keep it up, Dante. Just keep it up."

. . .

When we drove up to the Charcoaler and ordered, I saw Cassandra and Gina and Susie leaning against Gina's car and eating onion rings. When our order was ready, I parked next to them—and they were all screaming, "Mrs. Mendoza! Awesome!"

Sometimes I loved them so much. There was something about girls that guys didn't have—and would never have. They were amazing. Maybe one day, instead of always having to prove they were real men, guys would study women's behavior and start acting a little more like them. Now, that would be awesome.

Thirteen

SUNDAY MORNING, CASSANDRA AND I WENT FOR A run. I felt alive. It was as if Cassandra could read my mind. "I feel alive too."

Dante and I drove out to the desert. The desert was always there. Waiting for me. We took a long hike. Sometimes we'd stop and Dante would hold me. It was a wordless day. It was good to be free of words.

When the sun was about to sink, leaving the sky without its light, Dante and I leaned against my truck. I looked at Dante. "Hey," I said, "we're alive. So let's live."

"Let's live."

And I made love to him.

"Let's live," I whispered.

Fourteen

DURING LUNCH I TOLD GINA AND SUSIE AND CASSANDRA the story my dad had told me about my mom and the lizards. I found myself crying. I could hear my father's voice telling me the story. And I guess I was sad. But I was also a little bit happy. He left me stories to tell. Everyone has stories to tell. My dad had them. My mom had them. And I had them. Stories were living inside us. I think we were born to tell our stories. After we died, our stories would survive. Maybe it was our stories that fed the universe the energy it needed to keep on giving life.

Maybe all we were meant to do on this earth was to keep on telling stories. Our stories—and the stories of the people we loved.

Fifteen

THE NEXT WEEK, WE HAD A FIRE DRILL DURING SEC-
ond period. It was a little bit strange, though. It didn't seem like
a normal fire drill. It wasn't just the usual ten-minute thing. And
I could see some of the teachers talking to one another and I saw
Mr. Blocker, who was laughing his ass off—and some of the other
teachers too, and then another teacher chastised them, but I was
too far away to hear the conversation. And somebody said something about crickets. And I thought that was strange. And some
people were questioning Javier Dominguez, who was a smart and
hip kid everybody liked. But if Javier knew anything, he wasn't
spilling the beans.

After about twenty-five minutes, we were finally led back into
our classrooms. And then I thought maybe the day would be a good
day and distract me from the hurt I was carrying with me.

By lunchtime, the news was out. And our personal investigative
reporter, Susie, had the scoop. "Someone let out an army of crickets
in Mrs. Livermore's class."

"What?"

"Hundreds of them. Crickets everywhere. Apparently, Mrs. Livermore ran screaming down the hall and she was on the edge of having a breakdown."

"Crickets?"

"Hundreds."

"Now that's what I call genius," Cassandra said. "I'm sure Mrs. Livermore mistook them for cockroaches. So she went batshit crazy. And they were just crickets. It's brilliant, really."

"But how do you get ahold of so many crickets?"

"You order them."

"You mean like through a catalog?"

"Yeah. Or you could order them through a pet store."

"But why would anybody order crickets?"

"They're food—like for lizards or snakes."

"Oh, gross."

"Did the students in her class freak out?"

"I would've," Gina said. "It's making my skin crawl."

I found myself smiling at the thought of Mrs. Livermore running out of the classroom. It was nice to smile.

"Oh man," Susie said, "I would've sold my soul to have been there."

Sixteen

WHEN I DROVE TO SCHOOL ON MONDAY MORNING, I
was singing. Yeah, I was singing. I was up and I was down. And I was
up and I was down.

I was sitting in study hall and I heard Mr. Robertson's voice on the
intercom. "Would the following students please come to my office
immediately: Susie Byrd, Jesus Gomez, and Aristotle Mendoza." We
looked at each other. "You think they think we had something to
do with the crickets?" Susie looked at me. "I'd confess to that crime
even I didn't do it. I'd be a hero."

As we walked down the hall, we were laughing. "This is so
exciting."

"Susie, this isn't my idea of exciting,"

"Yeah, it is," Chuy said. "It's awesome. We're famous."

My friends were crazy—I mean, they were crazy.

Just as we arrived at Mr. Robertson's office, the door flung open
and two students stomped out. Mr. Robertson looked at his secretary.
"Make sure those two are signed in for detention starting today."

She took out a pad. "For how long?"

"Two weeks."

"We haven't had a two-weeker in a while."

"Is that English, Estella?"

"My version of it," she said. She spoke English with a Mexican accent—otherwise her English was excellent. She was clearly in a bad mood. I think Mr. Robertson was going to say something, but Estella wasn't quite finished. "I don't think you have a right to correct my spoken English—since I have to correct your grammar before I have you sign all the letters you send out."

She'd been his secretary forever, and she didn't take any crap. She knew how to handle students, and she knew how to handle her boss. She knew the value of her work. Mr. Robertson didn't speak any Spanish, and she had to be his translator as needed—which was every day.

"That's what I pay you for, Estella."

"That's what the school district pays me for."

"Estella, not today. I'm not in the mood."

"I understand," she said, "but if Mrs. Livermore calls one more time today, I'm going to forward you the call. She's called four times, and the last time she said that perhaps there was a language barrier. She calls again, I'm just going to speak Spanish and you can take it from there. And Mrs. Robertson dropped off your high blood pressure medicine." She handed him his pills. "I think now would be a good time to take one. I'll get you a cup of water."

Susie and Chuy and I just kept looking at one another.

Mr. Robertson made a motion for us to come into his office. "And I suppose you find all of this amusing."

"Amusing," Susie said. "I like that word."

"Do you always find it necessary to respond when no response is needed?"

He was definitely in a bad mood.

We all took a seat. Estella walked in with a cup of water and set it on Mr. Robertson's desk. He took out a pill and downed it with the water. He was looking old and a little weathered, and I wondered why anybody would want his job. He sat for a moment and he was obviously trying to calm himself down.

"So," Chuy said, "did we win an award or something?"

Mr. Robertson buried his face in his hands and started laughing his ass off. But it was more like he wanted to cry. And Chuy had this incredible shit-eating grin on his face. I loved that guy.

"What kind of award were you thinking you might be receiving, Jesus?"

"Chuy. It's Chuy. What kind of award? How about the speaking-truth-to-power award?"

"What truth?"

"We called Mrs. Livermore out on her racism."

"She is *not* a racist," he said firmly. "She's just stupid." He put his hand on his forehead, covering his face. "I never said that."

"And we didn't hear it," Susie said. "But racism and stupidity aren't mutually exclusive. And the two pretty much go hand in hand."

"I'm an educator. I know I'm an administrator now, but that doesn't make me less of an educator. And it's my responsibility to tell all of you that words like 'racism' shouldn't be tossed around casually. You should think twice, no, three times before you level those accusations at another human being. Am I clear?"

And then I had to jump in. "You're right," I said. "We should think three times before we make destructive allegations. But I think that you think we're not smart enough or that we don't know enough about the world to understand the meaning of the word 'racism.' You think that it's just that we don't like her. You think we shouldn't use the word 'racism' at all because we haven't earned the right to use it. So we should leave it to you and to other enlightened adults to decide when it is appropriate to use that word. But you disrespect us and you underestimate us. And you disrespect a lot of our teachers, who wouldn't dream of treating us the way she treats us. And *you* know and *I* know that this is not the first time you've heard this complaint. You didn't do your job. Just like you didn't grade our papers. You're the adult. And we're kids. And it's your job to take care of us. And you're not doing a very good job."

"The only reason I'm sitting here listening to all this is that I happen to know your mother, who is a credit to her profession. And that's the only reason."

"I think I already knew that." I was about to say something else, but I stopped myself.

He pointed at the door. "Go. And I don't want to see any of you in this office for any reason for the rest of the school year."

"You forgot to tell us why you called us in."

All of a sudden, he had this embarrassed look on his face. "Oh yes, that. Do any of you know anything about those crickets?"

"Crickets?"

"I wouldn't be surprised if you had something to do with it, Chuy."

"Well, if I had, I'd confess."

"Me too," Susie said.

Then he looked at me. "I've had other things on my mind."

"Oh, of course you have." He was very quiet. "I was very sorry to hear about your father. He was a good man."

I nodded. "Thank you, sir. I appreciate that."

He looked at all of us. "I'm not some kind of monster, you know."

"We know," Susie said. "You're trying to do your job. And we're trying to do ours."

He smiled. "Ms. Byrd. You're going to change a piece of the world. I know people like me get in your way sometimes. I'll try not to take it too personally. Now get out of here, all of you."

I remembered what my father had said, that there were worse men and worse principals. But I was still pissed about what Mr. Robertson had said: that the only reason he had listened to me was because he knew my mother. When I heard Mr. Robertson say it, it made me feel invisible. And that made me angry. He just didn't see us. He just thought of us as troublemakers. That was why he called us in. As soon as he heard about what happened in Mrs. Livermore's class, he thought of us. He just didn't see us.

There were only ten minutes left in the period. I headed for the nearest exit. I needed to get some fresh air. Susie and Chuy followed me. I closed my eyes and took a deep breath.

"Ari, you were awesome."

"Was I? He didn't hear a damn thing we said."

"Wrong," Chuy said. "He heard you. He heard you loud and clear."

"You know, I feel bad for Mrs. Livermore. I do. But how are we supposed to learn to look at the truth? Where are we supposed to learn right from wrong? Maybe that's it. They don't want us to go looking for the truth. They don't really want us to learn right from wrong. They just want us to behave."

Susie looked at me. "I like it when you're like this."

"Why? Because I'm engaging in Susie Byrd behavior?"

Chuy started laughing. And then Susie started laughing. And then I started laughing. But we all knew that what we really wanted to do was cry. We were so disappointed. Maybe we'd just expected too much.

The bell rang.

Seventeen

LEAVE IT TO SUSIE TO GET TO THE BOTTOM OF THE MYStery of the crickets in the classroom. "It was David Brown. I should have figured it out. He said he wanted to be an entomologist when we were in the fifth grade."

"Yeah," I said, "I remember that. I had to look it up."

We walked down the hall and she left a note in his locker. *Dear Cricket, you're my hero. And don't worry, I'm not going to out you. We all love you. Susie Byrd.*

The next day, he was passing by us with his lunch tray. "David," Susie said, "come sit with us."

He seemed startled. He just looked at Susie blankly. "I'm not very social."

"Who cares? We're not going to grade your social skills."

"You're funny," he said.

He sat with us, and he was awkward and uncomfortable, and I felt bad for him. Why was Susie always badgering the loners of the world when they wanted to be left alone?

"Why'd you do it, David? The crickets?"

"How did you know I did that?" He was trying to keep his voice down.

"It doesn't matter. Your secret is safe. So why'd you do it?"

"Like you're a big fan of hers?"

"Everybody hated her. Me included."

"Not everybody hated her. But I *really* hated her. And really, I sort of got the idea from Ari."

I looked at him with a big question mark on my face. "Well, I was sitting at the table right over there. And I heard you tell the story about your mother and the lizards some guy let loose in her classroom. And then I got this idea. It was like an *Oh, wow* kind of moment. And I knew what I was going to do."

"But why crickets?" Susie asked.

"Well, I like crickets. Crickets aren't really that scary. They're supposed to be good luck. Not like *cucarachas*. When I let the crickets loose, Mrs. Livermore had the most terrified look I'd ever seen on anybody's face—and you should have seen her run shrieking out the door. Everyone laughed, but some people felt sorry for her. I didn't feel anything."

He stared down at his plate.

"Maybe that makes me a bad person. I'm not sorry." He started to get up from the table.

"Stay here and eat your lunch," Susie said. "You should look at it this way. Those crickets were an army of demonstrators, marching and demanding justice."

"Are you trying to make me fall in love with you, or what?"

Eighteen

I DIDN'T KNOW WHY I WAS WATCHING THE NEWS.

There was a spokesman from ACT UP. And then the reporter was asking him, "Aren't you afraid that your strategies are threatening the very people you want to listen to you?" And the man said, "Nobody's listening. We don't have anything to lose. We're dying. You want us to be nice? You think we want people to like us? They hate us."

I was home alone. I turned off the television.

Nineteen

WE WERE SITTING IN MY TRUCK AFTER SCHOOL. DANTE had the day off, courtesy of some famous saint, and he was waiting for me in the parking lot.

He waved, that smile on his face. "I want to kiss you, Ari."

"Not a good idea."

"You're right. We're surrounded by privileged straight people who think they're superior. And they'd freak out. Why are straight people so oversensitive about things? Jeez, they're so fucking delicate."

"It's not all their fault. They're taught to think that way."

"Well, we were taught to think that way too. And we got over it."

"Maybe it's because we're gay."

"That's got nothing to do with it. And you just rolled your eyes at me."

"I have something in my eye."

"I love you."

"People are going to hear you." I opened the door to my pickup truck and got in. Dante jumped in on the passenger side.

"People are going to hear me? Really? High school students aren't people. They used to be people before they got to high school. And they will return to being people after they leave high school. For now, they're just taking up space."

"Not like me and you. We don't just take up space."

"Of course not. Gay people don't just take up space. We're better than that. And we're better at sex, too."

Yeah, yeah, that Dante, he was a riot.

A walk in the desert in the quiet. Sometimes the silence of the desert was a kind of music. Dante and I, we shared a silence between us that was a kind of music too. The desert didn't condemn Dante and me for holding hands. It seemed like such a simple thing, to walk somewhere and hold a human hand. A man's hand. But it wasn't simple at all.

We stopped and drank some water I had in my backpack. "You're like the water, Ari. I can't live without water."

"You're like the air, Dante. I can't live without the air."

"You're like the sky."

"You're like the rain." We were smiling. We were playing a game. And we would both win. There were no losers in this game.

"You're like the night."

"You're like the sun."

"You're the ocean."

"You're the dawn."

"I love you, Aristotle Mendoza. You think I say that too much. But I like hearing myself say it." He leaned on my shoulder.

. . .

We stood there in the silence of the desert—and he kissed me. And in that moment, I thought that we were the center of the universe. Couldn't the universe see us?

He kissed me and I kissed him back. Let the universe see. Let the sky see. Let the passing clouds see. He kissed me. Let the plants of the desert see. Let the desert willows, let the distant mountains, let the lizards and the snakes and the desert birds and roadrunners see. I kissed him back. Let the sands of the desert see. Let the night come—and let the stars see two young men kissing.

Twenty

MRS. LOZANO HAD WRITTEN HER NAME ON THE BOARD.
Mrs. Cecilia Lozano. "I'll be your teacher for the rest of the semester.
We're a little behind—but I'm sure we'll catch up. I'm sorry to hear
that there have been some problems in this class." She had this mischievous smile. "And I've been informed that some of you are uncomfortable in educational settings. Maybe it's the desks." She winked at us.

And we all fell in love with her.

"Why don't we begin with you telling me something about your-
selves. When I call out your name, tell us what you want to be when
you grow up. Ms. Susie Byrd, have you chosen a profession?"

"I want to run for Congress someday."

"Good for you. And good for us. Do you have a platform?"

"Make the rich poor and make the poor rich."

"You have your work cut out for you."

But I could tell Mrs. Lozano got a kick out of Susie's answer. Mrs.
Livermore would have given her a lecture.

Lucia Cisneros said she didn't want to grow up.

Mrs. Lozano shook her head and smiled. "I'm sorry to say you
don't get a choice."

"Then I want to work at Chico's Tacos."

Everybody laughed.

"Why would you want to work at Chico's Tacos?"

"My family owns it. I could take it over."

"I'd rather take over the L&J." Good old Chuy.

"Does your family own it?"

"No, ma'am."

"Well, then you'll be facing some difficulties."

Everybody laughed.

Teachers mattered. They could make you feel like you belonged in school, like you could learn, like you could succeed in life—or they could make you feel like you were wasting your time. As we went around the room, I was trying to think what my answer would be. And then I heard her call my name, and I heard myself say, "I want to be a writer."

Mrs. Lozano seemed very happy when I said that. "It's a very difficult profession."

"I don't care if it's hard. That's what I want to be. A writer."

"What would you like to write about?" I wanted to say, *I want to write a story about two boys who fall in love each other*. Instead, I said, "I want to write stories about the people who live on the border."

She nodded. "I'll be the first in line to buy your book."

"Ari, I had no idea you wanted to be a writer."

I looked at Susie. "Neither did I."

"No jokes. Do you really?"

"I think maybe I feel something inside that tells me that I'm going to be a writer."

"I think you'd be a wonderful writer."

"Do me a favor, Susie. Don't tell anyone—not even Gina."

She had a smile on her that rivaled a sunrise. "Oh, wow! I never thought that Ari Mendoza would ever ask me to keep a secret for him. You just made my year."

Spring break came around. The kids in our school didn't take trips to beaches or Las Vegas or places like LA or San Diego. That took money, and most of us didn't have any. But we liked spring break anyway. We hung out—which wasn't such a bad thing. We liked hanging out.

And everybody was all pumped up. Spring break—and then graduation. Commencement. The end. And the beginning. The beginning of what? For me, a life of trying to figure out who to trust and who not to trust.

I had a dream. I guess in the end, it was a good dream. Dante and I were running. There was a crowd of people chasing after us. And I knew they wanted to hurt us. Dante wasn't a runner, so he was falling behind. I ran back and said, "Take my hand"—and just like that he became a runner. Hand in hand, we ran. But the crowd was still after us. And then we reached the edge of a cliff—and below there were waves crashing into the rocky shore.

"We have to dive into the water," Dante said.

"I can't dive." I didn't think anyone could survive jumping into that water. And I thought Dante and I were going to die.

Dante wasn't afraid. He smiled. "We have to dive. Just dive when I dive." I trusted him—so I dived when he dived. And then I felt myself coming to the surface. The water was warm, and Dante and I smiled at each other. And then he pointed toward the sandy beach. And I saw my father waving at us and smiling.

That's when I woke. I felt alive. And I knew that part of the reason I felt so alive was because of Dante.

It was a good dream. A beautiful dream.

After I woke from the dream, I got up from bed and walked into the kitchen to grab some coffee. I smiled at my mom. "Why aren't you ready to go to school?"

She shook her head. "I don't know about you—but I'm on spring break."

"I knew that. I was just making sure you were, you know, in touch with reality."

"Ari, just have some coffee and be quiet. Sometimes it's better not to talk."

Dante and I were hanging out at his place and playing with Sophocles. That little guy liked to move around a lot. And he'd found his voice. He made noises, and he knew those noises were coming from him. I liked hearing him screaming with delight. That was the word, "delight." He was delighted to be alive. One day, he would be shouting out his name to the world. I hoped the world would hear it.

Twenty-One

SUNDAY NIGHT I WAS GETTING ALL SET TO BEGIN MY
last two months of high school. What had I learned? I'd learned that
my teachers were people—and that some of them were extraordinary. I learned that I had something in me called writing.

And I was learning that sometimes you had to let go of the people
you loved.

Because if you didn't, you'd live all your days in sadness. You'd
fill your heart with the past. And there wouldn't be enough room
left for the present. And for the future. Letting go—it was difficult.
And it was necessary. Necessary—there's a word.

I was also learning that loving someone was different from falling
in love with them.

And I was learning that there were a lot of people who were
just like me and they were struggling to find out who they were.
And it didn't have to do with whether they were straight or gay.

And, yes, we were all connected. And we all wanted to have a life
that was worth living. Maybe some people died asking themselves
why they had ever been born or why they had never found happiness. And I wasn't going to die asking myself those questions.

Twenty-Two

SUSIE AND GINA AND CASSANDRA AND I STUDIED AT my house in the evenings. Dante came to study with us too. Sometimes we held hands under the table.

"You don't have to hide," Cassandra said. "We know what you're up to."

"We're not hiding," Dante said. "We're just very private people."

Cassandra pointed at me. "He's private. You, on the other hand, are something of an emotional exhibitionist."

"Is that right?"

"That's right," she said. "It's what makes you so beautiful. You have a heart and you don't hide it. Ari still has to learn a few things on that front."

"Look who's talking," Gina said, "Miss Never Let Them See Me Cry."

"Women need to learn how to protect themselves."

"You could teach a class," Susie said. "And I'd take that class."

"How did this discussion become about me? I don't like where this is going." Cassandra picked up her notes and began going over them. "I have a test in the morning."

We all went back to studying.

That's the way we lived our lives the rest of the semester. On Fridays or Saturdays, we would all go to the movies or out into the desert and we would talk. We did a lot of talking. Sometimes Susie brought along the guy she was dating, "Cricket." We all called him that, and he took to liking it.

One night, we all went out into the desert and Cassandra brought along two bottles of champagne. "They were supposed to be for New Year's, but that didn't work out."

"It's not legal for us to be drinking alcohol at our age. We're breaking the law."

Susie just looked at me. "What's your point?"

"We are the criminal element that society wants to rid itself of."

"Maybe we're not committing a crime."

"Well, we are committing a crime," Dante said, "but I doubt the court would waste its time prosecuting us."

"Well, I say we commit this crime with intent—and to hell with it." Gina had this great evil laugh.

Cassandra popped open the champagne and brought out the plastic cups. Cassandra proposed a toast: "To Ari and Dante. Because we love that you love."

Sweet. So damned sweet.

We had fun. There wasn't enough alcohol to get drunk. Not even to get a buzz, really. I gave most of my champagne to Dante. I knew I wasn't going to grow up to be a champagne kind of guy.

I watched Susie kiss Cricket on the cheek. "My rebel with a cause."

"I'd kiss you too—but maybe that's not so cool," I said, "so consider yourself kissed."

Cricket had this goofy smile on his face. "That was a nice thing to say."

Our second toast was to Cricket. Before we toasted, he said, "Well, maybe we should toast Ari's mother. She's the one who gave me the idea. Well, via Ari."

"Here's to my mother," I said, and everybody toasted.

But then we went back to toasting Cricket. I hoped he grew up and changed the world. If he stuck with Susie, both of them might change the world together. I wanted to live in that world.

Dante and I escaped from the group so we could make out for a while. Who the hell invented the term "making out"? "Necking"? "Smooching"? The whole thing made me feel immature and silly. I hated the word "silly." And I hated to think of myself as being silly.

"This is so high school," Dante said.

"Well, yeah, but I'm too private to be an exhibitionist."

"Straight people make out in front of their friends—and we don't consider them to be exhibitionists."

"Shut up and kiss me, Dante. How are we supposed to make out if you're too busy talking?"

"Hey! Do you realize we've never had sex inside your truck? I mean, in the cab."

"Now, that's super high school."

"All the guys at Cathedral talk about car sex."

"You're kidding. All those good Catholic boys?"

"They're mostly smart Catholic boys. I'm not so sure how good they are. I mean, Catholic school boys are just guys—they're not altar boys."

And then we heard our friends calling out our names.

"We're coming," I yelled, "we're coming!" I twisted Dante's hand. "We didn't even get to make out."

"We don't have to get all sexual all the time."

"You'll live to regret those words, Mr. Quintana."

We walked back toward them holding hands.

"So, what were you guys doing?" Gina had this smirk on her face.

"We were chasing lizards."

I walked right into it—and Cassandra never let a good line get past her. "More like each other's lizards." And, yeah, they laughed and laughed, and when they stopped laughing, I said, "High school behavior doesn't appeal to me. Cassandra, you're regressing."

"I've spent my life playing at being a woman. Let me play at being a girl."

I loved Cassandra. There was something about the way she said things—not *what* she said but *how* she said them. I wondered how many hearts she was going to break.

"Do you think most people in high school have sex?"

"Some do," Susie said. "Most don't. The girls that have sex deny it. And most of the guys that say they've had sex are a bunch of liars."

"So," Gina says, "when is it morally acceptable to have sex?"

"Never," Cassandra said. "Maybe it depends on your religion. If you're Catholic, then it's never going to be morally acceptable—unless, of course, you're trying to have children."

"In America we're all messed up about sex," Susie said. "If you're having premarital sex, just don't tell anyone. They won't ask. And, really, they don't want to know. And everything will be fine. Just don't talk about it. Every time I see a pregnant woman, I want to walk up to her and say, 'I see you've been having sex. Good for you.'"

Cricket got a big kick out of that one.

And then Gina jumped in. "If a guy is going out with a girl, people don't assume they're having sex. But if a guy is going out with another guy, well, everybody assumes they're definitely having sex. Because everyone knows gay guys are oversexed."

"That's not fair."

"Well, that's what you get for being homosexuals."

Dante and I thought that was very funny. But why did people always talk about our sexual choice? *Choice?* It wasn't like we were choosing between two candidates who were running for president. It wasn't like that at all.

Twenty-Three

FRIDAY AFTERNOON AND I'D JUST COME IN FROM A run. It was good to run alone sometimes. Really good. I was sitting on the front steps, letting my heartbeat slow down, sweat pouring out of me. My mother came out the front door. She sat next to me.

"You look nice, Mom."

"I'm meeting some friends for a drink and dinner. I don't really feel like going—but I need to learn how to live my life without your father. And I'm sure I'll have a good time. I have lovely friends. And they know how to make me laugh. I could use some laughter in my life."

"Good for you, Mom.

"Dante's on his way here. We're probably gonna hang out at the Charcoaler. Have a great time, Mom. And if you drink too much, call me and I'll come and get you. And I won't even ask you to explain yourself to me."

She laughed. "Do I have a curfew?"

I watched her drive away. I heard Legs pawing at the front door. I opened the door for her, and she plopped herself down next to me.

Just then, I saw Dante hopping out of his father's car.

"Hi," he said.

"Hi. You wanna hang out at the Charcoaler and listen to some music on the radio?"

"Sounds good to me." We were smiling at each other. "Don't you ever take your shirt off when you run?"

"Nope." I know I was wearing a very mischievous smile. "My mom is out for the evening, and I have to take a shower—and I was wondering if maybe you'd like to join me. Or maybe you're not into that sort of thing."

"Meet you in the shower." He was already opening the screen door, with Legs following after him.

I laughed to myself. *I guess that's a yes.*

Twenty-Four

OUR LIVES RETURNED TO A KIND OF NORMALCY. *Normalcy*. There was a word. How could a gay guy even use that word? Dante and I were beginning to understand that our love for each other wasn't easy. And never would be easy. "Love" was no longer a new word. It was us that would have to keep that word new—even when it felt old.

One evening, Susie announced, "I got accepted to Emory University in Atlanta."

Dante clenched his fist in the air. "I knew you'd get in. And Ari already knows, but I got into Oberlin—with a scholarship."

I watched Dante. I loved it so much that he was happy.

"I got into UT," I said.

"Yessss." Gina did a little dance as she sat at my kitchen table. "So did I."

"Wanna be roommates?"

"Hell no! I'm not gonna be roommates with an impossibly handsome man. You'd scare away all my prospects."

"Good to know you're thinking ahead."

Dante and I exchanged looks. We were happy. And we were sad.

Twenty-Five

ONE THURSDAY EVENING, THE PHONE RANG. MY mother answered it. It was for her, not me. I was hoping it was Dante. Every time the phone rang, I always hoped it was Dante.

I walked out onto the front porch and Legs followed me, and for some reason, I felt a kind of calmness.. I just sat there as the sun began to set. I wished that I could breathe in all of this calmness and the portrait of a setting sun and let it live in me forever. I closed my eyes.

I felt my mother sitting down beside me. "Guess what?"

"How many guesses do I get?" And I looked at her, and she looked, she looked . . . "Mom, did something bad happen?"

"No, nothing bad. Something really good just happened to your mother."

"What's that?"

Her lips trembled, and tears fell down her face. "I've been named teacher of the year."

I couldn't help myself. I let out the loudest "Ajúaaaaaa" ever. I hugged and hugged her. "Ahhh, Mom, I'm proud of you."

She couldn't stop smiling. "But you know what your dad would have said."

"Yeah, I think I do. He would have said, 'It's about damned time.'"

"That's exactly what he would have said."

"Well, I just said it for him." I felt so happy I wanted to do something crazy, so I ran out into the empty street and yelled, "My mother is teacher of the year. Yes, sir, Liliana Mendoza, teacher of the year!"

"Ari, the neighbors are going to think you're crazy."

"I am crazy, Mom. I'm crazy about you."

Some of the neighbors did come out. "It's okay," I said. "I'm not crazy. I'm celebrating. My mom's been named teacher of the year."

Our next-door neighbor Mrs. Rodriguez, who was a super-nice old lady, just shook her head and smiled. "Oh, that's wonderful. And you've worked so hard, Liliana. Just wonderful." And the neighbors who had come out to see what the commotion was all about came over and said incredibly kind things like "We are so proud of you." And my mother, she looked as radiant as the setting sun.

After the neighbors left, my mother and I just sat there on the front steps. I realized we were both crying. "God, I wish your father was here."

"Me too, Mom. I miss him more than anything."

You know, I don't think I'd ever felt as close to my mother as I felt in that moment. It's funny how so many feelings can run through you all at the same time.

Friday morning, it felt like I was some kind of hero—and I hadn't done a damn thing. My mother's picture was on the front page of the *El Paso Times*. They quoted one of her former students, a young lawyer who'd graduated from Harvard Law School. "Throughout my college years and throughout law school, I often thought about her. She was the best teacher I ever had."

Mr. Blocker was all smiles. "Tell your mother she's my role model."

All my teachers said congratulations, as if I had had something to do with my mom's award.

After school, we were walking toward my truck in the parking lot. Susie and Gina and Cassandra kept looking at me. "You're so quiet, Ari."

I kept breathing. It was as if I couldn't catch my breath. I just wanted to reach my truck. I had to reach my truck. And then I saw it a few feet away.

"Ari, are you okay?" I could hear Cassandra's voice. I leaned on my truck like I was going to do a push-up and looked up the sky. "It's so blue," I whispered.

"Ari?"

"Susie, did anyone ever tell you that you have the kind of voice that could heal the world?"

"Aw, Ari."

"I miss my dad. He's never coming back. I know that. I keep thinking he'll walk through the door and tell my mom how proud he is. I'm happy for Mom. She's worked so hard. And I'm sad. There are days when I don't want to feel anything. I know there are seasons for everything. But why does every season have to hurt? The Bible doesn't tell you just how much each season costs you. The Bible doesn't tell you what you have to pay when it's time to refrain from embracing."

I leaned into Cassandra's shoulder and wept.

I heard her voice whispering, "'Those who sow in tears shall reap rejoicing.'"

Twenty-Six

DANTE CAME OVER AFTER SCHOOL, CARRYING A VASE with two dozen yellow roses. He handed the vase to my mother. "The Quintana family is very proud. This is from all of us—Mom, Dad, Sophocles, and me. But mostly from me."

"Is it your goal in life to make everybody smile?"

He nodded. "Mrs. Mendoza, it's better than working for a living."

We were standing close together and she said, "Stay right there." She came back into the kitchen with a camera. She took a few pictures. "Perfect," she said.

Dante and I were lying on sleeping bags that we'd laid out on the floor of my bedroom. Legs was right beside us. It seemed that there weren't any words living inside me. I was holding Dante, and then he kissed me and said, "I wish things could be different for us."

"Me too."

"Do you think we'll live together someday?"

"Isn't it pretty to think so?"

"That's the last line of *The Sun Also Rises*—and it's meant ironically. It's a tragic line."

"I thought you said you never finished it."

"Well, I thought since you were reading it, I might as well get all the way through it too."

"I'm not Jake and you're not Lady Brett—so maybe we have a shot."

"Isn't it pretty to think so?" he said.

And we laughed softly in the dark.

There was the sound of thunder. And then the rain started to fall. First softly—then it was a full rain beating down on the roof.

"C'mon," I said. I pulled him up. "We're going outside."

"Outside?"

"I want to kiss you in the rain."

We ran out in front of the house in our underwear. The rain was freezing, and we were both shivering. But when I kissed him, he stopped shivering and I stopped shivering. "You beautiful, crazy boy," Dante whispered as I held him. I could have stood there forever. Kissing him in the rain.

Twenty-Seven

THERE WAS A LOT OF COMMOTION AROUND MY mother's teacher-of-the-year award. The Catholic Daughters arranged for a street party in front of our house—complete with mariachis. Our house was flooded with flowers. My mother had a lot of admirers. Some of the flowers wound up in my room. I hated flowers.

And I even got to meet the lady with the pink Cadillac, who came over to congratulate my mother and gifted her with Mary Kay products. She was a trip. She loved Dante. "If I were forty years younger, I'd whisk you away and take you to Las Vegas."

Dante and I just looked at each other.

The school district had an award ceremony where my mother was given a really nice plaque and a nice big fat check. My mother said it was very generous of the school district. I told her, "Dad would have said it wasn't nearly enough after all the work you've put in."

My mom just smiled. "Is that how you're going to roll, Ari? Always reminding me what your father would have said?"

"I guess so, Mom. It's a tough job—but somebody's got to do it."

I thought the best honor my mother received was a letter she got from Lizard, her former student. My mother let me read it:

Dear Mrs. Mendoza,

I got some news from one of my old classmates from Jefferson High School. He said you'd finally gotten some recognition for your work in the classroom. Teacher of the year. I know you must be proud of the award—but you couldn't possibly be as proud as I am.

I might have mentioned this to you in one of my annual Christmas cards, but I keep a picture of you and me when I graduated from high school on my desk. I always hold that framed picture in my hand before I'm trying a case in the courtroom—and I talk to it. Well, I talk to you. And I say, "All right, Mrs. Mendoza, let's you and me go into that courtroom and show them how it's done." I always picture you in that courtroom. And I never make a move that you wouldn't be proud of. You have set a standard of excellence for me that I have always endeavored to live up to.

I'm often told that I am a very dedicated lawyer—something my wife admires about me. I learned what it means to be dedicated to your profession from you. I don't think I ever told you that I married a schoolteacher. She is every bit the educator that you are. I'm very proud of her commitment—and her love for her students.

I learned from you that you can't be a good teacher if you aren't a good human being. You also taught me that women should be respected and that teachers are undervalued by the society we live in. I have tried not to make the same mistake as our society by believing that my work is more important than hers.

I never tire of telling people of how I got my nickname. Even my nephews and nieces call me Uncle Lizard. When I think back, I have come to believe that setting those lizards out in your classroom was the smartest thing I ever did.

I know I have told you this before—but I will never stop thanking you for saving my life. I have nothing but respect and affection for you. I feel as if I will always be your student. I will always feel connected to you. Let me say again how proud I am, how happy I am, how blessed I am to have sat in your classroom.

I send you all my love,
Jackson (AKA Lizard)

Enclosed in the letter was a gold-plated lizard pendant on a gold chain. My mother put it on. "I think I'll wear this until the day I die."

Twenty-Eight

"MOM, YOU KNOW, SINCE I GOT BACK FROM VISITING Bernardo, I haven't really had any time to think about it."

"Do you want to talk about it?"

"I do. But I think maybe you don't."

"That's not true. Not anymore." My mother looked at me. "What are you thinking?"

"Do you know the name of the person that Bernardo killed?"

"Yes," she said. "That person's given name was Solitario Mendez."

"Do you know where he—where she's buried?"

"Mount Carmel Cemetery."

"How do you know these things?"

"The obituary page. That was the worst period in my life. To know that I brought a son into the world that killed another human being."

"You didn't do anything bad."

"I know. But it hurt. And I was so ashamed. So much of me died. It took me a long time to feel alive again. Life, Ari, can be an ugly thing. But life can be so incredibly beautiful. It's both. And we have to learn to hold the contradictions inside us without despairing, without losing our hope."

Twenty-Nine

SATURDAY MORNING AND I'D MADE UP MY MIND WHAT I
was going to do that day. I grabbed a piece of paper and wrote a
short note. I wrote it slowly and deliberately. I grabbed an envelope
and wrote the name I'd chosen.

I drove up to a flower shop and picked a bouquet of yellow and
white flowers.

I drove to Mount Carmel Cemetery. It turned out to be the
largest Catholic cemetery in the county. I panicked. I thought I'd
never find the grave. I drove to the office and asked where Solitario
Mendez was buried. The nice woman gave me a map and showed
me where the grave was located.

It didn't take long for me to find it. It was a simple stone with the
date of his birth and the date of his death. Her death. Twenty-four
years old. There was nothing to indicate a life or a horrible death. I
tried not to picture her last seconds.

I stood there and looked at the name. I placed the flowers in
front of the grave. I took out the note I'd written and read it aloud.
It wasn't exactly a prayer:

"'My name is Aristotle Mendoza. We never met. But we are

connected. Everything is connected. And not all those connections resemble anything that is good or humane or decent. The name on your gravestone reads SOLITARIO MENDEZ. But I wanted to give you another name. I hope this doesn't offend you. I'd hate to think that I would be inflicting one more cruelty on you. I know it's more than a little arrogant to give you a name you never chose—but I intend this gesture as a kindness. I think of you as Camila. I think of you as being beautiful, and I think Camila is a beautiful name. I will take this name everywhere I go. I can't undo what my brother did to you—but this is the only way I can think of to honor your life. In honoring your life, maybe I can honor my own.'"

I put my words back in the envelope I'd marked "Camila." I sealed it and tied it to the flowers with a string I'd brought with me.

I'd already decided that I would never tell anybody about my visit to Camila's grave—not because I was ashamed, but because it was something between me and her.

I sat in my truck for a long time. And then I drove back home.

Thirty

SCHOOL WAS ENDING. DANTE AND I WERE ON THE PHONE. "I don't know whether I'm happy or sad. I'm happy to be leaving high school. I'm excited to be going away to college. But I'm sad. I'm really sad. Everywhere I go when I leave, you won't be there. What will become of Ari and Dante?"

"I don't have an answer."

"We should have had a plan."

"Can we just be happy for right now?" It was like we'd exchanged attitudes.

"Yeah," he said quietly. "But maybe you don't understand how much I love you."

That made me mad. Like I didn't love him. "I thought you knew I loved you too." I hung up the phone.

He called me right back. And I just said, "Maybe you do love me more than I love you. I didn't know it was a contest. I can't really know what you feel. But you don't know how I feel. It makes me mad that we're playing this game."

Dante was quiet on the other end of the line. "I'm sorry, Ari. I'm not handling this very well."

"Dante, we'll be okay. Me and you, we'll be okay."

Thirty-One

I WAS DRIVING HOME FROM SCHOOL, AND I SAW SUSIE and Gina walking down the street. I'd know them anywhere. I always had my windows open because I didn't have air-conditioning. I stopped. "You ladies want a ride home? I promise I'm not an axe murderer."

"Even though you look like one, we'll take your word for it." I liked the dimples Gina got when she smiled.

They hopped in the truck. I had a question floating around in my mind. "Can you guys answer a question for me? How come you were always so nice to me for all that time when I wasn't so nice to you?"

"Don't you remember?"

"Remember what?"

"First grade? Swings?"

"What are you talking about?"

They just kept looking at each other.

Gina said. "You really don't remember, do you?"

I looked at her blankly.

"It was after school. We were in the first grade. Susie and I were on the swings, and we were having a contest to see who could swing the highest. And Emilio Durango, the class bully—do you remember him?"

Him, I remembered. He pretty much left me alone. Not sure why. And I didn't care. Because I liked being left alone.

"Well, he and two other boys told us to get off the swings. And Susie and I stopped swinging. And he said, 'These swings are for boys. Girls are not allowed on the swings.' And Susie and I were afraid, and we were about to get off the swings, and all of a sudden you were standing there, right in front of Emilio. And you said, 'Who says the swings are just for boys?' And he said, 'I do.' And you said, 'You don't make the rules.' And he pushed you and you fell down to the ground. And you got back up and he was about to push you again. That's when you punched him in the stomach as hard as you could and he was rolling on the ground like a crybaby. 'I'm going to tell the teacher,' he said. And you just looked at him like, *Who cares?* And they left. And you watched them walk away and you stood there to make sure they were gone. And then you just smiled at us and walked away."

"That's funny. I don't remember that."

"Well, *we* remember. Ever since then, Susie and I liked you. Because we're sweet girls and we remember the nice things people have done for us."

"Punching a guy in the stomach isn't exactly a nice thing."

"It was nice. It was very nice."

I parked the truck in front of Susie's house. Susie opened the door, and they both jumped out. I knew Susie had an editorial for me that she'd already written in her head. "Sometimes, Ari Mendoza, when you write the story of who you are, you have a tendency to edit out a lot of the scenes that make you look good. I have a suggestion for you. Stop doing that. Just stop. Thanks for the lift."

Thirty-Two

MR. ROBERTSON CAME OVER THE INTERCOM WHILE WE
were in our homeroom classes. "Good morning to all of you. I'd like
to congratulate all of you as we quickly come to the close of another
school year. And it's been a great year. Congratulations, seniors!
You've worked hard and we look forward to celebrating you at commencement. But first, as is our tradition, I would like to announce
this year's valedictorian and offer her our congratulations. We are all
very proud of her quest for excellence. I am happy to announce that
this year's valedictorian is Cassandra Ortega. Join me in offering her
our sincerest congratulations. And, as a reminder to all of you, we do
not want a repeat of last year, when some overenthusiastic members
of the senior class thought the destruction of school property was an
appropriate way to celebrate. Try not to follow that example. There
will be consequences."

Now I knew what people meant when they said, "I'm so happy
for you." I always kind of thought that it was just a lot of bullshit or
that people were just trying too hard to be nice. But at that moment,
I wanted to run and find Cassandra and hug her and tell her how
brilliant she was and that she deserved it and that I was glad we'd

stopped hating each other and that the fact that she was in my life meant something. She mattered to me.

Susie and Gina and I took off running down the hall to find Cassandra. I don't know what it is about girls and the way that they're friends, but they all knew each other's schedules. We reached Cassandra's first-period class, and Susie peeked in and she was sitting there. "We need to talk to you."

Cassandra's teacher smiled. "Take your time." Sometimes teachers were awesome.

When Cassandra stepped out into the hallway, we accosted her with hugs. "You did it! You did it!" Cassandra Ortega did not cry. She definitely did not cry at school. In front of anybody. But she *did* cry.

"Oh my God," she said. "Oh my God, I have friends who love me."

"Of course we love you," Susie said.

"Cassandra," Gina said, "why wouldn't we love you? You're brilliant and wonderful."

When I hugged her, I said, "You hit it out of the ballpark."

"Oh, Ari, I thank the universe every day for giving you to me."

Thirty-Three

MR. BLOCKER SENT ME A NOTE SAYING HE WANTED TO
see me after school.

I walked into his classroom. "Hi, Ari," he said. He opened one of
the drawers in his desk and took out my journal. "You left this on
your desk."

"I must have rearranged my book bag and taken it out and left it
there." And I was thinking, *Oh shit, oh shit,* because he had to have
read a part of it to make sure it was mine.

I couldn't look him in the eye. "So now you know who I am."

"I don't need that journal to tell me who you are. I know who
you are. And I happen to like who you are. But, Ari, be careful with
this. There are people who would like nothing more than to hurt
you. I don't want anybody hurting you. Look at me."

I lifted my head and looked at him.

"Don't ever let anybody make you ashamed of who you are. Not
anybody." He handed me my journal back.

Thirty-Four

DANTE QUINTANA WAS ALSO NAMED THE VALEDICTO-rian at Cathedral High School. "But I don't get to speak. They just call me up, I get a plaque, and I get to say thank you."

"So? Who cares about making a speech? You should be proud of yourself."

"I am. But I wanted to make a speech."

"About what?"

"I wanted to talk about being gay."

"What did you want to say?"

"That bigotry was *their* problem, not mine."

"Somehow I get the feeling that a speech like that wouldn't go over well at a Catholic high school."

"Probably not. Why is it always about what *they* want to hear? They don't care about what we want to hear."

"What do we want to hear?"

"That they're going to step aside and let us take over the world."

"I don't want to take over the world. That's not what I want to hear."

"What do you want to hear?"

"I want them to admit that they're not better than we are."

"Like that's gonna happen."

"Oh, like letting us run the world is gonna happen?"

"How can we make them change if we're not allowed to talk?"

"Why do we have to do all the work? It's like you just said, we're not homophobic—they are."

"Yeah, but, Ari, they don't think homophobia is a bad thing."

"You're right about that. Is heterophobia a bad thing?"

"There's no such thing as heterophobia, Ari. And besides that, we're not heterophobic."

"Guess not. But I bet your mom and dad are happy. Dante Quintana, valedictorian."

"Sounds important, doesn't it?"

I nodded.

"Yup. My mom and dad are over-the-moon happy."

"That's the only thing that matters."

I was lying in bed in the dark. I couldn't sleep. I remembered a conversation Dante and I had at the beginning of the semester. There was a fellowship for promising young artists at some institute in Paris that had a summer program. He'd told me he was thinking of applying. I told him I thought he should. But he'd dropped the subject and never mentioned it again. I wondered if he'd applied. I wondered if he'd heard from them. I wasn't going to ask. If he wanted to tell me, he'd tell me.

Thirty-Five

ON THE LAST DAY OF SCHOOL WHEN THE FINAL BELL rang I headed for Mr. Blocker's room. He was sitting there leaning against his chair, and he had a calm and pensive look on his face. He noticed me standing at the doorway.

"Ari, come in. Did you need something?"

"I just came—you were, well, when I think of learning, I'll think of you."

"That's a very thoughtful thing to say."

"Yeah, maybe."

We both just kept nodding.

"I just came to bring you something. It's a gift. I know we're not really supposed to give our teachers gifts—no bribing for a grade. But even though you're not really my teacher anymore—and even though you'll always be my teacher—ah hell, I'm screwing this up. I wanted to give you this." I handed him a little box I'd wrapped myself. Which was a big deal because I hated wrapping gifts.

"May I open it?"

I nodded.

He unwrapped it carefully and opened the box. He kept nodding.

He took out a small pair of boxing gloves. He held them up and laughed. And laughed. "You're hanging up your gloves."

"Yup, I'm hanging up my gloves."

I think both of us wanted to say something, but really there was nothing to say. Not everything was said with words. I was thanking him. I knew that he was thanking me. I understood that he loved me in that way that teachers loved their students. Some of them, anyway. He knew I knew. I looked at him. A look that said, *Thank you—and good-bye.*

Thirty-Six

THERE WE WERE, ALL OF US LINED UP TO MARCH IN. I stared at my maroon stole—top 5 percent of my class. There must have been a lot of students sleeping in class for me to have made that list. *No negative self-talk.* Now I had Cassandra's voice in my head too. I heard Dante's actual voice. "Ari!" He was all smiles. He hugged me. "I found you!" *Yeah,* I wanted to say, *you found me in a swimming pool one day and changed my life.*

"Dad and I are here. We're sitting with your mom and Mrs. Ortega. Mom was sad because she couldn't come. She sends love, and so does Sophocles." And then he disappeared into the crowd.

There were so many people, and I hated crowds. Still, I was happy, and I had butterflies in my stomach—but I didn't know why. I was just going to get a diploma handed to me. I was supposed to take that baton and begin my race toward wherever the hell I was going.

It was all a blur, sort of. I always halfway shut down around a lot of people. Gina was sitting in the same row—but still, too far away. The girl sitting next to me was talking and talking to the girl sitting next to her. And then she said to me, "You beat my brother up."

"He must be a real nice guy."

"I don't want to talk about it."

"Then why'd you bring it up?"

"Because."

Well, she'd really learned how to think.

"I'm going to be nice to you because it's graduation."

"I'll be nice to you too. I'm Ari."

"I know who you are. I'm Sarah."

"Congratulations, Sarah. You did it."

"Don't try to sweet-talk me."

So much for being nice. If there was one thing about the past, it didn't leave you alone. It liked to stalk you.

Mr. Robertson had been saying a few words as Sarah and I were having our whispered conversation—if that's what it was. He introduced the faculty as a group, and he had them stand. And we gave our teachers a standing ovation. They deserved it. They more than deserved it.

And then he introduced Cassandra. He ended by saying, "In every possible way, she has been a brilliant and extraordinary student. It's my distinct honor to introduce this year's valedictorian, Cassandra Ortega." As she walked toward the podium, the applause was polite—but it was hardly enthusiastic. I felt bad.

"The only reason," she began, "that I was selected to be this year's valedictorian was that the student body didn't get a vote."

And everybody laughed. I mean, *everybody* laughed. Brilliant. She had us in the palm of her hand.

Cassandra talked about how she'd always been hungry to learn.

473

"But not everything we need to learn can be found in a book. Or rather, I've learned that people are books too. And there are a lot of wise things that are contained in those books. I have friends. Yes, who knew? Cassandra Ortega has friends."

The laughs came. And they were friendly laughs.

"I have friends that have taught me—you know, good friends are also teachers—that you cannot consider yourself an educated person if you fail to treat others with respect. While my grades were excellent, I was often a failure when it came to recognizing the dignity of others—and that is something I regret. There is nothing we can do about the past, but all of us can change what we do and who we are in the future. The future begins tonight. Right now.

"My older brother, whom I loved, died of AIDS last year. AIDS is not something we discuss in our classes. Nor, many of us, at home. I think we hope it will just go away. Or maybe we don't care because most people who've died in that pandemic are gay men. And we don't care about gay men because we think horrible things about them, and we think they're getting what they deserve. We don't look upon the men who died or are dying of AIDS as real men, or as real people. But they *are* real men. And all of them are human beings. And they have brothers and sisters and mothers and fathers who mourn them or hate them or love them.

"It's easy to hate someone when we don't see them as being real people. But ignoring our differences isn't the answer, either. I don't think women are treated equally in this country, but in order to be treated equally, I don't want men to ignore the fact that I'm a woman. I like being a woman. And men like being men far too much."

She was interrupted by laughter and some clapping. I think the guys were doing the laughing and the women were doing the clapping.

"I have a friend. He belongs to the other gender. I don't need to reveal his name—but before we were friends, I hated him. I felt justified in hating him because he hated me right back. He wasn't a person to me. And then one day we got into an argument and that argument turned into a conversation—and I found that he was listening to me and I was listening to him too. And he has become one of the closest friends I've ever had. I learned to see him. I learned of his troubles, of his journey, of his hurts, and I learned of his capacity to love. And I learned about my own capacity to love.

"For the longest time, I have wanted to be an actress. Then I realized that I have been an actress all my life. But the question 'What do you want to be when you grow up?' is not just about what professions we choose. The real question is, what kind of person do you want to be? Do you want to love? Or do you want to continue the hate? Hate *is* a decision. Hate is an emotional pandemic we have never found a cure for. Choose to love.

"Class of 1989, please stand." And we all stood. "Hold the hand of the person sitting next to you." And we all held hands. "The hands that you are holding belong to human beings—and it does not matter whether you know them or not. You are each holding the hands of the future of America. Treasure those hands. Treasure those hands—and change the world."

There was complete silence—and then there was a thunderous applause for Cassandra Ortega. More than half of her audience had hated her before she'd walked up to that podium—and she had let us see her. She stood in front of that podium, and she looked out at us, and she was radiant. She was the morning sun. She was the new day we'd all been waiting for. And we fell in love with her.

The whole world wanted to take a picture with Cassandra. We were patient. Mrs. Ortega was so proud. I saw her watch her daughter as our classmates surrounded her. And I knew she must have been thinking, *This is my daughter. Yes, this is my daughter.*

My mother was standing next to me. "How does it feel to be someone's muse?"

"It feels okay."

My mom just laughed.

Thirty-Seven

WE WENT TO SOME PARTY, AND I WASN'T REALLY IN the party mood—but I was happy. Cassandra and Dante and Susie and Gina were having the time of their lives. And, in my own way, I was having the time of my life too. I guess I would always be the kind of guy that liked to celebrate things in a quieter way.

I wandered outside to the backyard. There was a great view of the lights of the city, and I wandered toward the back of the yard and leaned on the rock wall and gazed out at the view. I was out there alone, and I thought I heard something, and in the corner of the yard, someone was almost hiding behind a bush. And I noticed that whoever it was was crying.

I moved toward the person, and I could see that it was a guy. And I recognized him. Julio? Julio from the welcoming committee? "Hey," I said, "what's wrong? We're supposed to be celebrating."

"I don't feel much like celebrating."

"You made top ten percent of the class."

"Big fucking deal."

"It can't be that bad, can it?"

"You know, life isn't easy for everybody."

"Life isn't easy for anybody."

"But it's harder for some than for others. I hate my life."

"Been there. Done that."

"I doubt it. You don't know what it's like to feel like a freak. You don't know what it's like to know that you don't fit in and never will. And that everyone would hate you if they knew the truth about you."

And then I knew what he was talking about. And I decided that I was just going to trust the situation. I don't know why, but it didn't feel brave or anything like that; it felt, well, normal.

"Most people don't know this about me, because I don't like wearing a sign and I'm kind of a private guy, so only my family and my closest friends know, but I'm gay."

"You? Aristotle Mendoza?"

"Yup."

He'd stopped crying. "Are you some kind of angel that God sent me or something? I'm gay too. But I guess you figured that out by the way I was talking. And I've never told anybody. Not anybody. You're the first person I've ever told."

"I'm the first person you've ever told? Well, I guess I should be honored—but you should have given that honor to your closest friends."

"No."

"Why not?"

"What if they hated me after I told them? Then I wouldn't have anybody."

"But Elena and Hector are your best friends. I always see you together at school."

"They are my best friends. They've been my best friends since forever."

"I don't think they'd hate you."

"You don't know that."

"You're right. But I don't think I'm wrong. And what if I am wrong and they didn't want to have anything to do with you—wouldn't you want to know that they weren't worth hanging around with? Julio, never underestimate the people who love you. Tell them."

"I can't."

"Yes, you can. Whether you fucking like it or not, you're going to have to learn to be brave. Are they here?"

"Yeah, they're inside dancing."

"I'm going inside and I'm going to bring them out here. Look, I got your back. I'm not going anywhere. I'll be right here. Okay?"

"Okay," he said. He just kept nodding. "Okay, I might as well just get it over with."

I walked inside and spotted Elena and Hector. "Julio needs to talk to you."

"Did something happen? Is he okay?"

"He's okay. He just needs to talk to his friends." I cocked my head and they followed me outside.

"Julio, these are you friends. Talk to them."

"What is it, Julio? You're crying. What's wrong?"

"Everything."

"What, Julio? Tell us what's wrong."

"It's just that I don't know how to tell you that I'm—I'm gay."

And he bowed his head. I recognized that his tears came from an inarticulate shame.

"Oh, Julio, why didn't you tell us?" Elena reached for him and hugged him. And Hector put his arms around both of them—and they were all crying. "It's okay, who cares? We're your friends. Don't you know what that word means?"

"I'm sorry. I was afraid."

"Afraid we wouldn't love you?" Elena gave him that look. "I should kick your ass for not trusting us. I really should."

"And I should too," Hector said.

"Forgive me. Ari said we should never underestimate the people who love us. And he was right."

"We forgive you," Elena said. "Let's celebrate. It's a coming-out party!"

Julio had a horrified look on his face. "I'm just joking," Elena said. "We won't force you to make any public announcements." She turned to me. "You're full of surprises. For every bad thing I ever said about you, for every bad thing I ever thought about you—forgive me, Ari. I can be an asshole." She kissed me on the cheek. "I'll love you forever for this."

"Forever is a long time, Elena."

"I know what 'forever' means, Aristotle Mendoza."

I watched them as they walked away laughing and joking. I was happy.

I was about to go inside to join the party when I saw Dante walking toward me. "Are you being melancholy boy again?"

"No. I'm being Ari. I'm celebrating in the quiet. Look up at the stars, Dante. Even in the pollution of the lights, you can still see them."

He took my hand. He pulled me to the corner of the yard, where we could hide behind the large bush. He kissed me.

"I never dreamed a valedictorian would ever kiss me."

Dante smiled. "I never dreamed Cassandra's muse would kiss me back."

"Maybe life is made of the things we never dreamed of."

I wondered if I would spend my life hiding behind a bush and kissing men. I wondered if I would ever learn to stop raining on my own parade.

Thirty-Eight

THE PARTY WAS STILL GOING. BUT WE DECIDED TO ditch it. "Let's go to our place," Cassandra said. Dante hopped in my truck. Cassandra and Gina hopped in Gina's car. Susie hopped in Cricket's car. And we'd invited Hector and Elena and Julio, and they followed us to the desert, to that place that belonged to me and Dante and that we now shared with the people we called friends.

Cassandra brought a boom box and she found a good radio station and we listened to music and we were dancing. I introduced Elena to Susie. "You'll like each other. You can both spell 'feminism.'"

"Yeah, Ari, but can you?" Elena, she could give you some serious looks that could shut you down in a nanosecond.

"You see, Susie? A woman after your own heart."

And we outed Cricket to Elena and Hector and Julio.

Elena was ecstatic. "You're the cricket guy? You're our hero."

Cricket was a modest man. "I'm not anybody's hero."

"You don't get a say in this," Elena said.

And we started a chant: "We love Cricket! We love Cricket!" I don't think anybody had ever really celebrated his life. Everybody needed to be celebrated.

There was a slow love song on the radio. Dante and I danced, unafraid in the company of friends. And Dante, being Dante, asked Julio, "Have you ever danced with another guy?"

And Julio shook his head. "Well, you're about to." And he danced with him. And if anybody had ever worn a million-dollar smile, it was Julio.

We danced. We all danced in the desert. We danced in the desert that I loved. We danced until sunrise. And that dawn, the sun was shining on the faces of the people I loved. All of them, they were setting the world on fire.

Commencement. It meant something was beginning. The engines of the race were roaring in our ears. On your marks, get set . . .

Thirty-Nine

DANTE AND I WENT SWIMMING EVERY DAY AFTER
school ended. It was just me and him for a week. We hung out at
Memorial Park, across the street from his house. He was teaching me
how to dive. "Just watch me, you'll get the hang of it." I didn't care if
I got the hang of it. I was trying to memorize every move he made,
so I'd always remember.

After our swim, we were lying on the grass at Memorial Park.
Under what we called our tree. "Remember that summer art fellowship in Paris?"

"I was wondering about that the other day."

"Well, I got one. I got one of the fellowships. To the Paris School
of Fine Arts."

I jumped up in the air with a fist. "Yessss!" I hugged him. "Oh,
Dante! I'm so damned proud of you. Wow! That's amazing! Wow,
Dante! That's fucking amazing!"

But it seemed that Dante was hardly ecstatic. "I'm going to turn
it down."

"What?"

"I'm going to turn it down."

"But you can't."

"Yes, I can."

He got up from where he was lying on the grass and headed for his house. I went after him. "Dante?"

I followed him to his room.

"Dante, you get this special fellowship to study at an international program at the Paris School of Fine Arts and you're not going to go? Are you crazy?"

"Of course I'm not going to go. We're going to spend the summer together before I go away in September."

"And what do your parents say?"

"They say I'm throwing away a once-in-a-lifetime opportunity and that it will give me a chance to develop my art and give me a leg up if I really want to make a go of it as an artist."

"And I agree with them."

"What about us?"

"Us? We're still us. We're still Ari and Dante. What will this change?"

"You won't miss me?"

"Of course I'll miss you. Don't be stupid. But you can't say no to this—not because of me. I won't let you."

"So you don't care about spending our last summer together?"

"Who says I don't care? And who says it's our last summer together?"

"You'd rather me be in Paris than me be here with you?"

"I wouldn't put it that way. Don't say it like that. I want you to go because I love you. This is going to help you become what you've always wanted to be—a great artist. And I'm not going to stand in the way of that."

"So you want me to go."

"Yes, I want you to go."

I'd never seen that kind of disappointment and hurt on his face. "I thought you wanted to spend the summer with me. With me, Ari."

"I do, Dante."

"Do you?"

"Dante—"

The look on his face—he was so wounded. I looked into his eyes. He didn't say a word. He turned away from me and walked into his house.

I walked down the stairs and out the door. I felt lost—and then I told myself, *He'll calm down. He always does.*

Forty

I TRIED CALLING DANTE EVERY DAY FOR A WEEK. EVERY day, I called. "He won't talk to you," Mrs. Q said.

"I understand."

"Ari—" She started to say something, then sighed. "Sam and I miss you. I just wanted to say that."

I nodded into the receiver of the telephone—but I couldn't say anything.

I stopped calling. A week went by. Then another.

He didn't call.

Forty-One

MY MOTHER WAS STANDING IN THE DOORWAY TO MY
bedroom. "You have company," she said.

I looked at her blankly.

"Dante. He's sitting on the front porch. He wants to talk to you."

I sat next to him and Legs on the front steps. "Hi," I said.

"Hi," he said.

And then there was this long quiet.

"I didn't mean to overreact that way, Ari. I didn't. And I'm sorry
I didn't return your phone calls. I've been pretty lost without you.
But I've been thinking that this time apart is a good thing. We really
won't be a part of each other's lives in the same way when we start
college—and maybe it's good that we get used to the being-apart
thing. I mean, by the time we start the new semester, we'll be used
to living our own lives. Don't you think?"

I nodded.

"Ari, you and I don't have a future."

I shook my head. "Yes, we do, Dante. It's just not the kind of
future you imagined."

"You mean we can just be friends? Fuck that."

And again, there was a long silence between us. And just then I felt like we were two strangers. Two strangers who lived in different neighborhoods, different cities, different countries. I don't know how long we sat there—but it was a while.

And then I heard Dante's voice saying, "I'm leaving for Paris tomorrow."

"It's good that you're going. It's a good thing. A beautiful thing."

He nodded. "I wanted to thank you, Ari. For everything."

It's funny. Dante was always the boy full of tears. There were no tears in him now. But there wasn't any way I could hold mine back.

He looked at me. "I didn't mean to hurt you."

I stopped and took a deep breath and looked into his beautiful face, which would always be beautiful. "You know what, Dante? When you hurt someone, you don't get to say you didn't."

He got up and started walking down the sidewalk.

"Don't just walk away like that, Dante. I have one more thing to say to you."

"What's that?"

"I love you." And then I whispered it: "I love you."

He turned around and looked in my direction—but he couldn't look at me. He just looked down at the ground. And then he looked up at me. Those familiar tears were flowing down his face. The tears fell like the rains that fell on the desert sands in a storm.

He slowly turned around and walked away.

Forty-Two

I SAT DOWN TO WRITE IN MY JOURNAL. I STARED AT THE clean, new page. I started to write Dante's name. But I didn't want to talk to Dante. So I set my journal aside and took out a legal pad and started to write a poem. I didn't really know how to write a poem—but I didn't care because I had to write something to let out the hurt. Because I didn't want to live in that hurt.

> One day you said to me: I see a yearning.
> You saw the want in me that has no name.
> You're gone. There's a sky and there are trees.
> There are dogs and there are birds.
> There are waters on this earth and they
> are waiting. I hear your voice: Dive in!
> You taught me how to swim in stormy waters—
> Then left me here to drown.

Forty-Three

THERE THEY WERE, CASSANDRA AND SUSIE AND GINA, sitting at my kitchen table and drinking lemonade.

"I'm going to kick his ass."

"He's a complete shit."

"He's just like all the rest of them."

"He's *not* like the rest of them, Gina. He's not a complete shit, Susie. And, Cassandra, you're not kicking anybody's ass."

"But look at you. You're a mess."

"Yeah, I am. I have to learn to let go. We're just kids, anyway."

"Well, maybe he's a kid. But you're not."

"Can we just go to a movie and think about something else?" And that's what we did. We went to a movie. And then we went out for pizza. And we didn't talk about Dante, but he was there. He was like a ghost that was haunting my head. But mostly he was haunting my heart.

Forty-Four

A WEEK WENT BY. CASSANDRA AND I WENT RUNNING every morning. I'd spend my time reading. Getting lost in a book wasn't such a bad way to pass my days. I knew it would stop hurting one day. I ran in the mornings, read, talked to Legs, talked to my mom.

I had a lot of conversations with my mother—but I didn't remember what we talked about. I lived in that sadness that lay beyond tears. I wasn't exactly melancholy. I was more like lethargic or, what was that word Dante taught me? Oh yeah, "malaise." I was feeling malaise.

There was nothing else to do—except to live.

I tried not to think of the name that had been written on my heart. I tried not to whisper his name.

Forty-Five

I WOKE TO THE SOUND OF POURING RAIN. I WAS HAVing a cup of coffee when the phone rang. I heard Mrs. Q's voice. She said Dante had left a few things for me. I'd almost forgotten what a nice voice she had.

By the time I arrived at the Quintanas', it had stopped raining. Mrs. Q was sitting on the steps of the front porch and talking to Sophocles.

"What do you talk to him about?"

"Different things. I was just telling him about the day you saved his brother's life."

"Will there be a test?"

"Ever the smart aleck."

She handed Sophocles to me. "I need to get something for you. I'll be right back."

I took Sophocles in my arms. I stared at his deep, curious black eyes. He was a calm baby. He was happy just to be, and he seemed to understand what was going on around him, though I knew that wasn't really true. He was always sweet when he was in my arms. But he was fussy when Dante held him. I didn't know why that was.

Sam and Mrs. Q came out the door carrying paintings. Mrs. Q was carrying the painting Emma had given us, and I couldn't quite see the painting Mr. Q had carried out. Judging by its size, it was the painting Dante had been working on in his room. He'd wrapped it in an old blanket to protect it.

"We've missed you around here." Sam smiled at me. "Let me put this in the back of your truck." He came back up the steps and took the other painting and put it on my front seat. He bounced up the stairs, and right then I swear it was like watching Dante. He took Sophocles in his arms. "This little guy is getting big."

"Does he miss Dante?"

"I don't think so. But you do, don't you?"

"Guess it's written all over my face."

Mrs. Q handed me a letter. "He left this for you." She looked at me and shook her head softly. "I hate to see you so sad, Ari. Dante had that same look until the day he left for Paris. He never told us what happened between you two."

"I don't really understand what happened. I guess he just, I don't know, just, oh hell, I really don't know. Listen, I gotta go."

Mrs. Q followed me to my truck.

"Ari, don't be a stranger around here. Sam and I think the world of you. And if you ever need anything . . ."

I nodded.

"Whatever happened between you—remember that Dante loves you."

"The last time I saw him, it didn't feel like that."

"I don't think you really believe that."

"I don't know what I believe."

"Sometimes confusion is better than certainty."

"I don't really get what that means."

"Write it down—and think about it." She kissed me on the cheek. "Give my love to Lilly. Tell her not to forget about dinner tomorrow night."

"Dante used to think that when you had dinner with my mom and dad, all you did was talk about us."

"Dante wasn't right about that. He's not right about a lot of things."

When he fell in love with me—was he right about that? That's what I wanted to ask her. But I didn't.

I had always wanted to meet love, understand it, let it live inside me. I ran into it one summer day when I heard Dante's voice. Now I wished I'd never run into it. No one had ever told me love didn't come to stay. Now that it had left me, I was a shell, a hollow body with nothing in it but the echoes of Dante's voice, distant and unreachable.

And my own voice was gone.

I STARED AT THE PAINTING THAT DANTE HAD PAINTED for me as a gift. He'd asked me once, "Ari, if you could paint, what would you paint?" And I said, "Me and you holding hands and staring out at a perfect desert sky." That's what I was staring at—the painting I had imagined.

It took my breath away.

I sat on my bed and opened the letter Dante had left for me:

Ari,

I want you to know that I will always love you. I know it hurts you. It hurts me, too. Two guys in a lot of pain. I did want to stay with you forever. But we both knew that wasn't possible. You think you're difficult to love. But you're not. I'm the one who's difficult to love. I ask for what isn't possible. I'm more than a little ashamed of how I ended us—of how I ended Aristotle and Dante. You think I always know what to say—but that's not true. When I was walking away from you, you said, "I love you." I love you too, Ari. I don't know what to do—and I don't know what I'm doing. I know I broke your heart. But I broke mine, too. Ari, I know I can't keep you. But I just don't know how to let go. So I walked away—not because I didn't love you, but because I haven't learned the art of letting go with any kind of grace or dignity. I don't think I'll ever love anyone as beautiful as you again.

Dante

I read the note over and over and over.

And then I knew what I had to do.

I called Cassandra and Susie and Gina—and asked them to come to my house.

All three of them stared at the painting. "It's astonishing," Cassandra said.

Susie and Gina just nodded.

"Let me ask you something."

Cassandra put on her best English accent. "Well, there's never any harm in asking, darling. But you mustn't expect a pleasant answer."

"You're just trying to make me smile."

"It worked."

"What do you see when you look at that painting?"

Susie shrugged. "Is that a trick question? I see you and Dante holding hands and looking out into the desert."

"Does it conjure anything up for you?"

"It seems as though the two boys just might be in love," Gina said.

"Exactly. I see Dante's love. And that love is pointed in my direction. He painted it for me. For me."

Cassandra nodded. "What's this about?"

"He loves me. And he's afraid to lose me. That's what I think."

"So he just leaves? Because he loves you? And makes sure he loses you. Brilliant."

"It hurts too much."

"Letting go is that way," Susie said. "Who wants to let go when you love someone?"

"But you had to know that it wasn't going to be forever." Sometimes I hated Gina's brutal honesty.

"Who gives a shit about forever?"

"Dante let go. Maybe it's time for you to let go, too, Ari."

"Dante let go? The hell he did. I'm going to Paris."

Forty-Seven

"IS IT POSSIBLE TO GET A PASSPORT IN TWO WEEKS?"

"I think so. It costs more. But yes, why do you ask?"

"I'm going to Paris."

I was trying to read my mother's expression. "You're sure?"

I nodded.

"Okay."

"That's all you have to say?"

"I can't stand that look of hurt on your face. And I don't think it's going away anytime soon. You and Dante have some unfinished business. I'm not sure it's the right thing to do. And if it's the right thing, it may not be the right time. And I'm not saying it's the wrong thing to do either. As you recently reminded me, this is your life. But I know better than anyone that you can't fix everything."

"Mom, I don't believe Dante and I are broken."

My mom looked at me for a long time. Then she smiled. "Look at you, Ari: You're not afraid to love anymore."

She combed my hair with her fingers. "Why don't you and I go the passport office? And let's get you a ticket to Paris. Luckily, your father left you some money. And your aunt Ophelia's house will help you put yourself through school once we sell it. Graduate school, too, if you decide that's what you want to do. Though I'm not sure your father and Ophelia dreamed that they'd be paying your way halfway around the world chasing some boy."

"He's not just some boy, Mom. He's Dante Quintana."

Forty-Eight

I DIDN'T DRIVE TO THE QUINTANAS' HOUSE THAT EVE-
ning. I walked. We'd had an afternoon downpour, and it was cool
outside, the streets still running with rainwater. I breathed in the
smell of the rain and thought about that day when Dante and I had
gone out for a walk after the rain—and how that day had changed
the direction of our lives. It seemed like it happened such a long
time ago.

I rang the doorbell at the Quintanas' front door.

Sam held the door open for me. "Hi, Ari," he said, wearing that
kind and familiar smile on his face. He hugged me. "Come on in."

Mrs. Q was setting Sophocles down next to her on the couch.

"I understand you've decided to take a trip to Paris."

"And I understand that the two of you had a lengthy discussion
about this over dinner last night with my mom."

Mrs. Q laughed. "I wouldn't call it lengthy. We had other things
to talk about."

"Oh, yeah," I said. "UFOs."

Sam's grin—right then, he looked just like Dante. Though I'm
sure it was the other way around.

"You're sure about this."

"Yes."

I could tell Mrs. Q was trying to say the right thing—or at least trying not to say the wrong thing. "There's a part of my heart that's breaking for both of you. Dante can be very stubborn and unpredictable. He's all emotion, and sometimes his fine intellect gets thrown out the window. He was dead set on spending the summer with you.

"Dante has many fine qualities, but he's not selfless. And you are, Ari. I know that you wanted to spend the summer with him as much as he did. He sees how much he loves you, but he forgets to see how much you love him. He fails to understand how much you care about him because you care in such different ways."

"We have unfinished business. I have to be able to tell myself that I did my part. I know that the odds are that Dante and I will move on one of these days—because we're young. But I think I should have a say in when that moving on should happen. And I say, *Not today*."

Mrs. Q was shaking her head. "There are very few people in this world that can drag tears out of me, Aristotle Mendoza. And you happen to be one of them."

"That might be one of the nicest things anybody's ever said to me."

"Look at you. Look at yourself." Her voice could be firm and stubborn and kind all at the same time. "The first time I saw you come into this house, you hardly said a word—shy and unsure of yourself. Tell me, when did you become a man?"

"Who says I did?"

"I do," she said. "Even so, you don't know your way around Paris."

Sam said, "I've made some arrangements for you to stay with our friend Gerald Marcus. He's an American who's made Paris his home. He was once my mentor, and he's a kind and generous man. I've already spoken to him, and he's more than happy to have you as a guest in his apartment. And he even offered to pick you up at the airport. He'll be holding a sign with your name on it when you arrive at the airport. I understand you have a plan."

"I do." I held out an envelope. "Would you call Dante for me and read this to him? There's nothing all that personal in it. It's just the date, time, and place where I'm asking him to meet me."

Mrs. Q took the envelope from me. "I'll take care of it."

I nodded. "I don't know how to thank you. I really don't. Losing Dante doesn't mean just losing Dante. It means losing you, too." I felt those familiar tears running down my face. "I'm sorry. I mean, I hate that I've learned how to cry. I just hate it."

"You shouldn't ever be ashamed of your tears. Sam cries all the time. We love Dante. And Sam and I love you too. That will never change. What is between you and Dante is between you and Dante. You will always be welcome in this house. And don't you ever walk away from us, Aristotle Mendoza."

"I won't," I said. "I promise."

Forty-Nine

MY BAGS WERE PACKED, AND I WAS WAITING FOR SAM to pick me up to take me to the airport. My mother had a smile on her face. "You've never been on an airplane, have you?"

"No. Not ever."

She handed me two pills. "This one is for motion sickness—just in case. And if you get restless and start to fill your busy mind with thoughts that aren't going to do you any good except make you a wreck, then take this one. It will put you right to sleep. It's an eleven-hour flight."

"Mom, you're such a mom."

"Thank you. It's one of the things I'm good at."

As we were standing on the front porch. Gina's car pulled up in front of the house. And the three champions of equal rights got out of the car. "We caught you just in time. We had to give you a hug for luck."

"I don't deserve you. I don't deserve any of you."

"You don't deserve us? Sometimes I think you haven't learned a damn thing. Just shut the hell up. It's a good thing you've got a plane to catch or I'd be kicking your ass just about now."

My mother shook her head. "You've got to love these girls."

Just then, Sam's car pulled up in front of the house.

I hugged my mother. "*Que Dios me lo cuide*," she whispered. She made the sign of the cross on my forehead.

Susie and Gina gave me another hug. There was so much hope and love in their eyes. I would take their hope with me. All the way to Paris.

Cassandra looked into my eyes. "There isn't anything to say except I love you."

"I love you back," I said.

As we drove away, I asked Sam, "Where would we be without women?"

"We'd be in hell," Sam said, "that's where we'd be."

Sam helped me with my bag at the airport. I had a suitcase and a backpack. He handed me an envelope. "That's all the information you need." Of course, he'd gone over the itinerary twice on the way to the airport. And he told me at least three times that Dante knew where and what time we were to meet. And I kept reminding him that I was the one who'd set the time and place and I wasn't likely to forget. He was more nervous than I was.

He gave me a hug. "And give my love to Dante. And, Ari, no matter what happens, everything is going to be all right."

I thought I'd be a little scared on my first flight—but I was more excited than scared. I had a window seat, and as the plane took off, I got this feeling in the pit of my stomach—and a fleeting moment of fear. And then the calmness of the summer clouds gave me a sense of peace. I looked out the window the whole flight. I must have been really lost in what I was seeing, because it seemed like we were landing just after we'd taken off.

I didn't have a hard time finding the gate for my flight to Paris. I was getting more and more excited. I mean, like, little-kid excited. I didn't have much of a layover, and soon enough I found myself handing over my passport and my ticket as I boarded the plane.

I had an aisle seat, which was perfect. I guess I felt that sitting in a window seat staring out at the darkness might be a little frightening. I watched the people board, some of them laughing, some of them stressed. Some of them speaking English, some of them speaking French. They served us dinner soon after the plane took off. I got served a mini bottle of wine with my dinner. I ate the chicken and pasta, but I didn't taste it. I drank my wine.

I was restless and thinking about everything, and I was turning myself into a nervous wreck. I decided to take my mother's advice and take the pill that she said would make me sleep. And the next thing I knew it, the woman next to me was waking me up. "We're about to land," she said.

I felt the beating of my own heart.

Paris. I was in Paris.

A lot of people looked annoyed going through customs, but they must have been seasoned travelers. I thought going through customs was interesting. There were so many people, and the airport was huge. And I felt so small—but for some reason I wasn't at all scared. But, man, was I ever awake. I mean, I was super awake and curious about everything I saw. Paris. I was in Paris. It wasn't hard to know what to do and where to go. I just followed everybody. I did get confused once, but the woman who had been sitting next to me on the plane noticed the look of confusion on my face. "This way," she said. Her French accent was nice.

After I went through customs, I walked into the passenger pickup area. There was an older gentleman holding up a sign with my name on it. "I'm Ari," I said.

"I'm Gerald. Welcome to Paris."

Gerald looked like a distinguished, well-to-do older gentleman who had the eyes and smile of a much younger man. He was talkative and friendly, and I was glad because he made me feel at ease. Gerald took me on a practice run to the Louvre and back so I wouldn't get lost. But the Metro wasn't hard to maneuver. Not at all. I didn't feel as disoriented as I'd thought I would. Gerald said I was a natural. He took me to a nice café for lunch. He ordered wine. I told him I wasn't old enough to drink.

"American nonsense. Americans can be so ridiculous. I don't miss my home country. Not in the least."

It felt nice to have a glass of wine at an outdoor café. Everyone was so alive. "Adult" was the word. "How did you wind up in Paris, Gerald?"

"I retired very early. I came from a well-to-do family. I've had my share of suffering—but I always suffered in comfort." He laughed at himself. "I'd come to Paris and stayed for several months. I met a man. He became my lover. And then he jilted me for another man. Another American, as it happens. To add insult to injury, he was nearly as old as I was. Not that I was all that broken up about it. I don't think I loved him all that much. He wasn't remotely my intellectual equal. And that, by the way, has nothing to do with age.

"So, after my affair ended, I stayed. My real love was this city. It's my home now. Somehow it felt like home from the minute I got here."

"Do you ever miss America?"

"No. Sometimes I miss teaching. I miss engaging with young, ambitious, and brilliant minds. Like Sam's. I directed his thesis. He had a passion for poetry. Oh, and he was kind. The kindest man I ever met. He and his marvelous wife, Soledad. They were so alive, and I think half of their professors envied them. Sam was one of my favorite students. I know we're not supposed to play favorites, but we're only human. I met Dante when he first arrived in Paris. He's so like the both of them. Gifted."

I nodded.

"I understand you're on a mission."

"I am."

"Love at your age is rare. You're too young to know what you're feeling. And too young to know what you're doing. But that's all to the good. Love at any age is rare. It doesn't get any easier when you're older. No one knows what they're doing when it comes to love."

That made me want to smile. He asked me about my parents. I told him I'd just lost my father. We talked for a long time. I liked

Gerald very much. He was interesting, and he knew how to have a conversation and how to listen, and there was something very genuine about him. We took a walk afterward. And I could see why Gerald loved Paris. It had broad boulevards lined with trees and sidewalks that overflowed with people sitting, drinking coffee and talking with each other or just thinking alone.

The city of love. "Love" was such a strange word. You really wouldn't find the definition for it in any dictionary.

"Is there anywhere you'd like to go? I'm sure there are many things you'd like to see. There's no shame in behaving like a tourist the first time you come to Paris."

"The first time might be the last time."

"Nonsense. You'll come back someday."

"I'm here now—that's what matters."

Gerald patted me on the back. "It's an admirable thing, to travel so far. He must . . ." He stopped himself. "I was going to say that Dante must be a very admirable young man. But perhaps it's you who's admirable."

"Maybe we're both admirable, but I think that I was born with an idiot heart."

"What a lovely and endearing thing to say."

That embarrassed me. He noticed and changed the subject. "We can just walk. Paris is a city you get to know by walking its streets."

"I'd like to see the Eiffel Tower. Is that possible?"

"Of course. It's this way."

Walking through the streets of an unfamiliar city made me feel like a cartographer.

When we got off the Metro and headed for the Eiffel Tower, I pointed up ahead.

I saw a sea of people in a park—and most of them were carrying signs. I could see the Eiffel Tower in the distance. I'd never seen anything like it before. "What's going on, Gerald?"

"Oh yes, I forgot. Perhaps it wasn't the best idea to have come here today. It's a die-in. They're calling attention to the fact that so many people are dying—and the government doesn't seem to give a damn. I hope this doesn't upset you."

"No, no, it doesn't. It's amazing. Incredible. It's one of the most amazing things I've ever seen."

I looked out at the sea of people as we got closer and closer. Thousands of people. Thousands. I thought of Cassandra and Susie and Gina. If they were here, they'd be joining the protest. I had never seen, never dreamed of seeing anything like this. "They're so beautiful. God, they *are* so very beautiful."

Gerald put his arm around me. "You remind me of me when I was young. You haven't lost your innocence."

"There's nothing all that innocent about me."

Gerald just shook his head. "You couldn't be more wrong. Try to hang on to that innocence for as long as you can. As we age, we get cynical. The world wears us down. We stop fighting."

"You haven't really stopped fighting, have you?"

"I fight up here." He tapped his temple. "It's your turn now, to fight for yourself. To fight for those who can't. To fight for all of us."

"Why do we always have to fight?"

"Because we cling to ways of thinking that don't even qualify as thinking. We don't know how to be free because we don't know how to free those we enslave. We don't even know we're doing anything of the sort. Maybe we think that the value of our own freedom is worth less if everybody else has it. And we're afraid. We're afraid that, if someone wants what we have, they're taking something away that belongs to us—and only to us. But who does a country belong to? Tell me. Who does the earth belong to? I'd like to think that someday we'll realize that the earth belongs to us all. But I won't live to see that day."

There was a sadness in his voice. It was more than just sadness—a kind of weariness, a kind of hurt, the voice of a man whose dreams were slowly, slowly taken from him. I wondered if that would happen to me, too. Would the world conspire to take away my hope—to rip it from me? My dreams were just being born. God, I hoped I would be able to hang on to my hope, my dreams.

I looked at all those people speaking out, trying to make their voices heard among all the noise. *To rage against the dying of the light.* That was one of Dante's favorite poems. Dante.

"What do the signs say?"

"*'Sida La France doit payer.'* ACT UP Paris. Do you know ACT UP?"

"Yes."

"The words say: 'AIDS France must pay.'"

"What does that mean, exactly?"

"If we ignore something, then we'll pay the price. Governments love to ignore things that are not convenient. No one gains anything by pretending it isn't there. We all suffer for it. The AIDS pandemic asks our leaders to help, to invest in a cure. It takes compassion to lead. Some of our politicians do care. Most of them don't. And some of them don't even pretend to care."

I nodded. I liked Gerald. He seemed to know who he was. "That man over there. He's holding a sign. What does it say?"

"'AIDS took away my lover. France knows him as a number. I knew him as the man who was the center of my world.'"

"I want to talk to him. Will you translate for me?"

Gerald nodded. "Of course."

I walked up the man. He was young. Older than me—but young. "Will you tell him that it's a beautiful thing to love in the face of all this dying? Will you tell him he's very brave?"

"Excusez-moi, monsieur. Mon jeune ami américain voulait que je vous dise qu'il pense que c'est une belle chose à aimer face à tout ce mourant. Il voulait que je te dise qu'il te trouve très courageux."

The man handed his sign to Gerald and hugged me. He whispered in English, "We all have to learn to be brave. We can't allow them to take away our love."

He let me go. We nodded at each other. And then he said, "You're much too handsome to be an American."

I smiled at him. "I'm not sure I am an American."

The Ari I once was wouldn't have had the courage to speak to a stranger in a foreign country. He was gone, the old Ari. I didn't know where I'd left him—but I didn't want him back.

Fifty

I HEADED TOWARD THE LOUVRE AROUND NOON. I TRIED
not to think of anything. When I got off at the Louvre station, I
made my way to the entrance of the museum—then waited in line.
It didn't take longer than twenty minutes to get a ticket to enter one
of the most famous museums in the world.

I looked at my watch. I'd never worn a watch before. It was my
father's. Somehow I felt he was somewhere close. It was a strange
feeling. I had a map of the Louvre, and I followed it, and made my
way to *The Raft of the Medusa*. And then I found myself standing in
front of that painting. I wasn't disappointed. It was a huge painting.
"Magnificent" was the only word for it. I stared at it for a long time.

To have painted that. To have brought into the world a work of
art that could make a human heart feel alive. I wondered what it
would be like to have such a gift.

I looked at my watch. It was exactly one thirty. I stood in front
of the painting—and I felt so small and insignificant. And then I felt
him standing next to me.

Dante, who was always late, was right on time. For me.

I kept staring at the painting. And I knew he was staring at the painting too. "I come and look at it all the time. And think of you."

"The first time I saw that painting in a book, I fell in love with it. I didn't know I could fall in love with a painting. Just as I didn't know that I could fall in love with another boy."

We fell into a silence as if there were no words to say what we had to say. I knew he wanted to say he was sorry. And I wanted to say that I was sorry too. But it was so unnecessary to acknowledge the hurt because the hurt was gone now. And it was unnecessary to say "I love you" at that moment because sometimes it felt cheap to say such an obvious thing—so it was better to keep the silence because it was so rare and so sacred.

I felt him take my hand in his, a hand that held all the secrets of the universe, a hand I would never let go until I memorized each and every line of his palm. I looked up at the painting, the survivors of a shipwreck, fighting the waves of a storm, struggling to get back to the shore, where life was waiting for them.

I knew why I loved that painting. I was on that raft. Dante was on that raft. My mother and Dante's mom and dad and Cassandra and Susie and Gina and Danny and Julio and Mr. Blocker. And Mrs. Livermore and Mrs. Alvidrez, they were on that raft too. And those who had died too soon—my dad and my aunt Ophelia and Cassandra's brother, and Emma's son and Rico, and Camila, all the lost people that the world had thrown away—they were there with us on that raft, and their dreams and desires too. And if the raft collapsed, we would dive into the waters of that stormy sea—and swim our way to shore.

We had to make it to shore for Sophocles and all the newly

arrived citizens of the world. We had learned that we were all connected, and we were stronger than any storm, and we would make
it back to the shores of America—and when we arrived, we would
throw out the old maps that took us to violent places filled with
hate, and the new roads we mapped would take *all of us* to places
and cities we'd never dreamed of. We were the cartographers of the
new America. We would map out a new nation.

Yes, we were stronger than the storm.

We wanted so much to live.

We would make it to the shore with or without this ragged, broken raft. We were in this world, and we were going to fight to stay
in it. Because it was ours. And one day the word "exile" would be
no more.

I didn't care what was going happen to Dante and me in the
future. What we had was that moment, and right then, I didn't want
or need anything else. I thought of everything we had been through
and all the things we had taught each other—and how we could
never unlearn those lessons because they were the lessons of the
heart, the heart learning to understand that strange and familiar and
intimate and inscrutable word "love."

Dante turned away from the painting and faced me.

I turned to face him, too. I'd missed his smile. Such a simple
thing, a smile.

"Kiss me," I said.

"No," he said, "*you* kiss *me*."

And so I kissed him.

I didn't ever want to stop kissing him. But we couldn't kiss forever. "You know," I whispered, "I was going to ask you to marry me. But they won't let us do that. So I thought maybe it was best just to skip the wedding and get straight to the honeymoon."

"Have you decided where you'd take me?"

"Yes," I said. "I thought I'd take you to Paris. We'll spend our time writing our names on the map of the city of love."

Acknowledgments

It took me five years to write a book I never intended to write. Aristotle and Dante came from somewhere inside me and I thought I was finished with them. But they were not finished with me. I came to feel very strongly that I had left too many things unsaid and I became very dissatisfied with *Aristotle and Dante Discover the Secrets of the Universe*. Somehow, it seemed too easy. Slowly and reluctantly, I started entertaining the idea to finish what I had started. But what was it that I had left unsaid? I decided that only the writing of the sequel would I discover the answer to that. And I must be honest, this was the most difficult book that I have ever written.

Nothing in this novel came easily, which surprised me. At times, I felt that my heart was at war with itself. I was able to finish only because of the people who supported me with their love and their belief in me and their faith in my writing. I have said this before, and it bears repeating: No one writes a book alone. I would like to acknowledge those who were present to me in the writing of this book. It seemed, at times, the people who filled my life with a lovely and impossible affection were in the room with me as I wrote. Some were present to me almost as ghosts. Others were present quietly, almost silently. Still others were present to me in far more "real" ways. Mostly I heard their voices through telephone calls, texts and e-mails. Writing a book in the middle of pandemic changes things.

First on my gratitude list is my agent, Patty Moosbrugger. Through the years she was been so much more than an agent—she has become one of my closest friends. I do not know what I would do without her—nor do I wish to find out. As I wrote most of the book during the pandemic, I owe a debt of gratitude to the three people who were a part of my everyday life. Without their presence, I don't know how I would have survived. Danny, Diego, and Liz became my family—and the emotional support that I needed as I wrote. Without their presence, their patience, and their love, I am quite sure, this book could not have been written. My sister, Gloria, was always close, always in my heart, always a sentry watching over me. She was—and remains—my guardian angel. Through the past year I have seen very little of my friends, but there were many times I imagined each of them in the room with me, silently sitting as I wrote. These names are holy to me: Teri, Jaime, Ginny, Barbara, Hector, Annie, Stephanie, Alvaro, Alfredo, Angela, Monica, Phillip, Bobby, Lee, Bob, Kate, Zahira, and Michael. How many friends can a man have? As many as his heart can hold.

I think it important to thank those who devoted their lives as teachers and educators who are the heart of this and every nation. Their presence in this book is an acknowledgement of the contributions they have made to our society and the difference they have made in our lives. I would like, in particular like to thank the mentors who made me the writer I am today: Ricardo Aguilar, Arturo

Islas, Jose Antonio Burciaga, Diane Middlebrook, W. S. DiPiero, and Denise Levertov. I would particularly like to thank Theresa Melendez, who was my mentor when I first started my career. It was she who first encouraged me to become a writer. It was she who believed I had talent and should develop it. She had the kindest heart and the fiercest mind of all of my mentors—and I am grateful that she is still in this world. I don't believe I have ever given her the credit she deserves in my formation as a man and as a writer. Thank you, Theresa.

I would like to acknowledge the Catholic Daughters of America and the work they do. My mother was a proud member and in including them in my novel, I feel as if I'm honoring her. I would like to acknowledge all the men who fought in Vietnam. And I honor them with their fictional presence in this novel. I would like to honor all those victims of the AIDS pandemic and all those who suffered the loss of those they loved. Like so many others, I lost people I loved including my brother, Donaciano Sanchez, my mentor, Arturo Islas, and a close friend, Norman Campbell Robertson.

I would also like to thank my little dog, Chuy, who is the most wonderous creature. His boundless affection filled my days with his kind and boundless affection. He saw me through many nights of loneliness. I am every day filled with the hope he has given me.

And lastly, I am grateful for the work of a brilliant editor, Kendra Levin, who has elevated her work into an art. She is not only an admirable editor, but an admirable human being. It is an understatement to say that I loved working with her on this book. Her work on this book is anonymous—and I get all the credit. Thank you, Kendra.

Discover where it all began with the
international bestseller from

BENJAMIN ALIRE SÁENZ

BENJAMIN ALIRE SÁENZ is an author of poetry and prose for adults and teens. He was the first Latino winner of the PEN/Faulkner Award the recipient of the American Book Award for his books for adults. *Aristotle and Dante Discover the Secrets of the Universe* was a Printz Honor Book, the Stonewall Award winner, the Pura Belpré Award winner, the Lambda Literary Award winner, and a finalist for the Amelia Elizabeth Walden Award. His first novel for teens, *Sammy and Juliana in Hollywood*, was an ALA Top Ten Book for Young Adults and a finalist for the *Los Angeles Times* Book Prize. His second book for teens, *He Forgot to Say Goodbye*, won the Tomás Rivera Mexican American Children's Book Award, the Southwest Book Award, and was named a New York Public Library Book for the Teen Age. He teaches creative writing at the University of Texas, El Paso.